NEW ARRIVALS AT MULBERRY LANE

Rosie Clarke

First published in the United Kingdom in 2018 by Aria,
an imprint of Head of Zeus Ltd

Copyright © Rosie Clarke, 2018

9 7 5 3 1 2 4 6 8

A CIP catalogue record for this book is available from the British Library.

ISBN 9781786692993

Aria
c/o Head of Zeus
First Floor East
5–8 Hardwick Street
London EC1R 4RG

Chapter 1

The girl stood hesitating on the corner of Mulberry Lane, watching as people visited the pub and the shops, calling out and talking to each other, laughing in the manner of old acquaintances. Despite the blackened ruins of a building that had obviously been bombed during the Blitz and was still not completely cleared, it looked a friendly place and Rose was attracted to it because it was a pub and what she'd been used to, what she'd always known before. She'd grown up with the hustle and bustle of a pub and, in spite of things she would rather forget, it was drawing her on.

London was vast and had seemed, in the first hours of her time here, hostile to a girl from a small country village. The war these past years had left great dark scars, destroying whole streets in some areas and leaving rubble through which grass and weeds struggled for light, inhabited only by the rats and billboards on which posters had been pasted. After leaving the crowded railway station that first night, she'd spent hours sitting in a late-night café, shivering and afraid, until the man behind the bar told her about a hostel where she could get a cheap bed for the night.

Rose shuddered, still able to smell the stink of that night shelter but knowing that she could never go back to the life that had been hers. Nor did she want to, even though she'd had a warm bed, food to eat, her wages and people she'd known all her life – and yet she hadn't really known them at all. Friends she'd thought really cared for her had turned against her; she'd been shunned and even spat on and all for something that wasn't her fault… But she didn't want to think about that ever again. She couldn't go back, so she must go on – and that meant she had to find work. Since that first night, her wandering footsteps had brought her here, outside this public house, and she was conscious of feeling tired, cold and hungry, in need of food, somewhere to wash, and a bed where she could sleep in safety.

The Pig & Whistle was an old building, the paintwork peeling in places, but it was still attractive. The windows were clean and so were the nets at the upstairs windows. Pubs were usually warm and it was often easy to find work there. Rose could cook and clean and wait on tables. She'd done it all her life, for as long as she could remember – or since she was nine or ten years old and now she was nineteen, a pretty fair-haired girl with green eyes and a smile that had once come naturally but was now wary.

She crossed the road, which was cobbled and uneven, and went under the brick arch into the pub yard, pausing to admire the tubs of bright flowers that someone had put there, as if to defy the drabness of a world at war. It was a bright day, the 24th of January 1944, and the wind, which had begun to rise, was cold. The door at the back of the pub was open at the top like a stable door, the smell of cooking that floated out to her enticing and somehow welcoming. It was much like the pub she'd served in at home... but that was no longer her home. She was in London now and she'd chosen it because here they would not know her – or know that she was the daughter of a murderer. London was too war-torn and battered to bother its head about what happened in a small village hundreds of miles away.

She pulled at her crumpled grey skirt, trying to shake out the creases that were there because she hadn't changed since she arrived in the city; the hostel had no privacy and she hadn't wanted to take off her clothes.

'Come in,' a pleasant voice said as she knocked on the door and the girl reached over and opened the lock at waist-height. She walked into the large kitchen, which smelled delicious and was redolent of herbs and baking. 'Hello, I'm Peggy Ashley – who are you?' asked the owner of the voice.

Rose studied the pretty blonde woman. She looked as if she might be in her late thirties or perhaps early forties, very attractive, even enveloped in a large white apron, as she was; her hair was almost hidden beneath her cap, though it kept escaping to fall over her face in damp, curling tendrils.

'I'm Rose... Rose Marchant,' she said. Only the second part of the name was a lie. She'd thought that best. 'I've come to London looking for work... I can cook and clean and clear tables, but I'm not much good at anything else.'

Peggy Ashley laughed and Rose liked her at once. She was glad she'd been honest – as honest as she dared to be. 'Well, Rose Marchant, you've come to the right place if you're telling the truth. I have young twins and they're a bit of a handful to tell the truth, especially Fay. Her brother is quieter, but he does what she does so...' Peggy clearly adored them. 'They're resting for the moment but it won't last...'

'Do you want help with the children?'

'I want a girl who doesn't mind what she does,' Peggy said, her bright blue eyes seeming to pierce Rose's soul. 'Did you see my advert in the window?'

'No, I just thought it looked a nice place to work. Your tubs in the arch look so pretty – they make the rest of the lane brighter. What are the flowers? You don't see many at this time of the year.'

'Christmas roses. Haven't they lasted well? A friend of mine did that for me as a gift last month, and the lane needs something to cheer it up,' Peggy said. 'I don't know how it looks to you, but that derelict bakery is an eyesore – and the lawyer's office that burned down has never been fully cleared. They sent someone to make it safe at the time and that's all they've done. It's a shame...' She continued to look at Rose as if she liked what she saw. 'May I ask what made you decide to come here, to Mulberry Lane?'

'I... needed a change. I wasn't happy at my last place so I thought I would try to find work in London...' Rose was telling as much of the truth as she dare and she saw Peggy Ashley frown, because she'd sensed the lie behind the truth.

4

'Well, Rose, I'm in a bit of bother at the moment. My daughter Janet has taken her young daughter Maggie to live with a friend of hers in Devon for a while; her husband Mike died of his war wounds and it was awful for her. Janet helped me out when she felt up to it and my friend Helen has been working in the kitchen and the bar, but she just found work as a secretary and that leaves me with rather a lot to do... so I'll give you a try and we'll see if you settle here. You can have Helen's old room now she's gone...' Peggy was looking at the suitcase. 'Unless you've got somewhere to live?'

Relief flooded through Rose, because she felt unable to search further and didn't know where to go next. 'I couldn't afford it until I found work.'

'Well, you may as well live in until you find your feet or want to move on,' Peggy said. 'Bring that suitcase and I'll show you – and then I'm afraid I'm going to put you to work, but I shall give you a cup of tea and something to eat first...'

Rose smiled and nodded, feeling nervous. Peggy was friendly and it looked as if Rose had been lucky, but if her new employer ever discovered the truth it would probably all go sour. The best she could do was to work hard and hope that Peggy would forgive her if she ever realised just who Rose was...

Peggy watched the girl tackle the load of washing-up waiting in the large butler sink. She could tell by the way Rose rinsed the glasses in cold water after washing them that she'd done this sort of work before and thought that perhaps she'd been lucky. Peggy sensed that her new helper was basically honest, though she was obviously hiding something, but most people had secrets and she was desperate enough to take a chance on her.

The previous summer of 1943, Janet had decided to go and stay with her friend Rosemary in Devon, the widow of Mike's commander, she had two sons to bring up alone and she and Janet seemed to understand each other's feelings. After months of endless black despair over her husband's cruel death, Janet had decided she could not go on living in the place where he had died.

Peggy understood her daughter's terrible grief. Mike had seemed to be so much better, before suddenly dying in his sleep at Janet's side, and that had dealt her a hard blow. Peggy had heard her daughter weeping night after night and knew that Janet was bitter and angry – even with those she loved. The only person she seemed to want was Maggie, who would be four that March, her birthday a few days earlier than Peggy's twins. The little girl clung fearfully to her mother's skirts, and their grief was hard to watch so in a way it had been a relief when Janet had taken the child and left.

'I need to get away, Mum,' she'd said and her eyes had begged for understanding. 'I just can't bear to go on every day knowing that Mike died here in this house, in my bed. Losing him for a second time was too much to bear…'

'Yes, I know,' Peggy had replied, but of course she couldn't know really what that felt like and the accusation in Janet's eyes cut her to the heart.

For some three years now, Peggy had been estranged from her husband Laurie, with whom she'd previously spent years running this pub. He'd had an affair while away working on some hush-hush war thing he couldn't tell her about and Peggy had fallen in love with a young American officer, Able Ronoscki, in England on liaison work. Able had been reported dead more than two years before when his plane had been lost in foggy weather over the sea; Peggy hadn't even realised she was carrying his babies when he went missing. It had hurt Peggy terribly, and her grief had never left her, but it wasn't like having your husband back, only to wake and find him lying dead beside you in bed, and the twins had given her hope for the future, because they were his. Janet had been hysterical with grief after waking beside her dead husband.

Peggy had wanted to comfort Janet, to give her back the happiness she'd known for such a short time as Mike seemed to be regaining his life, coming back from the dark pit of forgetfulness that his severe wounds had cast him into. Perhaps the tiny shred of metal in his brain had moved, easing pressure on one part of his brain but then causing his death. The doctors hadn't been able to explain it, only to say that because it was there and embedded too deep for removal it was always going to cause trouble – but that didn't ease Janet's pain nor did it erase the questions they all needed answered.

Why had a cruel fate given Janet back her husband only to take him again?

Peggy had agreed at once when Janet told her what she wanted to do.

'I know it puts you in difficulty... with the twins and the pub to run...' Janet had apologised, 'but I can't bear to be here, Mum.'

'Helen will help me until she finds a job – and I've always got Nellie. She never lets me down and I can take on some part-time help. Maureen and Anne will come in when they can...' Maureen and Anne were Peggy's long-standing friends and they all helped each other in times of trouble.

Janet had accepted her mother's assurances, because Nellie had been like part of the family for years, and so she'd taken her clothes and her daughter and caught the next train. Her eagerness to leave had hurt Peggy, but she knew that because Rosemary had also lost her husband in the same sinking that fatal night when Mike was injured, she would be able to share Janet's grief – and perhaps it was what Janet needed, her friends rather than her family around her. Her letters in the intervening months seemed to suggest she was happier there and although she'd sent cards and presents she hadn't come home for Christmas. Peggy missed her daughter but seeing the excitement and happy faces of the twins opening their gifts had made it easier for her.

'I can't face it yet,' she'd told Peggy when she phoned to wish her Happy Christmas.

Helen had left the pub soon after Christmas 1943. She'd completed her training and wanted to live nearer her new job, which was as a secretary in a Government department in the city.

'I'll never forget your kindness, Peggy,' she'd said. 'I hope my leaving doesn't make things too awkward for you...'

'No, of course not, Helen. This was just a refuge for you – I'm happy for you to move on if you're ready.' Helen was the mother of one of Maureen Hart's friends; her daughter had perished in the early Blitz and she'd come seeking sanctuary when she could no longer bear to live with her cold husband.

Helen's husband had never come after her. Whether it was because he had no idea where his wife had gone or more due to his pride that would not allow him to chase after a reluctant wife, they neither knew nor cared. Helen had done her bit while she stayed at the pub and then she'd decided to move on.

Peggy wished she'd waited a bit longer to move out, because her efforts to find a new helper had not prospered. One young girl had come for three days and then complained the work was worse than the factory and returned to her old job. So Peggy had managed with help from her friends, but it hadn't been easy with growing twins, who were born in the spring of 1942 and would have their second birthday later that year. In fact, she'd decided to dispense with her annual Christmas party the previous year, asking just a few of her closest friends to celebrate with her on the day itself.

After Janet left, Peggy had employed an elderly man called Fred Dunby to help with the barrels on a temporary basis, but he'd succumbed to a nasty chill back in November the previous year and hadn't been in for weeks, and of course Fred was no help with the children at all. Alice, from across the road, did a bit of baby-minding sometimes, and Peggy had found various women to help with the washing-up, but they came and went and there was no one she could really trust to help with the pub and the children. Of course the wages Peggy paid couldn't compare with the wages paid in the munitions factories, most of which had now been moved out of London to secluded areas in the country so that accidents in the workplace would cause fewer casualties in the surrounding district. Rose turning up out of the blue was a stroke of luck.

She was clearly used to hard work and she seemed pleasant enough, but she had to learn Peggy's ways so they could work comfortably together.

Peggy sighed, because although she was managing to keep on top of most things, she missed her daughter and Helen too. Helen had promised to visit when she could and Peggy hoped she would, because they'd become friends. Peggy was feeling low and in need of something to cheer her. She fiddled with the radio, which was on the blink again, thinking about the marvellous new pocket-sized radios they were promising for after the war. So much was promised for after the war. If the end ever came. Thankfully, the Germans had turned their attention elsewhere after devastating London and the attacks had been spasmodic since then, though the papers warned of evil weapons preparing to wreak havoc on them again. Yet at the moment it was Berlin who was suffering as the Allies rained bombs on them, and the war seemed to be going their way as the USA launched the world's biggest warship. Peggy just wished it would be over and they could all start to live again without fear of those they loved dying violently.

A tap at her back door made her look round.

'Peggy... I just popped in to say I can work in the bar this evening if you want me?'

Anne Ross poked her head round the door and Peggy smiled at her friend, immediately feeling better. 'Lovely, thanks so much, Anne. Come and meet Rose – she's my new helper. Rose, this is my friend Anne Ross. Her husband is in the Army and she is a school teacher...'

'Nice to meet you, Rose,' Anne said, looking at her frankly. 'Peggy really needs some help. I hope you will be happy here.' She turned back to Peggy and once again she was smiling, happiness bubbling out of her. 'I've just heard from Kirk. He's coming home next week on a month's leave and then he'll be working and training here in England for a few months...'

'Oh, Anne, that is wonderful news,' Peggy cried, because Anne had hardly seen her husband since they were married. He'd been posted somewhere abroad and even his letters had been infrequent. It was no wonder that Anne looked so happy. 'I'm so pleased for you. Where will you stay – at his uncle's?' Kirk's uncle had a cobbler's shop next door but one to the pub and it was there that they'd met.

'Mavis would have us at hers and we are welcome to stay with Uncle Bill for as long as we like, but judging by Kirk's letters, he'll want to get away for a while. We'll probably go down to the sea for a couple of weeks...' Mavis lived across the road and Anne lodged with her.

'You'll enjoy that,' Peggy said, understanding that her look of delight was tinged with just a hint of nervousness.

Anne and Kirk had married a few days after meeting just before Christmas 1942 and had hardly any time together before he was sent overseas. 'It would be nice if you could find a proper home together...'

'I suppose we have one if we want it,' Anne said. 'My uncle left his flat to me when he died last year. I've been letting it out, but if Kirk thought it was right for us, I could take it over when the tenants leave next month...'

'Or you could sell it and buy something you both like,' Peggy suggested.

She saw that Rose had finished the washing-up and was now looking for another job. Nellie, her permanent guest and helper, entered the kitchen then and Peggy nodded to her.

'Go with Nellie, Rose. She's going to turn the bedrooms out this morning and she'll show you what to do – and when you've finished, you can come to the bar and help me serve until we close.'

'Yes, you must be about to open up,' Anne said and nodded. 'I'll get off, Peggy – but I'll see you this evening and we'll talk more then...'

'Yes, I'll look forward to it,' Peggy said and heard a cry from upstairs. 'Oh. That's Fay again... Will you see to her, Nellie? I must open the bar...' Fay and Freddie were Peggy's pride and delight but were at the stage of crawling and tottering, or in Freddie's case, running in spurts before falling over, and getting into mischief if left for five minutes.

'May I do it?' Rose asked. 'I like children. I used to look after... some children...'

'Nellie, go with Rose and show her everything,' Peggy said, giving her trusted friend a little look that told Nellie to keep an eye on the new girl. She seemed fine but it was best to take things slowly at first, especially where the twins were concerned...

'I was just talking to Maureen in the lane,' Anne said, following Peggy through to the public bar. 'She seems very happy. I suspect she has a little secret but she hasn't said anything yet... might not be sure...'

'She'll tell us when she's ready,' Peggy laughed as she caught Anne's look. 'I think you're probably right, Anne. I've seen her looking a bit broody again.'

Chapter 2

Maureen Hart was amazed each time she entered the grocery shop at the end of Mulberry Lane these days. It looked so different from the way it had when she'd worked there for her late father. Married now and with a young child to care for she seldom stood behind the counter, merely taking care of the ordering of new stock. The shop was hers now since her father died more than two years earlier, and Tom Barton, her young manager, was forever doing something to brighten it up and make it look different. One shelf was currently displaying wooden toys and trinkets, a new idea that he'd had, and she'd given him the authority to go ahead with. Ben Walker, a soldier who had been wounded and forced to retire from the Army early in the war, made the toys. His spine had been damaged and he needed a wheelchair to get around because he couldn't walk far, though he was able to walk a little and to look after himself. Unable to find the kind of work he'd done before the war, he'd used the skill in his hands to make toys from reclaimed wood he sourced in the junkyard. He'd come in for some cigarettes one day and shown Tom some of his toys. Impressed by the brightness and colour of some wooden bricks, the beautiful animal carvings, and the natural beauty of the wood in other pieces, Tom had asked if he could keep some pieces to show Maureen and he'd come up with his idea to sell them for the ex-soldier, taking a fifteen per cent commission.

'We might not sell many most of the year, but there are birthdays and at Christmas it should prove worthwhile; besides, it would help to fill an empty shelf.'

Since Tom's industry had cleared the backlog of tins and stock from the back room, there were unavoidably large spaces on the shelves as the war wearied on and shortages got worse. His new idea had filled a shelf and because there were wooden love spoons, trinket boxes, ashtrays and breadboards as well as the toys, they managed to sell a few items most weeks, and had done quite well the previous Christmas. Those sales hadn't made much difference to the shop's profits, but it helped the soldier and brought more passing trade, as toys were as difficult to find as anything else these days and Maureen had told Tom to buy more. Ben could only manage to make a few in a week and Maureen had told him that she would buy from him all the year so that he could earn a regular living.

Despite all the hardships, the year of 1943 had been relatively peaceful for the inhabitants of Mulberry Lane compared to the months that had preceded it. Now they were in January 1944. Peggy's twins, two months older than Maureen's son, were doing well, into mischief and running around until they tired themselves, and Ellie Morris, the young woman who worked for the hairdresser in the lane, now had a darling little girl named Beth with blonde hair and blue eyes. Her husband Peter was in the Army, but Ellie seemed happy living with Mrs Tandy, above the wool shop next door to her work.

Maureen's own son Robin was thriving and completely spoiled, because, between them, Gran and, her husband's daughter, Shirley, made certain he was never allowed to lie in his cot and cry. All he had to do was to yell and one of his ardent admirers would have him out of there and onto their lap. Maureen had given up trying to forbid it, because Gran refused to listen.

'Crying isn't good for babies,' she'd told Maureen in no uncertain terms when she'd said it would spoil him to pick him up every time he cried. 'It means he's wet, hungry or has the tummy ache and deserves attention.'

Of course, Robin was growing fast now, no longer a tiny baby but an unsteady toddler. His first words had been Dadda, Shirl... and then Mumma. Maureen had repeatedly told him about his daddy from the moment she held him in her arms, explaining that his daddy was a soldier. When Gordon had come home for a two-month posting and new training in late October 1943, Maureen had shed tears as she watched them together; because from the love and the pride in her husband's face, she believed her own fairy tale that Robin was indeed Gordon's son. Her belief in the myth had grown, because despite Rory Mackness' threats when she was in hospital just after Robin's birth that he intended to visit his son whenever he chose, he had not been to see her or his son since that day in 1942 and she could only hope it stayed that way.

'He's a beautiful child, Maureen,' Gordon told her when they made love the night before he was due to return to his regiment prior to his next posting. He'd finished his tour of duty in the desert before his leave and wasn't sure where his next posting might be after some further intensive training in the south of England. 'It was kind of you to let Shirley name him – and Robin suits him beautifully. He is intelligent and bright as a little bird.'

Gordon had changed so much since he'd joined the Army. He was stronger, fitter and far more confident than the man who had used to buy barley sugar for Shirley from Henry Jackson's shop. The days when she'd worked in her father's grocery business seemed far off now to Maureen. She'd trained as a nurse at the start of the war before falling for a child with a man who had let her down too many times, and then returning to the lane. Gordon had confessed his love and offered her marriage, even though she was carrying another man's child. He'd shown her what love really meant and she was so grateful that he'd loved her despite everything.

'It made her happy,' Maureen said, 'but I've realised it is perfect for him. We'll keep your name for our next son...'

Gordon had kissed her again, stroking the silken arch of her back. 'We might have a girl...' he said, but she'd shook her head and pressed against him, savouring every moment of their short time together.

'We'll have another boy. Shirley doesn't want a baby girl in the family.'

He had laughed at that. 'Well, she can't always have her own way. Not that she is spoiled, despite all the love you lavish on her, Maureen. My mother gave her all her own way when she was little, but you don't – and yet she is always laughing and happy. I don't know how you do it, but you seem to make us all happy… Gran, Shirley, Robin, all your friends – and Tom Barton worships the ground you walk on…'

Maureen had leaned up on her elbow so that she could look into his face. 'Do I make you happy, Gordon?'

'That goes without saying,' he'd murmured throatily and pulled her down on top of him, kissing her and then turning her so that she was beneath him and beginning to lavish her with his tongue and lips in a way that made her arch and moan with pleasure. 'Marrying you was the best thing I ever did, my darling… I promise you I have never been so happy or ever knew I could be.'

Maureen smiled at the memory, because she was certain that it was that night her baby was conceived. She had Gordon's child growing inside her now and that thought made her want to shout with happiness. At the moment her happiness was complete and even the slight complication of having Violet Jackson – her late father's second wife, and his widow – as the tenant above the shop wasn't enough to dim the glow inside her. She had hoped that Violet might move on after a while, but she seemed settled and Maureen felt obliged to let her stay for as long as she wished, if only in respect to her late father's memory.

'Is everything all right, Tom?' Maureen asked, noticing that Tom had begun to paint the wooden shelves a primrose yellow, which certainly made the shop seem lighter. 'Violet hasn't given you any more trouble?'

'Not since I made it clear to her that I wasn't having her clients coming through the shop to get to her. She can let them in through her door at the back...'

The flat had belonged to Gran and not Maureen's father, and Violet had taken up Gran's offer to remain in the property and carry on her trade as a bespoke corset maker. She'd been a bit sheepish and quiet on her return from hospital all those months ago, where she'd been rushed after she was attacked, robbed and left for dead by her own son, but she hadn't apologised to Maureen for what her son had done, nor would she ever admit that she'd put him up to robbing Gran and Maureen, and they'd never known for sure. Fortunately, they'd got most of the stolen pieces back, because of an honest pawnbroker, and Violet's son by her first husband was in prison, serving a fifteen-year sentence for burglary and assaulting her. She hadn't mentioned one word to anyone on the subject, and hardly ever spoke more than two words to Maureen or Gran. Her rent was paid on time each week, left in an envelope on the counter with Tom, and she'd had a few spats with him about who had the right to use the backyard and whether her customers could come in through the shop, but he was perfectly capable of standing up for himself. At seventeen years of age, Tom was tall and strong, though of a lean rangy build like his father, Jack. Jack Barton was serving in the Army abroad and kept in touch by infrequent postcards to his son and to Peggy Ashley. Jack was grateful to Peggy for helping Tom and he'd always found her attractive.

'You don't mind the new colour for the shelves?' Tom asked a little anxiously.

'I think it looks better than the old grey that Dad preferred,' Maureen said, smiling at him. 'You're always working overtime, Tom. I don't pay you enough for what you do...'

'You pay me what the shop can afford,' Tom said, looking at her with undisguised adoration. Maureen knew that he'd transferred his affections to her after he'd finally severed all connections with his mother. Tilly Barton's health and mental condition had deteriorated to the stage where she was now confined to a locked room in the infirmary, awaiting her transferral to an asylum. Tom had shed a few tears when he was told that he could no longer see his mother for the reason that she was mentally unstable and might try to harm him.

'I know she never loved me,' he'd told Maureen once. 'Sam was always her favourite, but she blamed me and Dad after he was killed on that bomb site – and then she seemed to hate us. Dad said it was because I was like him that she never loved me – but why did she marry him if she didn't love him?'

'I don't know, Tom. Perhaps it was because she thought your dad was her only chance and she wanted to be married...'

Tom shook his head. 'I think it went a lot deeper than that, but Dad doesn't know and she wouldn't tell me – and now she can't.'

'She may still get better...' Maureen had said, but she'd known, as Tom did, that it wouldn't happen.

Something inside Tilly– something she'd bottled up for years – had turned her mind sour and she'd dwelled on her bitterness until it took her over and she could no longer function properly. Maureen had visited the infirmary herself and been told that Tilly regularly soiled herself and wouldn't eat or drink, nor would she wash unless a nurse did it for her, and then she bit and scratched the poor woman. Tom could never have coped with her at home, and privately, Maureen thought he was a lot better off without the ungrateful mother who had never thanked him for all he tried to do for her, but she hadn't been unkind enough to say so and Tom had turned his affections to her. She imagined he thought of her as a big sister, because the friendship between them was much like being family.

Tom's father sent his son half of his Army pay and that meant he'd been able to stay in the family home, though it was too big for him and if his mother was never coming back he might be better taking a room. Peggy would take him in if he asked. Both she and Maureen kept a friendly eye on him, but he was perfectly capable of looking after himself.

Maureen picked up a newspaper lying on the counter and read the headlines:

Surprise American Landing at Anzio!

The Allied attack on Rome would weaken the Germans, robbing them of Mussolini's backing and perhaps shorten the war.

'Do you think this means the war is almost over?' she asked him.

Tom took the newspaper and read the article before replying. 'I think the tide is on the turn. When Eisenhower took over supreme command at the end of last year, I think it put the writing on the wall for the Germans, though I don't think they've accepted it yet – but if the RAF keep bombing their cities and towns, like the Luftwaffe have us in the past, that may weaken their morale.'

'I read somewhere that the RAF has bombed another secret weapons site in Germany...'

'Yes, I've read about that too.' Tom frowned. 'I don't know how successful it was – they're sure to have other sites in Germany. They say they're making unmanned rockets or flying bombs. I think they will have another go at London before they're finished...'

Maureen shivered, because a weapon like that could cause untold devastation, and London had never quite recovered from the intensive bombing of earlier years. There were spasmodic bombing raids now but mostly on the docks or industrial areas and nothing like the Blitz of earlier years. 'It was bad enough in the Blitz, but at least then we had plenty of warning; they say the first thing you hear with these is the bang when it lands...'

'Yes...' Tom looked grim. 'I went to try and enrol at the Army recruiting office again last week, but they asked for my birth certificate and then told me that I had a job and to stay where I was for the time being, although it's only a matter of a few months now until I'm eighteen. I might be called up for other work, but either way it won't be long now...'

'What kind of other work?' Maureen would be sorry to lose him, though she'd always known his job in the shop was temporary. Tom wanted a chance to experience life in the Army.

'He didn't say, but I read about Bevin's boys in the paper and they have posters up at the recruiting office about them needing miners. I think so many men went off to fight it has left them short of labour for things like the mines, even though it was always a protected job.'

'Oh, Tom! I don't think you would like being down a mine...' Maureen exclaimed.

'No, I shouldn't,' he said and grinned at her. 'I think if they get desperate it won't matter what I like – or a lot of other men either. We'll be called up and sent where we're most needed.'

'So if the fighting is going our way, they'll start putting more men to essential work here rather than sending them overseas.'

'That's what I was told, though not straight out,' Tom said. 'I think a lot of lads from down in Wales and also up north go into the mines younger than I am... and I'm strong for my age.'

'I shall hate to lose you,' Maureen told him. 'Especially, if I knew you didn't like your job. I know you want to join the Army but...'

'Yes, I do want to join the Army. I like working for you, Maureen. It's a good job and I'm sure once the war is over you'll be able to make this place really profitable – but I do fancy the idea of an Army life. Dad loves it. He told me last time he wrote that it was better than standing in line waiting for a job down the Docks any day. I'd like the chance to try it – although when the war is over, I'll probably think about a business of my own.'

'Well, let's hope you get your chance of both the Army and your own business.' Maureen didn't remind him of the dangers of being in the Army. Serving in the shop every day, he saw many soldiers; those in uniform, home on leave, and the wounded, who were disfigured, maimed and crippled. He knew that an Army career could be short in times of war and yet he'd still set his heart on it. Maureen wouldn't want to stand in his way, but she prayed he wouldn't be killed like so many others.

'I shall one day, even if I have to go down the mines first,' Tom said cheerfully. 'I've got the list for the wholesaler here, Maureen. The items at the top are the most urgent, but basically we need anything you can get... Sardines, chopped ham in tins, tea, flour, jam, dried rice, condensed milk...'

'I'll go in myself rather than phone,' Maureen said. 'If you're on the spot you sometimes get a few extra tins, but if you just ring up they don't bother to tell you what they've had in.'

'Good – and Peggy says please can you get some golden syrup?'

'Everyone wants that, not just Peggy. I'll do my best, Tom. Keep smiling and tell everyone we'll have new stock tomorrow. I'm sure to get a few extra bits.'

'You smile at them lot round the wholesaler, Maureen,' Tom said. 'That will melt their hearts...we can do with whatever you can scrounge.'

Maureen sighed as she looked at obvious gaps on the shelves. The war might be getting a little bit better for the Allies but she thought the shortages got worse all the time. 'You should learn to drive, Tom. I was thinkin' of buyin' a second-hand van. I'll pay for your lessons. We could save on the delivery charge from the wholesaler and it would make your home deliveries easier – and if you have a useful skill, it might help to get you into the Army.'

'Yeah, that's a good idea,' Tom agreed. 'Dad has learned to drive both trucks and tanks in the Army and he says he wishes he'd done it years ago. If he doesn't stay in after the war, he'll be able to get better paid work. I'll book up for lessons straight away – if you're sure about payin'?'

'Yes, I'm sure. I ought to pay you more wages, but if I give you this it sort of makes up for it.'

'You already gave me a good job when others would have thought me too young,' Tom said, 'but I'd love to be able to drive...'

He was still grinning to himself when a customer came in and Maureen left him to it. She would walk to the wholesaler and purchase whatever they would let her have, but if Tom learned to drive it would be better for all of them. Maureen would purchase a little vehicle and learn to drive as well, because with three children she needed to be able to take them with her wherever she went.

Chapter 3

'Come to Granny,' Mabel Tandy said, holding out her arms to the beautiful blonde-haired child in the cot.

Beth was so sweet and good that it was a pleasure having her in the house. One of Mabel's main regrets was that she had no sons or daughters to give her grandchildren. Her husband had died during the first Great War with Germany and she'd never wanted to marry again, despite several offers – but she knew that some of the offers were made with one eye on her profitable little business. The wool shop in Mulberry Lane had always brought in a good living, but these days it was more difficult to buy the bits and pieces she needed. To compensate, she'd started a sideline, taking in good-quality second-hand children's clothes, which she washed and ironed, to be certain they were clean, before she sold them. She took a shilling in the pound on most things and one and sixpence if she had to do repair work on them.

'Mo, Mo...' Beth bubbled at her, making her smile. She was very bright and intelligent, forward for her age in Mabel's opinion, but perhaps she was biased, because Ellie's little girl *was* her grandchild in all but blood and she certainly couldn't have been loved more if she really had been her own flesh and blood.

'Yes, darling,' Mabel said and touched her hands. 'Mummy will be home soon and then she'll take you out for a little walk.'

Ellie Morris now did part-time work in the hairdressing shop, just next door. It meant that she was finished early most days and could look after her daughter while Mabel cooked their dinner. Ellie did most of the housework too, either early in the morning or in the evenings. She'd lived with her mother-in-law when she was first married but they didn't get on and Mabel had offered her a home.

Mabel Tandy refused to take rent from Ellie these days. 'You're not earning as much now, and you should save. The Army sends you part of his wage, but one day Peter will come home and...'

She never finished that sentence, but they both knew what it meant. Peter Morris was Ellie's husband but not the father of her child. Ellie had been raped just before Christmas in 1941 and unfortunately fallen for a child – or it had seemed unfortunate then, but now neither Ellie nor Mabel would wish it otherwise. However, Peter had wanted her to give the child away to the Salvation Army for adoption by a childless couple. Ellie had promised him she would before he left to re-join his unit after a leave in the spring of 1942, but then, after an accident falling down the stairs, which had fortunately not resulted in the loss of her baby, she'd decided to keep it.

Ellie's tumble down the stairs had happened because she felt dizzy soon after Peter left, and she'd wondered if something in the drink of cocoa he'd made for her the previous night had caused the sickness that made her lose her balance. Afterwards, she'd told Mabel of her suspicion, but both of them had decided it couldn't possibly be true. Peter did have a violent temper; he'd shown it more than once, but he'd understood that the rape wasn't Ellie's fault and said that he'd forgiven her before he left. Yet both women were a little uneasy about his homecoming. He'd never written often, but since his departure after his last leave, not one letter or postcard had come for Ellie, which seemed strange.

'Letters often get lost,' Mabel told Ellie when she spoke of it. 'It doesn't mean anything...'

However, it lingered at the back of their minds. Peter might not have had Ellie's letter, to tell him she had a daughter, of course, but they had no way of knowing, because he did not acknowledge it – nor had he sent a Christmas card these last years, but none of that proved anything, because both letters and cards went missing in wartime.

Sometimes, Mabel knew, Ellie wondered who had killed Knocker James, the man who had raped her. He'd been found dead of knife wounds the morning that Peter had returned to his unit. Peter told her he would kill Knocker if he got the chance, but everyone said it had been a professional murder – and, besides, Peter had been with Ellie at the time Knocker was killed. So he couldn't have had anything to do with it, could he?

Neither Ellie nor Mrs Tandy was sure about anything to do with Peter these days. Mabel sensed that Ellie was unhappy and uneasy about her husband's return. When she'd married Peter in haste a few days before he was called up, she'd thought he loved her, but he'd changed when he came home on leave. Perhaps it was the war that had changed him. People said that war did change men, brutalising them, making them harder – but had that cruel streak always been there beneath the surface?

Mabel knew that Ellie lay awake at night and wondered what would happen when he came back on leave because she came down in the morning looking tired and listless. Mabel was apprehensive about it too. She had seen the violence simmering just below the surface. It wasn't her place to step in and say anything, but if he raised his hand to Ellie she would not stand silently by.

Rose nursed the little boy on her lap; Freddie was getting another tooth and had cried most of the night. She'd rubbed a little honey on his gums, just as her mother had told her to do with little Paul when he was teething, and it had seemed to ease Freddie for a while, but the tears were on his cheeks again.

'Poor little boy,' Rose said and rocked him gently. 'It hurts, I know... but it will be better soon...'

'Oh, you've quietened him at last,' Peggy said, coming into the kitchen with an armful of baby things that needed a wash. She took them to the sink, filled a bucket with hot water and left the clothes to soak. 'I got up to him three times last night but he just cried each time I left him.'

'I know, I heard him,' Rose said. 'Mum used to put a little honey on Paul's gums when he was teething, but the soothing effect only lasts for a short time…'

'Is that your little brother?' Peggy asked and took Freddie into her arms, smiling down at him as he patted her face and murmured, 'Mum… mum…'

Rose hesitated, and then inclined her head. 'Do you want me to clean or cook, Mrs Ashley?'

'Do you want to try making the cheese scones?' Peggy said. 'We might as well see what your cooking is like, Rose. I know you can make pastry. Those jam tarts looked and tasted good yesterday.'

'Mum always said I made the best scones and cakes she'd tasted.'

'Did your mother teach you to cook?'

'No – that was Grandmother, but she died when I was sixteen…' Rose turned away as her throat caught. She didn't know what had made her speak of her family at all – but it would seem strange if she never mentioned anyone from her past.

'I'm sorry. Were you very close to her?'

Rose closed her eyes. Her father's mother had been a strange, cold woman. They'd lived in her house over the pub, and she'd kept a long thin cane in the corner of the kitchen. Rose had felt that across her knuckles often enough in her early years, and on her legs.

'You will learn obedience or you will suffer for it,' Grandmother had told her. 'My son was trapped into marriage to a slut because you were on the way – and I'll not have you growing up to be like her.'

'Mum isn't a slut...' Rose had tried to defend her mother, even though Mum had shaken her head wearily. The sadness in her eyes and the unfairness of it had made Rose rebel too often and she'd learned to ignore the sting of her grandmother's cane. She'd learned to cook from sheer necessity, because she'd been told that unless she did things right both she and her mother would suffer.

Rose hadn't cried when Grandmother died of pneumonia. She'd seldom had a kind word from her, but she soon discovered that all the work her grandmother had done fell on her shoulders, because although her mother served behind the bar of their family's pub and flirted with the customers, when the pub was closed she went upstairs to her room and seldom came out until the bar opened again. Rose took her meals up to her, but she ate very little. It wasn't until a few weeks before her death that Rose realised her mother drank too much gin.

'No, I wasn't close to her,' Rose said, realising that her employer was waiting for an answer. The only person she'd truly cared for was little Paul – and his death had made her realise there was nothing worth staying for... 'I'd love to make the scones, Mrs Ashley. Shall we make some vegetable soup to go with them? We've got plenty of greens and potatoes, and there are some lovely carrots today. Reg brought you a box of vegetables from his allotment.'

'He's started to do that recently on his day off. Says he often has far too much for his family and so he thought of me...'

'Yes, that was so kind of him.' Reg was the postman and Rose liked him because he always stopped for a chat when he delivered the letters. Like most men who weren't in the Army, Reg kept an allotment, rearing chickens as well as growing vegetables. He was in his late forties and too old for the Army, but he reminded Rose of her father – as he had been, until Paul was born. It was after the child's birth that he'd turned sour and cruel...

Rose dismissed the painful memories swiftly before they could bring tears to her eyes. She'd left all that behind when she decided to come to London.

'I think vegetable soup is an excellent idea for today's lunch,' Peggy said. 'It goes well with the scones – and I'm going to make a rhubarb crumble for afters as well as some jam tarts. That plum jam I made last autumn is delicious; I must make some more this year if I can scrounge enough sugar from somewhere.'

'Then I'll make the scones and the soup,' Rose agreed and began to sort the vegetables for scrubbing and peeling. They were easy to do, because they were fresh dug. 'I helped Nellie clean the bar first thing. She's doing the bedrooms now, but I heard Freddie crying and came down to him...'

'Well, he seems to have settled for a while,' Peggy looked lovingly at her son in his cot; Fay was already fast asleep upstairs, for the moment untroubled by her teeth, of which she had almost all through now; Freddie's were taking longer. She glanced at Rose 'How old is your little brother now?'

'My brother died,' Rose said and her voice was so choked with emotion that it was a wonder anyone could hear her. 'Paul was found in his cot... the doctor said it often happens that the hearts of young babies just stop beating as they sleep in their cots.' Tears trickled down her cheeks and there was no way she could stop them.

'Oh Rose, my dear,' Peggy said and came to embrace her. 'I didn't mean to upset you. I'm so sorry. I shouldn't have asked...'

'Yes, you should. You have the right to know.' Rose sniffed and flicked the tears from her cheeks with the back of her hand. Peggy offered her a clean cotton handkerchief; it was large and white and had clearly belonged to a man. 'Paul died in his cot and my father said it was my fault for neglecting him, and some people believed him and called me names over it; one or two spat at me in the street. But I swear I didn't do it. I loved him. My mother said Father had suffocated the child – because he believed he wasn't his...'

'Oh, how terrible!' Peggy said and turned pale. 'The poor baby...' Rose saw her look at Freddie and there was an odd expression in her eyes. 'Your father couldn't have done such a thing – could he?'

'I don't know, but I think he might have,' Rose said, her eyes filled with grief and tears. 'He didn't believe the child was his and they had terrible rows over it – and then, suddenly, Paul was dead. He'd had a little cold, but I thought he was getting better and I was busy cooking and then when I went to pick him up, he was white and still...'

'How terrible,' Peggy said and nodded. 'It must have been an awful time for you – and your poor mother...'

Rose looked at her. She had wanted to keep her secret but it seemed the truth wouldn't be denied, even though she'd decided she could never tell. Peggy Ashley had been good to her these past two weeks since she'd come to the pub and she deserved the truth. It was best to get it out now, even if it meant she had to move on again. The words trembled on her tongue and then she was suddenly pouring it all out.

'My mother is dead... My father killed her with a hammer...' Rose stared into the distance, picturing the dreadful quarrel between her parents after Paul's funeral. 'We'd come from the church after burying Paul. They were shouting at each other. She flew at him with her fists. He thrust her away and then picked up his hammer and... there was blood everywhere...' Shudders ran through Rose and she covered her face with her hands as the dry sobs took her.

'Oh, you poor child,' Peggy said, looking at her in horror. 'Whatever did you do?'

'I ran outside and screamed as loudly as I could. One of our customers was passing in the street. He went in to investigate, but it was too late. We heard the shot and I knew what my father had done. He killed my mother and then shot himself with his pistol, which he'd kept cleaned and loaded from when he was in the Great War...'

Peggy was staring at her in stunned silence. Rose felt hollow inside. Her employer would ask her to leave now. Who would want to employ the daughter of a murderer? Especially one who had murdered his own son and his wife – because her mother had sworn that despite his doubts and accusations the child was his son and Rose believed he'd killed him out of spite, despite the doctors saying he had stopped breathing in his cot.

Peggy spoke at last: 'That is a terrible story, Rose. I knew you were hiding something when you first came to me, but I trusted you because I sensed you'd been unhappy...' Peggy was ashen, her face drained of colour. She looked at Rose and tears were in her eyes. 'I am so very sorry, my dear. Obviously, you've had a terrible life – but I want you to know that as long as I have the pub, you have a home with me.'

Rose looked at her, her throat closing with emotion as she held back a sob. 'I thought you would want me to leave if you knew...'

'No, Rose. You've already proved yourself to me. I would be sorry if you left. You are gentle and kind with the twins – and you help me in all sorts of ways. I think I was lucky you chose to come here...'

'Oh, Mrs Ashley...' Rose couldn't speak for her tears.

'Please, call me Peggy. You will be a part of our family now for as long as you wish...'

Rose smiled at her, nodding because she was too full of emotion to speak. She wished that Peggy was her mother, wished that none of the past had ever happened, but it had and it would continue to dwell with her for a long time, perhaps the rest of her life.

'Thank you... thank you so much,' she whispered at last. 'You don't know how much that means to me, Peggy.'

'I can't take away your pain, however much I might want to,' Peggy told her. 'But you can find happiness here, Rose. There are good people in the lane and they will all take you to their hearts if you let them. Once they get to know you and see that you work for me, you'll be accepted as one of us.'

Peggy hadn't been able to get Rose's revelations out of her mind since they'd talked the previous day. Watching her at work, noting how scrupulous she was in everything she did, Peggy thought how easily she'd become one of them. She was a pretty girl, fragile-looking but strong. Her eyes were an expressive grey and her hair had a smoky fairness that some people called ash blonde. Peggy's heart had been wrung by the girl's pitiful story: a mother that drank too much, a grandmother who treated her harshly, and a father who allowed bitterness to cloud his judgement to the extent that he had killed in anger.

It had frightened Peggy that Rose's father could murder a child in his bitter anger. Peggy's husband Laurie hadn't been home since before the twins were born. Laurie had been unfaithful to her before her affair with Able, but his fury when she told him she was having Able's baby had been unreasonable. His affair didn't matter, hers was unforgivable! After making sure that she allowed everyone to believe they were his children, Laurie had sent her a letter and a gift of five pounds to buy whatever she needed for the children after their birth – but he hadn't come home on leave. People assumed the twins were his, but her friends knew the truth and there was little point in insisting on making it public when Able was believed dead. Laurie wrote to her every few months, short, unemotional letters enquiring how things were in the lanes and if she was managing. She replied with equally brief letters telling him that they were still making a small profit, just enough to keep the pub ticking over until the end of the war – until he came home to claim it.

Peggy didn't really believe that Laurie would ever do what Rose's father had done, but it had made her wonder for a moment. His decision not to visit on leave showed her that she was not forgiven. For the moment, he considered it best to stay away and perhaps he was right – but he would return one day.

Peggy thrust the thought from her mind. The future could take care of itself; she had enough to do bringing up her twins and running this pub. At least she had the money Able had left for her. She remembered her brief visit to the lawyer's office.

'You can access the funds whenever it suits you, Mrs Ashley. There is no hurry whatsoever. I understand Captain Ronoscki also had some property in America, which would come to you through the terms of his will – but seven years needs to pass before you could claim it. The law considers that missing does not mean dead until seven years without a sight or a word from the person has passed. I understand his American lawyer is taking care of his affairs until such time as he is officially declared dead.'

Peggy had hesitated, then, 'It's just that I keep thinking Able might have been injured and lost his memory or something... don't you think? I know it happens...'

'It is always possible,' the lawyer had agreed, but she'd known by the tone of his voice that he believed Able was dead. Yet Mike had suffered a terrible accident at sea and been thought dead – and then he'd returned, although fatally injured. Peggy tried not to think it, but it might have been better had Mike not returned at all.

Sighing, Peggy put the unhappy thoughts from her and went upstairs. She could hear yelling from the twins' room and it was time she brought them down after their nap. She must concentrate on her twins. She had to accept that knowing Able had been a wonderful moment in her life, something to remember with a smile, but it had gone and she must move on. Hearing Fay scream as she entered the bedroom, she went over to the cot and found her daughter having a tantrum. Freddie was looking at his twin warily, tears on his cheeks.

Picking Fay up, Peggy saw a red mark on her arm. It looked as if she'd been pinched or bitten... But what would cause such a mark? Peggy kept their bedding and clothes scrupulously clean so it couldn't be a flea...

She shook her head. Rose would never hurt the children and Nellie certainly wouldn't; she loved them. Her gaze narrowed as he saw the guilty look in Freddie's eyes.

'Did you pinch Fay, Freddie?' she asked, but he shook his head in denial and his eyes filled with tears.

Peggy sighed. It seemed it was time she put them in separate cots. For a long time, they'd found comfort in being together, but if one was inflicting harm on the other, she would have to find another cot from somewhere.

Chapter 4

Tom wasn't sure why he'd overslept that morning. He was never late up, even if he'd worked long into the evening at one of his little jobs, as he called the decorating and small repairs he did in the lanes. These days it seemed that there was always someone at the door asking if he could just come and fix a tap or unblock a sink or clean a chimney, mend an electric kettle or fix a window.

Jack of all trades that's me.

He'd told his father in the latest letter he'd written. Tom wrote long letters to his dad, because he knew that he liked to hear all the news of Mulberry Lane.

Ma would say I was master of none, but I'm getting quite good at some things. Peggy says I don't charge folk enough, but it only takes a few minutes to do some jobs and I tell them a couple of bob will do. Sometimes, I don't charge at all...

The previous evening, and several before it, he'd been up late helping Alice, his neighbour, do up her small bedroom. A widow, who found it hard to manage on her meagre pension, she'd been harbouring her junk there for ages and some of it was saleable.

'I reckon I can take in a lodger if I get this room clear,' she'd told Tom. 'If yer take them old brass and iron bedsteads to Bert at the junkyard he'll give yer a few bob fer 'em and then yer can paint the room fer me.'

'Yeah, all right, Alice,' Tom said. Alice was a favourite with him and he didn't mind what he did for her. Every morning throughout the previous winter he'd fetched her coal in for her first thing and chopped kindling, but he never charged her for the little jobs he did, though she always tried to give him a bob or two. Alice often cooked enough dinner for two and fetched him round when he'd finished work at the shop to eat his share and he was glad to help her out.

He'd found several bits of brass and iron and had taken them to the junkyard, along with some broken wooden chairs, a big copper kettle with a hole in it and an old metal tea urn. After some haggling, Bert had given him two pounds, which was enough to purchase the paint for Alice's bedroom and more besides.

It wasn't a large room and he'd asked her whether it was big enough to let. She'd grinned at him and tapped the side of her nose, and then laughed.

'It's fer a mother and child,' she said. 'I'll get a cot and a chest of drawers in 'ere all right, and there's room for toys or a little table and chair, and the mother will 'ave the room you used. I went and asked down the council if they'd got anyone waiting for somewhere to live and the woman in the office told me it's the mothers and young babies they have trouble fixin' up. Lot of folk don't want 'em 'cos of the cryin', but it will suit me, long as they're decent...'

Tom suspected that Alice might be feeling a bit lonely. He'd stayed with her for a while when Knocker James had wrecked his home searching for stuff his brother Sam had taken from the bombsites, and he thought that's what had given her the idea of taking a lodger. Besides, Alice had very little money and often had to pop her silver teapot at *Uncle's* when the money was tight, though she always bought it back again, at so much a week.

When she'd asked him to clear and decorate her room, Tom had spent several evenings working on it and he'd stayed up late to finish the previous night, so perhaps that was why he'd overslept and was in a hurry as he left for the shop that morning.

He was fishing for his keys in his trouser pocket when the girl came up to him. He heard her before he saw her, asking if he was going to open that morning.

'Peggy has run out of margarine – and she needs some jam, flour and golden syrup if you have it...'

'She's in luck...' Tom's voice died away as he looked into a pair of smoky grey eyes and his heart gave the oddest leap in his breast, leaving him breathless with shock. He swallowed hard and forced the words out, 'Maureen got a dozen tins yesterday and told me to put two by for Peggy...'

'Oh, she will be pleased,' the vision said. Surely she was the prettiest girl Tom had ever seen? 'I know she wanted to make a big treacle tart today. It's one of her customers' favourites – though I think her apple pie is wonderful…'

Tom managed to concentrate enough to get his key into the lock and open the shop door. He stood back to let the girl enter and followed her in, putting up the shades on the glass half of the door so the light flooded in, but he didn't switch on the electric lights, because the government had asked everyone to save fuel. He took his jacket off and put on his white apron, giving her time to gaze about her. This was the first time she'd been into the shop, and though Maureen had told him Peggy had someone new working for her, Tom hadn't seen her in the lane.

'I'm Tom Barton,' he said. 'Are you Rose? My boss, Maureen, said she'd met you…'

'Yes, she's popped in to see Peggy a couple of times,' the girl said and smiled. 'I'm Rose. Nice to meet you, Tom.' Her smile widened. 'I've heard that if anything goes wrong round here, everyone comes to you…'

'Well, I'm asked to fix a lot of things,' Tom said, 'but I'm not sure I could fix everything… Fuses, leaking taps, a slate off the roof and decorating are all pretty easy, but I'm not sure I could fix a gas geyser or rewire the electrics of a house…'

'Who taught you to do all those things?' Rose asked as Tom gathered the items on her list and put them on the counter.

'Dad showed me some of them,' Tom said, 'but most are just a matter of common sense and working it out for yourself.'

'You must be very clever...'

'I wouldn't call it clever – just good with my hands...' Tom was aware that his cheeks felt a little warm. He'd never met a girl like this and she had him in a tizzy. 'How are you getting on workin' for Peggy? She certainly needed some help after Janet went to stay with her friend down in Devon.'

'Yes, it's a lot to do running a pub and looking after twins. They're a handful, especially Fay. She's got such a temper on her. Peggy's had to buy another cot, because they were pinching each other.'

'Kids always do that, don't they?' Tom said, remembering how Sam had liked to punch him when he was little and could get away with it. Tom had never been able to retaliate because Sam was his mother's favourite and ran to her crying if he gave him one back.

'I've never seen children's toys in a grocery shop before,' Rose said and Tom saw sadness in her eyes as she looked at them. *Was she thinking of a child who would like a toy?*

'They're made by a soldier who has to use a wheelchair to get around. He can't do hard manual work now, but he's clever with his hands. He showed me some of his things and Maureen said he could put a few bits here on the shelf. We take a small commission and we've sold quite a lot of pieces for him, especially just before last Christmas...'

'Those puppets look fun,' Rose said, 'and the trinket boxes are pretty. It was just a surprise to see them.'

'It's the war – we can't fill the shelves some weeks,' Tom admitted. 'Maureen was lucky this week, bought quite a few tins and things, but it's hard to get toothpaste at the moment. Most people say they use salt, but it's horrible…'

'Yes, it is,' Rose agreed. 'I'd love some silk stockings – or better still some nylons. I know girls who have American boyfriends sometimes get a pair or two from them. I wear little socks or nothing these days. I don't like staining my legs with tea leaves, and a line of eyebrow pencil down the back of my leg is worse, because it wears off in places and then looks awful.'

'Yeah, I know,' Tom said and grinned. 'I've seen the girls going down the dance hall on Saturday night and when they come back home, the line's gone all fuzzy…'

Rose laughed and paid him for her groceries. 'I can see you like to look at the girls' legs, Tom,' she teased. 'Thank you for the golden syrup – Peggy will be pleased…'

'No, I don't…' Tom felt himself blushing as she went out. He'd fallen right into that one! But no self-respecting man could resist looking at the girls' legs these days. The dresses they were wearing were so short! It was regulation to save material of course, but it did show off the girls' legs.

Now she would either think he was a lecher or a silly boy, Tom thought ruefully. He didn't know how old Rose was, but he imagined eighteen or nineteen. She would think a lad of seventeen was just a kid – but Tom had grown up fast. He'd had to take on the responsibilities

44

of a man after his father went to prison. Even when he'd been ill, after the bombsite explosion that had killed his brother Sam and injured him, his father hadn't been able to stay at home for long. He'd been given a choice of a return to prison or the Army – and naturally Jack Barton had chosen the Army. So with his mother fading away in the infirmary, Tom was on his own. He considered himself a man and his feelings for Rose were certainly not those of a boy. He fancied her something rotten already but knew he was just dreaming imagining her in his arms or thinking about the scent of her skin.

He grinned as he dismissed the thoughts as nonsense. He'd been thinking of asking her to the pictures until she laughed and said he obviously liked looking at girls' legs. Her remark had made him feel a bit foolish – which had saved him from making a proper fool of himself. Rose wouldn't want to go out with a lad like him; she could get any bloke she liked, so it was just as well he hadn't asked.

'No, you're not making the curls smooth enough,' Ellie said to the young girl she was training as her apprentice. Her name was Irene and she was fifteen, straight out of school. They'd had another apprentice named Janice and she'd just begun to cut the clients' hair really well and then she left to get a job with the Wrens when she was eighteen. 'Look, I'll show you again. Take your tail comb and select a small section, just a little square like this – and comb it right through to the tip, holding it with your left hand, and then you curl inwards with your right hand, but keep it very flat, and then pin it with these clips. Now you try…'

Irene took the comb back and selected the next small section of hair, curling it into an excellent flat curl before pining it.

Ellie smiled and nodded. 'Yes, that's right, Irene. The smaller and flatter you make your curls, the longer the set will last for the customer. What do you do when you've finished that line?'

'I take the curls back the other way, alternating them line by line…'

'Yes, well done, Irene,' Ellie approved and nodded to Irene's mother. 'She's learning, Mrs Wright. I'm very pleased with her…'

'I should like a nice auburn rinse next time I come – shall you do it or will you let my Irene have a go?'

'Colours are a big step forward,' Ellie told her, hesitating. 'Are you willing to risk it? I'll be supervising of course…'

'Well, if I don't, we can't expect your customers to let her experiment on them, can we?' Mrs Wright laughed, her double chin wobbling. She was a big lady but had a lovely nature and Ellie nodded, because Irene was an easy-going girl too and she was lucky to have her.

'All right, let Irene book it in for you before you go – I shall have to charge you cost price for the colour, of course, but the set will be free as usual. Guinea pigs don't have to pay!'

Mrs Wright chuckled and was told to keep her head still by her daughter.

Ellie turned away as her next client came in. Mrs Bull lived in Commercial Road and had passed at least two hairdressers on her way here, but she liked the way Ellie did her hair.

'You're having a perm today,' Ellie said, glancing at her appointment book and her client nodded, taking off her warm jacket and sitting down in the chair in front of the washbasin.

Ellie ran her fingers through her customer's hair, pulling it this way and that as she decided what it needed. Mrs Bull had grey hair, which she liked to have dyed ash blonde, and that meant it was only possible to do a very soft perm, because anything too strong would cause the ends to break off.

'I think I'll do a first cut but leave it a little bit longer in case we get any breakage. Your hair is slightly too brittle, Mrs Bull. I'm going to condition it first, but you know the perm will take a lot of the colour out.'

'Can't we colour it today?'

'It's a bit risky on top of the perm,' Ellie told her doubtfully. 'I'll do a cut and we'll see what it looks like when the perm is finished…'

'Well, you know best, but I'd like my colour as soon as possible,' Mrs Bull said and smiled trustingly at her. 'My hair has never been as good as it is now you're looking after it.'

'I like to make sure my clients' hair is healthy and that means taking extra care,' Ellie said. 'That's why I'm going to condition it before I do the perm.'

'Lovely…' Mrs Bull settled down, prepared for a long session. 'Have you heard from your husband yet? My son is coming home tomorrow and he has three weeks' leave… He says it's because they've had a rough time. I think he was wounded, but he's alive and that's all I care…'

'Yes, nothing else matters.' Ellie avoided the question about her husband. She didn't want to think about Peter and what would happen when he came home to discover that she hadn't given her baby away, 'You'll be glad to have him home at last,' she said and combed the hair right through, glancing at her apprentice.

'Do you want me to help you, Ellie?' Irene asked.

'If you've finished your mum's hair, you can come and hold the lotion for me now,' Ellie told Irene. 'Watch what I do as I curl the hair round the rollers. I always wrap the ends in these little papers. Not everyone bothers to do that, but I find it gives a much better result…'

Irene nodded, watching as Ellie applied the lotion and curled each section until the whole head was covered with the thin rollers, finally applying the machine that lent heat to the process. Irene's mother was ready to come out of the dryer by then and Ellie supervised as her apprentice finger-combed the hair, pressing in the nice deep waves and fluffing up the curls at the bottom before giving it a light spray of hair lacquer from the bottle they kept for salon use.

'Now, you can see why we alternate the lines of pin curls,' Ellie said. 'It gives far more bounce. Yes, that looks lovely… well, done.'

'Yes, it does look nice,' Irene's mother said. 'Thank you, love – and you too, Ellie, for showing her.'

Irene's mother left the shop and Ellie told her apprentice to pop next door and buy them a pound of sugar and a packet of biscuits from Jackson's.

'I should like some chocolate ones, but I doubt they've got any,' she said. 'Tell Tom it's for us and he'll see what he can do – I know he puts a few bits under the counter…'

'All right. Shall I take the money from the till?'

'No, that's not ours. We've got money in the cash box…' Ellie showed her where it was kept in the desk drawer and gave her five shillings. 'That should be more than enough – but if you want a small bar of chocolate you may have it…'

'Thanks, Ellie,' Irene said and took the ration card Ellie gave her. 'I'll be back in time to rinse the perm if you like.'

'This one has to be done very carefully.' Ellie gave her a little push. 'Don't stand talking too long.'

Irene almost ran the few steps to the grocer's at the end of the lane. It was called Jackson's even though Maureen Hart owned and ran it these days. She didn't often serve in the shop, but she went in and out a few times a week and everyone knew it was hers now. Mr Jackson's second wife had thought it would be hers, but she'd had her nose put out of joint when she was told the premises had never belonged to her husband.

Tom Barton was attending to a man in uniform when Irene entered. He was tall and had broad shoulders and his skin looked as if he'd been serving somewhere hot.

'Is that all, Mr Ross?' Tom said when he'd assembled the soldier's goods on the counter.

'Yes, thanks, Tom,' the man said and smiled. 'Anne asked me if I'd do the shopping for her to save time when she gets home from school this afternoon. We're off to the sea for a couple of weeks so this is for Mavis – she gave us a good breakfast and supper last night, so Anne wanted to give her a few bits to thank her.'

'I bet you're glad to be home, sir.'

'Yeah, I couldn't wait to see my wife,' Kirk Ross answered with a grin. 'But I like the life in the Army, Tom.'

'I wanted to join, but they won't take me until I'm eighteen,' Tom said. 'It's only a few months to go and I reckon I could fight as well as most men…'

Kirk smiled and then inclined his head. 'I reckon you could too, Tom – but I've seen some of the young recruits in tears when we're under fire. They don't realise what hell is like until they're in the thick of it. Best you wait a bit longer.'

'You reckon I'll get a chance at them then?'

'I don't think it's anywhere near over yet…' Kirk said, picked up his goods and left, nodding to Irene.

'Is he Anne Ross's husband?' Irene asked Tom when the door had closed behind him. 'She's lucky – he's so good-looking!'

'Is he? – Yeah, I suppose so,' Tom agreed. 'Are you busy this morning? I've had customers in non-stop ever since I opened.'

'I set my mum's hair and Ellie is in the middle of a perm – we need sugar and some biscuits. And I'd like a Cadbury's milk chocolate flake – if you've got any…'

'Sorry, Irene. I haven't seen any of those for months,' Tom told her. 'I've got some Rich Tea biscuits and also some bourbon creams...'

'We'll have the bourbons,' Irene said, 'and a pound of sugar please. Ellie said I could have a bar of chocolate – if you've got any?'

'I've got these...' Tom showed her a box of Fry's chocolate cream bars. 'If you've got the coupons...'

'They're Ellie's, but she lets me have something sometimes, because she doesn't bother with sweets much, and she knows I've got a sweet tooth.'

'Right, they'll be OK, because I know you, though you're not supposed to use other people's coupons unless it has been pre-arranged – they could be stolen, you see. There's a lot of that going on, and forged coupons too...' He inspected the coupons Irene offered and nodded. 'Yes, these are all right.'

'I didn't know people forged ration books,' Irene said, looking at him in awe. 'You must be clever to run this shop and do all the other things you do, Tom...'

'I'm just doing a job,' he said and handed the book over after marking the necessary coupons with his blue pencil to show they'd been used. Tom hesitated for a minute and then said, 'Do you like goin' to the flicks?'

'Yeah, I love it,' she said. 'Especially if it's a nice story...'

Tom hesitated. Irene was younger and he hadn't taken much notice of her until now, but Rose's mocking smiles had left his confidence a bit bruised.

'I think there's a film with Cary Grant on at the Gaumont at the moment – would you like to come with me?'

'Yes, please,' Irene answered a little too quickly, but she really liked him and had been hoping he might ask her out one day. 'When?'

'This evening – or tomorrow?'

'I could go tonight...'

'All right. I'll meet you after work – about six-thirty and we'll catch a bus up town...'

'Thanks...' Irene blushed. 'I'll see you later then...'

Gathering up her things, she bolted before he changed his mind. If she asked Ellie to let her go a bit early, she could pop home and change her clothes and be back for six-thirty.

Chapter 5

Rose finished making scones and started on the custard to go with the rhubarb crumble Peggy had made earlier. Peggy used a packet of custard powder these days for quickness and because it wasn't possible to buy all the ingredients for what Rose thought of as a proper custard. Grandmother had taught her how to make it, and the day she'd produced a flawless, free-of-lumps custard, at the first attempt, was the only time she remembered her grandmother smiling at her as if she were proud of her.

'The scones look lovely,' Peggy said as she poured the custard into a jug. 'I think people liked that Bakewell tart you made yesterday. I've had a dozen customers ask me for it this morning...'

'Would you like me to make one now?'

'No, but you can make another tomorrow. As long as the almonds and the essence last out, we'll keep offering it on the menu.' Peggy smiled at her. 'I was lucky to get you, Rose. You're not just a cook; you're a very good one. I should think you could get a job in a really decent restaurant – but I hope you won't leave me just yet.'

'I've no intention of leaving,' Rose said and looked at Nellie as she entered the kitchen. 'I've got the kettle on, Nellie – are you ready for a cup of tea and a bun? I made some almond muffins for us.'

'You'll spoil us,' Peggy said. 'I'd better get back to the bar. Maureen is holding the fort at the moment. She popped in for a chat but she can't stop long and I'll need you in the bar as soon as you've had your break, Rose.'

'Why don't I take over in the bar while you and Nellie sit and have a chat for five minutes?' Rose said. 'I had a cup of tea while I was waiting for the scones to cook...'

'Go on through,' Peggy said, looking pleased. 'It's ages since Nellie and I got a chance to sit down together'

Rose left them to it. It was amazing how easily she'd settled into the life here and she was beginning to feel better as the shadow that had hung over her since the deaths of those she'd loved began to lighten a little.

She could see at once that the bar was twice as busy as it had been recently and she was asked for a half of pale ale and a cheese scone immediately. Maureen was serving too and she kept at it until the little queue had been dealt with and then smiled at Rose.

'We haven't seen a rush in here like that for a while. I think there must be a lot of troops on the move. Half of them are soldiers I've never seen before – some of them American or Canadian.'

'They've probably been sent here from their base as part of a new initiative,' Rose said. 'I haven't read anything in the papers and no one has said anything, but I suppose it is all hush-hush as usual...'

'Yes, I expect so,' Maureen sighed. 'I keep hoping something will happen – we'll have a big victory and the war will end.'

'No hope of that yet, missus...' a soldier had returned to the bar to ask for another drink. 'We're all off in two days. All we know is they're bringing us in from all over the show...'

Rose took his order and he pushed the money across the counter to her, his hand catching her wrist as she moved to take it.

'How about coming to the flicks with me tonight?'

'I'm sorry, I'm working,' Rose said and tried to remove her hand. He held on to it, his eyes narrowed and fixed, as if he thought he could bully her into submission. 'Please let go...'

'Not until you promise to meet me – ask for a night off...'

'I can't – we're busy...' Rose wouldn't have gone out with him if it had been her evening off because she sensed he was a bully, but his grip tightened. 'Please let me go.'

'You heard what the lady said, Private Thompson,' a man wearing the stripes of a sergeant commanded and the soldier glared at him but let her hand go. 'I'm sorry about that, miss. Some of the men get a little overexcited when they have leave – especially after a few drinks.'

'It's all right – but thank you for the intervention,' Rose said. 'I expect it makes the men nervous not knowing where they're being sent next.'

'That is no excuse for trying to force yourself on a respectable young lady,' the soldier said and smiled. 'I'm

Sergeant Jimmy Morgan – I'd have liked to take you out myself, but I heard you tell Thompson that you couldn't get the night off...'

Rose might have asked Peggy for some time off if he'd asked first, but she wouldn't go back on what she'd said. 'I get a few hours to myself in the afternoon...' she said without thinking and then blushed. He was tall, dark-haired and spoke in a pleasant English accent.

'Rose... I think your friend called you Rose...' Sergeant Morgan smiled at her. 'Will you think I'm as bad as Thompson if I ask you if we could go out to tea – somewhere up the West End? I'd have you back for when you open...'

'Oh...' Rose hesitated, because it was a long time since she'd gone out with anyone. 'Well, we close at two – and I needn't get back until seven...' Her blush deepened as he grinned in delight. 'Yes, I should like to have tea with you, sergeant.'

'Great. I'll hang around until closing time and then we'll go. I'll have some of that rhubarb crumble and custard while I'm waiting please.'

Rose served him and he carried his food away to one of the tables, joining some other soldiers. She didn't have time to wonder if she'd done the right thing, because Maureen had to leave and Rose was kept busy serving various customers until Peggy came through to help with the lunchtime rush.

'It's almost like old times,' Peggy said when there was a lull at last. 'We used to be like this every day before the war started. Nowadays, it's up and down. Some days we're busy and others it's quiet, but we manage to keep goin'.'

'We always had our regulars at home, though since the war started all the young men left to join up,' Rose responded with a smile. 'And then, of course, the Brewery asked me to leave. I'd had to close down until things settled after the funerals and they wouldn't let me have the licence…'

'Probably considered you too young,' Peggy remarked. 'Their loss is my gain.' She glanced at her watch. 'It's a quarter to two, Rose. I'm going to ring the bell for last orders in a minute – and you can leave as soon as we finish serving.'

'Is it all right if I don't get back until seven?'

'Yes, of course,' Peggy said. 'Nellie will help me until you get back – are you going somewhere?'

'I've been asked out to tea by Sergeant Morgan,' Rose said and her gaze moved in the direction of the sergeant. He was wearing his Army uniform but managed to look more interesting than most of the other soldiers who had been in for drinks. As he glanced her way, she realised how blue his eyes were and noticed the tiny scar at his temple.

'Do you know him?' Peggy looked a little surprised as Rose shook her head.

'No, but he seems nice, a gentleman, and he stopped another soldier annoying me, so I thought why not? Having tea isn't going to cause me any harm, is it?' She looked at Peggy anxiously. 'If you think I shouldn't…'

'No. I was just surprised. I know several of the customers have asked you out but you always say no…'

'They always ask me out at night, but tea is different...'
Rose looked at her, searching for approval. 'If you think I
shouldn't go...'

'I think you should go and enjoy yourself,' Peggy said.
'As you say, having tea isn't going to get you into trouble,
Rose. It's time you had a little fun, my dear.'

Rose smiled. 'Yes, it's my first date for years. My father
frightened all the local men away so I never went out...
not after I left school. I did have a boyfriend at school, but
when he went away to work, he never wrote, even though
he promised he would.'

'Men aren't much good at writing letters as a rule,'
Peggy said, 'though Maureen's husband is the exception.
She says he writes her wonderful letters – the bits the
censors leave anyway.'

Rose laughed. Peggy rang the bell and for a couple of
minutes they were busy serving last drinks, but the pub
was gradually emptying, until only Sergeant Morgan was
left. He brought his empty glass and dish up to the bar.

'Shall I wait outside?'

'No,' Peggy said. 'Come through to the kitchen, Sergeant
Morgan, while Rose pops upstairs to change her dress.
You can tell me all about yourself and I'll give you a cup
of tea while you wait.'

'Did Peggy give you the third degree?' Rose asked, laughing
up at her companion as they boarded the underground
train that would take them to the West End. 'I think she
wanted to make sure you weren't going to kidnap me...'

Jimmy laughed at her saucy remark. 'Your employer thinks highly of you, Rose. Some of the men that drink in her pub aren't to be trusted – and I'm glad you've got someone like her to look after you.'

'I'm not sure I need to be looked after,' Rose said as Jimmy took out his cigarettes and offered them. 'I am grateful to her for taking me in and giving me a job and a home, of course.'

'Where do you come from, Rose? I'm from Cambridge myself. I was at university when the war broke out and I decided to finish my course, and I got a first class degree, so I was a few months late joining up – but it paid off, because they made me a sergeant straight away. Apparently, I'm officer material and can expect to make my way up the ranks.'

'We lived in Suffolk,' Rose said. She wondered briefly what he would think if he knew her history and felt nervous, because she didn't like to deceive him but was afraid he might look at her differently once he knew. 'My family had a pub – but I'm on my own now. That's why Peggy thinks I need looking after.'

'She's only being motherly and that's her nature I guess,' Jimmy said. 'I want to be an architect when all this nonsense is over.'

'I was never allowed to think about the future. My life was the pub and that was it – I suppose that's why I chose to try for work at another pub when I came to London.'

'Well, I'm told you're a wonderful cook,' Jimmy said and grinned. 'You should think about running a tea shop of your own one day...'

'Oh, one day,' Rose said vaguely. 'When the war is over – that's all everyone says these days, isn't it? It's as if all our lives are on hold… as if we're just waiting for permission to live again.'

'I shouldn't wait for permission if I were you,' Jimmy told her, serious now. 'Make the most of your life, Rose. I intend to, because every time we start a new tour of duty the odds get shorter…'

'That sounds cynical?'

'I've seen too many mates die,' Jimmy admitted. 'It either makes you bitter, mad or cynical. I think I'd rather take the detached view and if that sounds cynical, so be it.'

'We don't really understand what you have to go through out there,' Rose said and the laughter had gone now. 'We see wounded soldiers once they've been patched up, but we never see the hardship or the horror that you men have to endure.'

'I thank God for it,' Jimmy said. 'That's why we fight. Our women: mothers, girlfriends, sisters, families… you are all the reason we go through it again and again, because we know that unless we stand up to be counted when needed, the Germans will sweep into this country and everything will change. There will be no freedom if we let them walk over us. I'm fighting to keep things the way I like them… sleepy villages and cows in the fields and no jackboots or guns.'

Rose felt her throat tighten with emotion. She'd never really thought about it from the men's point of view before; they were called up and they went, whether they liked it or not – but what kept them on their feet when things were so bad that it was almost unbearable? It could only be love of home and family, of course.

'Have you got a girl who writes to you?' she asked impulsively.

'No, I've never had a girl for more than a few dates... none of them ever made me want to settle down and I didn't want to break hearts.'

'Would you like me to write – just as a friend? No ties on either side... just friendship.'

'I would like that very much. You're a lovely person, Rose,' Jimmy said. 'My mother writes occasionally, and my brother sends me a card now and then – he's still at school and itching to leave and join up.'

'What about your father?'

'He was killed on night-watch,' Jimmy said and pain flickered in his eyes. 'He worked at a factory making munitions as the watchman and they bombed the place to smithereens.' He hesitated, and then smiled at her: 'So friendship and letters then – no broken hearts if a German bullet has my name on it?'

'Cross my heart,' Rose said and laughed at him. 'If I'd had an older brother I should have liked him to be just like you, Jimmy.'

'Yeah? Well, I'm not sure I want to be your brother, Rose – but I'd like to be your friend, and I'll write to you, if you write to me...'

'That's a deal,' Rose said as the train pulled into their station. 'Come on, I'm looking forward to my tea. Where are you going to take me?'

'Nothing less than The Savoy lounge will do for a girl like you,' Jimmy said and laughed as her eyes widened in shock. 'We're going to spoil ourselves, Rose – after all, this is a treat, so we might as well go the whole way.'

Rose lay in bed that evening thinking of the laughter and fun she'd shared with her new friend. Despite the fact that they'd had only a few hours together, she felt that she knew him – much better than he knew her. Jimmy had told her all about his life in Cambridge, about the beautiful colleges, the punts on the river and the pubs where he drank with his friends. She knew of his ambition to build beautiful buildings – big places like public libraries and town halls.

'I expect the work will be to rebuild homes and infrastructure when we start to repair what the Germans knocked down, but one day I want to design more adventurous buildings…'

Rose had laughed, because his face lit up when he spoke of his ambition. The more Jimmy talked, the more Rose liked him, but she hadn't told him about her parents or her little brother – somehow she couldn't find the way – and so she spoke about her schooldays, which had been happy, and let him talk. Jimmy had lots to say and Rose was a good listener.

Their time together flew past and before she knew it they were outside The Pig & Whistle saying goodbye.

'I may get time to pop in tomorrow for a quick drink,' he'd said, 'but no promises. There's a lot for us to do before we embark and I'll probably be kept busy checking lists and moving supplies – but I shall write with an address for you to reply to, Rose – and I shan't forget you.'

'I've had a wonderful afternoon,' Rose replied and impulsively kissed him softly on the cheek. 'I shall write – and I'll keep my fingers crossed that one day you'll come back and visit me again.'

'Keep everything crossed, Rose,' Jimmy had said and grinned at her. 'When is your birthday? I'll send you something if I'm able…'

'Not until July – the nineteenth. I'll be twenty then. When is yours?'

'December the ninth,' he'd answered. 'It was a lovely afternoon, Rose. Thank you so much for giving up your time to me. Goodbye, my dear. Fall in love and be happy… and get that tea shop.'

Rose had watched him walk away. She'd made a friend and a little smile touched her lips, because now she had something to think about when she wasn't working. Her visit to The Savoy had been exciting and opened her eyes to the way things were done in exclusive restaurants. Perhaps she *would* have a tea shop of her own one day and make dainty little cakes and sandwiches like those she'd eaten that afternoon. She would enjoy writing letters to Jimmy and sending him little parcels of sweets and cigarettes, which were what all the troops wanted when they were on duty abroad. For the first time since her father had destroyed all their lives, she felt better about things.

Chapter 6

'Here you are, Peggy,' Reg said with a cheerful grin. 'Three letters for you this mornin'. Proper letters, mind. I reckon that's from Janet, and that's from your old man – and I think this might be Pip…'

'You've brought me riches this morning, Reg,' Peggy smiled at him and slipped the envelopes into her pocket for reading later.

'I'll bring you some veg on Sunday,' he said. 'I've got plenty of carrots and cabbages left in store, and I'm sure you can do something with them.'

'I'll make you an apple pie to take home,' Peggy promised.

Reg's wife had died a few months back. She'd had a weak heart for years and the bombing during the Blitz had made her worse. She'd suddenly dropped down unconscious while shopping in the market one day the previous November; she'd been rushed to hospital but of course it was too late, despite all the attempts to resuscitate her. Reg's married daughter Susan cooked dinner for him every Sunday and he coped for himself every other day of the week. Peggy suspected he ate a lot of fish and chips or pie and mash from the shop up by the market.

'See yer on Sunday then, lass,' Reg said and went off whistling.

Peggy frowned as she started on the pasties she was making for lunch. Reg never stepped over the bounds, but she'd have to be blind not to see the way he looked at her these days. He, like everyone else in the lanes, knew that Laurie hadn't been home in nearly three years, and perhaps there was a thought in his mind that Peggy might be lonely? Doctor Michael Bailey still called occasionally, but Peggy *was* married so she never gave any of the men who looked at her the slightest encouragement – perhaps because the memory of Able never left her. How could it when she only had to look at Freddie to see him?

She was lonely at times – lonely and bored. It seemed as if she never did anything these days but work, and much as she loved to cook, she was in need of something more. Some nights she lay in bed and ached, not for Laurie, who seemed little more than a stranger now, but for Able. She'd wondered at the start if her feelings for him were just midlife crisis and thought they probably wouldn't last, but instead of fading away, the memories just got sweeter and made her wish that he would walk into the bar and smile at her. She might as well wish for the moon!

She sat down while the kettle was boiling, opening Pip's letter first. Her son wrote about once a month these days, normally breezy letters about his life and the fun he was having. Not once did he complain about anything other than the food, though she knew the young men who flew spitfires round the clock to protect the airfields and other strategic targets were going through a rough time, but Pip only joked and said he missed her cooking. He'd written in his untidy scrawl:

Well, Ma, I'll be home on Saturday. They've stood me down for a rest, so I'll have several weeks twiddling my fingers and I thought I'd come home and plague the life out of you. I hope it's all right to bring Sheila. She'll only be staying for a week, after that she has to get back to work, but I'll be home for at least a month – if you can put up with me?

If she could put up with him? Peggy's smile was wider than a mile at the thought of having her son home for more than one night, which was his usual visit, and she loved the idea that she would at last meet his girlfriend. She knew he was serious about Sheila, even though he was still only twenty; of course, he'd grown up fast since he'd joined the RAF and was certainly not a boy these days.

She opened Janet's letter next. The tone of her daughter's letter was definitely more cheerful than it had been of late.

Hope you're coping all right, Mum, and that the twins are well. I'm giving Rosemary a hand with all her charities down here, which keeps us all busy, and Maggie goes to a nursery school for a few hours three mornings a week. It's just playing with other kids and toys, but I think it's good for her, because she has been spoiled – and she was very jealous of the twins. That was part of the reason I came away for a while, and at nursery she's learning she can't always have her own way.

I'm not sure how long I shall stay here. Rosemary says I'm welcome to make my home with her, but I'm not certain it would work in the long run. She seems to be getting over her husband's loss and her sons like her new friend, Jon. Captain Jon Mendlesham is a pilot and he told me he knows Pip. Captain Mendlesham plays cricket with Rosemary's boys and he took us all out to lunch the other Sunday. Rosemary says he's just a friend, but he wants to be more. I can see it when he looks at her. If they got married I couldn't stay on with her, and although I've made friends here, I think I'd rather come back home if it happens.

I think I ought to take a job once Maggie goes to proper school. I know I've helped you, and as I said, we do a lot of charity and volunteer work down here, but I'd like to work for one of the women's volunteer units on a full-time basis. I'd rather wait until Maggie can start the infants' school though, which will be next year if we come back to London. I could get her into St. Martin's when she's four, and then you or Nellie could collect her at three in the afternoon for me when I'm at work, couldn't you? I'd be able to help you at night, give you some time to go out with Maureen or Anne – I hope they're both OK and the children?

Anyway, I know you have lots to do. I hope you've forgiven me for leaving you in the lurch, but I had to get right away, and I'm glad I did. When I come back, can I have a different room please? Perhaps Helen's old room.

Love always, Janet. xxx Maggie sends a hundred kisses to her granny.

Peggy sighed as she folded the letter. Janet was feeling better at last and she thanked God for that but was disappointed that she didn't want to work in the pub when she got back. Of course once Maggie was at school, Janet would be expected to do a useful job. Serving behind a bar wasn't a reserved job, even though it was necessary, but unless she found herself war work of a kind, she might be called up to factory work. The choice had been there at the start, but these days every woman was expected to do at least part-time war work of some kind. Staying home to look after a child wasn't considered an excuse, especially if there was an older relative who could do the childminding for you. Peggy was exempted because she ran the pub and had two children under five, but Janet might find herself being asked to do some form of war work as soon as she put Maggie in school, so it would be best if she found a job she wanted to do first.

Peggy thought she ought to speak to Rose about doing some form of war work as well as her work here. If she signed up on a voluntary basis, either for night work a couple of times a week or did one day a week with a women's voluntary association, she would be fine. Otherwise, she might find herself being asked to enrol for factory work. Every young woman had to be seen to be doing her bit these days. Even Nellie went to help at a forces' relief club two nights a week. She helped sort through donations of clothes, shoes and other items, which were then sold to raise money to send comforts to the troops. She said it made her feel she was helping her son and daughter, who had both signed up to the forces in the early days, as soon as it became apparent that war was inevitable.

Peggy had left Laurie's letter to last. It was always a chore to read them and each time she told herself that next time she would put it straight in the bin, but she never did. Laurie's first words startled her:

I've been given a long leave. It means I'll have to come home, Peggy. There has been a bit of an upset here... and I'm not sure I'll be returning. For the moment I'm suspended and so I shall come back to the pub and make myself useful.

I know this may be a bit awkward, because we've been estranged for a while now, but I really have no choice. I'm sorry... sorry that I caused you hurt, because I know you would never have gone with that young American if I hadn't been such a pig to you, Peggy. It isn't easy to forgive. I've been bitter and angry towards you, and no doubt you felt the same towards me. Yet I hope we can be civilised – even friends.

If my war work is finished here, I should like us to try to make things work again. We both want the pub to do well, and it's time you had help there. So I'm coming home next Sunday and I'll sleep in the spare room. Please try to forgive me and accept what has to be...

Laurie.

Peggy stared at the letter in dismay. She'd thought her husband would be away for the remainder of the war and now he was coming home in a few days. Her thoughts

ROSIE CLARKE

worked swiftly. Rose was using the room Laurie was expecting to occupy. She'd already decided to put her into Janet's room so that her daughter wouldn't have to sleep in the bed where her husband had died; that meant Janet would be relegated to one of the rooms they'd let to guests years ago. There was one large one that had room for a small bed for Maggie, but it needed clearing out and a complete spring clean. Pip would have his old room, of course, and there was another single for Sheila, because they were also coming to stay. The bedrooms would be full to bursting! She would have to ask Tom Barton if he would give her a hand in the evenings after he'd finished at the shop. Alice had been full of praise for the way he'd decorated her little room, and she now had paying lodgers – a young widow called Mary Jenkins and her three-year-old daughter Julie.

'Tom's such a good lad,' Alice had told Peggy the previous evening. 'He worked until nearly midnight to finish that off fer me so I could get me lodgers.'

'Yes, he is,' Peggy said. 'How are you gettin' on with your lodgers then?'

'It's marvellous,' Alice had replied and grinned at her. 'Should've done it long ago, Peggy girl. I get fifteen bob a week for the two rooms and breakfast, and extra if I cook dinner for them – and that means I can cook for meself as well.'

Peggy was glad it had worked out so well for Alice. She would have to ask Tom if he had time to decorate her large guest room for Janet. Her daughter wasn't planning on returning just yet, so there was plenty of time...

'Something wrong, Peggy?'

She turned to look at Nellie, who must have entered the kitchen without her hearing. 'Oh, I was lost in thought, that's all...'

'You've let yer tea go cold,' Nellie said. 'Yer can't fool me, Peggy love. I can see by yer face yer worried over somethin'...'

'Laurie is comin' home on Sunday,' Peggy said. 'He's being released from his post... I suppose he's done his bit for the war...'

'Well, I never thought he should have been asked to go,' Nellie said, nodding her head. 'Laurie Ashley did his bit in the last war. Keeping a pub is a necessary job. Everyone needs somewhere to drink or we'd have folk up in arms...'

Peggy laughed. 'You're right, but you know things haven't been happy between us...'

'He let yer down,' Nellie said staunchly. 'I know yer, Peggy Ashley. If yer man had been straight with yer, you'd 'ave been straight with 'im'

'Would I? I'm not so sure,' Peggy replied. 'I loved Able – I still do. I don't want Laurie back as a husband, but this was always his pub, even though I've been running it these past years; he paid for the licences and the lease and he has a right to come home. I wouldn't stand a chance of getting the licence if Laurie wants it. We shall just have to work out a way of living and working together.'

'You'll manage that all right,' Nellie said. 'Besides, he was a warden before they called him up to do whatever he's been doin' up there – and I shouldn't wonder he'll go back to it. It will keep him out of yer hair fer a while, girl.'

'Well, it should be all right for a few weeks. Pip is bringing his girlfriend here for a week and he has a month's leave... I'm not sure where we're goin' to put everyone.'

'Well, you can 'ave my room,' Nellie said and grinned at her. 'I was goin' ter tell yer today, Peggy. The council 'ave come up with a little flat for me at last...'

'Oh Nellie, I'm so glad for you – if it's what you want? You mustn't think you have to leave. I wasn't intending to ask you to give up your room.'

'I know that,' Nellie said, 'but it's a nice little place, just a tuppenny bus ride away, so I can afford to come into work every day same as usual.'

'I'm glad; I should hate to lose you, but I know how much this means to you...' Peggy was surprised. 'You thought you didn't stand a chance – what happened?'

'My daughter is coming home...' Nellie frowned. 'She's been thrown out of the Wrens because she's pregnant. Her bloke is in the Navy and he's goin' ter marry 'er as soon as he gets back, but we don't know how long that will be...'

Peggy was taken aback. 'Nellie! I don't know whether to congratulate you or say I'm sorry...'

'Don't be sorry, Peggy. The silly girl should've got the ring on 'er finger when 'e was 'ere, but she ain't done nothin' a load of other daft girls ain't done – and at least it means I'll 'ave her 'ome and it put us in line fer a flat...'

'Well, in that case, I think it's wonderful,' Peggy said and darted at her, giving her a hug and a kiss on the cheek.

'Think of it, Nellie – you'll be a grandmother, and you'll love that...'

'Yeah...' Nellie grinned. 'That's the only reason I didn't knock 'er block orf. I shall love 'aving the pair of 'em, Peggy.'

'Yes, of course you will,' Peggy said. 'When is the baby due?'

'Around the middle of July,' Nellie replied, her eyes sparkling. 'I'd better get my knitting needles out. I thought my girl was a confirmed career woman but this changes everythin'... even if she wants to go back to work once the baby is old enough to leave with me.'

Peggy could see how excited Nellie was even though she was trying to hold her excitement in check. 'I think we deserve a drop of sherry,' she said as Rose entered the kitchen. 'You're just in time to celebrate with us, Rose. Nellie is goin' to be a grandmother and my son is bringing his girlfriend to stay – and my husband is coming home for a while too.'

'Oh...' Rose looked a little startled. 'Does that mean you won't need me?'

'No, it certainly doesn't, but it does mean you need to enrol for volunteer work a few evenings a week. We'll get to keep you if we can prove that you're doin' some war work. Otherwise they'll be after you to join one of the forces or the volunteer brigades...'

'Maureen suggested I join the WVS with her,' Rose said. 'She does three nights a week for a few hours – and she does two mornings a week at the hospital. I can't do that, because I'd have to sign on full-time as an auxiliary, but I can join the WVS. I'll go along with Maureen and put my name down.'

'Good for you, Rose. We all have to do our bit. Anne does ambulance driving on Saturdays and Sundays,' Peggy told her. 'She is considered to be in a reserved job, because she's a teacher, but she still does her bit when she can...'

'I can't drive, but I'd like to learn...'

'Both Maureen and Tom are learning to drive,' Peggy said. 'They're very busy people – in fact we all have to be these days. With so many of the men away in the forces they're crying out for volunteers, and it's the law that every woman who can needs to work.'

'Yes, that's what Maureen says...' Rose smiled. 'I got a letter from Jimmy Morgan this morning. He says they're embarking for somewhere warm. He doesn't think it's the desert this time, but the kit they've been given is lightweight so that has to be somewhere warm, doesn't it?'

'Might be Egypt or Malaysia, or anywhere come to that. We've got men serving all over the place now,' Peggy said. 'They can't tell us where they are in their letters, but when they come home they have plenty to say...'

'Well, I'm going to join one of the volunteer services and then I can tell Jimmy I'm doing my bit, can't I?'

'Yes, you can,' Peggy agreed and handed both her and Nellie a glass of sherry. 'Let's drink to the new baby – and to victory for the Allies...'

'And let's hope the war is soon over,' Nellie added.

'Yes, let's hope they all come home soon...' Rose said and sipped her sherry just as they heard a wail from upstairs. 'That's Fay. I'll go, Peggy – it must be nearly time for you to open the bar...'

'Goodness me, you're right,' Peggy said and looked at the clock on the wall. 'In all the excitement I'd forgotten. I'd better get through there right now.'

Chapter 7

'Are you desperate for anything?' Maureen asked when she popped into the shop that afternoon and found Tom rearranging his shelves. She'd just finished one of her two mornings at the hospital. Maureen considered she was lucky to get even two shifts a week, because a married woman with a child was very seldom taken back. However, Sister Morrison had put in a good word for her, telling her privately that the latest batch of new recruits were the worst they'd had. Maureen took this with a pinch of salt, remembering that she too had been considered useless when she first started in the hospital at Portsmouth, but she was grateful for the shifts she was given. As yet her pregnancy was in its early stages and she wasn't suffering any of the aches and pains that she'd had with Robin towards the end of her term with him.

Her various jobs meant that she was constantly busy, and that Gran was asked to look after Robin while she worked. Maureen usually took him with her in the pushchair when she visited friends or the shop, but not when she went to the wholesaler, because she needed to seem efficient and business-like there. Gran never minded babysitting at night, and when Shirley was home from school no one was allowed to do much for her brother; she ran after him, spoiling him as if he were a little king and he only had to point at something and she would give it to him.

Tom looked at his list, then, 'No, we're just short of the things you couldn't get last time, but we need all the usual stuff. I've made a list, but if there's anything going just bring it – we need to fill the shelves.'

'Did you order some more toys and trinkets? Anything that helps to keep trade goin' at the moment is a good thing.'

'Yes, but Ben has been into hospital for treatment on his back and it made him very sore so he hasn't been able to do much recently.'

'Oh, poor Ben,' Maureen said sympathetically. 'I know he suffers but he's always so cheerful you forget what he has to put up with…'

'He's only twenty-two,' Tom said. 'The injuries he suffered have aged him and he looks older, but that's all he is…'

'Well, tell him we love his toys and will keep stocking them for as long as the war lasts…'

'Yeah, I shall,' Tom said and pulled a face as he saw a customer coming. 'It's Irene from the hairdresser's. She's always popping in for a few sweets or some biscuits these days. I took her to the flicks and she never stopped chattering the whole time. I think she considers herself my girl now – but we're just friends.'

Maureen laughed and then said, 'Make it clear to her now, Tom, or she will claim you've broken her heart.'

'I've tried to,' Tom said ruefully, 'but— Hello, Irene. What can I do for you?'

'I'll get off then,' Maureen said. 'Don't forget you have a double driving lesson this evening…'

'Oh… no, I won't…' he shot her a grateful smile, because his driving lessons weren't until the weekend, but it would serve as an excuse if Irene asked him out again.

'I wish I could learn to drive,' she said wistfully as the door closed behind Maureen. 'I could never afford lessons on my wages…'

'Nor can I,' Tom said. 'Maureen is paying because she wants me to drive the van she's bought. She's going to use it for ferrying her kids about – and I'm going to deliver groceries with it sometimes.'

'You could take us to the sea next summer,' Irene said, giving him a hopeful look, but Tom shook his head.

'It's not my van, it's Maureen's. I wouldn't ask her if I could use it just for a pleasure trip. Besides, you'll have a proper boyfriend by then, Irene. A girl like you will be courtin' in no time… and I hope to be in the Army.'

Irene frowned, because it wasn't what she wanted to hear. She asked for biscuits and Tom told her they had some plain ones or some ginger snaps.

'No chocolate biscuits,' he said. 'We've got some penny bars of milk chocolate though. Maureen got a box last week and I've kept them under the counter for those that ask…'

Irene bought a packet of ginger snaps and two penny bars of chocolate. She took them and the ration book and went out, giving him a look that accused him of breaking her heart, but he steadfastly ignored it. Irene was only fifteen and she would get a crush on a lot of men before she found the right one – and Tom certainly wasn't it. He'd only taken her to the pictures as a friend on an impulse, but she'd clung to his arm and tried everything she knew to get him to kiss her, but he'd simply taken her home, thanked her and said goodnight. Irene was still a little girl to Tom, even if she thought differently.

His thoughts were suspended as the girl he most admired walked into the shop. Rose looked lovely. She was wearing a pink jumper and a grey pleated skirt, and her hair was brushed back off her face showing her ears in which she wore tiny silver earrings.

'Hello, Tom,' she said and smiled at him. 'Peggy wants you to call round this evening if you can. She needs a room redecorating... it's for Janet when she comes home. I'm having her old room and Pip is bringing his girl home for a week – and Mr Ashley is coming back too...'

'Mr Ashley is coming back – is that for good?' Tom asked, a little surprised.

'Peggy just said he was coming back.' Rose looked at some magazines and picked one. 'I'd like to buy this – and a quarter pound of fruit sweets, please.'

'We've got raspberry drops, barley sugar or Tom Thumb drops,' he said. 'Which would you prefer?'

'I think the Tom Thumb drops,' she said. 'I like to suck several different flavours in one go...'

Tom laughed, because he liked that too. 'Yes,' he said. 'Nothing else tastes like them... A quarter pound then?'

'Please…' Rose said and hesitated. 'What can I send to a soldier? I'd like to send small gifts every now and then – what is easy to post and would keep?'

Tom's heart sank, but he'd always known she would think he was too young for her. 'Well, you could send a few cigarettes – but we've got some small tins of mint humbugs in at the moment. You could send ten ciggies and a tin of the humbugs. It makes a nice parcel… Oh, there are some toffees as well in rolls…'

'I've got all my sweet coupons,' Rose said. 'I'll take the humbugs, two of those toffee rolls – and twenty Players. Jimmy smoked those when he took me out to tea.'

Obviously Rose thought a lot of her friend, if she was prepared to sacrifice her sweet coupons and buy him twenty cigarettes. She couldn't earn much at the pub helping Peggy.

He grinned as he put the various things on the counter in front of her, because Tom liked her too much to hold a grudge just because she had a boyfriend. 'Your boyfriend will be pleased to get these…'

'Jimmy is just a friend,' Rose said. 'I like him and he took me out to tea – but he only wants to be friends, because he isn't sure he'll come back.'

'Of course he will,' Tom said. 'Any man would come back for a girl like you, Rose. I'd make sure I didn't get myself killed if I was out there and had you waiting for me.'

Rose went into a peal of delighted laughter, making Tom colour up again. 'Oh Tom, you are lovely,' she said as she paid for her goods and scooped them into her pocket. 'If you were a bit older, I'd let you take me dancing…'

It was on the tip of Tom's tongue to say he would take her dancing that Saturday, but before he could build up the courage to say it she had gone, throwing a mischievous look at him as she closed the door.

Tom knew she was teasing him. Rose was a bit of a flirt, he thought, but it didn't stop him liking her and wishing he was older. If he was in the Army, perhaps she would take him seriously. It was the wrong time in his life for Tom to fall in love with a girl, especially a girl who already had a soldier friend she was keen on. Yet he couldn't help himself wanting to take her in his arms and kiss her.

'Daft lad,' he told himself and laughed. Rose was too beautiful, too intelligent and wonderful to be interested in a bloke like him, but one day he would be older. He just had to hope that by the time he was old enough to go courting, she wasn't already married with children of her own.

Tom returned to rearranging the shelves. He thought it best if everything wasn't in the same place all the time. There was nothing he could do to fill empty shelves, but most shopkeepers were in the same boat these days. He wasn't sure this life would suit him forever, but he had to be patient. The recruiting officer had hinted that if he kept going down there to pester them about taking him in the Army, he'd find himself down the mines.

Maureen was right about him learning to drive. If he had a skill like that the Army would have more use for him and be less inclined to send him off to a job he knew he would hate.

*

Maureen was walking home from the wholesalers. She was hurrying because she'd spent a long time looking round the large warehouse; they'd had a lot of stock come in that morning and Maureen had been lucky. The boss liked her and told her it was a case of first come first served these days.

'You all get your share of the rationed stuff,' Malcolm had told her. 'But you're a regular, Maureen, and have been for years – all that stuff over there is fresh in, so pick whatever you need.' He'd pointed to a large trolley that they used to move stuff round the warehouse.

Maureen had found things they hadn't been able to get for ages, including a box of knicker elastic, pins, needles, cottons, writing paper and envelopes and – joy of joys! – a box of fully fashioned silk stockings containing two dozen pairs in cellophane packets. She'd bought an assortment of bits, knowing that Tom worried about his empty shelves and making use of Malcolm's generosity to stock up on everything she could, including tins of black treacle, condensed milk, tinned fruit cocktail, packets of custard powder, some fresh eggs and a side of bacon, also several large tins of corned beef, which Tom would slice for the customers as needed. She was smiling as she thought of his pleasure when the delivery van unloaded that little lot tomorrow. It would keep him busy for a while and stop him thinking of running off to be a soldier for a few months longer.

So, as she walked briskly home through the lanes, Maureen was smiling, content with a good day's work and the prospect of getting home to her children and Gran. There might even be a letter from Gordon…

'Hello, Maureen – did you think I'd forgotten all about you?'

A shock ran through Maureen as she heard the voice – a voice she'd once dreamed of with longing but now dreaded. 'What do you want, Rory?' she said warily and looked at him. He looked tanned and healthy, which probably meant he'd been abroad for a while. Rory no longer served with the fighting forces, but the last thing she'd heard, he was working with the Army logistics, moving equipment for the troops.

Rory's eyes were hard as he met hers. 'I told you I should want to see my son – and I've come to London for that purpose…'

'Robin isn't your son,' Maureen lied. 'I don't care what you say, Rory. He's mine – and Gordon's. Nothing to do with you at all…'

'I'm not a bloody fool,' Rory said and grabbed her arm, looking down at her fiercely. His fingers bit into her arm but she didn't cry out. 'I'll be round tomorrow and I want to see him – there will be trouble if you try to stop me. I'm warnin' you…'

'Leave me alone…' Maureen pulled back from him, but he held her tightly and she gave a little yelp of alarm.

'What do yer think yer doin', mate?' a man's voice startled Rory and he relaxed his hold on her arm. 'The lady wants to go – let her or yer might find it's you getting' a taste of yer own medicine… I don't like bullies.'

'You and whose bloody army?' Rory grunted, but as the man came nearer, his face paled as the large shadow loomed over him and he let go of her arm. 'I ain't hurtin' her – I'll be round tomorrow, Maureen, so be there…'

Rory turned and walked off abruptly and Maureen glanced up at the man-mountain that was her rescuer. He was wearing the uniform of a sergeant in the Army but she didn't know him.

'Thank you so much…'

'I can't stand bullies,' the soldier said. 'I'm lookin' for Mulberry Lane – can you show me the way please, Mrs… sorry, I don't know yer name?'

'I'm Maureen Hart. I live just round the corner of Mulberry Lane. It's on my way home. Walk with me and I'll show you…'

'Right, thanks,' the soldier said. 'My name is Sid Coleman. I'm looking for a pub by the name of…'

'The Pig & Whistle?' Maureen said and the soldier nodded. 'My friend Peggy runs it… Do you know her?'

'No, but I've met her son; he told me to call in and have a drink, when I was in town.' He looked thoughtful. 'I was in hospital for some months and I've been convalescing – they were finding me a job because my spine was damaged and I can't go back to the front line…'

'You should tell Peggy you know Pip,' Maureen said. 'If she knows you're a friend of her son's, she'll be pleased to see you.'

'We know each other, but we're not exactly mates. We meet at the same pub now and then and play darts. I'm

84

the leader of the Army team and Pip is the best man on the RAF side – so it's a sort of friendly rivalry, but you could say we get on all right.'

'Well, Peggy will be delighted to meet you, I'm sure,' Maureen said, 'and it was lucky for me that you happened along…'

'Who was the bully threatening you?'

'A previous boyfriend,' Maureen said, flushing. 'He doesn't like it that I found someone else…'

'Everyone has the right to change their mind,' the soldier said. 'Ah, I can see the pub… Are you all right to get home now?'

'Yes, I'm fine,' Maureen lied. 'I'm not frightened of Rory – he just won't take no for an answer.'

'You should be wary of him,' the soldier said. 'I've seen plenty of his type – and they can be nasty. You take care, Maureen…'

'Yes, I shall, thanks again…'

Maureen turned away to her home in Gun Street, leaving him to cross the road and enter The Pig & Whistle through the front door. She quickened her step because Gran would be getting worried.

'The bed ain't been used for a while, mate,' Tom said to the soldier he'd met at Peggy's that evening. His name was Sid Coleman and he was looking for somewhere to stay for a few days. Pip had told him that Peggy would put him up, but she had everyone descending on her at once and couldn't manage it, so Tom had offered him somewhere to sleep. 'I can give yer toast and stuff in the morning – but you'll have to eat out somewhere…'

'I'll eat at the pub,' Sid said and grinned. 'Don't worry about changing sheets for me, Tom. If you'd been sleepin' where I have recently, you'd know this bed was sheer luxury.'

'It was my brother's…' Tom said. 'I've changed the sheets recently and I don't think they're damp…' He shook his head. 'Well, you're welcome to stay for as long as you like.'

'Thanks.' Sid looked appreciative. 'It's just a few days this time, half business, half on leave – but if I'm seconded to the general, I may want to come back again on a more permanent basis.' Seeing Tom's curiosity, he grinned. 'I've been recommended as a driver for a general; his name's confidential, but they think he needs a bodyguard-cum-dogsbody and I'm it. It means driving him wherever he wants to go and lookin' after him twenty-four seven. Still, it's a picnic compared to where we've been…'

'Where have you been – were you at El Alamein?' Tom asked eagerly.

Sid laughed good-naturedly. 'I was certainly at Tobruk and a few other places in Africa,' he said. 'Keen on joinin' up are yer?'

Grinning, Tom said, 'I've been down the recruitin' office so many times they practically threatened to send me down the mines if I didn't stop botherin' them.'

Sid threw back his head and laughed so hard his whole body shook. He was dark-haired with a square chin and a big nose but had the kind of looks that people trusted and liked.

'I wish I'd had you in my troop,' he told Tom and clapped him on the shoulder. 'I think you'll make a fine soldier, Tom. How old are you?'

'Seventeen, eighteen in April...' Tom sighed. 'I know it's goin' to be all over by the time I get in – and I'm itchin' to give the Germans a whacking.'

'You'll get yer chance,' Sid said. 'I reckon we could get you into the cadets – hasn't anyone spoken to you about joining the reserves? They're blokes could be called up quick if needed, and they give yer all the regular trainin'.'

'I'll join anythin' if it helps me to be a soldier...' Tom was all eagerness.

'I'll see what I can do if I get seconded to that general. He could get you in with no fuss, but there are other ways – leave it to me, Tom. You're a big lad for yer age. I reckon we should be makin' use of a lad like you...'

Tom thanked him, leaving him to settle into his room. It was good having someone in the house again. He'd come very close to giving his home up recently, because it was a waste just for one, and Ma wasn't ever coming back, but he'd hung on for his father's sake. It was a place for Jack to come when he was home on leave and he paid the rent, but he might decide not to bother if he knew for sure that Ma wasn't coming back.

Tom had been to the infirmary again asking to see her, but they told him she'd been transferred to a secure hospital where she would get treatment for her mental problems. Now he'd got himself a lodger, temporarily, but there was a possibility he'd want to keep the room and return whenever he was in London with his general. Tom would enjoy the company of a man who had done his bit for the Army.

Chapter 8

Ellie bought the items Mabel had asked her to pick up after work and Tom had shown her the silk stockings, letting her buy a pair. She was feeling very pleased, because he'd told her they were rationing them to a single pair each for their regular customers, but only a few pairs remained so she was lucky to get them. She would have liked to be going to a dance somewhere to wear them, but that was only wishful thinking.

As she turned to leave, Ellie almost bumped into the soldier patiently waiting for his turn at the counter. He grinned and caught her arm, steadying her as she tried to avoid stepping on his toes and dropping half her purchases.

'I'm sorry,' she said and bobbed down to retrieve them. He did the same and their heads almost touched. Ellie blushed, embarrassed. 'I'm an idiot. I was so excited about getting some silk stockings and didn't notice you there...'

The soldier laughed, and Ellie laughed too, because he was rather too big to miss. 'Well, I must have shrunk a bit in the night,' he said. 'Don't you worry, miss – you couldn't hurt these great clodhoppers of mine if yer stamped on them.'

'I'd better go,' Ellie said, sobering as she remembered what had happened the last time she'd laughed and talked with a soldier.

'You get right on, little lady,' the soldier said. 'I've only come in for some ciggies and to tell Tom I'll need my room for at least three weeks this time...'

'Are you stayin' for three weeks?' Tom said and looked pleased. 'You got the job then?'

'Yeah, I start tomorrow – the only thing is... security might want to vet you, Tom. You won't take offence if they come round and ask a few questions?'

'Nah, course not,' Tom said, still looking delighted.

Ellie left the shop before she heard any more. The large soldier was called Sid and he was obviously all right or he wouldn't be staying with Tom Barton. She thought about the way he'd smiled at her and felt wistful, because there was something nice and comforting about him.

Going round to the back of Mabel Tandy's property, Ellie entered the kitchen and put her bits and pieces on the table. She could hear her little daughter crying and went quickly upstairs. Mabel was trying to feed her some milky rice pudding, but Beth was red-faced and miserable, which wasn't like her.

'Why won't she feed?' Ellie asked. 'I had difficulty feeding her this morning – but she did take some milk. Is she ill? She looks very red in the face...'

'Yes, I know. I think she might have a little temperature, Ellie. Do you want to take her round the doctor's? You'll be in time for the evening surgery and I'll get on with supper while you're gone...'

'Yes, all right,' Ellie said and reached for her child. Beth felt hot and there was a little rash on her cheeks. She picked up a blanket from the back of a chair and wrapped it round her. Beth might be feverish and over-warm, but it was cold out now towards the end of February. She didn't want her little girl to get a chill, because despite the way Beth had been got on her by force, she loved her to bits and couldn't imagine how she'd ever considered giving her away. 'I'd have come home earlier if I'd realised…'

'I was just thinkin' of phoning the doctor and askin' him to call, but you'll get seen sooner if you take her round,' Mabel said, looking serious.

Ellie nodded and went quickly down the stairs and into the lane. The soldier she'd seen in the shop was standing by a large black car parked across the street and rubbing at the shining bonnet with a duster. He looked at her as she crossed the street and seemed to pick up on her anxiety instantly.

'Is the kiddie ill?' he asked as Beth started screaming.

'Yes, I'm taking her to the doctor's.'

'Is it far? I'll take you in the car if you like…'

Ellie hesitated. She wouldn't normally get into a car with a man she didn't know, but this one seemed genuine and the fact that he was staying with Tom made her feel safer.

'Yes, please. The surgery is at the end of Commercial Road. I can direct you…'

'I know the road,' Sid said and smiled encouragingly at her. He took a peep at Beth and nodded. 'Don't worry, love – we'll soon have you there. Poor little mite looks proper poorly…'

'Yes…' Ellie swallowed a sob. 'I knew she was off her food this morning, but I was busy at work and Mabel, my landlady, looks after her until I get home and she didn't call me…'

'Probably thought it was just a little chill. Babies get lots of them and most aren't serious but upsetting for them and their mums.'

Ellie settled into the front seat beside him. The seats were leather and smelled of polish. She glanced shyly at the obliging man at her side as he drove.

'You sound as if you have kids of your own?'

'No, but my elder sister has four, up to the age of nine – and I've often been roped in for nappy changing and bottle feeding.' He smiled and Ellie realised he was really nice-looking when he smiled that way. 'Don't worry, Ellie – hope you don't mind my usin' yer name. Tom told me who you were when I asked.' He laughed. 'I was sayin' how pretty yer were and he told me you was married…'

'Peter is in the Army like you,' Ellie said, her cheeks pink. It was a good thing that Tom had told him she was married, because Peter would kill her if she was seen with other men. Ellie wasn't in the least afraid that Sid would do what that awful Knocker had done to her. He just wasn't the sort of man that would rape and beat a young woman, but perhaps that made him even more dangerous, because Ellie was very much in need of some loving kindness. Mabel Tandy loved her and treated her like a daughter, but that wasn't like being with a man who loved you. With Beth whimpering in her arms, Ellie couldn't help wishing that the man driving her to the doctor's was someone she could turn to and cry on, but she had to be careful and remember strangers could be dangerous.

She was thoughtful as the car slowed to a halt. Sid jumped out and opened the door for her and then took the baby while she climbed out. He gave her back and looked around.

'There's a place I can park just around the corner. I can't leave the car, but I can wait if you want a lift back...'

'No, you go,' Ellie said. 'I'll be all right to walk home. I wanted to get here quick, but I'll be fine now...'

'Just as you like. I hope the child is all right...'

Sid got back in the car and drove off as Ellie went into the doctor's surgery. It smelled of stale sweat and sickness, also strong drink on the breath of an old man who looked like a tramp. Ellie went to the reception desk and told her she was worried about her little girl, because she was hot and had a rash.

'Take a seat over there. Doctor will see you as soon as he can...'

Ellie did as she was told, jiggling the child in her arms as she tried to hush her, but Beth had reached the screaming stage and she saw the receptionist look at her several times. At last she came over to her and looked at Beth.

'I've moved you up the list, Mrs Morris. Beth is clearly very unwell and I think the doctor needs to see her now...'

'Thank you,' Ellie said, her throat tight with anxiety. 'I can't quiet her – perhaps I should have stayed home and asked for a call.'

'No, it's best you brought her. You'll be in in a moment…'

The doctor came out a minute or two later and called her name. Ellie followed him into the surgery and explained the situation. He told her to put Beth down on his couch and then he examined her while Ellie watched anxiously over her.

'I'm glad you brought her in, Mrs Morris. I'm going to send Beth along to the hospital immediately, and of course you must go with her…'

'What is wrong with her?' Ellie was frantic with worry now.

'I'm not certain, but I think it could be meningitis, though I haven't seen many cases, so I'm not sure, it might be a form of sepsis, which is a kind of poisoning…' He paused, looking worried. 'I've heard of a treatment – a kind of vaccine called Flexner's, but I don't know if it works in all cases…'

Ellie had never heard any of the words before, but she could see that the doctor thought it was serious. 'Will she be all right?' she asked, beginning to tremble.

'I won't lie to you, Mrs Morris. I fear your little girl is very ill and it will be touch-and-go. We're not very good with illnesses like this as yet…'

His answer terrified her. Beth couldn't die, not after all she'd been through to keep her.

'No! Please, don't let her die…' Ellie was crying, the tears slipping down her cheeks.

'Is there anyone who can take you to the hospital?' Ellie shook her head. 'Go and sit in the waiting room. My receptionist will give you a form to take with you and an ambulance will come…'

The doctor escorted her back to the waiting room, but as he was telling the receptionist what to do, Sid came up to them.

'I found a place to park safely. Is it serious, Ellie?'

'She has to go to hospital. They're sending for an ambulance…'

'I can take you quicker,' Sid said and looked at the doctor. 'Just tell me where and I'll take her now…'

Ellie was crying as Sid took the form she needed and guided her out to the car, which he'd parked at the back of one of the better shops in the road. He opened the door for her and she got in obediently, feeling numbed.

'He says it might be meningitis or sepsis. I don't know what either is – do you?'

'I know they're not good,' he said and looked at her sideways. 'The sooner we get Beth to the hospital, the better. Try not to worry, Ellie. Babies are stronger than everyone thinks. And it may not be that… it could be just a nasty rash of some sort…'

'Why did the doctor send her straight to hospital?'

'Because if she is really ill, it's the best place.'

Ellie nodded. It was stupid, but she felt so much better now that Sid was with her. 'You'll stay with me at the hospital – won't you?'

'Yes, of course. I have to report for work at eight in the morning, but I'll stay as long as I can…'

'Thank you…' Ellie looked at him shyly. 'I love her so much. I don't want to lose her.'

'We're getting to the hospital now,' he said and gave her a reassuring look. 'We'll know soon… Keep your chin up, love. It may not be as bad as it seems.'

Ellie had never been as anxious or as distressed as she felt when the doctors took her little girl away to examine her. She kept looking at Sid, her eyes brimming with tears, begging him silently to tell her it was all right. After half an hour with no word from anyone, she was shaking and Sid put his arm about her, holding her tightly as they saw the doctor coming towards them. He looked at Ellie and then at Sid.

'I'm pleased to tell you, Sergeant Morris – Mrs Morris. It isn't meningitis…'

'Oh, thank God,' Ellie said and swayed, not even noticing that the doctor had mistaken Sid for her husband, or that he'd accepted it without comment. Sid put his arm around her and held her, comforting her. 'What is it?'

'It is a kind of food poisoning, which causes symptoms that can look like a more dangerous illness,' the doctor said and frowned. 'It means that it is still serious, but fortunately we are able to treat this sickness – and she will be kept in hospital for a couple of days until it's under control. I think it is better if you go home for now, Mrs Morris. Is there some way we can contact you?'

'Yes, Mrs Tandy – my landlady has a telephone,' Ellie said and gave him the number. 'But can't I stay with her, please?'

'It would be too distressing. Beth is in the best place, Mrs Morris. Nurse will take good care of her and we'll let you know how she is in the morning.'

Ellie wanted to plead with them to let her stay, but hospitals were such daunting places and she knew they would not relent. Beth was in their care now and relatives were not allowed into the wards except at strict visiting times. She felt close to collapsing. The doctor seemed to realise that she was distraught.

He looked at Sid. 'Please take your wife home, sergeant. She really can't stay here...'

'Come on, Ellie, we'd better go,' Sid said. 'The doctor and nurses will look after her – and you would just be in the way...'

Ellie nodded, but looked back several times as Sid took her out of the hospital. 'What if she dies?'

'She won't, Ellie. The doctor told you, it is something they can treat...'

'How could she have got food poisoning? We sterilise her bottle and boil her nappies...'

'I don't know, Ellie,' he said. 'Maybe, she got dirty hands somehow herself and put them in her mouth – who knows. She's ill, but it isn't the worst...'

Ellie mopped her tears on the hanky he gave her. She looked at him as he opened the car door for her to get in. 'I'll never be able to thank you for this,' she said. 'I don't know what I'd have done on my own...'

'I'm glad I was there and you don't need to repay me. I've only done what any decent bloke would do...'

Ellie didn't answer, but she knew Peter wouldn't have done as much. He wouldn't have tried to comfort her and he would have been glad if the child died. She swallowed hard, knowing that she was facing the truth at last. She'd tried to believe that everything would be fine when Peter came home, but she knew it wouldn't. He would be angry that she'd kept Beth – and, if she was honest, she didn't want to live with him ever again.

'Cheer up, love,' Sid said gently as they pulled to a halt in front of the wool shop. 'I'm sure your little girl will be all right – the doctor seemed confident and that's a good sign.'

'Yes, it is,' she whispered. 'Thank you – thank you so much for everything…'

'I really did nothing,' Sid said, but Ellie suspected that he had risked getting into trouble because of what he'd done for her. 'I shan't see you in the morning – but may I come and ask how Beth is when I've finished for the evening? It might be nine or even ten…'

'Yes, please come,' Ellie said and smiled at him. 'Goodnight, Sid.'

'Goodnight, Ellie.'

He smiled at her, watched as she went into small passage that led to the back of the house and then got back into the car, driving off round the corner to the garage that had been arranged for his general's official car… He'd taken some risks with it, driving her to the doctor and then the hospital and leaving it parked where anyone could have tampered with it or even stolen it. And he'd done that for her sake, when he knew that if anything had happened to it he could have lost the job he'd only just been given.

★

Maureen walked home quickly the next morning. She'd left Gran to look after Robin while she went to the shop. She'd warned Gran that Rory might call and hoped that he hadn't forced her to let him in so that he could see his son. Perhaps if he'd been more respectful and asked rather than demanded she might not have minded him just looking at Robin – but if he thought he was going to have any say in how her son was brought up, he had another thing coming...

As she rounded the corner, she saw him leaning against the lamp post on the opposite side of the street, smoking a cigarette, and knew he'd waited for her. Maureen squared her shoulders, because there was no one to help her this time. Twice when Rory had been rough with her someone had turned up, but she couldn't expect it to happen all the time. She had to stand up for herself.

'So you're back then,' Rory said, crossing the road to meet her. 'You know what I want, Molly...'

'Don't call me that,' she said coldly. She'd liked it when he called her that once but not anymore. 'Robin's my son and Gordon is his father... so there's no point in you wantin' to see him.'

'I have to get back to my unit this evenin', but I'm not leavin' until I see him – you know he's mine, so don't deny it.' He looked at her stubbornly, but he wasn't aggressive this time. Maureen realised she wasn't afraid of him and her tension eased.

'I could've been cheatin' on you while you were cheatin' on me with Carol,' Maureen said, her head going up proudly. 'I think you've forfeited all the rights you ever had as far as I'm concerned – and that goes for my son, too.'

'I know you hate me now and maybe you've got a right,' Rory admitted. 'I'm not goin' to try and take him away from you, Maureen – I just want to see him before they send me overseas again. Please... I know you loved me once.'

Rory had always been able to turn on the charm when it suited him.

'Yes, I did and you broke my heart more than once,' Maureen said. 'Don't think you can walk back into my life and take over again...'

'I don't and I *am* sorry. Believe me; I've regretted what I did. I was a bloody fool, Molly... Please, just let me see him. I shan't trouble you often, but he is mine, I know it in my guts.'

Maureen hesitated and was lost. He was Robin's father despite her denials and perhaps she'd been unfair to forbid him. At least he hadn't been drinking this time.

'You can look but you can't touch...' she said and he smiled in the way that had once had the power to make her heart turn over. 'I mean it, Rory. If you try to snatch him, I'll kill you... I'd stick a knife in you rather than let you take him.'

Rory nodded, but she saw a gleam in his eyes and wished she'd stuck to her guns as she allowed him to follow her into the house. Gran was in the kitchen and Robin was in his playpen, sitting on a blanket and making bubbles as he chewed at the ear of his ragged old teddy bear, which had been hers as a child and Gran had kept.

'He's been hanging around outside all mornin',' Gran said when she saw Rory and shook her head. She held up a heavy cast-iron ladle and thrust it at his face. 'Any funny business and you'll feel this, my lad.'

'I just want to look at him...' Rory kneeled down on the peg rug that covered half the kitchen floor and stared at the child in the playpen. There was such hunger in his face that Maureen's heart caught. She'd suspected him of all sorts of things, but it seemed he only wanted to see his son – and perhaps he had the right after all. 'Hello, Robin... I'm a friend of yer mum's, see...' He took a small bar of chocolate from his pocket and broke a piece off. 'Can he have it?'

'I suppose so...' Maureen said and watched as her son took the offering and put it in his mouth, chewing and smiling because he liked the taste. 'He does like milk chocolate.'

'Here,' Rory gave her the rest of the bar. 'For when he wants it later...'

He put a tentative hand through the bars and Robin grabbed it, biting his fingers and making Rory yelp in surprise.

'He bites everything at the moment,' Maureen said. 'His teeth are coming through and it hurts when he gives you a good nip.'

'Yes...' Rory rubbed his hand. He got to his feet, then bent and tussled the little boy's hair, which was redder than his own. 'He's a fine boy, Molly – take care of him, won't you?'

'Of course we shall. He's spoiled because we all love him...'

'He is mine, isn't he?' Rory looked at her pleadingly.

'Yours may have been the seed that gave him life, but he's mine, Rory – and I'm married to someone else. He will be brought up as our son. You have to accept that...'

'I do,' Rory said surprising her. 'Velma turned up again and now she's claiming she's still my wife. She now says her first husband was a bigamist and so, according to her, we're still married. It's all a pack of lies and when I get back after the war I'll sort her out, even if I have to get a divorce to be rid of her. Whatever she says, I shall never live with her after the way she neglected my child and let it die... and I couldn't take care of my son while there's a war on. I wouldn't let her near him! So it's best that you keep him safe, but I'm reserving the right to see him sometimes. I know he won't die of neglect in your house—'

Maureen understood his anger for she had seen the way Velma neglected their child, leading to its death.

'No, we shall keep him healthy and safe if we can,' Maureen said. 'You can rely on that, Rory – but why let yourself be ruled by Velma? Surely you do have enough cause to divorce her?'

'Yeah, I might if I come back,' Rory said. 'I'm being sent abroad again, Molly – not as a soldier, but as part of the maintenance and logistics team at base camp. I think it's pretty dicey where we're goin' and I might not get back.'

'I thought you would be safe here in England now...' Maureen was doubtful. 'Your eyesight isn't as good as it should be – is it?'

'I can see well enough to do my job and I volunteered,' he said. 'They didn't want to take me, because they say

I've done my bit, but I pestered them and now I'm goin'. To be honest, I don't care if I come back... I've got nothin' much ter live for – and if I stay here I'll probably end up being hung for murder...because, I'll do fer that bitch afore I'm done.'

'Oh, Rory...' Maureen felt a moment of sadness. He looked so alone and even desperate, and she had loved him once. 'You shouldn't feel like that – one day you'll find someone you can be happy with...'

'And what if I did? I'd probably let her down again. I know I didn't deserve you, Molly – but you were the only one I loved. If I come home I may visit to see how my son is, but I promise I shan't harm either of you. You didn't need protection the other day. I would never hurt you... more than I already have. And I love him as much as I could love anyone.' His voice broke on a muffled sob.

Maureen's throat was tight, but she refused to let herself be swayed. Rory had always known how to charm, but she wasn't going to give him an inch, because underneath the charm, he was selfish and thoughtless and he would hurt them again without trying if she let him.

'I'm sorry you're unhappy,' she said, 'but I can't change things. I love Gordon and he's my husband and the father of my unborn child. We have three children, or we shall have when this one is born. You should divorce Velma and find someone to give you children of your own...'

'I only ever wanted you...' he said and then turned and walked out of the kitchen. Maureen heard the street door close behind him.

'Well, that's a turn-up for the books,' Gran said, looking at her oddly. 'What made you let him in, Maureen?'

'I don't know – perhaps he has the right. I deny it, but Robin is his son.'

'Now you've started it, he'll come back again and again.' Gran shook her head. 'Don't trust that one, Maureen. He laid it on thick about Velma, but I wouldn't believe a word he says. He's just trying to play on your sympathy. You take my word for it. He's a bad penny and they always turn up...'

'I know, Gran. I'm over him now, I really am, but I'm not sure I could've stopped him. He was determined to see Robin – and he could've forced his way in if I refused. I thought it better to get it over.'

'Well, just be on your guard all the same,' Gran said. 'He couldn't look after the boy yet, but if he ever gets a decent home, look out. He hasn't done with you yet, I'll swear.'

'When the war is over, Gordon will be home again. He'll keep us all safe...'

'Oh, there's a letter on the dresser,' Gran said. 'I didn't say anythin' while that Rory Mackness was 'ere, but I'm sure it's from Gordon, although the writin' is a bit odd...'

'Lovely!' Maureen swooped on the letter and tore it open. 'Yes, it's from Gordon...' She caught her breath on a sob. 'Oh no, he's been wounded badly. He didn't write this Gran – a friend has done it for him. He sends his love and says he should be home soon... in a hospital anyway...' She stared at her grandmother, one hand going to her stomach as if to protect her child. 'Oh, Gran.

I've been longing for him to come home – but not badly wounded…' Tears spilled over as she held the letter to her breast. 'What am I goin' to do if—'

'You can stop that nonsense at once,' her grandmother said. 'Cryin' won't solve anythin' and it's bad for the baby. You need to be healthy and strong to bear a healthy baby…'

'Yes, I know…' Maureen swiped the tears from her face with the back of her hand. 'I don't want to lose Gordon, Gran. I didn't realise how much I loved him until he had to go back last time and then it really hit me…'

'Well, I dare say he'll get over whatever it is – he didn't say what injuries he has?'

'No, just that he's being sent home, but it must be serious. It has to be to get a Blighty pass…'

'Yes, I know that, my girl – but keep your chin up. He'll want you smilin' and happily awaitin' the birth of your child when he sees you, not weepin' all over the show.'

Maureen bit back her tears. She'd been worrying over Rory the last few hours and now Gordon was injured. If anything happened to him, she didn't know if she could bear it. It had taken her a while to really love him, but she did and she didn't want to lose him.

Chapter 9

'Oh thank God,' Mabel said when Ellie gave her the good news the next day. Beth was responding to treatment; her fever had gone and the spots were fading. 'I should never have forgiven myself if anything had happened to her.'

'It wouldn't be your fault,' Ellie told her. 'Honestly, Mabel. She must have picked up somethin' when she was crawlin' around and put it in her mouth – no one can watch a lively child all the time. It might have been an infection off that old tin toy I found in the pawn shop. I've thrown it out just in case.'

Mabel mopped at her eyes with a lace hanky. 'I'm so glad she's gettin' better – and it was fortunate that you got her to the hospital so quickly.'

'That was Sid's doing,' Ellie said. 'He was so kind, Mabel. Taking us to the doctor's surgery and then the hospital – and he stayed with me when I was goin' out of my mind with worry, and brought me back...'

'Yes, that was kind of him,' Mabel Tandy said, looking a bit anxious. 'I know I don't have to tell you to be careful, love, but...'

'Yes, I know what you're goin' to say,' Ellie replied, 'but Sid isn't like that awful man who raped me...'

'I'm sure he isn't,' Mabel Tandy said. 'From what you've told me, he's a lovely man – the kind of man I wish you were married to, but you're not, Ellie. You have a husband and if he heard you'd been seein' someone... well, I'm already nervous of what he'll do when he realises you've kept Beth.'

'Yes, I know,' Ellie said and then looked at her seriously. 'Divorce is awful, but so is livin' with someone you don't love or even like...'

'Oh, Ellie...' Mabel looked at her sadly. 'I'm not a prude and I wouldn't stop you havin' a divorce if it was up to me, because you rushed into marriage without truly knowing him – but Peter would never agree. I think he might kill you...'

'Yes, I know,' Ellie agreed and a shudder ran through her. 'It's wicked of me, I know – but last night I thought how much better our lives would be if Peter didn't come back.'

'Ellie, you mustn't, my love,' Mabel chided gently. 'I know things weren't right between you when he was home – but you have to give your marriage a chance. No man would have taken the news that you'd been raped easily. I can understand why he wouldn't want that man's child...'

'He wanted me to lose my baby,' Ellie said and her face was cold and proud. 'I know it in my heart, Mabel. I can't prove it and you don't want to believe me – but he put somethin' in my cocoa, I know he did...'

'If he hurt you...' Mabel looked fierce. 'If he hurt you or Beth, I think I would kill him myself...'

Ellie looked at her and suddenly laughed. 'Oh, Mabel, of course you wouldn't and nor would I – but I'm not sure I can live with him. He wasn't the man I married when he came back last time...'

'War does bring out the worst in men,' Mabel said thoughtfully. 'But it seems to me he was bad through and through from the start, even though you didn't see it.'

'No, he was lovely to me at first,' Ellie contended, 'but his mother told me he had a temper. She warned me what he would do if he thought I was goin' with other men. I thought she was just being mean to me, because she didn't like me – but now I think she really was tryin' to warn me.'

'Then you must be very careful,' Mabel said. 'I know you like this Sid – and he sounds nice, but be very sure what you're doing. If Peter came back and heard stories...'

'I know. I didn't intend to get involved with him, Mabel, but he helped me with Beth – and I like him. I can't be rude to him after he was so kind to me, can I?'

Mabel shook her head and went through to open up her shop. She only opened up for a few hours a day now, because the stock couldn't be readily replenished so she was eking it out, a few ounces of wool for her regular customers as they needed it. Ellie knew she must be using her savings to manage, but she wouldn't admit it and she wouldn't take a penny from Ellie, except for the food they shared. Ellie paid for as much of it as she could, but she knew that Mabel would soon be in difficulty if things didn't pick up… but there wasn't very much she could do, because she earned very little herself.

'Well, Peggy, I'm home at last,' Laurie Ashley said and put his suitcase down in the kitchen; glancing round, he thought nothing much had changed. 'They've told me I shan't be needed again – so I reckon that's it for me as far as the war goes, apart from some night-watch duties with the ARP.'

'That must be a relief for you,' Peggy said and took a deep breath. 'Welcome home, Laurie. I'm sure you'll soon get used to bein' here and servin' behind the bar. I hope it won't seem too dull and boring after what you've been doing…'

Laurie grimaced. 'Obviously, I can't tell you what I've been doin'. I signed the Secrets Act and if I broke my oath I could go to prison – or even be shot… but I'll admit it was exciting at first. However, I did somethin' wrong and they've sent me home.'

'Are you in disgrace?'

'Not exactly, but they think I might be a security risk in the future and so they don't want me.'

'Should I say I'm sorry?'

'No, not unless you don't want me back?' He looked at her quizzically and for a moment she saw the old Laurie, the man she'd loved for years – and believed had loved her.

'I think we've both done things that hurt the other,' Peggy said, her eyes meeting his honestly. 'I enjoy workin' here amongst my friends and I don't want to leave the lanes, so if you can accept things the way they are I see no reason why we shouldn't make a go of it. We can surely be civil to each other and keep the business goin' as best we can – at least until after the war.'

'And what then, Peggy? Will you go off with your twins and find a new life?'

'I really can't answer that, Laurie. It all depends how we get on. I don't want to live with you if we're constantly sniping at each other – but this is your home as much as mine and I wouldn't dream of makin' it uncomfortable for you. It's up to you to do the same and to treat the twins decently.'

'If I'd wanted a divorce I'd have said so when you wrote and told me you were havin' a baby. I want us to try to live with each other...' Laurie broke off as Pip walked in with a young woman just behind him. 'Hello, son – I didn't realise you were home...' His gaze went to the girl standing just behind Pip. She had light brown hair, which she wore in a knot at the back of her head and heavy-rimmed glasses. No one could call her a beauty, but she did have a nice smile and he thought she would look attractive if she let down her hair. 'Are you goin' to introduce me to this young lady?'

'This is Sheila,' Pip said. 'I did tell you I had a girlfriend when I wrote last Christmas.'

'Yes, but young men change their minds often, so I wasn't sure.' Laurie offered his hand to the serious-looking young woman. 'It's nice to meet you, Sheila. What do you do? All young women work these days, don't they?'

'I drive an ambulance and work part-time with a women's voluntary unit at the hospital. I'm not a nurse, but I visit and write letters for wounded men who can't manage it, take drinks round and generally make myself useful – and then I help out in my parents' pub in the evenings…'

'My word, you are a busy person,' Laurie said. He wondered what had attracted his son to her because she looked and sounded years older than Pip. He hoped that it wasn't serious on his son's side as already he wasn't sure that she was right for him.

'Dad, I should like a word later,' Pip said and smiled. 'Mum said you were comin' home. Sheila and I are off for a look round. I'm taking her up West for a meal and to see the shops. She's never been to London before.'

'Mum and me usually go into Hastings or sometimes Eastbourne,' Sheila said. 'Pip says the shops are much better in London. I've yet to be convinced…'

She gave Pip a teasing look, her grey eyes suddenly filled with mischief and Laurie saw the attraction, but it didn't make him warm to her. She was too old, too sophisticated for his boy – but he would have to be careful. He didn't want a fiasco like they'd had with Janet when she wanted to marry Mike. Peggy had gone against him and he'd been very angry with her – and he'd been right. Mike's injuries and subsequent death had ruined Janet's life. If he'd had his way, she would still be single and probably already forgetting the man she'd thought she wanted to marry, and that could have saved her a lot of grief. His granddaughter was a stranger to him and at this time he felt little interest in her, though that might change once he got to know her – but it wouldn't change his opinion that Janet should never have married.

'Shall you be home for supper this evenin'?' Peggy asked Pip. 'I'm makin' a big casserole so it will keep warm in the oven and not spoil…'

'I'm not sure, Mum,' Pip said. 'We might go to a show or the flicks while we're up the West End…'

'It doesn't matter, it will taste even better tomorrow,' Peggy said and turned as Rose entered. 'Ah, Rose, can you watch the oven and take out my pasties and scones when they're ready? It's time for me to open up…'

'I'll do that, Peggy,' Laurie said. 'I can unpack later. Have a nice time, you two…' He looked at Rose, who was staring at him uncertainly, but didn't ask, because he could guess all he needed to know. Peggy had found it too much to do all the cooking and the bar work as well as looking after the twins. Now he was home she would have more time – and perhaps they didn't need to employ this young woman at all, but he would make up his mind about that once he'd had time to observe her. His first impression was that she was a sexy young madam with a twinkle in her eye. He found her attractive and thought he might try his luck with this Rose if he got the chance.

Laurie was back and the sooner he stamped his authority on things the better. He would ring the Brewery later and let them know he was in charge once more, make certain they were getting their fair share of beer. While he was away Peggy had had to do it all, but now he was home and he intended to keep a firm hand on the reins. This was his pub and Peggy was useful, but he didn't intend to let her stand in his way. He'd had a taste of freedom and she'd been with that damned Yank so she couldn't complain. As long as she behaved he'd let her stay, but otherwise...He smothered the thought. For the moment she was useful to him and he'd better keep her sweet... and that meant tolerating the Yank's bastards.

Peggy joined her husband in the bar for the lunchtime rush that day. Everyone was delighted to see Laurie back and he bought several of the customers a drink, making himself instantly popular again, she thought a little sourly. It wasn't like Peggy to be resentful, but she couldn't help feeling a bit that way, because Laurie had made it so plain that he was in charge now. After more than three years of being the boss, Peggy felt she was being put in her place and it annoyed her, though she fought the anger inside her. Laurie had every right to step back into his old shoes as the owner of the pub lease. It was his pub and even though Peggy had kept it going almost single-handedly for a lot of the time, she was now relegated to the kitchen, cleaning, and helping out when required.

She ought to be grateful that Laurie was back home. He could rise first in future and get the range hot before she came down and it would be as it had been for years before the war – and yet a part of her resented the way she was suddenly just his wife instead of an independent woman, able to run the business with some help from Nellie and her friends. Yet that was stupid, because it would give her more time to be with the twins, something she'd wanted – and she would be a fool to let her chagrin spoil things.

Perhaps it was that the scales had fallen from her eyes and now she saw Laurie for the selfish man he was – perhaps always had been, and her love had blinded her to his faults, though she thought the change had been gradual, made worse by whatever had happened in Scotland to make him bitter. It might be that he'd become disillusioned with life – or her. What she did know was that she didn't want to be his wife again, though she could work with him for the good of their family.

Putting her annoyance to one side, she turned to greet Alice, who had come for a second glass of milk stout.

'Did you hear about the King and Queen havin' a shillin' lunch with the miners?' Peggy shook her head. 'They said it was a long time since they'd had a better meal…'

'I could give them something better – but they wouldn't come here.' Peggy frowned. 'Still, I bought some lemons for Shrove Tuesday, but they were sixpence-halfpenny a pound.'

'No wonder you look a bit glum at that price, Peggy love,' Alice said, jerking her head towards Laurie. 'Bit strange 'avin' 'im about, is it?'

'Yes, just a bit,' Peggy agreed. 'But he has a right, Alice. It is his pub.'

'And where would 'e be if you 'adn't kept it goin' then?'

Peggy smiled, her friend's belligerent question making her feel instantly better. She was being daft. Folk were making a fuss of Laurie because they were pleased to see him back. Once things settled down it would feel like the partnership it had always been, and make things easier all round. She hoped he wouldn't want to sack Rose, because she liked the girl and knew she'd settled here. Rose wouldn't find it easy to get another job she liked as much.

Chapter 10

Laurie looked at his reflection in the bathroom mirror that evening. He'd managed to get through the day without coughing more than once or twice, but he'd had a little bout of it again this evening as he was using the toilet. It must be that the air in London suited him better than up in Scotland, because he hadn't been able to stop coughing for weeks prior to his return home. Once, when it was really bad, he'd almost passed out and one of his colleagues had reported it to the major. He'd been ordered to report to the doctor just before everything went awry and he'd had an appointment, which he hadn't bothered to cancel after he was summoned to the major's office that last afternoon and given a dressing-down.

Laurie bitterly resented the way he'd been treated. Anyone would think he was a damned German spy. He had never once told Eileen anything that could remotely affect the work they did up at the house, but just because he'd upset her she'd written that filthy letter, which had led to the unpleasant interview.

Hearing someone try the bathroom door, Laurie wiped his hands on a towel and went to unlock it. He found himself face to face with the girl Peggy had taken on. She blushed bright red as he opened the door, wearing only his vest and trousers.

'Forgive me, I'm sorry…' she said, looking embarrassed. 'I didn't mean to disturb you, sir.'

'I've finished anyway,' Laurie replied, letting his eyes travel over her, because she was wearing a silky dressing gown over her nightdress and he could clearly see the outline of pert breasts. He reckoned that she must have known he was in there because he'd been coughing and she must have heard the water flush in the toilet. Right little flirt she was! Laurie knew the sort and was in no doubt that she was up for it. 'You're welcome to use it now, Rose.'

'Thank you…' she blushed again and avoided looking at him as she went in and locked the door after her.

Laurie grinned as he walked down the hall to the bedchamber he was using. He didn't like it that much, but it was the best other than the one Peggy was using and for the moment she wasn't going to invite him to share her bed. Perhaps he couldn't blame her for that, because he hadn't been exactly faithful to her in Scotland. Marie had been his first affair, but she'd been special, and if she'd lived— But to let his thoughts travel that path was too painful and he cut them off swiftly. After Marie, he'd had a one-night affair with another operator at the house and she'd left immediately afterwards and Laurie imagined she'd asked for a different posting, though he had no idea why.

He'd never thought about being unfaithful until he met Marie; he'd felt a bit guilty over that at first but then, after

Peggy's affair, he'd been angry and determined to make up for all the lost chances over the years. Why shouldn't he make the most of things, after all no one knew what would happen from one day to the next?

Laurie had been more careful in looking for a sexual partner after that and he'd settled down with Eileen, the local landlady for a while, but he'd begun to get bored, because she was too demanding, and then he'd seen that lovely young brunette who was on leave from the Wrens… Meredith, she'd told him, and she was on fire for an affair. Laurie had been happy to oblige her, but unfortunately Eileen had seen him kissing her late one evening and then the fireworks had started. They'd had one hell of a row that night and Laurie had told her straight that he had no intention of giving up his home to move in with her after the war ended. The next thing he knew was that someone – he believed Eileen – had written a spiteful letter to his boss hinting that he drank too much and was of a loose character and talked about his work when he was drunk.

None of that was true. Laurie had never drunk large amounts, but the letter had thrown him into a dark light and it was considered that, in the circumstances, he could not be trusted with secret codes. He'd argued for more than an hour, but the result was the same. Major Harris had told him that if he could be compromised he was a security risk and he was therefore being let go.

'You've done good work for us, Ashley,' he'd said as he shook hands. 'I'm sorry for this and I don't want to let you go but once a doubt is raised against your name I have no choice but to act on it.'

Laurie had wanted to shove the words back down his throat but a coughing fit had overtaken him, and the major had kindly advised him to get himself to a doctor and sort his life out. He'd ignored those wise words, packed his bags and returned to London and funnily enough he'd been fine until this evening. His chest felt a bit tight but he reckoned a dab of Vicks would cure that and he had no intention of wasting time or money on doctors.

Rose wished she hadn't chosen that particular moment to visit the bathroom. She'd needed rather urgently to visit the toilet and the only other alternative was the one in the pub yard, which was cold late in the evenings. Yet if she'd thought a little more she might have known it was Mr Ashley coughing – a harsh hacking sound that reminded her of one of the customers at her father's pub. Josh Barrow had been consumptive and she'd seen him coughing in the lane, spitting blood-flecked phlegm and once he'd gone so red in the face that he'd almost keeled over.

She didn't think Mr Ashley was ill though, because he was clearly still interested in sex – and with any woman that took his fancy, if she was not mistaken. Rose had read the look in his eyes the first time she saw him, and he'd made her feel hot and flustered when she met him at the bathroom door. His eyes had gone all over her, making her uncomfortable.

Oh bother the man! Rose had been settled at the pub. She liked Peggy and Nellie, and she enjoyed caring for the twins, and working at the pub. The customers were a friendly bunch and it was a pleasant life, but Rose wouldn't be able to stay on if Mr Ashley got too interested. She'd had enough of men trying it on in her old life and she didn't want it to start here. Because Rose's mother had been flighty, the men imagined her daughter must be the same and she'd had to fend off their hands for years.

Rose sighed as she finished brushing her teeth and put her bits and pieces back into her sponge bag. It would be unfortunate if she had to move on just as she was beginning to make friends; she'd hoped in time she might find a place for herself in Mulberry Lane amongst these people, but if Laurie Ashley continued to look at her like that she would have no choice but to leave.

Peggy sat on the edge of her bed, re-reading the letter that Able had left for her in the event of his death. It told of his love and of the money he'd left for her in case she wanted or needed a home of her own.

Had the time come to use that money? Peggy was reluctant to do it and yet she wasn't sure she could live the rest of her life under the same roof as Laurie. He seemed like a stranger sometimes and Peggy wasn't sure she wanted to cross that divide. It was easy to stay and just accept that things would go back to the old way, but she'd become used to making her own decisions while Laurie was away and it irritated her now that he was back and assuming that everything would be as he ordered it.

'Oh, Able,' she whispered and got to her feet, wandering over to the window to look down at the dark lane. She'd switched off her light because otherwise she would have the warden round banging on the door. It was a long time since they'd had a raid round this way, but the government was warning that it could start again, and the wardens were as strict as they had always been.

Peggy wished the war was over, but even more she wanted something good to happen. It had all been dark and gloomy for too long. Too many deaths, too many widows, too many orphaned children... and too much heartache.

Sighing, she closed the curtains, finding her way back to the bed before switching on her bedside light. Until this evening, Peggy had faced up to all her problems as they came, but tonight she just felt swamped. She had Able's children and she loved them, but she wanted... Her body ached for the touch of the man she loved and she knew that she was lonely. Oh, she had many friends, and there were men who felt more than friendship for her, but deep inside, she was alone, because the one man she wanted wasn't here to touch her and kiss her.

'I love you, hon. I always shall...'

The words were so clear in her mind that Peggy could have sworn Able had spoken to her, but it was because she'd been re-reading his last letter of course.

'Able, I love you...' A tear slid down her cheek because the years ahead seemed long and empty.

Chapter 11

'I wanted to ask you, Dad – will you sign for me to get married this summer? I intended to marry Sheila last year, but her father was ill so we put it off – but I'd like to be married this July,' Pip said. It was early morning and he'd come down to find his father lighting the range. It wasn't cold enough to light fires in the rest of the house yet, but the range always had to be kept going to keep the oven hot for Peggy, and they would probably light up in the bar that evening, because in February the evenings could be cold. 'I know the law says I can't marry until I'm twenty-one without permission, but I feel older – and I'd like to marry Sheila now. After all, we don't know whether I'll come through the war or not. I've flown too many sorties to be certain. They say your chances get slimmer with each raid you go on...'

'Don't talk like that, Pip,' Laurie said abruptly. 'I never heard such rubbish. We all know you pilots do a dangerous and wonderful job – but that doesn't mean it makes sense for you to rush into marriage with this girl...' He poked angrily at the fire, sending a shower of sparks up the chimney.

'You're not going to deny me the way you did Jan, are you?' Pip looked at him in disbelief. 'I thought you'd learned your lesson over that – and thank God Mum saw sense. At least Jan had a little bit of happiness with Mike before it happened…'

His father glared at him. 'Don't you think it would've been better if your sister had never married him? She would probably have settled down with someone in a secure job by now instead of being a war widow…'

'So Maggie should never have been born? Well, I think you should be ashamed of yourself,' Pip said, looking at him in disgust. 'That's bloody insensitive rubbish and I'm only glad that Jan isn't here to hear you. She's breaking her heart over the way Mike died – and all you can say is that it would be better if they'd never got married. Do you never think of anyone's feelings but your own? There's a war on, Dad, and that means we should all do exactly what makes us happy while we can.'

'So if you're a burglar you can go out and break into as many homes as you like as long as it makes you happy?' Laurie shovelled some coke onto the range fire.

'Don't be ridiculous! You know very well what I mean,' Pip said and looked angry. 'You may see me as a child still, but I can assure you that I'm not. I intend to marry Sheila in the summer, July we thought. I wanted your permission, but if you won't give it…'

'You'll ask your mother, is that it?' Laurie glared at him. 'I'm sure she'll give it to you – but you're a fool to tie yourself down too soon. That's what I did and I've regretted it all my life. You are in a good job and if you get a chance after the war you could make a brilliant career for yourself, Pip. It is better to wait and marry when you're older – thirty-something... Besides, Sheila is too old for you in her ways.'

'Sheila is a few months older than me that's all. She is a serious girl that's why you think she's older, but I like that – I'm not interested in silly girls who giggle and make eyes at everything in trousers.'

'Well, you won't get my permission or my blessing if you marry that girl,' Laurie said. 'I know I probably can't stop you – but my advice is to wait for a few years and then make your mind up...'

'You're impossible,' Pip said in disgust. 'I took your side against Mum when... I thought she was wrong, but now I understand perfectly. If I'd been her, I should've told you to clear off.'

'As it happens, this is my pub, my house – and my business. If anyone has the right to say leave, it is me – but I don't want to push your mother out...'

'Because she is too useful to you,' Pip said angrily. 'She's worked herself half to death all these years and then you have the cheek to say it's yours. She has a right to half of all of it in my opinion and any decent lawyer would support her if she divorced you...'

'Well, I think you've made yourself plain,' Laurie said, his lips white with fury. 'Now, if you don't mind, I'll get on with these fires. I've got two more to light...'

Pip stalked out of the room and went up the stairs two at a time. He wished he'd never asked for his father's permission, because he knew his mother would have given it with a smile.

He found his mother making coffee in the upstairs kitchen, the delicious smell of it making his mouth water. His mother had managed to buy some real coffee at a small shop in Commercial Road and she'd kept it for her family as a treat. Sheila was with her, so he bit back the angry words, but when Sheila smiled at him and took her coffee cup back to the bedroom, he sat down at the table and put his head in his hands.

'Somethin' wrong, love?' his mother asked.

'It's Dad – he refuses to give me permission to get married in the summer...'

'Oh dear, I was afraid of that,' his mother said and poured him a cup of coffee. 'I'm sorry, love. I know his blessing meant a lot to you.'

'Not anymore – not after what he said.' Pip sipped the hot drink. 'Sheila is going home tomorrow and I'm going with her, Mum. I'll be asking you to sign for me when we set a date – you will, won't you?'

'Yes, Pip, if it's what you want. I'm sorry you've fallen out with your father. It's a pity he came back too soon. Maybe if he'd still been away he would have signed for you...'

'I'm sorry if it means he'll be awful to you again.'

'He won't,' she said and smiled. 'He can't hurt me anymore, Pip. I love you and Jan, Maggie and the twins, but I don't love Laurie now. So he can be mean to me and I'll get angry, but it won't hurt – and if things get too bad, I'll find somewhere else to live and work.'

'I don't want you to lose your home over this…'

'Able left me a lot of money,' Peggy said. 'It's at the lawyers and in an account I can access when I want. I haven't yet, because I hoped Able would come back, even though I know it won't happen – but if I can't live with Laurie, I shall find a business I can make my own.'

'You're a wonderful cook, Mum. You could set up a tea shop anywhere…'

'Yes, perhaps,' she admitted. 'I've had my eye on the old bakery for a while now. I could have a shop and a small tea room in that place…'

'That's a wreck…' Pip looked astonished. 'It would cost several hundred pounds to make that fit to use…'

'I have quite a bit of money,' Peggy said. 'I would've kept it for the twins, but if I need it I shall use it to make a home for all of us – somewhere you and Sheila can come and stay.'

'I shan't stay here again unless Dad's gone back to where he was…'

'I doubt he will. I think he left under a cloud, though he can't or won't tell me what happened. Laurie is back for good and he's made it plain he owns this place and everything in it.'

'That isn't fair, Mum. You've kept this place going for years. People made it their local because of you and your food – any lawyer would say you were entitled to half or a big chunk of what he owns anyway.'

'What is that, Pip? He has a bit of cash in the post office and very little stock in the cellar. We make a profit after we pay the Brewery's rent and the bills, but not much these days. I could claim some of that cash in the post office, but I don't need it. At the moment, Laurie is saying he wants to make a go of it and I'll give him his chance... perhaps we can manage to work together for the sake of the family.'

'You're a saint, Mum.' Pip grinned at her. 'I'm glad you're independent of him – and I'm delighted that you like my Sheila.'

'I do. I think she's a lovely girl,' his mother said and kissed him. 'I'll try to bring your father round, Pip – but if I can't, I will sign your form, my darling. The last thing I want is for you to be estranged from your father, but he can be a bit of a fool and stubborn. He isn't a bad man, just a selfish and sometimes thoughtless one.'

'Yeah, and I'm stubborn too,' Pip said. He stood up and hugged her. She protested that he was too strong and he laughed. 'Not a boy anymore, am I?'

'No, you're a man and you do a man's job,' she said. 'I'm proud of you, Pip...' They heard Fay shriek and Peggy got to her feet, but Sheila poked her head round the door.

'I'll see to her, Peggy. You have a nice sit-down and talk to Pip...'

'She'll make a good mother,' Peggy said, 'but not too soon I hope. I can't keep up with all the knitting. What with the twins and Maggie...'

'We both want kids but not just yet,' Pip replied. 'Sid is popping in this evening for a drink and I want a word with him...'

'I'll tell him to come through and you can entertain him in private.'

'I think I'll go down and visit Jan in Devon while I'm on leave,' Pip said. 'It's ages since I've seen her and I should like to see Maggie. I bet she's grown...'

'She is growing fast. I haven't seen her for nearly eight months now, but Janet says she's had to make new dresses for her again... It has done your sister good being with her friend, Rosemary. I think she is learning to live again after her husband's loss and Janet will see that – and she will learn from it. And I know she'd love to see you.'

'When I visited last time, I didn't know what to say to her.'

'It takes time to recover from bereavement. Janet felt it more because she woke up and found him cold in her bed, when she'd thought he was getting over it – but in time the horror of it will fade.'

'Perhaps Dad was right then – he said it would've been better if she hadn't married Mike.'

'That is rubbish,' Peggy admonished. 'If something awful happened to your Sheila, you wouldn't think it was a pity you'd ever met her, would you?'

'No, I'd just wish I'd had her longer...' Pip nodded. 'Yes, that's what I thought – but I wasn't sure Jan would ever get over Mike's death.'

'Some people don't, of course, but I think your sister is stronger than that – she's very like Laurie in some ways. I think she's tougher than any of us realise. She didn't behave like a wilting lily when Mike died, she got angry – angry and bitter, but she sounded less bitter when she last wrote to me. I think she's beginning to come to terms with her loss.'

'I hope so, Mum. I'm very fond of Jan, even if we don't always get on.'

'I know,' Peggy said and smiled at him. 'You're a lovely lad, Pip. You deserve to be happy.'

Peggy went down to the kitchen. She was sorry that Pip was leaving sooner than he'd planned, but it was better than having constant quarrels between him and his father. She'd been afraid Laurie would refuse his permission and she'd learned better than to go straight into the attack. It was best just to leave it for a while. Laurie would think things through and maybe he would realise the futility in denying a man what he wanted, because Pip certainly wasn't a boy now.

Laurie looked at her as she started preparing the scones and shepherd's pie she was making for the pub lunch, but Rose entered the kitchen a few minutes after her and began to cook their breakfasts. There was sufficient bacon in the pantry to make a nice meal for all of them as well as some ripe tomatoes for frying and some mashed potato that would make a delicious bubble and squeak with the cooked cabbage that Peggy had set aside the previous day.

'Are you thinking of staying with us long, Miss Marchant?' Laurie addressed Rose formally as she was slicing the tomatoes. 'I'm sure Peggy was grateful for your help while I was away, but I'm not sure how long we shall need help here – after all, we have Nellie, and there are women who come in part-time…'

'Laurie...' Peggy was distressed that he'd spoken to Rose as if she were a stranger. 'I promised Rose a job for as long as she liked...'

'Well, I'm not sacking her,' Laurie said. 'I suppose you could let Nellie go – but we don't really need two cleaners now I'm back.'

'Rose is a lot more than a cleaner,' Peggy said, holding on to her temper by a thread. 'She cooks and looks after the twins, as well as helping in the bar.'

'Well, perhaps part-time then,' Laurie said. 'She can cut her hours to, say, three hours in the morning. We're not making enough profit to employ two women full-time, Peggy...'

'Mrs Tandy might give me a couple of hours or perhaps I could get a job at the hairdresser's...' Rose looked uncomfortable. 'I'll find somewhere else to stay as soon as I can...'

'That's a good idea, Rose,' Laurie said. 'We shan't throw you out – but we really can't take in everyone who needs a place to stay. Peggy has a generous nature, but it's as well I'm back...'

'What is the matter with you?' Peggy demanded as Rose slipped from the room, leaving the breakfast uncooked. 'You've upset Pip and now you've upset Rose. I don't know you anymore, Laurie. You don't seem to care about anyone.'

'Surely, you can manage to cook and look after the twins, and do a few hours in the bar when they're asleep. It's either her or Nellie – you can't keep them both now I'm back. You can cut the hours for both if that makes you happier – but you've been taking in all and sundry from what I hear: Tilly Barton, some woman called Helen, her daughter Sally, Nellie and now this girl…'

'Helen did her share of the work while she stayed here.' Peggy flared up at the injustice of his accusations. 'Tilly was only here a few days, and Sally one night. Surely I can have a friend to stay in my own home?' She glared at him. 'Who has been stirring up trouble, I'd like to know?'

'No one in particular, but I've been hearing what a generous woman you are to everyone. It has to stop, Peggy. We've no more than anyone else and we need to make up for all we've lost because of the war.'

'I've always given a free drink occasionally and you've never complained before.'

'One free drink is all right, I do it myself – but you can't cook meals for neighbours and give your food away. I'm back now and I want to see this place making a profit again.'

Peggy bit her lip. Laurie had a point in a way, because she did help anyone in need, but it was only in a small way, and people helped her – it was give and take and he ought to know it. He did know, but he was just letting her see who was boss. Laurie was obviously in a bad mood because of the quarrel with Pip. She would just let it all blow over and see if things got better – and if not then she would investigate the old bakery premises a bit further. In fact she would make an appointment to view it one day soon; in the meantime, she'd take a look through the back windows of the bakery, because the gate to the yard wasn't locked.

She'd made inquiries and knew that the lawyer looking after it was prepared to let it for a very small rent, but it would need a lot of doing up – and it might be better to buy if she could get it cheaply. Yet it was a big step so she would wait and see if things calmed down a bit before making the change, but a peep in the windows wouldn't hurt.

Laurie went through to the bar, which Nellie had already been in and cleaned. He knew she did a lovely job and he didn't really want Peggy to get rid of her, but he didn't want Rose in the house. She was young and attractive and her body was seductive – and, to tell the truth, he was tempted. However, he realised that he couldn't afford to get involved with another woman under Peggy's nose, because that would be pushing things too far. As Pip had told him, his wife would surely be entitled to a slice of whatever he owned.

He'd felt humiliated at being asked to leave his job and bitterly angry with Eileen for writing that foul letter. He'd been tempted to give her a good hiding, but that would most likely have ended in a prison sentence for him, so he'd simply packed his bags and come home to The Pig & Whistle. Except that it didn't feel like it used to. Peggy had made it her own. Everyone told him how marvellous she was, how she'd taken folk down the cellar during the Blitz, giving them food and drinks to help bolster their courage while the bombs rained around them.

In truth, Laurie was jealous and angry. Peggy had managed without him, but he knew he couldn't run the place without her. She and Nellie and Rose were like a family, and even Pip was on her side – telling his own father that his mother was entitled to half of everything if they split up. Laurie felt like something the cat had dragged in and he didn't enjoy knowing that everyone thought the world of his wife.

Laurie was damned if he was going to walk away and make things easy for her. Peggy hadn't taken him back to her bed yet, but he thought she might in time – but not if she knew— Laurie shut the thought out. The letter he'd taken from Reg only the previous day burned a hole in his pocket. It was Peggy's letter, meant for her eyes only, and he'd read it. He'd opened the seal of the thin envelope, which had come all the way from America, and he'd read what it said, every telling word.

It was sod's law that this letter, written several months earlier, should finally make its way here just as he had come home. If Peggy knew what was in it, he thought she would leave him instantly – and he couldn't run this damned place without her.

He supposed he was a fool to try and get Rose out, because if Peggy left she might have taken over the cooking – but she didn't like him. He'd sensed it when he'd stared at her in her bathrobe, which was opened at the front and revealed white skin and a hint of delicious curves. Her unspoken rejection stung his pride and it had made him cruel in the kitchen. After the quarrel with Pip, he'd wanted to lash out and hurt someone and Rose happened to be there. Besides, even if he'd been wrong to believe Rose was asking for it, he had no thought of apologising.

Peggy wasn't going to leave, not yet anyway. Laurie had no intention of ever giving her the letter. As long as she never knew the truth, he was safe. Once the war was over, things might change, but by then the pub would be on an even keel again. The customers would be used to him and not devoted fans of his wife – and he could find a girl to cook and clean and work in the bar. As for that bloody American's brats, well, he would just ignore them. Seeing Peggy fussing over them made him angry, but so far he'd hidden it. Better folk should think them his than lose face in the lanes.

He looked at the range, his hand curling about the thin paper in his pocket. It had been sent airmail, which made it unusual. Supposing Reg mentioned it to Peggy and she asked where it was? He couldn't say he'd burned it. He might lie and say he'd never seen it, but would she believe him or Reg?

He would keep it hidden for the moment – and he'd find a way of getting round Reg. He'd tell him it had contained bad news and he'd kept it from Peggy for that reason... Yes, that might work, because Reg had a soft spot for Peggy. If he treated him to a few free drinks, got the chatty postman on his side, Peggy would never learn about the letter that had come from America – the letter that might make her decide to leave him.

Chapter 12

'You don't have to leave, Rose,' Peggy said as she entered the girl's bedroom and saw her packing later that day. 'Laurie was just in a bad mood because he argued with Pip. I'm not going to sack you – but I may have to cut your hours...'

'That's all right, Peggy,' Rose said. 'I liked living here with you – but I'll be honest, I don't like your husband. I popped over the road and asked Mavis if she had a spare room and she has. Mrs Ross is going to move into her uncle's flat so I can have hers when she does. Until then, I can have the box room at Mavis's house. It's very small, but it means I can stay here in the lanes. I've got two mornings a week at the hairdresser's helping Ellie, and Mrs Tandy said she would like to give me some work but can't afford it – so I'll try somewhere else in the lanes...'

'You might try the bakery round the corner, Rose. I think they need a girl on Saturdays. I was hoping you would stay with me, because I have an idea for the future, but I'm not ready yet...'

'I'll still come in and help for a few hours if you want – but I think it's best I don't live in...' Rose's cheeks were pink and she couldn't meet Peggy's eyes.

Peggy looked at her in silence for a moment. 'Yes, I understand, Rose. Well, if you can come four mornings a week to help me with cooking and the twins. I hope you find something nearby if you need more hours...'

'I've been saving most of my money so I'll be all right for a while,' Rose said. 'I'm really sorry, Mrs Ashley. I did like it here.'

'I'm still Peggy to you, Rose. I hope we can be friends – despite my husband?'

'Yes, of course we can,' Rose agreed. 'It's only that he – reminds me of someone. His temper and his black looks... just like my dad.'

'Is that all, Rose?' Peggy looked her in the eyes. Was Rose telling her the truth? Surely Laurie wouldn't try to seduce her under their own roof? If he had, he was disgusting! She could scarcely believe he'd sunk so low and yet Rose wouldn't lie.

'He – he looks at me too much...' Rose's face was flaming. 'Please don't hate me, but I don't want to sleep under the same roof...'

'Did your father look at you like that?'

Rose nodded and looked down at the floor. 'Sometimes, yes. He never touched me like that – but he wanted to and it made me feel awful...'

'Yes, I do see, Rose,' Peggy smiled and squeezed her hand sympathetically. Peggy wished she didn't have to leave; she would rather Laurie had stayed in Scotland but he was here and there was nothing she could do. 'You'll be all right with Mavis. Anne has been happy there, but she and Kirk will have more privacy in her uncle's flat – of course it's hers now. She might sell it and try to find somewhere closer to the lanes and the school when she gets around to it…'

'I'll come down now and help you in the kitchen – and then I'll take my case over the road later.'

'No, you take it now,' Peggy said. 'You can come in at nine o'clock in the mornings and leave at twelve. That's three hours, four days a week. I'm sorry I can't make it more, but Laurie is the boss…'

'He's not the one people like,' Rose declared outspokenly. 'Oh, they'll slap him on the back and say they're glad to see him back while he buys them free drinks, but you'll see – if you ever leave, he'll only have a few old men to keep him company of an evening…'

Peggy nodded and left Rose to finish her packing. Laurie's behaviour made her angry but for the moment her hands were tied – and it was difficult to believe that the husband she'd once known and loved could have changed so much. Was Rose imagining it – or was Laurie really so lost to decency that he'd embarrassed a young girl he ought to have protected as one of his staff?

Sheila was carrying the twins downstairs; she'd dressed them both and they were laughing. Peggy would miss her when she went back home – and she would miss Rose, but Laurie had known that she couldn't part with Nellie. There had been no contest. A choice between them must always mean Nellie came first, because they'd shared too much. Still, it would mean more work for Peggy, even if she didn't serve in the bar as much – and she'd miss that too, because all her customers were her friends.

Rose looked round the tiny room and sighed. It was nowhere near as nice as the room at Peggy's pub. However, she couldn't stay at the pub, not when Laurie Ashley looked at her the way he had. She'd never dreamed he would be like that, but the looks he'd given her had sent shivers down her spine.

Rose wasn't interested in men who looked at her like that. Laurie Ashley wasn't the first. Her father had sometimes touched her arm in passing, his eyes conveying a message he would never dare to speak. Rose had felt sick when he looked at her in that way, because she'd believed he was her father; it was only when she'd read her mother's diary after her cruel death that she'd realised Roger Martin was just the man who had married her mother when Rose was on the way, though he'd always spoken of himself as her father – but that was just to discipline her, to make her do as she was told.

It explained his wild jealousy, of course. It made sense of his obsession that Paul wasn't his son – and it made his lusting after Rose a little easier to understand, but it didn't make her feel any less dirty. The thing she'd liked so much about Jimmy Morgan was that he'd made her feel special, put her on a pedestal and treated her like a lady, something she'd never known before.

Her father's customers had sometimes looked at Rose with those hot eyes that seemed to pierce her very skin, stripping her bare. She'd had to fight off more than one – and it was because they'd known she was the daughter of a woman who was no better than she would be. They'd believed that her mother had gone with other men, both before and after her marriage – and so they'd taken it for granted that Rose was the same, but she wasn't interested. Rose's mother had never confided in her and so she didn't know who her real father was or whether the gossip was true or false – what she did know was that she wouldn't allow men like that to get near her.

At the Pig & Whistle, Rose had received only respect from Peggy's customers. One or two soldiers had tried to flirt with her, but none of them had looked at her in that sly hot way that told her they thought she was easy. Jimmy had taken her to tea at a posh hotel and told her she was special. Rose had begun to think she was special – until Mr Ashley looked at her that way. She couldn't have stayed under the same roof as him after that because she didn't trust him to stay out of her room. She hadn't liked having to tell Peggy, but she'd had to make her see – and perhaps she ought to know what kind of a man her husband was. She hoped she hadn't hurt Peggy or made her unhappy, and yet she'd sensed the tension in the house ever since his return. It was a pity he'd come back.

'When did you get back?' Peggy asked as Anne knocked at the kitchen door and then came in. 'I wasn't sure if it was today or tomorrow…'

'We came back on the earlier train because it was so cold,' Anne replied. 'My uncle's flat has a good range to heat it and Kirk is getting it going now – and I'm going to fetch our things from Mavis's house and take them home…'

'I shall miss you popping in and out,' Peggy said. 'But never mind, I'll see you as often as we can manage– did you have a lovely time at the sea?'

'It was wonderful,' Anne said and her eyes sparkled. 'Even better than our honeymoon, if I tell the truth. Kirk is just the man for me. I was right to marry him, even though I did it in such a hurry that Christmas we met.'

'You're lucky to have him home again so soon, some of the men don't get back for ages, and those in a prison camp can be unheard of for years,' Peggy said. 'You've got another week to get settled into the flat before he leaves. Do you think you'll stop at the flat or will you sell?' For a moment Peggy's thoughts went to Able. She'd often wondered whether the enemy might have picked him up when his plane ditched in the sea… but perhaps that was wishful thinking. *If* he was alive he might return one day and she longed for him with all her being.

'Kirk says it's fine until we have children, but then he wants a house with a garden for them. He's going to be based down south for a while now, Peggy, so perhaps he'll get home for short breaks – and maybe I'll be lucky this time.'

'It's going to happen,' Peggy assured her, because she knew how much Anne wanted a baby. 'Just be happy that Kirk is around for now, and then, before you know it, you'll be making baby clothes.'

'Yes, I know you're right,' Anne agreed. 'It's just that I want a baby so much.'

'Yes, of course, and I'm sure it will happen for you...' Peggy smiled at her.

'Maureen didn't look too happy when I saw her going into the shop just now,' Anne said. 'She hasn't lost the baby, has she?'

'Gordon has been badly injured,' Peggy said. 'She's very worried about him. They haven't told her much yet, but he's being transferred to a military hospital. She will go down as soon as they let her know he's settled.'

'Oh, that's awful for her,' Anne said, obviously upset. 'I'm so sorry. I'll go and see her as soon as I can...'

'She needs a bit of comfort.' Peggy sighed. 'Like you, she hasn't had much time with her husband. He got home in the autumn for a couple of weeks but... well, we mustn't look at the bleak side of things. We have to hope he will get better once he's here in a good hospital.'

'Whatever would she do if anything...' Anne stopped abruptly and shook her head. 'No, he has to get better. He can't die... she couldn't manage with three kids if Gordon wasn't around...'

'We've had enough sorrow and death in the lanes these past years. I don't think I can bear another death – it's too soon after Mike and the others...' Peggy's voice broke on a sob.

Anne nodded, her eyes spiked with tears, because Mike's death had affected them all. 'Alice told me Laurie is back. That means you won't need me to come in in the evenings, or will you?'

'I might.' Peggy shook her head. 'Maureen was saying we should all go out together – but she won't feel like it now.'

'She might if he's not too bad – to cheer herself up. I know I was glad of her company while Kirk was away. It just gets so damned lonely, especially at night when you draw the curtains…'

'Yes…' Peggy sighed. 'That's exactly what it feels like – lonely. You can have friends, but if the person you love has gone…' She shook her head, swiping away a tear. 'Laurie is back but I miss Able…'

'I'm sorry, Peggy. I didn't think…'

'It's harder than I thought it would be, Anne. I've always thought Laurie would be away until the war ended, so I had plenty of time to make up my mind what I should do when he got home – but it happened so quickly… You'd think it would be easier with him home, but Rose has moved out and the twins have been playing up – and I'm not sure whether I can carry on as if everything is fine.' Tears trickled slowly down her cheeks.

'Oh, Peggy, I'm so sorry, love.' Anne came over and hugged her. 'I'm always on the end of a phone if you need me.'

Peggy nodded and brushed away her tears. It was stupid, but she felt as if everyone had suddenly left when she needed them the most. Maureen would be away for days at a time visiting her husband in hospital; Anne had been just across the road but now she would be a bus ride away; Nellie wasn't far off and she'd see her every day and Rose would come in for a few hours in the mornings... but it wasn't the same. It would be just her, the twins and Laurie sleeping in the pub at night and somehow it didn't feel right... and she was a bit nervous of being alone with him.

No, she was being stupid! Peggy struggled against the feeling of oppression that had come over her since Laurie returned. Something was wrong; she knew it but didn't know what it was or what to do about it.

Oh, Able, she thought as Anne left her to fetch her things from across the road. *Able, why did you have to leave me? I need you... I really need you here with me now.*

She heard a sound behind her and turned to see that Tom Barton was standing at the kitchen door armed with his paintbrushes and a can of paint.

'I bought pale blue, Peggy,' he told her with a cheerful grin. 'They'd got white, cream or a ghastly mauve and this blue is pretty, so I thought you would like that better.'

'Oh Tom,' Peggy said, relief flooding through her. She was so pleased to see him that she wanted to hug him. 'I'd forgotten you were going to start on the spare room tonight. I'm so pleased you've come... and I'm sure whatever you've picked will be lovely.'

Tom grinned at her and said, 'Shall I go straight up? I'll stay late for a couple of nights and get it finished for you – just in case your Janet decides to come home sooner...'

'Yes, thanks, Tom,' Peggy said, her spirits lifting slightly. She wasn't entirely alone. Tom was always there, as were Alice and Maureen's grandmother – and Doctor Michael Bailey. She hadn't encouraged his visits, but he still popped in every now and then to ask if she was all right, and she knew she only had to lift the phone and he would come. Besides, Laurie wouldn't harm her. She'd known for a long time that he no longer loved her, but he counted on her to help run the pub. Peggy hadn't decided what to do with her life yet, but she would hang on here until she made up her mind.

Chapter 13

'You know I'll look after Shirley while you're away,' Gran said when Maureen asked a little diffidently. 'Are you certain you can manage Robin? It isn't easy takin' a young child on the train and the hospital won't let you take him into the ward…'

'I know. I thought perhaps I could find a nursery for him while I visit Gordon – or perhaps the hotel will have a service…'

'Robin is used to me,' Gran said. 'Please let me take care of him for you, love. You shouldn't have the worry of a young child when you have a sick husband to think about, Maureen. You don't know how bad he is yet. No, Gordon is your first concern for the moment – and the child you're carryin'. Besides, Peggy would always help me if I asked.'

'Peggy has enough to do,' Maureen said.

'Everyone has enough to do these days,' Gran said, 'but I'm here for you, my love. You don't need to do everything yourself.'

Maureen looked at her uncertainly, because she didn't like putting so much responsibility on her grandmother, but what she said made sense. 'Yes, perhaps it is best if I leave him with you, at least this first time. I'll find out what facilities there are in Portsmouth for childcare and perhaps I can take him next time – if Shirley wasn't at school I'd take her, because she is so capable with him…'

'Exactly, so she will help me in the mornings and when she gets home after school. Stop fussing, Maureen. It's bad for you and the baby.'

'I know…' Maureen's eyes filled with tears. 'I'm just so worried, Gran. Gordon has been badly hurt…' She caught back a sob. 'I keep thinking about what happened to Mike. Janet was so happy to have him back and then…'

'Now stop that this instant!' Gran said sharply. 'Your husband hasn't lost his memory… but he may have lost something else. You have to be prepared, Maureen love. He didn't tell you what the trouble was and that means he's nervous about telling you… so it may be bad burns or the loss of a limb…'

'Yes…' The feeling of loss and distress threatened to overwhelm her but she held back her tears. 'I know I have to be strong for him, Gran. It won't stop me loving him, no matter what has happened… He will need reassurance.'

Gran looked at her with her wise old eyes and nodded. 'Yes, very likely. It's hard for men who are desperately wounded. They lose their pride too if they can't work the way they used to. I knew quite a few who came back from the last war; it was pitiful to see them losing the will to live. You make sure your Gordon knows he has plenty to live for Maureen.'

'Yes, I shall,' Maureen said and checked her bag: purse, ration card, comb, a handkerchief, her compact with face powder and lipstick, and her gas mask. Also, she'd packed some cigarettes, matches and a packet of humbugs for Gordon, plus a small case, with underwear, socks, towels, shaving kit, soap, shoes, slippers, trousers, shirts, jumpers and a dressing gown. 'I think I have everything I need…'

'Paint a smile on your face when you visit him, love,' Gran advised. 'He's alive and the rest of it can be faced, however bad it is…'

'Yes, Gran, thanks…' Maureen hugged her impulsively. 'I've no idea what I'd do without you. You've always been here for me.'

'And always shall be while I can,' Gran said stoutly. 'Now, stop fussing, go and catch your train – and you can ring me and let me know how things are when you have time.'

'Of course I will.' Having left her adored son sleeping in his cot, Maureen picked up her case and left. She walked to the bus stop, but she hadn't been there five minutes when a large sleek black car drew up and a man leaned over to open the passenger door.

'Can I give you a lift, Mrs Hart? I didn't know your name the other day when I scared that brute off, but Ellie told me about your husband…'

Maureen remembered the large man who had helped her when Rory grabbed her arm. Ellie had told her how good he'd been when her little girl had to be rushed to hospital.

'Sergeant Coleman,' Maureen said and smiled as he got out and lifted her suitcase into the boot. 'This is so good of you. I have to catch the train down to Portsmouth... Gordon has been taken to the hospital I nursed at for a while at the beginning of the war.'

'At least you know he's in good hands,' the soldier grinned. 'I was in hospital abroad for some weeks and it is much better when you get home. He'll be feeling more like himself already – and when he sees you it will cheer him up.'

'I hope so,' Maureen said. 'This is a lovely car. I've never been driven in anything this posh before.'

'It belongs to my general, but he's in a meeting until six this evening and he told me I could take a couple of hours off, so he wouldn't mind my doing a good turn – and after I've dropped you at the station, I'll get it cleaned and polished for him.'

'But it already shines like a new pin...' Maureen smiled.

'My general likes it that way – and he's an important man, so I make sure everything is just so for him.'

'Yes, of course you must,' Maureen agreed. 'Do you like your job, Sergeant Coleman?'

'Please, call me Sid. We're all friends in the lanes, aren't we? And yes, I do like what I'm doing. It makes a nice change from being shot at by the Germans and the Japs.' He grinned at her. 'Almost worth gettin' injured three times for... but once I'm fully fit again, I'll ask for overseas service.'

'It sounds to me as if you've already done your share,' Maureen said. He was a big man and seemed strong, and he wouldn't have been sent home and given a job like this unless he was considered to have done as much as any man could be asked to do, and a lot of battle wounds didn't show on the outside.

'Let's say I know my way round a military hospital.'

'You've been hurt a few times then?'

'In and out of theatre like a dose of salts, I was,' Sid confirmed. 'My lungs failed at one time and they thought I was a goner – might've been if it hadn't been for the tenacity of one doctor who was determined he wouldn't let go. I pulled through after some months of intensive nursing so don't despair over your husband. He will probably come through fine. If we manage to get back home, it makes us fight for life.'

'Yes, and talking to you has made me feel better.' She smiled.

They had arrived at the station. Sid got out, opened the passenger door for her and got her case for her.

'Thank you, Sid. It was kind of you to bring me here.'

'No trouble,' he said and tipped his cap to her. 'Good luck. I'll be sayin' me prayers for your Gordon – and so will everyone on the lanes…'

Maureen's eyes filled with tears as she walked away. Her friends had all wanted to help her, but what she needed was for Gordon to come back to her and be strong and well again, and only the doctors and nurses could tell her how likely that was.

Tom was unpacking a box filled with cigarette packets and chocolate bars when the shop door pinged and he turned round to see Laurie Ashley standing there. He was surprised, because the pub sold cigarettes and it was unlike Peggy's husband to do the shopping.

'Morning, Mr Ashley,' he said. 'What can I do for you, sir?'

'I wondered if you'd got a nice box of chocolates for Peggy, please? I've not been around to buy her presents for a while now and I wanted to give her a surprise.'

'Ah, I see…' Tom grinned and reached under the counter. He knew it wasn't Peggy's birthday, because that was in June, and still three months away, but a surprise gift was even better. 'I keep these out of the way, because we can only ever buy a few at a time. You'll need coupons, of course, but the price is seven shillings and sixpence…'

'Yes, I've got the ration card they gave me when I was released from service…' Laurie Ashley coughed slightly, putting a handkerchief to his mouth and turning away for a moment. He turned back to Tom afterwards and frowned. 'It's my chest. The cold weather didn't suit me up there and it has got steadily worse, so they said I'd done my bit. I dare say you'd like to join up, wouldn't you, Tom?'

'I'm going to be in the reserves soon,' Tom said because he couldn't keep his excitement inside. 'I got the word this mornin'. I've got to go along this evenin' and be enrolled and then I'll be given a uniform and I'll go regular for drills and trainin' – on Sundays they take us to a shooting range and teach us to fire a rifle. I'm eighteen next month so I hope to get in the Army…'

'Well, that is good news,' Laurie said and paid for his purchase. 'You won't have so much time for helping everyone out once you start your training, Tom.'

'No, but I'll finish Peggy's room for her on Saturday,' Tom said. 'After that, I might not have as much time as before – but if I'm needed I'll fit it in somehow, as long as I'm in London.'

Laurie nodded. 'You're a good lad, Tom, but I'm home to help Peggy now, so she won't need to call on you.'

'What about your chest, sir? I don't mind givin' you a hand...'

'No, that's all right, Tom. I can still do most things – and not a word to Peggy, remember. We don't want her worryin', do we?'

'No...' Tom frowned as Laurie Ashley took the large box of chocolates and left the shop. There was something odd about the way he'd told Tom he could manage – almost as if Tom was being warned off, as if Laurie Ashley didn't want him going round there too often. Surely he wasn't jealous of Tom? Tom would have laughed, it was so daft, and yet he had a cold feeling at the nape of his neck. There was something he didn't quite like about Laurie Ashley since he'd come home.

Rose had told him that Mr Ashley had demanded Peggy either sack her or Nellie or cut the hours for both of them – and now he was warning Tom off. Was he trying to cut Peggy off from her friends? Surely not! Why would he do that? It didn't make sense to Tom. Everyone was so friendly in the lanes; people just went in and out of each other's houses. He thought about how good Peggy had been to him and his father when his mother was first taken ill and his brother Sam had died. Tom wasn't sure what Peggy's husband was up to, but nothing would stop him going round to make sure Peggy was all right, at least until he joined up.

Tom shook his head. Perhaps he was imagining things, but he was pretty certain he was being discouraged from visiting too often – but it had had the opposite effect, because he would make sure to call in as often as he could just to be sure she was all right. And when Maureen got back he might tell her of his suspicions – but that depended on how she was getting on at the hospital. If Gordon was very ill, she couldn't be worried by Tom's doubts even though he knew she was fond of Peggy.

It was a pity that Anne had moved away from across the road, and that Rose was no longer living over the pub. Peggy was hoping her daughter would come back to the lanes and Tom thought it would be a good thing if she came sooner rather than later. If Pip had been around, he might have told him that he was uneasy, but he'd gone back to where he was stationed with his girlfriend rather than staying on as he'd first intended. Tom knew he'd fallen out with his father over something, though he had no idea what – but that made him even more wary. He would certainly keep an eye on Laurie Ashley while he could – and when he left, he'd tell one of the other residents he could trust.

Maureen's stomach was churning as she asked which ward her husband was on and was told it was Critical 2. That meant he was very ill but not under intensive nursing. She walked up the stairs, wondering whether she would see any of the nurses she'd known when she was working on the wards, but as yet she hadn't seen a friendly face. The nurses all looked about sixteen to Maureen and she realised that many of the girls she'd known would have been sent overseas or moved to other hospitals and new recruits were being trained to take the place of those who had left.

'Maureen... I've been expecting you...' the well-remembered voice of her tutor, Sister Matthews, reached her, stopping her in her tracks. At least there was someone here she knew! 'I should like to have a word before you see Sergeant Hart...'

'Sister...' Maureen followed her along the hall into her office and closed the door. 'It's so nice to see you; all the nurses seem so young. Why do you need to talk to me?'

'Please sit down, Maureen, I can see you're expecting again and I think this has been a terrible strain for you.'

'I haven't been told what is wrong with Gordon, except that he was badly wounded...'

'Yes, it is his injuries that I wanted to talk to you about,' Sister Matthews said. 'I have him on my ward – and he has suffered superficial burns to his face, hands and legs, which are still painful, though healing well. He also has a broken shoulder, which will need exercises when he is able to start them – and I'm very sorry, but your husband has a badly infected left leg from the knee down. The wound is open and suppurating and we're not sure if it will heal. Doctor is trying some new treatment, but it is painful and

Sergeant Hart is suffering. He is going to need a lot of care and love when we send him home. It will take months to get him walking again and, as you know, a lot of the men suffer great pain with such serious wounds. Being a nurse you will be able to keep an eye on his leg and treat it properly. So many men let their wounds get raw and infected before they come back to us for help and by then it's too late. However, providing we can save the leg, there is nothing to stop Gordon making a full recovery – and, of course, the war is over for him.'

Maureen felt as if she were going to faint. She'd seen enough of these types of cases to know how much pain the men suffered afterwards, also the humiliation, anger and despair most of them felt at becoming an invalid. It was as if they felt less of a man because of it, losing their confidence and becoming angry and sullen. 'I'm glad you told me yourself, Sister. I need a few moments to come to terms with it and I wouldn't want Gordon to see my shock…'

'Exactly. I know you, Maureen, and I know that you won't think any the less of Gordon because of what he has suffered, but he may well think less of himself. He will need all the help you and his family can give him. It is going to give him pain for some time. We must think ourselves lucky that the surgeon didn't cut his leg off over there. It happens in a lot of cases, because gangrene sets in, but Sergeant Hart has been lucky, even though it may not seem so just now. He will learn to manage very well for himself and not be stuck in a chair for the rest of his life – but that will demand great patience from you. You have to stand up for him and to him, Maureen.'

'Yes, I understand, Sister,' Maureen said and lifted her chin. 'He has to fight through the pain or he will be stuck at home in the chair – but Gordon is strong and determined and I'm sure he can do it.'

'That's the spirit,' Sister Matthew said and smiled at her. 'I've missed you, Maureen. You were always one of my best prospects. I do hope you will go back to nursing once your family is older and Gordon is on his feet again.'

'It is my intention, Sister – and I've been told that the no-married-nurses rule is being relaxed in several hospitals. So I have every hope of finishing my training in a few years' time, when the children are older, and becoming a staff nurse.'

'Good, good; the service can always do with nurses like you,' Sister said. 'Off you go now. You know what to expect.'

'Yes, thanks to you,' Maureen said and left her office. What she'd been told had shocked and hurt her, because it meant the man she loved was suffering terribly and his ordeal wouldn't be over for months, perhaps even years. It took time, courage and patience to get patients with such injuries able to live a normal life, but Maureen was determined that she would get Gordon through it.

Outside the ward, she paused and put a hand to her stomach, thinking of her unborn child. Gordon's son needed a father to watch over him and play football with him in the garden and she needed her husband by her side. It was up to her to give Gordon the strength to carry on.

She was smiling as she walked into the ward and looked for him. He was in the second bed and lying back against the pillows with his eyes closed, his face white and strained. His injured leg was bare and supported by a pulley, the wound open and raw, a great hole in the calf, which meant most of the muscle of that leg had gone and would need building up once it had healed. Breathing deeply to steady herself, Maureen walked up to him, bent down and kissed him softly on the lips.

'You shouldn't do that, nurse, my wife wouldn't like it,' Gordon said and smiled as he opened his eyes. 'Hello, love. You look lovely. How is everybody?' He hesitated, then, 'Well, I came back like I promised – but I'm a bit the worse for wear, I'm afraid.'

'We'll get you better, my darling,' she said. Her mind was teeming with questions, but they could wait until he was home and on the mend. 'The nurses and doctors will give you a good start, but when you come home to Shirley, Gran and me, you'll be so well looked after you won't know yourself. Shirley takes good care of Robin and she'll be over the moon to have her dad home.'

'Going to smother me with love, are you?' he asked and there was a slightly defensive note in his voice.

'Oh no, not at all,' Maureen said and made herself tease him, though inside she wanted to weep. 'We have proper hospital rules in our house. Shirley keeps us all on our toes. She asked me to show her how to make hospital corners and woe betide me if I just pull up the bed in the morning. Gran is sure your daughter will be a nurse one day or perhaps a doctor. She's so bright and clever at school these days.'

'Yes, she is intelligent and happy, thanks to you and your gran,' Gordon said and visibly relaxed. 'They tell me it will take months before I can walk properly again, but they say I shall do it....'

'It helps if you take proper care of yourself and the wasted leg,' Maureen said, ignoring the way he flinched as she spoke of it unemotionally. 'Once you leave hospital, it will be much better than it is now, but it will still need lots of attention. We have to bathe it and help the skin heal and keep it supple with creams, and then it will mean exercise to build the muscle again.'

'I'm lucky to have a nurse in the family...'

Maureen caught the hint of bitterness in his tone. 'I'm your wife, Gordon, and I love you. That is all I care about – but I know you and I know you'll want to get out of the wheelchair as soon as you can. If you let me help you in the way they taught me here, it might just be that bit sooner – but don't imagine I'm going to fuss over you all the time. It's your life and you will find the motivation yourself.'

'I already have tons of it,' he said and grimaced. 'It's just so bloody painful. They give me stuff to kill the pain but it wears off and then it's the very devil.'

'Yes, I know. All my patients said the same when I was working here; the medication was never quite enough.' Maureen blinked to stop the tears of sympathy. She mustn't let him think she felt pity when what she felt was love and a desire to hold him in her arms and kiss him until the paid eased. 'It will get better gradually as it heals,

Gordon. I promise you it will become less painful... but it will take time.'

She looked at the red marks on his face and hands, but they were already healing, the skin taut in some places and spotted with brown marks.

'At least the burns aren't awful,' she said. 'I've seen much worse...'

She thought she saw his lips twitch even though his lashes were wet. 'You're not going to let me feel sorry for myself, are you?'

'No point in that, is there?' she said. 'Let's get this clear now, Gordon. I'm so glad you've come back to me, darling. You're alive and that might not have been the case. I know we have a lot of battles to fight – I know better than you how hard it will be – but we can do it together.'

A reluctant smile spread across his mouth. 'Yes, Sister Matthews told me you would keep me up to the mark. I shall try not to be too difficult a patient, Maureen.'

'You're not my patient; you're the man I love. Very much. The doctor and nurses will visit even when you come home – but if I can help just a little, you will let me, please?'

'Yes, of course I shall,' he said. 'The sooner I'm on my feet again and working, the better...'

Maureen smiled and touched his uninjured hand. Gordon was determined now, but she knew that there would be many hours of terrible doubt and pain ahead, when he would wonder if it was all worthwhile, but all she could do was keep showing him love and helping him as much as he would let her.

Chapter 14

'This letter came for you,' Peggy said as she handed Rose the brown envelope. 'It looks as if it came through the forces network?'

'Yes, it is from Jimmy,' Rose said, a tinge of rose in her cheeks as she took it and slipped it into her pocket. 'I'll read it later and I'll have to send him my new address...'

'I'll always keep any letters for you. Remember, I'm your friend, Rose. We'll have a cup of tea and you can have a quick look at Jimmy's letter now.' Peggy hesitated, and then lowered her voice. 'I'm thinking of making a change and if I do manage it, I'd like you to work for me full-time again, caring for the twins, cooking and perhaps living in. I haven't looked into it fully yet, but I'll let you know as soon as I can.'

'That's very mysterious?' Rose's eyes sparkled and she glanced over her shoulder. 'But I do like the idea, Peggy – and the answer is yes...' She moved away to put the kettle on as Laurie walked in, deliberately turning her back on him.

'Gossiping again?' Laurie said in a teasing tone. 'I bought you some chocolates, Peggy. You may have forgotten it was our wedding anniversary last week, but I hadn't...'

'Oh... No, I hadn't forgotten,' Peggy said, taken back because he hadn't remembered their anniversary for years. 'That is very nice of you, Laurie, thank you.' It was so long since he'd bought her a present of any kind. For years all he'd given her on birthdays and at Christmas was money to get something for herself, and that wasn't quite the same. 'I shall enjoy them. We'll all have some when we have our morning break – chocolates are such a treat...'

Laurie gave her an odd look but didn't say anything, merely asked if there was any food ready to take into the bar.

'Yes, I've made some goat's cheese and chives tarts, also mince and potato pies – and I've prepared a winter salad of white cabbage, carrots, onions and leeks in vinaigrette to go with them.'

'Sounds a bit odd to me,' Laurie said. 'I shouldn't think anyone would buy it, but I'll take it through if you like; a good steak and kidney pie was always a favourite as I remember...'

'Actually, the salad has been a bestseller recently,' Peggy said defensively. 'We can't provide all the meat and puddings they used to love.'

'No, I suppose not,' he said. 'In the country there's quite a bit of game and farm butter and stuff, so I suppose I haven't noticed the shortages as much as you have here...'

'Lucky for you, milord,' Rose muttered and Laurie looked at her sharply, not quite catching the words.

Peggy smothered a laugh, because she'd heard and she liked Rose's sharp humour, but she also knew that Laurie would not appreciate her poking fun at him.

'I'd better open up,' he said. 'I expect Nellie has finished cleaning by now...'

'Oh dear,' Peggy said after he'd gone. 'I think he will find our meals not quite up to his standard. He's forgotten what it was like to live on pie and mash, and bread and butter pudding, as we often did in the old days... Actually, I might make a bread and butter pudding tomorrow...'

'That salad is really tasty,' Rose said. 'I love it and the goat's cheese tarts, and so do a lot of your regulars.'

'I'd like to run a café or teashop,' Peggy said, deciding suddenly to confide in her now that Laurie was out of hearing. 'Perhaps doing light lunches and afternoon sandwiches and cakes. I'm not sure about the future, Rose, but it's what I'd like one day...'

'I'd work for you tomorrow,' Rose said, 'but I'm not sure that I like working for Mr Ashley. I have to be truthful, Peggy...'

'You're not going to leave me in the lurch?' Peggy looked at her in alarm.

'No, of course not! I would give you plenty of notice if I did leave – but I want to stay in Mulberry Lane, and I'll work for you as long as I can.'

Peggy understood why Rose was thinking about finding work elsewhere. She didn't hit it off with Laurie and he hadn't been exactly friendly towards her. Laurie had come back talking about working together in harmony, but he was always criticising these days, sniping at her, as if he wanted to undermine her confidence.

Leaving the pub would be a big step to take. It was not the easiest of times to set up her own business, and living close to the pub would make it more difficult, because Laurie would not take her desertion lying down. Yet she wasn't prepared to let him treat her like a doormat...

Putting the abandoned bakery into good order would take a lot of what Able had left her and that meant she would have to make a success of her business almost straight away. If she could buy all the sugar, butter and other ingredients she needed to make delicious cakes and puddings, it wouldn't be a problem, but at the moment she was limited in what she could offer her customers.

The clothing restrictions had recently been lifted, because everyone had hated the austerity suits. Now men would be able to have turn-ups again and choose the style they liked, and women too would have more choice. The clothes were still rationed, of course, but if you saved your coupons you could have more choice. Once the food restrictions lifted a little, she would think seriously about making the move towards a business of her own.

According to the news they heard, it seemed that the Allies were beginning to make some advances against the enemy. The Americans had launched a big assault in the Pacific and the Russians had trapped ten enemy divisions. Perhaps it wouldn't be too long before life began to get back to normal and then she would have to make a decision.

Peggy felt guilty that she might be using the pub to keep her going until she could branch out on her own, but on the other hand, her industry had kept the pub ticking over for years, and especially while Laurie was away.

The chocolates had been a surprise and if it was Laurie trying to mend fences, then Peggy ought to give him a chance – but gifts didn't make up for all the harsh words. She hadn't liked having to choose between Nellie and Rose, though, as it turned out, Nellie had asked if she could work fewer hours now that she had her daughter at home with her.

'I'd never let yer down if yer needed me, Peggy,' she'd told her, 'but if I get the cleanin' done first thing, yer don't really need me after that, do yer, love? You've got Mr Ashley back and Rose is good with the twins...'

Peggy could hardly insist that she did need her, even though she missed having Nellie around all the time. It was only natural that Nellie wanted to be with her daughter and it was true that Laurie could manage the bar most of the time. Yet Peggy liked serving her customers, talking to them and hearing all their news.

She smothered a sigh as she heard a wail from Fay. The twins had woken her just after five. She'd bathed them, fed them and played with them, and they'd fallen asleep again, giving Peggy time to get on with her work.

'Do you want me to see to them, Peggy?' Rose asked, but she shook her head.

'No, I'll go up, Rose. You read your letter. I'll bring them down and then you can make the scones and soup. I wondered if we could use those green tomatoes I bottled last summer to make soup – what do you think of the idea?'

'I think it would be lovely with a little dried basil,' Rose said. 'I might put a little sugar in to sweeten it if it's too sharp. Tomato soup is always red... but this would be different...'

'I got a tin of pink salmon the other day and I'm going to make us sandwiches for lunch.'

'Lovely,' Rose said. 'Let me experiment with the soup. I'll see what it tastes like and then decide if it needs anything else to make it tasty... we do have some lentils in the store cupboard.'

'I'll leave it to you...' Peggy made a dash as Fay's screams increased. She didn't know how Laurie thought she would manage the cooking and the twins if Rose left her.

Rose was on the stool searching the top shelf for the lentils when she heard a noise behind her. She turned and saw Laurie Ashley looking at her legs. She'd been stretching up and must have given him an excellent view of her underwear. Anger made her bold and defiant.

'Gentlemen don't look at a lady's legs when she's in a vulnerable position.'

'Are you a lady, Rose?' he asked and she felt coldness at the back of her neck. He was leering at her, a menacing expression in his eyes.

'What is that supposed to mean?' she asked, getting down from the stool with the stone jar in her hand. He was so close that her skin prickled and she felt a surge of fear.

'I read the papers. My wife might not bother, but I read them from back to front and I remember faces. Your father murdered your mother – and some reports implied it was your fault... and you lied about your name. It's March, not Marchant.'

Rose froze as he saw the leer in his eyes. 'I told Peggy about the murder and she said it didn't matter. It wasn't my fault...'

'Perhaps not, but you had quite a reputation locally, didn't you?'

'You have no idea what you're talking about.' Rose raised her chin defensively. 'Besides, I've made a new start and I like living in the lane.'

'Oh, I'm not saying you should leave,' he said and moved a little closer. 'But you could be a bit nicer to me, Rose...' the threat was implied rather than spoken and Rose itched to throw something at him. He might be Peggy's husband, but she wouldn't put up with this from anyone.

'Keep away from me or I'll tell Peggy,' she hissed. 'I don't want you near me and if you think you can blackmail me...'

'Who said anything about blackmail,' he asked and looked a little uneasy.

'If Peggy didn't need help I'd find work elsewhere – and if you bother me like this again, I will...' Rose looked at him coldly.

He raised his hands and backed away, his eyes mocking her. 'Enough said. I've never forced a woman, but I know a lying little tart when I see one... so behave yourself or

I'll let a few people know about your background.' He walked out of the kitchen grinning as though he thought he'd won the prize.

Rose made up her mind to look for alternative work and when she found it, she would give in her notice. Peggy had spoken about making a change and Rose guessed she was unhappy, but it was unlikely that she would just walk away from a business that she'd spent years building up, and Rose wasn't prepared to be around a man she despised as much as she despised Laurie Ashley.

Maureen phoned Peggy that evening. She'd just returned home and wanted to talk but didn't feel she could leave the children with Gran again.

'Gran's been so good,' she said. 'She looked after them for two days while I visited Gordon…'

'How is he, Maureen?'

'In a lot of pain, as you might imagine,' Maureen told her. 'He was in reasonable spirits considerin', but it will be a long job, because the wound isn't healing properly yet. I feel so sorry for what he has to go through, Peggy, but of course I shan't ever tell him…'

'No, of course not,' Peggy said. 'Sayin' I'm sorry wouldn't help either of you, but you know you have my support and my love. If I can do anythin' – anythin' at all…'

'I know,' Maureen replied and smothered a sob. 'I've got good friends to support me, but Gordon has to do it himself, Peggy. I can help; you can help by keeping his spirits up when you see him, but he will have to go through it and we can't bear his pain for him.'

'He isn't bitter, is he?'

'No, not that I've seen – at least, not yet, but it may come when he realises all the things he won't be able to do for a long time, if ever, like playing football with the kids...' Maureen sighed. 'Anyway, how are things with you – is Laurie all right? I know it can't be easy havin' him back...'

'The first thing he did was to quarrel with Pip and he made me cut Rose's hours. She's livin' over the road with Mavis now and I miss her. Nellie moved into her flat, so it's just Laurie, the twins and me at night...'

'Oh, that's a nuisance, Peggy. Rose was such a big help to you.'

'She doesn't like Laurie,' Peggy said. 'I can sense an atmosphere whenever they're in the same room. From what she's said, I think he must have done something to make her uncomfortable. Perhaps some heavy flirting... but from him not her.'

'You won't put up with that – in your own home?'

'What else can I do – unless I just take the twins and leave everything I've worked for?'

'Oh, Peggy, I don't know what to say...' Maureen sighed unhappily. 'I'm here most of the time and I'll call in when I can – but I shall be in Portsmouth this weekend again. We hope Gordon can be moved to London soon, but he needs some special treatment first so it may not be for a few weeks yet... but we could let you have a bed in the sitting room if it gets unbearable...'

'And let him have everything? No, I can give as good as I get…'

'Be careful, love…'

'Oh, Maureen love, I don't want you to worry about me – you've got enough to worry about yourself; what with Gordon and the new baby on the way. You've got to take care of yourself too.'

'Gran and Shirley make sure of that – but you would always do the same for me and if you feel somethin' is wrong, just tell me. Remember Tom is around – and that nice Sergeant who is staying with him. Sid would throw the fear of God into anyone…'

'Laurie would never hurt me physically,' Peggy said. 'He's been impossible to live with, even though he bought me some chocolates. He said it was for our anniversary, but he hasn't bothered with that for years! He's so sharp with Rose and he finds fault with me and I see him frownin' when the twins cry…'

'I expect he feels awkward too,' Maureen said. 'He has been away for a long time – and the twins aren't his…'

'It worries me that he won't accept them,' Peggy said. 'They don't notice that he ignores them at the moment, but when they get older it is sure to cause trouble. I'm not sure what to do for the best… Divorce is such a huge step…'

'Peggy! Would you really leave him?' Maureen hesitated. 'What about the pub – all your years of work?'

'I'd have to give that up… he'd never let go…' Peggy's voice lowered. 'I'll see you tomorrow then, Maureen. I've got to try to get to grips with this wretched new PAYE tax system. I'm damned if I understand it…'

'I'll give you a hand one day if you're stuck. I think I'm on top of it.'

'Thanks. Take care of yourself, love…'

Maureen looked at the receiver as Peggy put it down abruptly. She frowned as she realised that her friend must either have suspected that Laurie was listening in or he'd walked into the room. She would call round in the morning and see what was going on. Peggy said Laurie wouldn't hurt her – but he wasn't exactly kind to her either, and if she were Peggy, she would be worried about his attitude towards the twins. It must be very irritating for a proud man to know that his wife had given birth to a younger man's twins.

Peggy was sleeping. Laurie had heard the boy start whimpering in his cot and listened for his wife to get up to him, but she hadn't and now the girl had started to cry. Laurie wasn't sleeping well because he'd found it harder coming back to the pub than he'd imagined. His wife's influence had grown too strong in his absence and it annoyed him that when he'd phoned the Brewery they told him what Peggy had been ordering and questioned his choices. The travellers who called in to tell him about new products asked for Peggy and seemed doubtful when he gave them an order for sauces or cigarettes, and the customers kept asking if Peggy was well and saying they missed her when she wasn't in the bar.

He waited for a while but Peggy didn't wake, so he got up and went into the twins' bedroom. It was Fay who was crying, though Freddie was also awake and looked up at him with wide eyes as he bent over Fay's cot. Laurie hesitated to pick the crying child up. She wasn't his and he felt no affinity for her and yet as he looked at her red face, he remembered Janet when she was small. He'd spent night after night nursing her when she was teething and he'd been the only one who could comfort her. Peggy hadn't been able to quell her tears.

'What's wrong then?' he asked in a soft tone. A part of him wished the twins had never been born, but that was only his pride – and now he remembered what it was like to be a father. Laurie had always wanted to have more babies, but after Pip they hadn't come. He'd thought it was Peggy's fault, but he realised now that it was more than likely his inability rather than hers. He'd had a bad bout of the measles in his late thirties and that could ruin a man's chances of having more children. 'Come on, girl, there's no need to take on so...' He bent down and lifted Fay up, catching the tell-tale odour of a dirty nappy. It was acidy and very strong, and he guessed she had an upset tummy. He stroked her cheek with one finger. 'Well, let's see what we can do to make you more comfortable.'

Laurie removed the soggy nappy and dropped it in the bucket Peggy used for soiled linen. He wiped the little girl's bottom with some cotton wool and a drop of cleansing lotion, noticing there was a bit of a rash on her tender skin. Hunting for some healing cream, he found a pot and smeared a good dab on before replacing the nappy with a soft clean one. Fay had stopped crying after he'd removed the wet cloth and was looking at him with Peggy's eyes. He thought she looked beautiful and it wrenched at his heart when she smiled up at him and blew bubbles.

Memories of Janet as a baby flooded back and some of the anger and pain eased away. When he'd told Peggy to let everyone think he was the twins' father, he'd thought he could cope, but it had been hard to come back to a home that no longer seemed his and discover that neither his wife nor her children appeared to need him.

'There we are then,' he said and placed Fay back in her cot. She looked at him for a moment and then said, 'Dadda...'

Laurie felt a little shock and a tug at his heartstrings. She wasn't his daughter but she seemed to think she was and for some reason that brought tears to his eyes.

'Yes, little one,' he said. 'I'm your daddy. I can see you haven't had all the attention you need, but I'm back now and your mummy will have more time to look after you...'

Laurie turned to look into the other cot. Freddie was just staring up at him, his thumb in his mouth. He wasn't crying, but he picked him up anyway and checked his nappy, which was dry.

'Are you going to call me Dadda too?' he asked, but Freddie didn't speak; he just looked at him with those wide, faintly accusing eyes, as he was put back into the cot. 'No? Well, that's a shame...'

Laurie turned to leave and then saw that Peggy was watching him from the doorway. She had a wary look in her eyes.

'What were you doing?'

'Fay has a tummy upset and I changed her nappy. You need to take her to the doctor in the morning, get something for that tummy. Freddie doesn't have it – he's fine, but I checked him just the same.'

Peggy walked to the cot and looked down at the twins. Freddie smiled and held out a hand to her. 'Mumma...' She bent down and kissed him and he patted her face, laughing. Returning to Laurie, she gazed up at him. 'Why didn't you call me?'

'You were obviously tired or you would've woken when they were crying. Besides, I always helped with the others when they were ill or teething...'

'Yes, but...' she stopped. 'I wasn't sure how you would feel... I mean it isn't quite the same, Laurie.'

'It can be if you want it to,' he said and smiled at her. She looked sexy in her nightgown with her hair tumbled. He'd forgotten what a good figure she had and surprisingly found himself aroused. 'We just have to want things to come right, Peggy, that's all...'

'Thank you for changing her,' Peggy said. She hesitated, then, 'I want us to be friends, Laurie – but you've been so prickly and nothing I do is right for you.'

'I felt as if I was in the way,' he said. 'You didn't need me – you had everything worked out and I was just a nuisance...'

'Of course you weren't,' Peggy said. 'This is your home and your pub – but you made it so clear that I was just the woman who cooks and cleans and I've wondered if you would prefer me to leave...'

'Don't be an idiot!' he said harshly and then frowned. 'No, I'm the idiot for making you feel like that, aren't I? I'm sorry, Peggy. I'll try to do better in future.'

'Why did it all go wrong, Laurie?' Peggy asked and looked sad. 'I thought we had a good life but then... It wasn't enough for you, was it?'

'I'm not sure what went wrong,' he said. 'I hated it that you made such a fuss of your stepfather, Percy. He was never faithful to your mother, even though you thought he was so good to her.'

'Mum loved him and he brought her back from the edge,' Peggy said. 'She'd lost her husband and her son and was sinking fast until Percy stepped in. If he went with other women, she didn't know about it and nor did I – so when he was ill I wanted to help him. It was never more than that...'

'I know but it annoyed me – and I suppose I wanted a change. And then you took Janet's side over her marriage...'

'She was in love,' Peggy said. 'Why don't you admit it, Laurie? These things wouldn't have mattered if you'd still loved me, but you were bored.'

'Yes,' he admitted it finally. 'Well, I tried changing my life, but it wasn't a bed of roses. I'd like to make things up with you – I'd like to be your husband again. Oh, I'm not demanding a place in your bed immediately, but I'd like to think it could happen one day.'

'I'm not sure,' Peggy said truthfully. 'I'm not the same person either, Laurie. Things can't ever be as they were...'

'No, you're more independent, more confident than you ever were,' he said. 'I was sincere when I said I wanted to try again, even if it is only as friends and partners – but I felt shut out, not needed. I thought you could manage without me... but I helped just now, didn't I?'

'Yes, you helped...' Peggy smiled and Laurie realised that she had a new beauty about her, a serenity that made her seem above him. He'd got bored with the woman who was a mother first and a wife second, but he didn't know the new Peggy, and he was intrigued. 'Thank you for being so gentle and kind with Fay and Freddie. I was afraid you would resent them and hate me because of what they represent. You were awful to Pip and his girl – and he really loves her. You shouldn't take anger against me out on your son.'

'I just didn't want him to make a mistake,' Laurie confessed. It was a night for confessions, for getting words out that were hard to say. 'And I did resent the twins – but when Fay was in such distress I thought of our Janet when she was teething. A baby isn't to blame just because her father was not married to her mother. I shan't hurt them, Peggy. I'd never harm an innocent child...'

Peggy relaxed. She'd been feeling anxious lately, but now she knew she had nothing to fear. Laurie had been like a bear with a sore head these past few weeks, but he wouldn't harm her twins. He wanted to be the boss and to give out favours, as he had in the past – for her to be grateful to him and look up to him. Peggy wasn't sure she would ever feel that way again, but she could be pleasant and treat him as a friend rather than a stranger.

'Let's see how things go,' she said.

'I don't like that girl you've taken on,' he said. 'She's a slut – I rang the pub where she used to live and they told me. Everyone says she was sleeping with her own father… and other men…'

'Laurie! I'm sure Rose isn't like that…' Peggy sighed. She liked Rose, but Laurie obviously didn't, and that was because Rose had made it clear she didn't want his attentions. 'I think you should give her the benefit of the doubt. She seems honest and good-hearted to me.'

'She came out of the bathroom, her robe opened at the front and the way she looked at me – well, it's up to you, but I should get rid of her. You've got Nellie to help you and you can get someone else if you need them.'

Peggy sighed, because he was being unfair, but for the moment she was tied, though perhaps it didn't matter. 'Rose is thinking of leaving soon anyway. She doesn't like you either, Laurie.'

'The sooner she goes, the better, as far as I'm concerned. There's bad blood there, Peggy. Let her go and ask Nellie to come in more…'

'I shan't argue with you, Laurie. Rose will leave and perhaps Janet will come home if I ask her to.'

'Yes, you do that,' he said and smiled. 'She should be home with us – until she marries again. If Janet was here we could go out sometimes. It's years since we went to the flicks or a meal.'

'I'm not sure she ever will…'

'Telephone her and ask…'

'Why don't you? You could tell her you want to get to know Maggie…' She saw the doubt in his face. 'You need to try to build bridges, Laurie, with Pip and Janet. Otherwise this family will fall apart.'

'Janet married Mike to defy me,' Laurie said. 'You wait – in a year or two at the most she'll get married again.'

Chapter 15

Janet stood at her bedroom window and looked down into the large garden. It was like spring that morning in March with the first early bulbs beginning to flower everywhere. She didn't blame Rosemary for wanting to come back to her home in Devon; it was a much nicer property than she'd had in Portsmouth. A large Victorian building of red bricks and a slate roof, it had lots of space for her children to play in the gardens, and the extensive attics, if it was wet. The boys went to day schools now rather than the boarding school they'd hated and seemed much happier. They'd shown no outward signs of grieving for their father and eagerly played football with Rosemary's new man. The whole family had got excited when Oxford won the third wartime boat race on the River Ouse, leaving Janet feeling like an outsider.

Janet had imagined that Rosemary would still be grieving for her husband, but seeing her with the tall, handsome man in the garden that evening, she suspected that her friend was considering marriage.

It was time Janet thought about returning home to the pub. She'd been here for more than seven months now.

Janet didn't want to be in the way of a couple on the verge of making a new life together. It would be embarrassing for them if she walked in on intimate moments.

She'd warned her mother she might come back and asked to be given a different room. Janet couldn't sleep in the bed where Mike had died. She hadn't known what was happening until she started dressing and then turned to find him cold and still in her bed. Perhaps that was what hurt the worst, she thought, because she ought to have been aware – she ought to have held him in her arms as he slipped away, and it felt as if she'd let him down. Everyone would tell her that was stupid, because there was nothing she could've done; the doctor said it would have been quick and Mike hadn't felt pain. It was his opinion that her husband had never known what was happening, but that didn't make it any easier for Janet.

Mike had seemed to be so much better for a few days before that night. He was remembering little things, feeling loving and close to her and Maggie – and he'd gone chasing after Jack Barton when that awful man who had raped Ellie had been seen in the lane. Jack had intended to teach him a lesson and if Mike hadn't chased him, he might have killed him. At first Janet had blamed Ellie for telling him: it was her fault Mike had gone off like that and Janet had felt that the furious running was the reason he'd died. She'd stopped thinking like that since she'd talked to Rosemary. It was strange how she could tell her friend things she could never have told her mother, which was unfair because Peggy was a loving, caring person and always ready to listen. Maybe it was that she cared too much, while Rosemary was able to look at things from a distance. Janet had needed that and she'd enjoyed helping with all her friend's good causes. Maggie had been happier down here too, though she never asked about her father. Janet wasn't sure if she remembered him, because he'd been around so seldom in her daughter's life, and she'd been too distressed to talk to her about him. It had been easier to live here, away from the pub, but now she knew it was time to go home.

Rosemary needed to have time alone with the man she was falling in love with, and Janet needed to get on with her life. She'd stopped blaming herself for Mike's death and she'd stopped blaming Ellie and the rest of the world. Her anger had burnt out and she'd reached the numb stage when she just managed to get through each day. If it hadn't been for Maggie, she might have just sat in a corner and given up all interest in life, but her daughter was a lively child, always into mischief and asking for something.

'What's that, Mummy?' was her favourite question. And, 'Can I have...?'

Janet would tell Rosemary in the morning. She'd telephone her mother and tell her she was coming home – and she would stay for a while – but it was probably time she started to plan for the future. Janet knew that there was always a home for her in her mother's house, but it was time she thought about finding a job that would support her and Maggie. She had a small pension from the Navy, but she would need to work – and she wanted to work. Like all women these days, she did part-time war work, a few hours with the WVS or working with the Red Cross, packing first-aid kits and parcels for men in prisoner-of-war camps. With a young child, Janet couldn't do a full-time job, but with her pension and some part-time office work, she might be able to afford a small house in the suburbs – somewhere within a short bus ride or a train journey to see her mother once a week. Maggie liked train rides and she liked Grandma Peggy. She'd asked for her a few times lately, questioned when she was going to see her, and that was a part of the reason Janet had decided to go home for a while – just until she could find a home of her own.

Janet heard the telephone ringing and went to answer it.

'Janet Rowan here,' she said. 'Rosemary is in the garden, I'll fetch her for you if you wish, unless I can take a message...'

'Janet... I heard you were staying with Rosemary...' She felt a little tingle at the back of her neck as she heard Ryan Hendricks' voice. He'd been a good friend to her in the past and she knew that he'd wanted to be much more, but when Mike had come home he'd taken a step back. 'How are you?'

'Ryan...' She took a deep breath. 'I'm all right – but it has been very hard. I knew what could happen, of course, but it was so sudden...'

'Yes, I was terribly sorry when I heard. I didn't like to telephone too soon, because I knew how you would be feeling – but I'm in Exeter this next week. May I come and see you one day?'

Janet hesitated. She liked Ryan but she'd put him out of her mind when Mike was ill. 'I'm going back to London soon…'

'I could take you home?' Ryan suggested. 'I'd like to meet for tea or something… and I'd be happy to take you and Maggie home. It would save you a long train journey. If we start early, we can break for lunch and drinks… and it's ages since I've seen you…'

'Yes, it is,' Janet agreed. 'All right – when do you want to come here?'

'Say Thursday? I could put up overnight at a small hotel and then we can start out early on Friday morning…'

'Very well,' Janet agreed. 'We've acquired quite a bit of stuff since we came down here. Rosemary has given Maggie some of the boys' old toys and I was wonderin' how best to get them home.'

'I'm glad to be of service,' Ryan said. 'I'll call on Thursday afternoon. We can all go out for tea – Rosemary too if she would like that – and then we'll pack the car and be ready for an early start.'

'Thank you – you always seem to turn up when I need help,' Janet said. 'Who told you I was stayin' here?'

'I've kept in touch with Rosemary all this time,' Ryan said. 'She told me she thought you were feeling a little better?'

'Yes, being here has done me good,' Janet said and there was a little break in her voice. 'I had to get away from there…'

'I do know what you've been through, Jan,' Ryan said and his voice was a caress.

'Yes, I know you do,' she said, remembering the night he'd come to her in utter devastation after his family and his home had been destroyed by a bomb. 'I didn't ask how you are. I know you were abroad for a while…'

'I had to sort out a problem for the Army. A lot of equipment and stores were going astray – and I'm glad to say that that particular problem is now behind bars and likely to stay there a very long time.'

'It's hard to imagine that someone would steal from our troops,' Janet said, her interest awakened. 'Surely, everyone knows how important it is to get equipment and food to our men?'

'You would think that,' Ryan said. 'But it happens all the time, though not in such a big way – a stolen pig or some eggs going astray is one thing, but hundreds of pounds' worth of stores is another matter.'

'It's what you do, is it?' Janet said. 'You're an inspector of some kind, making sure the black market doesn't flourish…'

'Something like that,' Ryan said and she could hear the smile in his voice. 'You know I can't say too much – but I like to think of myself as a troubleshooter for Government departments.'

'I don't need to know,' Janet said. 'I always suspected you did something like that – your regular visits to Portsmouth – but I shan't ask any more questions.'

'Will you be putting Maggie in nursery school soon?' Ryan asked. 'Only I know of a decent place that takes young children for a few hours…'

'I'm thinking of finding part-time work,' Janet told him. 'When I can afford it, I'll look for a small house with a garden for Maggie. Rosemary has a wonderful garden here and Maggie loves it – but I don't want to be too far from Mum. Somewhere we can visit her at least once a week…'

'We'll talk about it when I come down,' Ryan said. 'It's lovely to talk to you again, Jan. I've thought about you a lot…'

He replaced the receiver at the other end without waiting for her reply. Janet frowned as she put down her end. She'd been surprised to hear his voice and it would be nice to be looked after on the journey back to London instead of having to struggle on and off a train with luggage and a small child – but she hoped Ryan didn't expect anything more, because she wasn't ready for a new relationship just yet.

'I'm sorry to see you go,' Rosemary told Janet when she gave her a basket filled with vegetables from the garden that had been stored over winter. 'Although, I can tell you now that I'm going to be married – perhaps in the summer so that that the boys can enjoy the wedding and a seaside holiday – and then we'll have a trip to Scotland nearer to next Christmas… Mack treats the boys as if they were his own and they all like skiing and hill walking. We can't go to Austria at the moment. He's a bit doubtful of Switzerland, because they're neutral and that means we could meet Germans there so we'll try Scotland… We can walk and enjoy the good food, salmon and game, even if the skiing isn't brilliant...and there will be lovely log fires and good whisky.'

'I suspected marriage might be on the cards for you,' Janet said and hugged her. 'Thanks so much for havin' me all this time. I'm feeling a bit better, so I'll go home and give Mum a hand – and I'll look for a place of my own. It's time I went to work I think...'

'Yes, I had the same idea, but Mack had others and I gave in for the sake of the boys... they miss having a father and they've been happier since Mack started coming round. I like him an awful lot, but he isn't John – if you understand what I mean?'

'Do you love him?' Janet asked.

'I like him a lot and I enjoy being with him,' Rosemary said in her forthright manner, as honest as always. 'He's attractive, a good lover and very attentive – and he gives me all the things I was missing. I don't feel the way I did when I first married John, but I don't think it's necessary to be madly in love. I'm older now and I want the kind of life I would have had if John had lived. Mack will take me dancing, to the theatre and for holidays abroad once the war is over...'

'I understand, well, I hope you'll be very happy, Rosemary.'

'I intend to be,' she said and kissed her cheek. 'We're staying in the house. Mack is going to sell his property and we'll buy a flat in London – or something overseas when this nonsense is finished... Mack's aunt has a house in the south of Spain and he enjoys the life there.'

Janet nodded, turning to greet Ryan, who had finished stacking her luggage in the car and was waiting for her.

'Maggie wants to sit in the front – shall you have her on your lap or take turns?' he asked with a smile.

'Oh, I'll let her have a turn until we stop. She'll get tired later and want to sleep on the back seat. Bye, Rosemary, thank you so much for having me to stay.' She hugged her and Maggie gave her the small box of chocolates they'd managed to buy as a parting gift. 'I really needed your help and I do feel better.'

'I'm so glad, my dear,' Rosemary said. 'Remember what I told you...' she whispered in Janet's ear. 'A passionate love affair isn't necessary – take what you can get...'

Janet nodded, but she was frowning as she walked away, getting into the back seat as Maggie excitedly claimed the front seat next to Ryan. She seemed to have recognised him, though it was a long time since she'd seen him, and was quite happily calling him 'Uncle Ryan' and singing to herself. Janet realised that Maggie had seen far more of Ryan as a young child than she ever had of her father.

Rosemary's confession had shocked her a little, because her friend had been so devastated by John's death. Janet would never have expected her to remarry so soon or for the reasons she'd indicated. Janet didn't think she would marry unless she fell in love again, and her heart still felt numbed and sore after the pain Mike's tragic death had caused.

'Are you all right in the back?' Ryan turned his head to look at her.

'Yes, I'm fine,' she said. 'The question is, will *you* be with Miss Chatterbox beside you?'

'I'm happy as a sandboy,' he said and smiled down at Maggie. He put his hand in his pocket and pulled out a brown paper bag, giving it to her. 'I hope you like raspberry drops and barley sugar? I bought a mixture of sweets for you, Maggie.'

'Clever thinking,' Janet said and a soft laugh escaped her as Maggie popped a red sweet in her mouth. 'Nothing else works half as well.'

Janet turned to wave as Ryan drove away. Maggie didn't look back: she was perfectly happy because she felt safe with Ryan and her mother and she had some sweets. She'd talked excitedly of seeing Grandma Peggy but hadn't mentioned the twins. Janet hoped she would be over her jealousy of them now and there would be no more clandestine visits to the cots to pinch their arms. She'd had to scold Maggie and smack her arm when she'd caught her pinching Fay, but she was nearly four now and hopefully it wouldn't happen again.

Chapter 16

'Jan will be home this evening,' Peggy told Maureen when she popped in for a cup of coffee before catching her train down to Portsmouth. 'I didn't ask her to come, she rang me and told me she was on her way – and a friend is driving her up, so she doesn't have to struggle with the luggage. Rosemary gave Maggie several toys and she wouldn't have willingly left them behind.' She sighed. 'Apparently, she has a little present for the twins. I wasn't able to give them much on their birthday, except for the knitted toys you made for me and a carved donkey and a rabbit that soldier made...' Ben Walker had made several toys for Maureen's shop, but most were too big for the twins' little hands.

'Maggie is a lucky girl,' Maureen said. 'Robin has had only a couple of new toys. All the other things he plays with were Shirley's. It was her idea to give him her teddy, but he throws it out of his cot.'

'I've given the twins some of Pip's things, and I gave a few of his toys to the church sale so that other mothers could buy them; it's sad for little ones whose mothers can't even buy them a teddy bear...'

'Well, I suppose some families don't have the money, even if they were available,' Maureen said and Peggy nodded. In the lanes there were families who struggled to pay the rent and put food on the table. 'But I've given some of Shirley's old clothes to the church, because lots of kids could do with them.'

Peggy nodded. Times were hard and they all had to do what they could to help each other. Peggy had given all her mother's old clothes away now and things she'd had when she was young. Enterprising young mothers could turn them into clothes for their kids.

'How are you feeling, love?' Peggy asked.

'I'm fine, thank goodness. I need to be fit, travellin' up and down on the train every few days.'

'Let's hope Gordon is transferred to London soon. It will make all the difference and you might even get him home by the summer.'

'That would be wonderful,' Maureen said. 'What about you, love? Are things any better with Laurie?'

'Yes, a little. We talked the other night and he was good with Fay – changed her nappy when she had tummy trouble. Laurie does most of the bar work and I just go in for an hour or so in the evenings, when the twins are asleep. It's workin' better than I thought. I'd forgotten how good it was to come down and have all the fires lit...' She smiled. 'It will be nice to have Janet back, though.'

'I'm glad,' Maureen said. 'I wasn't sure how you'd be when he first got back...'

'I'm taking it one day at a time – and Rose is leaving, because they don't get on – so I'll be advertising for some help in the mornings. Nellie does all the cleaning and I need to look after the twins, so if I can get someone to muck in with the cooking a bit that will help…'

'Won't Janet will help with the kids when she gets back?' Maureen asked. 'I should think Maggie will go to school next spring. She'll have plenty of time then.'

'I think she might find herself a proper job once Maggie is at school – and she might want a home of her own, but she'll be here for a while and that gives me time to find the right person.'

'I manage my jobs and the children because I have Gran – but Jan would be on her own… I don't think she's realised how hard that can be.'

'No, I'm sure she hasn't,' Peggy said. 'But I'm not sure Jan could ever settle at the pub after what happened.'

'No, that was so upsettin' for her,' Maureen sighed. 'Well, I must go and catch my bus or I'll miss the train. I'll talk to you when I get back.'

'Give my love to Gordon, and tell him we're all thinkin' of him.'

'Yes, thanks,' Maureen said. 'I'd better get off…'

Peggy smiled and watched her leave through the kitchen door, waving as she went under the archway. She picked up a paper that Laurie had fetched earlier and read some of the headlines. There was a picture of a young German boy of fifteen-years-old in a soldier's uniform. At least in Britain they hadn't got to that stage, Peggy thought; eighteen was plenty old enough for young men to have to fight.

Peggy washed the teacups before returning to the cooking she'd started before Maureen arrived. She'd made a shepherd's pie with buttered greens to go with it, mince pasties, scones and some fresh crusty bread, which smelled so delicious that it made her hungry, and she'd peeled the green cooking apples for a pie. She started to flour the board for her pastry, feeling her throat tighten, because every time she made apple pie she thought of Able and the longing for him almost overcame her.

'I wondered – do you know if Peggy Ashley still runs the pub?' the man asked Rose as she came out of Mavis's house and prepared to cross the road. She stared at him for a moment, because his uniform was strange and she thought he was American or Canadian, though she wasn't sure which.

'That's a matter of debate,' Rose said, feeling rueful. She'd lost a good job she loved and was not particularly looking forward to working in the cardboard factory. 'Most would say her husband runs the pub since he came back from the war – and she has to look after the twins. They've not long had their second birthday and are quite a handful – especially Fay…'

'Peggy has two-year-old twins, you say?' The man in the strange uniform looked at her oddly for a moment and then nodded. 'I see – thanks for telling me, ma'am… I didn't know her husband was back…'

'Yeah, he's been away for ages…' Rose began, but the man had turned and walked away and didn't hear her as she said, 'He's a brute and a beast and she would be better off without him, if you ask me.'

Rose stared after him for a few moments, wondering who he was and why he'd wanted to know if Peggy was still at The Pig & Whistle. He'd walked off in the opposite direction, so why had he wanted to know? Perhaps Rose should tell Peggy someone was asking about her.

Crossing the road, she stopped as Ellie came out of the hairdresser's.

'Hi, Rose,' she said. 'You asked if I could fit you in for a trim this afternoon and I said no, but I've had a cancellation and I can fit you in at two thirty if that's all right.'

'Yes, that's lovely,' Rose said. 'I'm looking forward to starting work with you on Saturday.'

'I shall be pleased to have you, Rose. It means Irene can start to have her own customers and not just her mum.'

'Where's your little girl today?'

'Mabel is looking after her for me. I'm really lucky to have her. Sid brought round a huge teddy bear for Beth last night. I don't know where on earth it came from, but he says it isn't pinched so I'm happy for her to have it.'

'Sid is a nice person,' Rose said. 'I've seen him in Tom's shop – he lodges with him, doesn't he?'

'Yes…' Ellie looked pensive, a little sad and Rose spoke impulsively.

'I wondered if you'd like to go out sometimes in the evening…'

Ellie looked surprised. 'Where were you thinking of going?'

'I've been given two free tickets to a dance, but I think it's more of a social do. We could watch, listen to the

music, have a drink, and play cards or the tombola...
shuffle round the dance floor together if no one asks us.'

'I like tombola,' Ellie said. 'I used to go to that when I
lived at home with my friends...'

'Well, we could try that,' Rose said. 'You don't seem to
get out much – and I don't have many friends. I thought
we might go out together sometimes...'

'Well, yes, I can't see why not,' Ellie said. 'Mabel
wouldn't mind me goin' with you now and then. She
never grumbles when I go out with Maureen – but she's
too worried about Gordon at the moment...'

'I haven't met him, but everyone says he's lovely. I hope
he will soon get better.'

'We all do,' Ellie assured her. 'All right, I'll come to the
social do with you, Rose. I'll ask Mrs Tandy if you can
come to lunch one Sunday. It's not a lot of fun when you
don't have many friends.'

'It was all right at Peggy's...' Rose felt a surge of anger
against the man who had made it so uncomfortable for
her that she'd had to find another job at a factory. Rose
knew that the reason he'd wanted her out was because he
knew she wouldn't have let him have all his own way. He
was determined to put Peggy in her place and Rose would
have stood up to him and told her to tell him where to
go – and that's why he wanted her gone; that and the fact
that he fancied her and she'd turned him down. Well, even
though she couldn't work in his pub she would be around
for Peggy, whether he liked it or not...

Waving goodbye to Ellie, Rose walked into the pub
yard. It was her last but one morning and meeting Laurie

Ashley as he crossed the yard, she was glad she'd made the break. He'd been hostile towards her since that day in the pantry and she would be glad when she didn't have to see him every day. All thought of the man she'd met in the lane had gone from her head as she walked into the kitchen and Peggy told her that Janet would be there that evening.

'You'll be happy to have her back,' Rose said and smiled, because she really liked Peggy and she would never have let her down if it hadn't been for her husband. 'It means you'll have some help with the twins, doesn't it?'

'Yes, I shall be fine now,' Peggy said and poured her a cup of tea. 'But don't be a stranger, Rose. I'm sorry you had to leave – but Laurie…' Peggy sighed and shook her head.

'I'm not going anywhere, Peggy. I'll still be living at Mavis's house and around a lot of the time if you need me…'

'Thanks,' Peggy said. 'Can you pop upstairs and help Nellie with the bedrooms, Rose? She wants to get away early, because her daughter is due at the maternity clinic this afternoon and she'd like to go with her…'

'Yes, of course,' Rose said. She thought fleetingly then of the man in the lane but pushed it aside. Peggy was too busy that morning to be bothered with someone who had just walked away. After all, if he'd wanted to see her, he would have gone to the door of the pub and asked after Rose told him she was there.

'Oh, Jan darling, it's lovely to have you home,' Peggy said and embraced her daughter as she carried a sleeping

Maggie into the kitchen. 'It must have been such a long day for you…'

'We started very early,' Janet said, 'but we stopped for a drink and some sandwiches a couple of times, and Ryan's car is so comfortable, much better than clambering on and off trains. Is Maggie in her old room? I'll take her straight up and say hello to the twins… I've got a belated present for their birthday… some things Rosemary gave me out of her attic.'

'I haven't moved Maggie's things – but I've had the large guest room decorated freshly for you, love, and there's room for her with you if you prefer. I hope you like it…' Peggy saw a flash of grief in her daughter's face but Janet said nothing, merely carrying her daughter out into the hall and up the stairs as Ryan entered the kitchen loaded down with their belongings. 'Goodness me! It's just as well Janet had you to bring her home… She'd never have got that lot on and off the trains by herself.'

'I was delighted to bring them both back to you, Mrs Ashley.'

'Please, call me Peggy – I think we've known each other long enough now, Ryan. How are you these days?'

'Much better and happier to be back in England,' he said. 'It's so long since I saw you. I understand you have twins? Your husband must be over the moon.'

'Yes…' Peggy turned her head aside, as she always did when anyone spoke of the twins as Laurie's. It was what he'd asked for in return for her remaining at the pub, but sometimes she felt she was betraying Able's memory. 'Can I give you a drink – or a cup of tea?'

'I could murder a cup of tea,' Ryan said and laughed as he deposited an old and much-loved rocking horse in the kitchen. It had been in Rosemary's attic, but she'd brought it down for Maggie and then given it to her as a parting gift. 'I can see fights over this once the twins are old enough to want their turn. I don't think Maggie is too keen on sharing…'

'No, perhaps not,' Peggy said. 'I think that may be why Janet is planning on finding a home of her own…'

'She would be silly to move too soon,' Ryan said with a slight frown. 'This is a lovely comfortable home, Peggy. I know I would be quite happy living here if it was mine. I'm looking for something in the suburbs. I'd like to be a short ride from the city on the tube. I have a lot of contacts in this area…'

Peggy looked into his eyes and then nodded. 'I wish you lots of luck with your plans,' she said and smiled, because she was glad Janet had a friend like him. 'And please call whenever you wish…'

Peggy turned away to pour boiling water into the large brown pot as Janet returned to the kitchen. She was smiling and looked much less tense than when she'd left them to stay with Rosemary in Devon.

'The room is lovely, Mum, thank you,' she said and went to hug her. 'I'm really glad to be home. It's been awkward at Rosemary's the past few weeks. I felt in the way when Mack was always there.'

'This will always be your home while I live here, Jan…'

'Yes, I know, but I shall find a place for Maggie and me when I can afford it, Mum.'

'Of course... Tea for you, Jan?' Peggy asked. 'I've got some fresh scones ready – or there is a ham salad if you would rather... and Ryan is welcome to stay, as I hope he knows.'

'Mum, you shouldn't have gone to any trouble,' Jan said. 'We ate snacks on the way. Rosemary sent a huge basket of stuff from her garden too, winter greens, eggs from her chickens – and a chicken. Her gardener plucked it for us...'

'Roast chicken this weekend then,' Peggy said and turned to Ryan. 'I'd like you to stay...'

'I have several appointments this weekend,' Ryan said, 'but I'd love to come another time. I'll leave you now, Jan. If there is anything you need – just ring me. I'll give you my new number...' He took a little white card from his inside pocket. 'It was nice talking to you, Peggy. I'll call another day.'

'Ryan – thank you,' Janet said and moved towards him. She took his card and held it in her hand. 'It was so good of you to bring us.'

'I'll always do anything for you, Jan. Goodnight – and I'll see you soon.'

Jan stood watching as he left by the back door, closing it behind him. She sat down at the kitchen table and pulled her cup of tea towards her.

'Ryan didn't have his tea—'

'No, I expect he wants to get home. Do you know where he lives now?'

'He uses hotels and lodging houses for the moment.' Janet looked at her mother. 'I'm glad to be home, Mum.

I'm sorry if I made things difficult for you, goin' off the way I did.'

'I understood, my darling,' Peggy said. 'I'm glad to have you back, but you must do whatever suits you. It's your life and I shan't stand in your way. I can manage with Nellie's help – and your father's.'

'Is Dad helpin'?' Janet asked and sipped her tea. 'Pip told me they'd had a row…'

'I wish he hadn't fallen out with Pip – but you know what he's like,' Peggy said.

'I think Ryan wants to marry me…' Janet blurted it out and then looked flushed. 'I don't know how I feel. Rosemary thinks I should if he asks me – but I have to be sure. She's not in love with Mack, but she thinks he'll give them all a better life.'

'Yes, you must think carefully,' Peggy agreed. 'Don't marry just because it would make your life easier, Janet.'

'I thought once I was fallin' for Ryan,' Janet said. 'There was one night when I almost went to bed with him… but then Mike was found alive and I made my choice.'

'Yes, but things are different now, my love. You have another chance – but you must take your time and think carefully. I want you to be happy whatever you choose.'

'Yes, I shall take my time,' Janet said, got up and put her arms around her mother and kissed her. 'I do love you, Mum. I just couldn't show it because I was hurtin' too much.'

'I know that,' Peggy smiled and gave her a hug. 'You are my daughter and I shall always love you whatever you do. Never forget that…'

'I don't think I forgot; I just didn't want to let any form of love in – it was easy to be angry and shut it all out, except for Maggie. I clung to her because without her I should have gone under...'

'Yes, I know.' Peggy stroked her hair and smiled at her. 'I'm so glad you've come back to me, Jan. We'll make it a good spring and summer for everyone – and then we'll talk about the future when you're ready.'

Chapter 17

Maureen looked anxiously at Gordon's pale face as he lay back against the hospital pillows. Sister Matthews had told her he'd been having some intensive treatment, which had exhausted him. Tears pricked behind her eyes, but Maureen refused to let them fall. She must never show Gordon pity because he would hate it.

'I'm a bit late,' she said and smiled as he opened his eyes to look at her. 'The train was diverted due to damage on the line, because the bloody Germans have decided to start making our lives difficult again – so it took half an hour longer…'

Gordon nodded wearily. He'd read the papers and knew that the Germans had suddenly decided to bomb London and things like railway lines again. The RAF was bombing the hell out of their towns and cities, so it wasn't surprising that they'd decided on another mini Blitz.

'As long as you're safe,' he said and looked at her with a mixture of love and concern. 'You need to look after yourself now you're having our baby. If the travellin' becomes too much for you, you mustn't come so often…'

'I might come down and stop for a while, unless they find a bed for you in London,' Maureen told him. 'Shirley wants to see you, and Robin would like to see his daddy – and Shirley is so good with him. I can trust her as much as I trust Gran these days. She's growing up so fast, Gordon.'

'I've missed seeing them both growing up,' Gordon said and reached for her hand. 'It has been touch-and-go about whether they needed to take my leg off, Maureen. I should hate that, but it is at last responding to this new treatment and the infection is under control. I've been told I may be moved to London in a couple of weeks or so. I shan't be home, but you'll be able to visit me more easily…'

'That's wonderful news, love,' Maureen said and bent to kiss him. 'We've all been very worried about you, but I had confidence in the nurses here. Shirley will be so happy to see you. She's making you a present – but I'm not allowed to tell you what, of course.'

Gordon reached for her hand and held it. 'How did I get to be so lucky? I dread to think where Shirley would be now if you hadn't taken her on.'

'Gran has looked after her a lot of the time, but she loves her – we all love her, Gordon. Shirley is my daughter and all we need to be happy is to have you home with us again.'

'I wasn't sure I would make it,' he admitted. 'The pain nearly sends me mad at times, but I can see the healing is happening and so I'll put up with the agony of the treatment.'

'I know they're giving you penicillin, and the papers are full of how wonderful that is, and I expect they give you salt baths...' The worry inside belied her calm tone, but she couldn't let him see that she'd been fearful for his leg and his life.

'That hurts like hell,' Gordon said, 'but it is helping the wound to heal. They packed it with maggots and they ate out the rotten flesh, but the doc says it will gradually restore itself now that all the puss and infection have gone.'

'Yes, I know it all sounds horrible and the treatment is controversial, but it works. Had the gangrene set in, you would've lost your leg.'

'I know. At first, I shouted at the doctor for the pain he was puttin' me through, swore and called him all the names under the sun, but he's done me the world of good.'

'We must be thankful they didn't just chop your leg off over there,' Maureen said. 'The field surgeons are so busy, they don't have time to wait in most cases. You were lucky – even though it doesn't feel that way.'

'I know I'm lucky to be alive. It was fierce fighting when the Allies landed at Anzio, Maureen. I was lucky to be near an American unit when I was hit; they got me out when I was wounded, otherwise I might have died, I kept thinking about you and the children and it kept me goin', though it meant I was longer before I was able to get home.'

Maureen nodded. There hadn't been much in the papers, because it was all hush-hush and Gordon was wounded soon after the landing, but perhaps that was luck, because the Americans had still been landing their troops and they'd sent him back from the conflict on one of their ships. 'You're here now. I pray you'll never have to fight again.'

'I'll be lucky if I can work or return to the Army,' Gordon said wryly. 'I doubt I'll be sent overseas again, even if I can manage to hobble about on two legs.'

'You will in time,' Maureen said and took his hand, holding it firmly. 'I promise you that you will in time. I've bought a little van and both Tom and I are learning to drive it so that he can deliver the goods and I can go to the wholesaler.'

'I don't want you overdoin' things in your condition...'

'I'm fine, really well,' Maureen said and laughed. 'Driving will make things easier for all of us. You learned in the Army, didn't you?'

'I wanted to drive years ago, but I could never have afforded a car, but I took the opportunity to learn when the Army offered to teach me – and perhaps one day we'll be able to afford a car...'

'We make a few pounds from the shop these days – though not as much as we could if we were able to buy all we need. It makes me wonder why Dad didn't leave more to Violet. He must have made good money all the time I worked for him, but I don't know what he did with it,' Maureen said.

'Perhaps he spent it on his wife?'

'Violet doesn't seem to think so,' Maureen said. 'It's odd really, but Dad always kept his secrets. I wouldn't be surprised if he has money hidden somewhere...'

'Have you looked?'

'I'm sure Violet has looked in the flat, but I haven't bothered. I wouldn't know where to start...'

'Oh well, it's a mystery,' Gordon said and grinned. They heard the bell ring and his smile disappeared. 'Why does an hour go so fast when you're here and every minute drags when you're not?'

'I'm staying overnight, so I'll be back for the evenin' visitin' and in the mornin',' Maureen said and bent to kiss him. 'Have a good rest, love, and I'll see you later...'

Maureen smiled as she left him, turning back at the swing doors to wave. He was watching her and she saw the longing in his face, and the pain. Her heart wrenched and she wished she could stay with him, nurse him, and help him through all he had to suffer, but there was nothing she could do until he was allowed to come home.

Rose left the factory after a busy day, feeling tired and irritable. She wished she'd never had to leave the pub. It had been lovely living with Peggy, cooking and taking care of the kids, but the factory was hard, dirty work and she hated it. Trudging down the lane, she felt the knobbly cobbles through her shoes and sighed, because they needed repairing again.

'Hi, there, beautiful,' a voice said and Rose halted, looking up at the man in uniform in amazement.

'Jimmy – is it you?' she asked. 'Is it really you?'

'I went to see Peggy and she told me you'd taken on factory work...' He grinned at her as he noticed the turban that covered her hair and the streaks of dust on her cheeks. 'I was going to ask if you wanted to go to the flicks or something, but you look tired.'

'I was until I saw you,' Rose said and laughed. 'Give me fifteen minutes to wash and change and I'll meet you – in the pub if you like.'

'Are you sure?'

'Yes, of course. It's wonderful having you home. I wasn't expecting it...' Her eyes travelled over him anxiously. 'You're not hurt, are you?'

'No, I've been promoted and sent back for some special training. I'll be a captain after this, Rose – are you impressed?' His smile made her laugh for sheer joy.

'Very,' she said. 'I'll join you as soon as I've had a wash and changed these filthy clothes...'

'What made you change jobs?' he asked and Rose shook her head.

'I'll tell you later.'

She sprinted to her lodgings and hurried in, stopping to say hello to Mavis before rushing upstairs to wash and change into a nice skirt and twinset. She ran a comb through her hair and fluffed it up, thanking her lucky stars that her hair was naturally bouncy even when it needed a wash. Applying a little lipstick and a dab of face powder on her nose, she picked up her best coat and went dancing out to meet Jimmy, feeling happier than she'd been for weeks.

'I've missed you, Rose,' Jimmy said as he walked her home later that evening. They'd been out for a meal at a nice restaurant where they'd actually been able to choose between roast pork and duck in orange sauce with potatoes and vegetables, followed by a delicious bread and butter pudding. 'I've thought about you a lot – and it was great gettin' your letters and the parcels. You shouldn't have spent your money on me, though…'

'I'm so glad you're home,' Rose said, ignoring his comment. 'How long have you got?'

'Only a few days and then I'll be away training, but I may get a few hours off now and then. It means I can at least phone you and send you a card,' Jimmy said. 'I've got a week's leave now, so we can go out a few times – if you want?'

'Of course I want,' Rose assured him. 'I love being with you, Jimmy.'

'Have you been out with anyone since I left – any passionate love affairs goin' on?'

'No, of course not,' she said. 'I'm fussy about who I spend time with, Jimmy.'

'That's my girl,' he said and looked pleased. 'I thought I'd be away for years when they told us we were goin' overseas, but I only got as far as Anzio – you know the Allies landed in Italy to put Mussolini in his place?' Rose nodded. 'And then my promotion came through and they said they were sending me home for trainin'… some sort of special mission later this year, no idea what yet, but I know there's a flap on, all hush-hush.'

'It's lucky for me you've been sent back for a while,' Rose said and sighed. 'I haven't had much fun recently. I liked living at the pub – but not since Laurie Ashley, Peggy's husband, came home.'

'He sounds a right monster,' Jimmy said, because she'd related the whole saga of his rudeness over dinner, and frowned. 'Why do you think he took a dislike to you?'

Rose sighed, realising that she had to tell him, because if she didn't he might hear it from Laurie Ashley and believe the worst.

She took a deep breath, then, 'My father killed my mother because she used to flirt with other men. She was unhappy and drank too much – and Dad thought his son Paul was someone else's. Paul died in his cot and Mum believed Dad had suffocated him and they quarrelled violently after the funeral – and he killed her...'

'That must have been awful for you...' Jimmy said shocked, then squeezed her hand. 'You've had a rotten time, love – but you're all right now. You've got friends to look out for you here.'

'Thank you...' Rose paused, tears hovering, then, 'Some of the men who came to the pub used to try it on with me, because they thought I was like her – but I wasn't. Mr Ashley had got hold of part of the story. Peggy said he read lots of newspapers and I think he must have read about the murder and believed a lot of lies about me. At the time, there were rumours that my parents quarrelled over me, hints that I had an intimate relationship with him. One paper made me out to be a slut. It wasn't true – and I think Mr Ashley had his own reasons for wanting me out of the pub...' She lifted her head, meeting Jimmy's gaze. 'He wants to rule Peggy and he knew I would take her side, stand up for her – also he made a pass and I told him no... I haven't been with anyone. I'm waiting

for the right man... someone that I can love and respect.'
*Someone who wasn't disgusted by her story, someone
who would understand and love her – and she hoped that
someone was Jimmy.*

'You don't have to tell me that, love. I never thought
you were like that...'

'Laurie Ashley seemed to think it...'

'Mucky bugger,' Jimmy said and looked angry. 'I noticed
the way he looked at you this evening when we had a
drink at The Pig & Whistle. No wonder you left, love.'

'I don't like factory work, but the other girls are good
fun and the pay is better,' Rose said. 'Peggy spoke about
getting her own place one day. If she did, I'd work for her
like a shot – but not for him.'

'You tell me if he gives you any trouble,' Jimmy said,
looking fierce. 'I'll knock his block off if he lays a finger
on you.'

'Oh, Jimmy...' Rose laughed and hugged his arm,
relieved that her confession had not given him a disgust of
her. 'Thank you, but I'm sure he won't. I've made it clear
I'm not interested. I pop in to see Peggy now and then, but
he never comes near me.'

'Good, because I'd kill any man who upset my girl...'

Rose stopped walking and looked up at him. 'Am I
your girl, Jimmy?'

'I think so – don't you?' he asked. 'It's Saturday
tomorrow. Why don't we go down the shops and pick out
an engagement ring?'

'Oh Jimmy!' Rose hugged him excitedly. 'This is so
sudden! Are you really asking me to marry you?'

'Sounds like it,' Jimmy said and grinned because he sensed her excitement. 'I know I said I was against it, Rose, because of the risk that I might not get back, and although I fell for you right away we didn't know each other. Well, that risk hasn't changed, but while I was away I thought about you all the time. Your letters gave me somethin' to live for. I love you and I need to know you're waitin' for me. None of us know how much longer we've got and… well, I've realised you're the one for me.' He looked into her eyes. 'That's if you feel the same?'

'Oh yes,' Rose said and went into his arms as he pulled her in for a passionate kiss. 'I'd love to be your wife, Jimmy. And I'd love to go shopping for a ring.' It was all happening so fast she couldn't believe it, and yet they weren't the only couple to marry in a whirlwind these days; the war made everyone grab what happiness they could.

'Good,' he said. 'Once people know we're engaged it will stop jerks like that Ashley bloke from gettin' ideas – and if it doesn't, I'll kill him with my bare hands.'

Rose snuggled up to him. She'd been afraid to tell him her history, but Jimmy didn't care. He loved her and he wanted to marry her – and Rose was ridiculously happy. She'd fallen for him right at the start, but she'd had to hide it. Now she could let him see that she thought he was the most wonderful man in the world. Jimmy was right, no one knew how long they had left and you had to grab what you could with both hands.

'I love you, Jimmy,' she said and lifted her face for his kiss, 'and I always shall.'

Chapter 18

Maureen met Rose as she was on her way to the pub on Monday morning. Rose came bouncing up to her and waved her left hand at her.

'What's this then?' Maureen asked as she saw the lovely sapphire and pearl three-stone ring. 'Who is the lucky man?'

'Jimmy is home,' Rose told her. 'They're making him a captain and he's having training before he goes anywhere overseas again, so he'll be home for a while...'

'Well, that's lovely for him – and for you,' Maureen said and smiled at her. 'I'm happy for you, Rose. What did Peggy say?'

'I haven't seen her yet,' Rose said. 'I'll pop round this afternoon and show her my ring.' She was about to walk on, but then placed a hand on Maureen's arm. 'I haven't asked about your husband. Is he any better?'

'Yes, just a little,' Maureen said. 'He hopes they will be movin' him to London in a few weeks, which means I'll be able to see him every day...'

'Oh, that's lovely. I'm so pleased for you,' Rose said. 'I expect he's pleased about the new baby. If there's anything

I can do to help ever – look after the children – you only have to say.'

'That is kind.' Maureen gave her an appreciative look. 'Gran is managing pretty well – and Shirley is marvellous with Robin. She's not eleven yet but she acts like a little woman, taking her brother for walks and changing his nappy. I never worry about him when she's around.'

'Well, I'll let you get on. I've got an extra shift this morning. We've been on full-time, making cardboard recently. I don't know what they need it all for, but we never seem to make enough.'

'Someone told me they use it for coffins for the troops,' Maureen said. 'We can't get enough wood for other things, so they've been making lots of cardboard coffins somewhere down on the coast. It was supposed to be a secret but it got out… of course, I don't know if it's true…'

'Yes, I'm sure that's right,' Rose said. 'I hadn't thought about it being used for something like that – but it fits the sizes we've been making recently…'

'What an awful thought,' Maureen said and shuddered. 'Do you think they're gettin' ready for another big push somewhere?' The British had gone into Burma in force recently and every newspaper told of a new action somewhere in the world: each big fighting initiative, meant a lot more wounded men and thousands of deaths.

'I've no idea. I just wish it was all over,' Rose said. 'I should hate it if…' She shook her head. 'No, I'm not going to be negative. Tell Peggy I'll see her later…'

Maureen nodded and went under the arch and round to the back of the kitchen. Peggy was sitting at the table nursing Freddie, who had the sniffles, but looked up with a smile as she entered.

'You're back then, love. Tell me at once – how is Gordon?'

'He's a little better. His wound still looks raw, but it seems to be healing and responding to treatment. I think he's in a lot of pain, but he was happy about coming back to London and seemed more concerned about me than himself.'

'Gordon is always like that,' Peggy said and smiled at her. 'You were so lucky you married him and not the other one, Maureen. I think he would've made your life hell. You would never have been able to trust him.'

'I know.' Maureen held out her arms to Freddie. 'Can I hold him for a minute? Have they all got this chill?'

'Maggie was the first, but she's over it now, but Fay still has a nasty cold.'

'Poor little mite… it makes a lot of work for you if they're restless.'

'Freddie isn't too bad.' Peggy put her son into Maureen's arms. 'I'll pour us a cup of tea and I've made a carrot cake. Try a piece and see what you think; it's a new recipe.'

'All your baking is good,' Maureen said and smiled at the little boy who was patting her face and attempting her name. 'Yes, Auntie Maureen… aren't you a clever boy then…'

Freddie burbled at her and then clamoured to be put down. Maureen put him into the playpen and looked round for his twin.

'Where is Fay?'

'She's upstairs in her cot. Her cold is worse than Freddie's, so I left her to sleep, because she was grizzling half the night...' Peggy brought the teapot to the table. 'You must be pleased that Gordon is coming to a London hospital soon.'

'It makes things so much easier for me, but I haven't pressed for it because they're so good with wounds down there. I just hope the improvement continues when he's transferred.'

'I expect it will,' Peggy said, 'or are you worried about it, love?'

'Not worried, just a little anxious,' Maureen said. 'It was touch-and-go for a while whether he would lose his leg...'

'No wonder you're upset,' Peggy said and reached for her hand to give it a squeeze. 'Try not to dwell on what might happen, love. I firmly believe that Gordon will come through whatever. He's a strong man and he has you, so he's going to fight even if the worst happens.'

Maureen wiped a tear from her cheek. 'That's more or less what Gordon said to me. He's so brave, Peggy. I've seen other men weep when they were in the kind of pain he is, but he doesn't let me see his despair – and I'm sure he feels it sometimes. Even if his leg heals it will take ages before he's anythin' like back to normal...'

Nellie entered the kitchen then, bringing Fay with her. 'This one was demanding milk and cake so I brought her down, Peggy. I think she's feelin' better.' She looked at Maureen. 'Hello, lovey. How's that husband of yours?'

'He's a little better, Nellie. I was just tellin' Peggy that he hopes to be transferred to a London hospital before the summer.'

'That will be better for all of you,' Nellie said and sat Fay in her high chair, busying herself with cutting a tiny slice of cake for her. 'I'll be glad when we can have all our lads and lasses back home.'

The talk turned to the war, which had been looking better for the Allies of late. Since the landing at Anzio, the British and American troops had made good progress, and the Russians had smashed the siege line at Leningrad in January. The RAF had some wonderful new jet engines, which were giving them the advantage in recent skirmishes with the enemy, and the Government had even turned its thoughts towards what needed to change at home after the war.

'I read in the paper that Mr Churchill says over sixty German U-boats have been sunk since last summer – I reckon that's more than in the rest of the war,' Nellie said. 'The tide is turnin' – you mark my words. We'll 'ave them buggers on the run soon enough…'

'Let's hope you're right…'

Nellie gave Fay her milk just as Janet entered the kitchen with Maggie. 'What do you reckon, Jan – have we got them bloody Germans on the run at last?'

'Let's hope so,' Janet said. 'Ryan says there's somethin' big on the cards, but no one knows what – so we just have to hope for the best.' She'd set Maggie down, and she was now pulling at her skirt and asking for cake. Janet didn't respond immediately and Maggie darted to where Fay was sitting and snatched her half-eaten cake, stuffing it into her mouth and eating it so fast that she almost choked herself. Fay started screaming and threw her glass of milk over Maggie. 'You naughty girl,' Janet said, pouncing on her daughter and giving her a good slap on her bottom. 'You mustn't take what belongs to Fay. Say you're sorry now.'

Maggie set her mouth stubbornly, then hid her face against her mother's skirt and started to sob noisily.

'Stop it, Fay,' Peggy said and tapped her on her hand. Fay's eyes opened wide and she gave her mother a look of such indignation that Maureen would have laughed if she hadn't sensed that it was a sensitive situation.

'I'll take Maggie for a walk,' Janet said and scooped her daughter up; she bundled her into her coat and bonnet and fastened on leading reins, because Maggie had a habit of darting off if she could. 'Sorry, Mum. I don't know what got into her. She can't be hungry. She had bread and jam before I brought her down.'

'I don't think being hungry has anything to do with it,' Peggy said. 'These two are rivals and we need to keep an eye on them...'

'Maggie is bigger and should know better,' Janet said and buttoned her own coat. 'I'm going to see about that nursery place... I'll be back in a couple of hours...'

'I'll walk with you,' Maureen said. 'I'll see you later, Peggy. Bye, Nellie.'

Janet was quiet as they left the pub yard and crossed the lane.

'I shouldn't worry about it,' Maureen said. 'All children go through this stage, Jan. The terrible threes I've heard it called – and she's bound to be a little jealous of the twins.'

'I shall have to find somewhere of our own,' Janet said and sighed. 'In a way I'll be sorry, because I can help Mum and I like being at the pub – but the children need their own homes. Maggie isn't too bad with Freddie, but she seems to hate Fay. I don't think I can stay beyond the end of summer…'

'It's hard for you,' Maureen said. 'I've always had Gran and I'm so grateful for her. It means I have time for my nursing, though I've given that up until the baby is here, and for my friends, as well as the kids. If you're on your own it's a twenty-four-hour job…'

'Yes, I know.' Maureen saw she was looking thoughtful. 'I understand why Rosemary decided to marry Mack, even though she admits she doesn't love him the way she did her first husband – but I'm not sure I want that…'

'Don't marry unless you're in love,' Maureen said. 'I know some people think I married Gordon just because it was easier, but that isn't the case. I knew that I cared for him, but I didn't realise how very much until he was wounded – but I think it would have been harder to take if I hadn't been in love with him.'

'I care for Ryan,' Janet admitted. 'There was a time when I believed I was in love… but then Mike came back and died…' She drew a sobbing breath. 'That took so much out of me, Maureen. Finding him that morning in my bed just tore me to shreds. I'm not sure I could ever feel anything as strongly again. I don't think it would be fair to Ryan to marry him unless I can give him all of me – do you?'

'That's something you have to work out for yourself. I was over Rory when Gordon asked me to be his wife. When I fell for Rory it was like a bolt from the sky, but it wasn't the same with Gordon, it happened gradually – and yet now I feel as if he's my world... apart from the kids, of course, but that's a different kind of love, isn't it?'

Janet smiled and looked at her. 'You've cheered me up, Maureen. I'm glad I'm not the only one who doesn't always know her own mind. Ryan is a good man and he could give me a wonderful life – but I have to be sure.'

'Yes, you wait until you are sure,' Maureen said. 'And don't worry about the kids too much. Children fight each other all the time. Shirley came home with her dress ripped the other day. She'd been fighting over something in the playground. She wouldn't tell me what it was, but knowing her someone was rude about me or her dad. She's a proud little thing and a fighter when it's necessary.'

'Maggie is just the same,' Janet said. 'Mike could control her – I think perhaps it was losing him that made her more possessive of me and whatever is hers.'

'Yes, perhaps,' Maureen agreed. 'Give yourself a little time, Jan. If you can enrol Maggie in a preschool group it will do her the world of good. Being with other children should teach her to share...'

Maureen had reached Gran's house. She said farewell to Janet and went in, stopping to take off her coat. Gran came out of the kitchen.

'I'll put the kettle on, love. Shirley's teacher popped round to see us in her lunch break. She says there's some trouble between Shirley and one of the other girls in her class. They've both been punished for fighting, but Shirley pulled Jilly's hair this morning and she's been caned for it...'

'How dare they?' Maureen was angry. 'I will not have my daughter caned. She had enough of that on the farm. Don't bother about making me tea, Gran. I'm going straight down there and I'll sort this out once and for all...'

'You ought to rest...' Gran said, but Maureen was already on her way.

'Can't you tell me what the trouble is?' Maureen asked Shirley as they walked home together. 'I've told your teacher she is never to hit you again – but she says you have to stop picking on this Jilly... What makes you do it, love?'

Shirley hesitated, then, 'I didn't start it, Mum. She kept jeering at me – said Robin wasn't my brother, only my pretend-brother. I told her she was a liar, but she said her mother told her and her mum doesn't lie...'

'Oh dear...' Maureen drew a deep breath because it was her lie that had caused this problem. She'd wanted everyone to believe that Robin was Gordon's son, but obviously Jilly's mother had worked out that he couldn't be Gordon's and had told her daughter. Shirley was only ten years old – how could she tell her the truth? Yet she had to sort this out somehow. 'Shirley darling, you know how much I love you, don't you?'

'Yes...' Shirley looked up at her happily. 'You're my mum...'

'I wasn't always though, was I? You had a mother before, didn't you? She loved you too but she couldn't stay to look after you – and so you came to me. You're my daughter now and I love you as much as if you'd always been mine. You do believe that...'

'Yes...' Shirley was thoughtful now. 'Is it the same for Robin?'

'Robin is my baby and so he's your step-brother in the eyes of the law, but you love him as a brother, don't you? Just the way he loves you – just as your daddy loves him and me but still loves you as much as he always did...'

'Robin came out of your tummy...'

'Yes, but he was there before daddy and I were married.' Maureen took Shirley's hands, bending down to look into her eyes. 'The baby in my tummy now will be mine and daddy's – and he or she will be your half-brother or sister in the eyes of the law – but in love he or she will be just your brother or sister. The baby will be yours in blood and love, but Robin is your brother in love... do you understand?'

'Sort of...' Shirley said hesitantly. 'Did you have another daddy for Robin before you married my daddy?'

Maureen looked directly into her trusting eyes. 'I thought I loved someone and we made a baby, but then he hurt me and I knew I'd made a mistake. Gordon, your daddy, had been growing in my heart, but I didn't really know it for a long time – but now he's there with you, Robin, Gran and the new baby. You see, I love you all, so it doesn't matter who is what – just how much we all love each other...'

'I'll tell Jilly I'm sorry for hitting her,' Shirley said and nodded. 'She was my best friend, but I hated her for saying things about you and Robin – but now I can tell her. Robin is my brother in love and we all belong together…'

'Yes, darling, we all belong together.'

Maureen straightened up. 'Shall we go and see what Tom has in the shop? We can buy some sweets for you – and if there's any chocolate we might get a little bar for Robin…'

Shirley's face lit up and Maureen realised that her daughter had been suffering from uncertainty. The term of pretend-brother had worried her, making her fear that her relationship was not secure, so she'd taken it out in anger on her erstwhile friend. Hopefully, she would make it up and the crisis would be over. Perhaps if Janet explained to Maggie that she was in no danger of being supplanted in her mother's affections by the twins, she might stop being aggressive towards them… but of course Shirley was older and she'd learned to know how lucky she was.

Chapter 19

It was Thursday morning, and Tom was loading some boxes of chocolate bars on to the shelves when Rose entered. He'd been busy all morning, unpacking what Maureen had managed to bring from the wholesaler and setting his shelves out. His heart leaped as he saw how pretty the girl he admired looked and he moved closer to the counter to serve her.

'Mornin' Rose, how are you?'

'I'm wonderful,' Rose said and held out her left hand for him to see. 'I got engaged last Saturday, Tom. What do you think of that?' Her eyes were sparkling and he managed to keep his smile in place, even though she'd taken his breath away.

'I think he's a very lucky man,' he said and Rose laughed. 'Have you known him long?'

'Only since I came to the lanes. He went abroad but he's been promoted so they sent him back for more training... and he asked me to marry him.'

'Congratulations. I hope you will be happy...'

'I think I shall,' Rose said. 'Jimmy loves me – and he respects me. What about you, Tom? What have you been doin' recently?'

'I joined the reserves,' Tom said, lifting his head proudly. 'I'm trainin' with them four nights a week – and on Sundays. If Hitler invades I'll be ready…'

Rose went into a peal of laughter. 'I'll bet he won't dare, now you're in the reserves,' she said, teasing him as she always did. 'I'd love to see you in uniform, Tom.'

'I'll get it next week,' he said and grinned at her. Tom didn't mind Rose making fun of him because he liked her. He wished he was older, because if he had been she would have been his girl not this Jimmy's. 'So when are yer gettin' married then?'

'I'm not sure. Jimmy is going away for a couple of weeks. He thinks he'll be back this way when he can and then we'll make plans…'

'Well good luck.' Tom smiled at her. 'What can I get for you?'

'Oh, Mavis wants a pot of jam of some kind, anything you've got. A half a pound of tea, some tinned meat – and a tin of peas, if you've got any?'

'Yes, we've got everything on her list for the moment,' Tom said. 'I think someone is releasing a bit more stock. I haven't heard anything official, but the wholesalers suddenly have extras and that's good for everyone… We've actually got some tins of peaches today.'

'I'd better take one for Mavis then – but I'll pay for it. I get far more every week than she does now I'm at the factory.'

Tom placed the items on the counter in front of her. Rose paid for them and then asked for some sweets and settled on a quarter of a pound of treacle toffees and a small bar of chocolate, as well as twenty Players cigarettes.

'Taking up smoking?' he asked.

'No, these are for Jimmy. He's always giving me something...' Rose nodded as she paid for her purchases. 'I'll see you around...'

'Are you comin' to the church social?' he asked.

'Oh yes,' Rose said. 'Ellie is coming with me. I don't think Jimmy will be here, so I shall keep my promise to go with Ellie... See you, later...'

'Yeah, see yer later,' Tom said and grinned. His smile vanished as the door closed behind her. He couldn't let Rose see that her being engaged hurt him, because she saw him as a youth and not as a man. She was in love with a soldier.

Tom pushed the knowledge from his mind as the door opened and Sid Coleman entered, followed by Irene from the hairdresser's. Sid stood back and Tom served her first, smiling at her as she dithered over her choice of chocolate or biscuits, because he still felt a bit guilty about only asking her out once. She chose a bar of Fry's chocolate, paid and left. After Irene had gone, he turned to Sid.

'Packet of fags, Tom, and some mints...'

'How's things with you then, Sid?' Tom asked his lodger. 'Job still all right?'

'Yeah, it's good,' Sid said. 'I like driving my general and I like livin' round here – only one fly in the ointment...'

'Anythin' I can do, mate?'

'Nah, it's female related,' Sid replied and winked. 'Trouble is she's married – and she ain't one of them what play away, if yer know what I mean.'

'Yeah, I do,' Tom said knowingly and arched his eyebrows. 'Women are the devil – ain't they?'

'You got love problems too?'

'She don't know I exist – thinks I'm a kid...'

Sid laughed shortly. 'I know the feelin', Tom. The girl I want knows I exist, but she won't give me any encouragement. I know she's got a husband and I shouldn't expect anythin'... but yer can't help yer feelings, can yer?'

'No, yer can't,' Tom agreed, taking Sid's money. It had cheered him up hearing his friend's problems. He'd thought it was just him who couldn't get the girl he adored, but Sid was in the same boat – and he was a fine man so perhaps there might be hope for Tom after all.

Ellie picked up her little girl and kissed her. Beth was so beautiful and she loved her so much – and Sid thought the world of her too. He was always bringing her little presents and he would have her on his lap in a minute if he could. A sigh escaped Ellie, because she wished so much that Sid was her husband.

There, she'd admitted it at last. Ellie had tried to control her feelings for the big man who had helped save her daughter's life. She was convinced that if he hadn't got them to the hospital so quickly her little darling would have died and her gratitude had been gradually turning to something warmer ever since. Yet she knew it was wrong and foolish, because she was Peter's wife and even though she no longer loved Peter, divorce was still a dirty word. Not only that as Mabel Tandy had explained to her, divorce was difficult to get and would cost too much money.

'Peter would never agree to it,' she'd told Ellie. 'And he hasn't done anything to warrant it – or at least we don't have any proof. You think he deliberately made you ill so that you would lose the baby, but he would deny it – and I'm afraid the court would believe him; especially if you were known to have a new lover.'

'Sid is just a friend.'

'He comes here often to see us all – and if you didn't live with me, folk would be gossiping over it.' Mabel had looked at her sadly. 'You were only just seventeen when you married Peter, my love. It was too young to know what you wanted…'

'I loved Peter as he was then,' Ellie had said, her lashes wet. 'I didn't know how violent he can be – and my aunt didn't want me at home. She couldn't wait to push me out. I think she was more pleased than I was when Peter asked to marry me…'

'I know things were hard for you, Ellie,' her generous landlady had said. 'I just don't want you to make things worse for yourself. Peter can be bad-tempered and if he thought…'

'I know. I shan't do anything silly. I promise.'

Ellie was well aware that her husband would make her suffer if she got involved with another man. He hadn't truly forgiven her for putting herself at risk of rape – which he held was what she'd done by going alone to the pub and accepting drinks from strangers. He was right, of course he was, and she blamed herself for being so stupid – but her loneliness had driven her to seek company and she'd been too young and innocent to realise the trouble she could land herself in.

'Any girl who lets a man she doesn't know buy her a drink is asking for trouble,' Peter had told her when he'd come home to find her pregnant with a child that couldn't be his. His fingers had dug into her arms, making her wince. 'The bugger who raped you will pay for it – but it was your own fault for bein' there in the first place…'

Ellie had seen the resentment and anger in Peter. She'd been frightened of him, but then he'd seemed to relent towards her and he'd been good to her, taking her out the night before he left for the Army and making love to her – but had he put something in her drink to make her unwell in the hope she'd lose the baby? Ellie couldn't know for sure, but the dark doubts lingered at the back of her mind – including one that she hardly dared to name.

Knocker James had died horribly the night before Peter returned to his regiment. Her husband had been with her, so he couldn't have done it – but had he caused it to happen? It was such a dreadful thought that Ellie hadn't been able to speak of it even to Mabel. Peter had a clear alibi, but the police had never discovered the killer and everyone said it was a professional assassin – so someone had paid for it.

Ellie thrust the thought to a far corner of her mind, where it joined others. She wished she could somehow break free of the man she'd married so hastily at seventeen, but she couldn't see any way out… and now Peter was coming home on leave again. His letter had come like a bolt from the blue, shattering her peace. Her husband expected to be here by the end of March, which meant she couldn't invite Sid to have his dinner with them that week... something she really looked forward to on Sundays, when he was usually free from his duty. She ought to tell him not to call round anymore and she must definitely let him know that her husband was coming back, because otherwise there would be ructions from Peter.

'I'll see you on Saturday, but I shan't be able to come for lunch on Sunday,' Sid told Ellie when he took her some flowers and a few tiny jelly sweets for Beth that evening. 'My general is going to stay with friends for a few days and I'll have to take him and be on call while he's away...'

'Oh... so you wouldn't have been able to have dinner with us anyway...' Ellie said and her disappointment showed through despite her determination to hide it.

'Perhaps it's just as well since Peter's coming home on leave...'

'I wish he wasn't...' Ellie's eyes filled with tears. 'I'm frightened of what he'll do when he sees Beth. He didn't want me to keep her, Sid. He wanted me to give her away, because of what happened...' She'd confided her terrible secret to Sid once when he'd been talking about how beautiful Beth was – and, to her surprise, he'd been completely on her side, declaring he would have thrashed the bugger that raped her if he'd been around then.

'He's a stupid fool,' Sid growled, angry because she was upset. 'If Peter hurts you, you let me know. I'd kill him if he touches you, Ellie love...'

'Oh, Sid, I wish—' Ellie gasped and held back the words she'd almost said because she mustn't let him see, but Sid was looking at her and her expressive face told him all he needed to know.

'You do care for me, don't you, Ellie?'

She bit her lip, not daring to look at him as she gave a little nod. 'Yes, but I mustn't – we mustn't,' she whispered. 'Peter... he is so jealous and he can be violent...'

'I'm not frightened of him, Ellie love... I know he's your husband and I have no rights, but he doesn't deserve you after the way he's treated you.'

She looked up at him then and the fear was in her eyes. 'You don't know what Peter is capable of, Sid. The man that raped me... he was violently murdered and I think... I think Peter may have arranged it.'

Sid looked at her in silence for a moment. 'I would've killed the bugger that raped you with me bare hands,' he told her fiercely, 'but I'd cut them off before I'd hurt you, Ellie. If Peter hurts you let me know and I'll sort him – and that's a promise. No matter who he is involved with, I ain't afraid of him or his kind...'

'Oh, Sid...' Tears trickled down her cheeks as she looked at him and then he bent his head and kissed her softly on the lips. It was just a sweet kiss of comfort without passion or lust and it made her sob harder, because she wanted Sid's arms about her. She wanted to be loved and protected – safe from violent men who inflicted pain as a way of making a woman do as they wanted. 'I wish – but we can't…'

'Not yet,' he agreed and smiled at her. 'You need lookin' after, Ellie – and from now on I'm the one to do it. If you say the word, I'll face Peter down and speak to him man to man. When you're ready, we'll get you divorced from him – and don't be afraid of what he'll do, because I'm not…'

Ellie scrubbed her tears away. 'You'll be away for a while and I'll try to talk to him… but he's my husband and people will think I'm easy, Sid. He's been fightin' the enemy to keep me safe and I feel bad about lettin' him down – but I don't love him. He frightens me and I wish… I wish I'd never met him and you were my husband…'

Sid grinned from ear to ear. 'That's all I needed to know, love. Just go along with him as best you can until I get back and then I'll sort things…'

Ellie gave a little nod, but she was thinking about Peter being home and what she would do in the bedroom. She didn't want her husband to touch her ever again, and yet she knew what would happen if she refused…

'I'll try,' she promised and then Mabel walked in with her tray of cocoa and the opportunity for private talk was over.

Ellie knew Mabel wouldn't approve, but *she* didn't have to be with Peter once the bedroom door was closed.

Chapter 20

Anne looked at herself in the mirror and saw the excitement in her eyes. She wanted to pinch herself to be sure that she wasn't dreaming, but she was three weeks late with her period and because she'd always been as regular as clockwork, it made her think that she was pregnant. She wished Kirk was with her so that she could tell him, but he'd gone away on his training course. Perhaps it was best that she went to the doctor's and had her suspicions confirmed, she thought, but her happiness was bubbling away inside and she knew she had to tell someone – and she needed to make that appointment.

It was difficult to get through until lunchtime, and Anne was in a hurry to leave during her break. She popped into the surgery and was told she could have an appointment that afternoon after she finished work.

The afternoon had never seemed so long, but the last bell rang and Anne was sharp about seeing her class out and leaving. She walked swiftly to the surgery and took her place in the waiting room until she was called.

'And what can I do for you, Mrs Ross?' the doctor asked.

'I think – I hope I may be pregnant…' Anne said a little breathlessly.

'I see it would please you,' the doctor smiled at her. 'I'll give you a little examination, Mrs Ross – and then we'll do the urine test to be certain, but I often think women know themselves when this particular little miracle has taken place.'

Anne submitted to the gentle examination, was told he thought she was right, but would only confirm it once the test had been completed. She thanked him and he shook her hand and wished her well.

Her feet were dancing on air as she caught a bus. She couldn't just go home to be alone, because she needed to tell someone and she wanted to talk to Peggy. Her friend had given birth to twins and she was a few years older than Anne, so her point of view was very valid. Younger women gave birth regularly and easily, but it wasn't quite as straightforward for older mothers.

Peggy was in the kitchen when Anne knocked on the door. Laurie was standing near the table, but when he saw her, he picked up a dish of tarts Peggy had made and walked out without speaking. Peggy smiled with pleasure and invited her in at once, asking if she wanted tea and apple pie.

'You're really cold,' Peggy said, touching her hands. 'Come to the fire and sit down, Anne.'

'I wanted to tell you…' Anne said, because she couldn't keep it inside a moment longer, 'I've been to the doctor – I believe I'm pregnant, Peggy…'

'Anne! That is wonderful,' Peggy said and hugged her. 'I know how much you want a baby, love. Has it been confirmed by the test yet?'

'Not yet, but Doctor Phillips thinks I'm right so fingers crossed...'

'I'm sure it will happen,' Peggy said and kissed her cheek. 'Does Kirk know yet?'

Anne shook her head. 'I shan't tell him until I'm absolutely sure – besides, he's on a course and I can't contact him for the moment, but I know he'll be thrilled. We both want children.'

'That is the best news I've heard in ages,' Peggy said. 'I ought to offer you sherry or something...'

'No, just a cup of tea, please. I'm going to be very careful what I eat and drink from now on. I wanted to ask you whether you took any special precautions when you knew you were expecting.'

'I carried on the same as always, working up to the last minute and eating whatever I felt like – though I didn't drink much alcohol. My doctor advised against it on my second visit, so I took notice – but lots of my customers do and they seem all right...' Peggy smiled at her. 'I know this is your first baby and you're a little bit older than I was when I had Jan – but you're strong and healthy. I don't think you need to worry too much.'

'It's just that the women in our family either don't conceive or they have miscarriages,' Anne said apprehensively. 'I don't think I could bear it if I lost my baby...'

'You won't,' Peggy said and put an arm about her waist. 'Think positive, Anne love, and it will all come right – believe me.'

'I wanted to hear you say those words,' Anne said and laughed. 'It makes me feel more confident. I half wish I was still living with Mavis, because if Kirk is away when the time comes…'

'You will come and stay with me when it's near your time,' Peggy said instantly. 'We'll look after you, Anne. You have friends and we care about you.'

Tears sparkled in Anne's eyes but she blinked them away, because it was foolish to cry when she was so happy, and it would be silly to let her irrational fears spoil her pleasure in being pregnant.

'Yes, I know you and Maureen are always here for me,' she said and took out her hanky, blowing her nose. 'I'm all over the place with my emotions.'

'That's how we all get,' Peggy said and laughed. 'One minute you want to shout for joy and the next you're in tears – but when the uncomfortable bit is over, you'll have your own child and that's worth whatever you have to put up with in the meantime.'

'Yes, I know…' Anne was smiling again as Peggy brought over tea and home-made biscuits. She was so glad she'd come to her friend, because Peggy's no-nonsense attitude would help her get through the lonely nights until Kirk was home again.

Janet entered the kitchen at that moment, carrying a struggling Maggie in her arms. She set her daughter down and the little girl ran to the table, pulling at Peggy's skirt to demand milk and cake.

'Sorry to interrupt, but can you keep an eye on her while I pop to the shop?' Janet said. She looked apologetically at Anne. 'Maggie is full of energy this evening. It has been a long day...'

'I'll look after her for a little while,' Anne offered and bent down to offer Maggie her hand. 'Do you want to hear a story, Maggie?'

Maggie stopped pulling at her grandmother's skirt and looked at Anne with interest. Her years of teaching had not been for nothing, and Maggie pressed up against her knee as she started to tell her the story of Goldilocks and the three bears.

Janet shot her an appreciative look, grabbed her jacket and purse and left quickly. Peggy watched with a smile on her face and then went to answer a scream from Fay.

'It's like Bedlam here at times,' she told Anne ruefully. 'At least you know how to handle small children...'

Anne smiled and stroked Maggie's curls. She was a pretty child but tended towards a sulky attitude and was very demanding. Anne wasn't sure whether Peggy and Janet had spoiled her or whether it was the lack of a father. She felt so sorry for Janet losing her husband in such a cruel way and admired her for the way she was pulling her life back together.

For a moment Anne allowed herself to think of what she might do in Janet's place but dismissed the idea. Every woman in Britain must have the same thoughts at times, but they could not allow the horror of the war to destroy their lives. Jan had crumbled in grief but was now fighting back – and like so many other women she was learning to live again. Anne knew that she would do the best for her child whatever life threw at her.

'Is Anne pregnant?' Janet asked her mother later that evening when they were alone in Peggy's bedroom for a few minutes. 'Only I saw somethin' in her face when she offered to look after Maggie that made me think she might be.'

'She might be,' Peggy said and smiled at her daughter. 'I'm sure she will tell you when she's ready – and when she's sure.'

'I thought so.' Jan looked thoughtful. 'There's a kind of contentment about her... I know she felt out of it when both you and Maureen were havin' babies...'

'Anne's mother miscarried several times and so did her aunt. I think Anne was anxious in case she was barren – a dreadful thing for a woman who wants a child.'

'Oh, poor Anne! I hope she is pregnant and that everythin' goes well for her,' Janet said and hesitated, then: 'I've been thinkin', Mum. I went down the council but they said they've got hundreds on the waitin' list and with just one child and a home I wouldn't get on to it for ages. I'll have to rent from a private landlord and the rents are high on anythin' decent, so I think I'll stop on here for a while, if that' OK? I need to save for a deposit and some rent in advance...'

'Good.' Peggy was pleased. 'I'd rather you stayed until you're sure you can manage properly. There's no reason why you shouldn't do part-time work and save for a few months. You can still take a turn in the bar sometimes and help with the twins if I'm busy.'

'Yes, it works well this way,' Jan said. 'I still think I'd like my own home one day, but there's no rush...'

'I'm glad you're thinkin' that way,' Peggy answered. 'I was afraid you might rush into somethin' unsuitable and be miserable.'

'Yes – and there's Ryan,' Janet said. 'He asked if he could take me out one night, Mum. I've never been out with him alone in the evening; it has always been tea or during the afternoon – what do you think I should do?'

'You have to think carefully before you make a choice,' Peggy said. 'If you turn him down flat you might regret it in time – on the other hand, you mustn't agree to anything that isn't what you really want.'

'I told you, I'm not goin' to marry again unless I feel that I'm in love. I didn't have much time with Mike, but what I did have was wonderful. I want that again, Mum – and I don't want to end up in a boring marriage that makes me feel the way you did...'

'Oh, Jan...' Peggy looked at her unhappily. 'You mustn't confuse what happened between Laurie and me with your own life. We had our good times – and they *were* good, love. For years I was perfectly happy. I'm not sure what happened, and I don't think Laurie knows either if he's honest. Maybe it's just a midlife crisis – a feeling that if you don't have a fling it will be too late...'

'That's not how you felt about Able?'

'Oh no, I loved him. I still love him.'

'That's how I want to feel,' Janet said. 'I know I could be safe and protected with Ryan – but I want to feel passion and…' She laughed and shook her head in embarrassment. 'I shouldn't be sayin' things like this to my mum…'

'You're a woman not a child now, Jan. I'm glad you can tell me how you feel and I think you're perfectly right to wait. At the moment you're still grievin', but one day you will be ready to love again – wait until then and then grab your happiness with both hands…'

'You're so wise, Mum,' Janet said and went to give her a hug. 'I love you so much – even though I don't always show it.'

'I think you're a bit like your dad in that way,' Peggy said. 'At times I thought he didn't care for me at all – but since he came home, he's been so good with the twins and he keeps lookin' at me – as if he's hopin' I'll forgive him and take him back.'

'And shall you?' Jan raised her eyebrows.

'I don't know,' Peggy replied honestly. 'Perhaps I should take what I can and accept that all marriages have their ups and downs – but I can't forget Able…'

'Oh, Mum, I do wish there was some hope. I keep thinking Able might come back the way Mike did – but you've never had a letter or anything, have you?'

'Only from the lawyers,' Peggy said and sighed.

'Is there no one you could approach… ask if there's any news?'

'Able would've written or come here if he could,' Peggy said. 'I know it happens all the time that men reported as missing turn up – but surely he would get in touch?'

'Unless he's too ill to come himself? He might ask someone else to visit you or write... let you know he's alive.'

'I wish I'd asked those friends of his to keep in touch...' Peggy sighed. 'But I know this is all foolish. I have to let go.'

'Everyone told me to let go when Mike was missing, but I didn't believe he was dead...' Janet looked thoughtful. 'I think I'll accept Ryan's invitation, Mum. He found Mike for me – he might just be able to get some definite news about Able.'

'Janet...' Peggy stared at her. 'Do you think you should ask?'

'Mum, I want more than anything to see you happy and if Able is alive – well, I'd like to know about it.'

Standing outside his wife's bedroom, Laurie listened to her talking to Janet. He frowned as he heard that she was still in love with that damned American – no doubt she would go to him if he turned up!

The letter from America was well hidden where Peggy would never find it. For a while, he'd never let it out of his sight, because if Peggy read it she would leave him and Laurie wasn't ready to let her walk out of his life, but now he'd tucked it away in a place she would have no call to look. Besides, Peggy wasn't suspicious. She'd been pleased by the way he'd taken his turn with the twins and he'd thought he was gradually winning her round. It made him angry to think that Peggy would still walk out and leave him for that American.

If Rose had accepted his advances he'd probably have given Peggy the letter and let her go, because there was very little real affection left on either side. Peggy tolerated him and he needed her for the moment. Laurie had seen enough to know that if folk in the lanes thought he'd let his wife down he could kiss goodbye to half of his trade. The regulars came to see Peggy and she was serving in the bar most evenings again, leaving Janet to respond to the twins and Maggie if they woke.

He turned away as he heard his wife and daughter saying goodnight, passing the twins' room as he made his way to his own. He rubbed at his chest, feeling the urge to cough again. They were his kids – that damned American! The thought crossed his mind that if ever he wanted to punish his wife he could do it through them.

Chapter 21

Ellie finished brushing out her last customer of the evening's hair and showed her the back of her head in the hand mirror. She nodded and smiled, and Ellie sprayed liberally with lacquer to preserve the set and then turned off the radio. Mr Churchill had recently given a speech saying that the hour of Britain's greatest effort was approaching and the mood was sombre, too much so for Ellie.

'I'll give it a good spray, Mrs Brown,' she said. 'It's damp out this evening and we don't want the bounce falling out before you get home.'

'Oh, I've got a waterproof rain hat,' the customer said and took it out of her bag, tying it carefully over the crisp waves and curls. She paid Ellie, gave her a sixpenny tip and left. Ellie pocketed the sixpence. Tips were important to her because her wages hardly paid her expenses each week, despite Mabel forgoing the rent. Ellie always brought food for the larder anyway, because she couldn't just take all the time, so it still left her reliant on Peter's wage. If she did leave him, she would have to manage without it – and she might have to move away from the lanes, because Peter wasn't going to let her go without a fight.

The telephone rang just as she was leaving. Ellie answered it. Her boss, Mrs Stimpson, was on the other end and wanted to talk about trade and how the stock was holding up. Ellie put down the phone at last with a sigh. Why couldn't she have rung earlier instead of when it was closing time?

It was as she was locking up for the night that a figure loomed up out of the gloom and Ellie jumped. For a moment she thought it was Knocker James come to grab her again, but as the man spoke she knew he was human not a ghost.

'Finished for the night, Ellie?'

'Yes, I've just locked the door...' Ellie answered and looked up at her husband. Her heart raced madly and she felt sick inside. 'I didn't expect you yet... I thought your letter said you would be home the beginning of April? That's not until next week...'

'Sorry to spoil your plans...' The sarcasm in his voice cut at her like a knife. 'Planning on going somewhere were yer?'

'Peter! Please don't talk to me like that,' Ellie protested. 'I wasn't planning anythin'. I was just surprised to see you...'

'Yeah, I know.' Peter's face came close to hers. She could smell strong drink on his breath and knew he'd been to a pub somewhere. 'You lyin' little cheat! If you think I don't know what you've been up to, think again. I know you've picked up with another bloke... he comes here often ter visit yer and the bloody kid.' His hand closed on her arm. 'I thought you were goin' ter get rid of the brat?'

'I couldn't...' Ellie smothered the cry of pain that rose to her lips. 'Beth is so lovely. I wanted to keep her – and I'm goin' to...' Her head came up then and she looked at him defiantly. 'You can't make me give her away. I shan't...'

The pressure of his fingers increased, hurting her so much that a little moan escaped her. 'You're my wife, Ellie, and you'll bloody well do as I tell yer – or there will be trouble.'

Ellie felt herself being pushed up the little alleyway that led to the back of Mabel's shop. Halfway along, Peter slammed her against the wall, banging her head and pressing his knee against her body to imprison her.

'Stop it, you're 'urtin' me...'

'I will bloody 'urt you...' Peter snarled and slapped her across the face once. 'This is just a warnin' – it's nothin' to what you'll get if you defy me again.'

Anger surged as Ellie looked up at him, uncaring for the moment that he was hurting her. 'You can't treat me as if I were dirt,' she challenged him. 'I don't 'ave to take this, Peter. I'm not goin' to let you hit me or bully me – and I want a divorce.'

Peter struck her so hard that her senses reeled. She was terrified as he put one hand round her throat, his face close to hers. 'I'll kill you and the brat before I let you make a fool of me,' Peter hissed, his spittle spraying into her face. 'And don't think that bloody fool you've got runnin' after yer will save yer. I've already arranged for him to be put out of action – and unless you do as you're told, I'll kill the brat and make you wish you'd never been born.'

Ellie shuddered, all the fight draining out of her as she heard the threats against both Sid and Beth. 'Please, you mustn't kill Sid...' she gasped. 'He hasn't done anythin' except help me take Beth to the doctor. We're just friends...'

'I know that or you'd already be dead,' Peter said. 'But he's hopin' – and I want him out of the way. He'll get a sharp warnin' and if he comes near yer again, he'll get it... just like the other one...'

Ellie's eyes filled with tears. 'I don't know what 'appened to you...' she choked. 'You used to be fun and lovin'...'

'Oh yes, you liked all the gifts and the goin' out – where did you think the money came from? Not from working down the docks like the other donkeys!'

'You were in with criminals?' She stared at him in shock.

'You silly bitch,' Peter snarled. 'It's time you grew up. I only have to snap my fingers and you and that brat will disappear for good.'

Ellie turned her face aside. She knew what her life was going to be like in future whenever Peter was around, and it seemed he had spies who told him everything she did. Her only chance was to appease him while he was home and then make a run for it – if only she could protect her child and herself from his brutality until he was recalled to the Army.

'Stop snivellin',' Peter said. 'I don't want yer bloody landlady callin' the police 'cos I've hit yer. And don't think yer can whisper to her behind me back – if she steps out of line, I'll give her a belt as well.'

Ellie raised her head, wiping her face with the back of her hand. 'Mabel has been good to me. Just leave her alone, Peter, or I'll be the one goin' to the police. You can threaten me all yer like, but I'm not a doormat and I won't let you hurt Beth or Mabel...'

'Well, maybe I'll just make you suffer, bitch,' Peter said with a cruel leer. 'Just do as I tell yer and we'll see... I'll be back later, and if you tell that interferin' bitch that I slapped yer, she's for it.'

He pushed her ahead of him and she heard him walking away. Ellie hastily wiped her tears from her cheeks. Mabel would see the bruise and it was no good lying to her – but Ellie had to make her see that they couldn't do anything about it until Peter returned to his unit or he might kill them all.

Sid parked the car into the generous space, locked it and left the garage, making certain the door locked behind him. His general was important and he'd been warned not to leave the car where anyone could damage it or even put a bomb under it, because, as unbelievable as it seemed, there were those in the country who would risk a lot to get rid of men like Sid's boss – men who were making a difference to the war.

He left the garage and started to walk down the road, feeling pleased with life. Ellie would be expecting him later, because he'd told her he would call in and he had a present for Beth – and something for Ellie too. Sid wanted to give her a ring and all the nice things that were missing from her life, to take care of both her and the child. He'd seen enough to know that she didn't have much money to spare and he was pretty flush these days. Ever since he'd started work, Sid had been savin' for the day when he got a home of his own and then a wife and kid. He wanted things nice when he got wed, because his own parents had struggled to bring up half a dozen youngsters. Sid was determined that Ellie and Beth would want for nothing – though it would cost a pretty penny to get that divorce. They needed proof of Peter's mistreatment of his wife.

Sid wasn't sure when he became aware that he was being followed. He sensed rather than heard the footsteps behind him but knew that while he was in the busy street he was safe enough. If he was going to be attacked, the assassin would wait until he was in a dark lane. A little smile touched his lips, because Sid knew something the man tracking him didn't.

He was quite capable of tackling any normal assailant with his bare hands, but the pistol in his pocket would come in handy if there was more than one. He'd been issued with it as an official bodyguard and any attempt on his life would be linked with an attempt to get to the general... so if he shot to kill, no one would kick up much of a fuss over it. Not that he would intentionally kill, but he had no qualms about defending himself or his general.

As he turned into the dark lane, Sid tensed, his alert hearing picking up the sudden rush of steps and he turned to meet the attack as the knife came at him. He was struck in the fleshy part of his arm but still managed to pull out the gun and fire... his bullet hit the mark and he saw the man fall.

'Oh, Ellie, what are we goin' ter do?' Mabel looked at her in dismay. She'd seen the swelling on her cheek as soon as she walked in and Ellie had told her what Peter had said and done to her in the lane. 'I should've believed you when you told me what he did before... He's a bully and a brute and you have to get away, love. You have to leave now, before he comes back...'

'He would take it out on you,' Ellie said and bit her lip. 'I'm goin' to leave him, Mabel – but not until he's gone back to his unit. He would just come after me...'

'Not if he doesn't know where you've gone. I've got a bit of money saved. If I give it to yer, it will take yer a long way off...'

Tears filled Ellie's eyes. 'I want you to answer the door if Sid comes tonight – you must tell him to stay away, because Peter will have him killed. I know he will...'

'Oh, Ellie, I can't believe...' Mabel wiped her own tears. 'If he hits me, I don't care – but I don't want him to beat you like this... and Beth. What will he do to Beth?'

'I don't know...' Ellie looked at her and the tears trickled down her cheeks. 'I don't know what to do...' She broke off as they heard someone at the back door and then it opened and a man entered. Ellie's cry died as she saw it was Sid. He was wearing his uniform but the blouson was stained with a brownish patch that looked like blood. 'Oh, Sid – what happened? Was it Peter?' she asked.

'Someone attacked me on my way here,' Sid told her. 'It's been taken care of, Ellie – but I wanted to see if you were all right. I can't stop and I haven't brought your present, because I have to report what happened...'

'You were attacked?' Ellie was horrified as she saw the rent in the sleeve of his uniform and the dark stain of blood. 'Are you badly hurt?'

'I'm not sure whether it was an attempt at murder or just a warning – but I came off best, Ellie...' Sid looked grim, his mouth hard and his eyes glinting in the lamplight.

'Peter said he'd arranged to have you sorted...' Ellie whispered. 'He was here earlier...'

'Whoever it was that attacked me is now fighting for his life in hospital,' Sid said. 'He knifed me and I shot him in the shoulder, but then I called an ambulance and they took him away – and so I came straight here, because you're not safe with that madman on the loose.'

'You shot the man that attacked you?' Ellie's eyes opened wide. 'Will you get into trouble if he dies?'

'I'm reporting it as a plot to kill me in order to get to my general,' Sid said. 'If you hear anything, just keep quiet – and I'll deal with it. Remember, I'm not afraid of your husband and if he hurts you...' He looked at the red mark on her cheek, suddenly realising. 'He already has! Where is the devil? I'll thrash him to within an inch of his life...'

'Sid, you mustn't,' Ellie said. 'Just be careful because Peter is violent and he's determined to harm you...'

'I told you, I can take care of myself,' Sid said and frowned. 'It's you I'm worried about – let me take you away. You and Beth. I'll put you on a train this evenin' and you can stay with my sister… he won't find you there, Ellie.'

'Go with him, Ellie,' Mabel urged. 'Please, go with Sid now, tonight. If you and Beth are safe, nothin' else matters…'

Ellie hesitated, because she didn't like leaving Mabel alone, but then she realised that if she'd gone, Peter would be too busy looking for her to bother with her friend.

'Just be careful, Mabel, because he threatened to harm you,' she said and then looked at Sid. 'I'll fetch Beth down…' Ellie looked fearfully at the back door, because if Peter returned there would be a fight and someone would be hurt. She had to be quick.

Upstairs, she thrust as many of Beth's things into a suitcase as she could and some undies and a dress for herself, snatching up her sleeping child and hurrying back down to the kitchen, where Mabel had the pushchair ready. Beth stirred and whimpered but didn't wake.

'Write to me when you're settled and I'll let you know when it's safe to come home,' Mabel said and thrust some notes into Ellie's hand. 'Take care of her, Sid. Don't let that devil hurt her…'

'If he tries to touch her, I'll kill him,' Sid said and Mabel nodded her satisfaction.

'Sid will look after you, love,' she said and kissed Ellie's cheek and then Beth. 'I shall miss you, but don't think of me – just look after yourself and Beth…'

'Don't open the door to him,' Sid advised. 'He's a nasty so-and-so – and you need to take care.'

'I love you…' Ellie hugged Mabel and then allowed Sid to usher her out of the door.

They walked swiftly down the lane, Ellie looking over her shoulder constantly, fearing that Peter would come after them, worrying about her friend. Surely Peter wouldn't take it out on Mabel just because she'd run away? She hesitated, half inclined to go back, but Sid took her arm and urged her on. When they saw a taxi standing at the side of the road, Sid spoke to the driver. He was reluctant to take them at first because he was finished for the night, but then agreed, and in a few seconds they were speeding towards the railway station.

Ellie drew a deep breath. Peter wouldn't come after her immediately. He might look for her at her aunt's house, but she would be far away in the country with Sid's family.

Sid wrote an address on a piece of paper from the notebook he carried in his pocket and gave it to her. 'I'll come down when I can and if he's gone back to his unit I'll take you home, Ellie.'

'Thank you,' she said, looking at him anxiously. 'I don't know exactly what happened tonight, but please take care of yourself – I'm afraid of what he might do to you, Sid, especially if he can't find me…'

'You just take care of yourself,' Sid said and smiled at her. 'I'll come for you when it's safe and not before…'

Ellie nodded. The taxi had arrived at Liverpool Street Station. Sid got out and saw to the pushchair and her case. He paid the driver and then accompanied her into the busy station, where he paid for her ticket and gave her ten pounds. Ellie tried to refuse, but he forced it into her purse.

'You may need it until I can look after you,' he told her. 'I love you, Ellie, and I wish I could come with you, but there are things I have to take care of…'

Ellie took his arm and saw him wince. 'You're hurt badly,' she said. 'You should go to the doctor, Sid – please take care of yourself… for me.'

'It's all right, I tied a bandage round, but I will see the doctor,' he said and bent his head to kiss her. 'I love you, Ellie. Listen, that's the train you need pulling into platform three. Stay with Christine until I come… she will understand if you tell her I sent you…'

Ellie nodded and went past the barrier. It was all noise and confusion but Ellie had sometimes travelled on the underground when she lived with Peter's mother and trains held no fear for her. A young soldier saw her struggling with her case and lifted it onto the train for her while another lifted the pushchair in.

'That your old man over there?' he asked and Ellie nodded, allowing him to think it as she thanked him for his help. 'We help each other out, missus.' He saluted Sid, who nodded to him.

Sid waited beyond the ticket barrier until she was on the train, waving as she looked back. Ellie blinked hard. It felt as if she were running away and deserting both Sid and Mabel – and yet they both feared for her and Beth. Looking down at her sleeping child, Ellie's expression hardened. She found a seat and took Beth in her arms as the obliging soldier put the pushchair up on the luggage rack. She couldn't stay and let Peter take out his anger on her child. She had no choice but to get away until it was safe to return… but she was so anxious for both Sid and Mabel. Peter was ruthless and if he guessed what they'd done, he would be violent and vindictive.

Peter was running scared. He'd been watching as the paid assassin had attacked the bugger who had dared to go after Ellie and it had shocked him to see how easily the soldier had dealt with a man who had killed many times – but a knife was never any match for a gun.

Who would have thought Sid Coleman carried a gun? As soon as he saw the knifeman go down, a man known by the scar on his face, a man who had killed for him before, Peter had taken to his heels and run. He felt confused, but anger was burning deep down inside him. The man who had been shot that night was a long-time friend; he'd helped Peter out more than once in the past and he'd counted on him being there when he got back after the war. Many of Peter's plans for the future revolved around being able to inflict fear into others – and now he'd have to look for a new hard man to back him.

Peter's life of extortion and power over others had come to an abrupt end when he was sent to war. He'd been well on the way to making a name for himself in the East End and had seen himself as rich and powerful once he got a grip on the empire he was set on building. Outwardly good-looking, with a smile that charmed most people, Peter had learned early in life that he could get most of what he wanted with a lift of his finger. He'd left most of the rough stuff to his friends, particularly Scarface. Peter was the brains and they were queuing up to work for him until bloody Hitler got in the way. However, the Army had taught him how to kill and he wasn't squeamish, but neither was he a fool. He wasn't risking his life against a damned gun when he was unarmed. There were other ways to get his revenge.

That bloody Sid Coleman was going to get it! Peter had his army-issue weapons and he'd give the man who'd pinched his wife and killed his friend a taste of his own medicine – but first of all he was going to teach that bitch a lesson.

The anger was seething inside him the whole time he was walking. It was dusk and most shops and businesses were closing. Peter liked the night, because it made it easier to hide and he had no intention of being caught. This mess was all of Ellie's making – her and that bloody interfering landlady of hers. They would be sorry they'd got on his wrong side when he'd finished with them! Peter could be generous when he chose and he'd loved Ellie when he married her, never letting her see what was underneath the pleasant face he showed to the world, but she'd seen the other side of him now. She'd be kneeling at his feet and begging him by the time he finished with her – but he wouldn't kill her, because he still wanted her. She was his, but that bloody brat wasn't...

He walked up the narrow alley between the two shops, trying the back door handle of Mabel Tandy's kitchen. It was locked and that made him angrier than ever. The bitches had locked him out. He banged on the door loudly, calling out to be admitted, thumping again and again until it was suddenly opened and Mabel Tandy stood there looking at him. She was wearing her pink wool dressing gown and a hairnet and something about her stance made him blow his top.

'Get out of my way, you old hag,' he said and thrust her to one side. He pushed his way into the kitchen and looked about him. 'Where is she?'

'Ellie isn't here,' she said and there was contempt in her face. 'She's gone where you will never find her. You've forfeited the right to be her husband, Peter. She's left you…'

'No! She can't!' Peter roared and lunged towards her. She backed away, but he was quicker and he had her by the throat. 'Tell me where she's gone, bitch, and I might let you live…'

Mabel looked him in the eyes and she was like a lioness protecting her young. 'I don't care how much you threaten or what you do – I shan't tell you, because I can't. I have no idea where she is – just that she's gone and she's safe from you…' she ended on a gasp as his grasp tightened, blocking her air.

'Bitch!' Peter's hands closed round her throat. There was a red mist in front of his eyes, the anger filling his head so that he hardly knew what he did as he kept on pressing and pressing until she went limp. As he let go of her, suddenly aware of what he'd done, she fell to the floor, eyes bulging and her face purple. 'Wake up, you old hag…' Peter kicked at her body, but there was no response. He'd killed her! The bitch was dead…

Suddenly, panic set in and he couldn't think what to do. He had to get away – away from that staring lump of flesh on the floor. If anyone knew what he'd done he would hang... but no one would know. Ellie wasn't here. She might guess if she read about the murder in the papers, but she wouldn't dare to point the finger, because she knew he'd go after her...

Peter's thoughts were all over the place. His wife was going to get her comeuppance one of these days, but for the moment he had to think of himself. No one had seen him come here, so if he just went he was in the clear...

He rushed from the kitchen and nearly collided with a woman at the end of the alley as he made his escape. Peter vaguely recognised her, but it didn't register who she was and he just ran blindly. His kit was still at the station where he'd left it in a locker. He would get back on a train tonight and no one would ever know he'd been here.

Maureen watched the man running away. He'd knocked into her but hadn't apologised and she doubted he'd even noticed her. Peter Morris had seemed to be in a panic over something... A chill started at the back of Maureen's neck because she sensed something was wrong. Ellie was frightened of her husband. Maureen had known it for a while now and she felt anxious about her.

'Ellie...' Maureen walked swiftly up the little passageway to the back door of Mabel's property. It was open and a light was showing through, ignoring the blackout. Her throat tight with apprehension, Maureen approached the door, pushing it back a little to see inside and then she gasped in horror as she saw the body lying on the ground. 'Mabel…' she cried and ran to kneel by the side of the woman who had been a friend to everyone in the lane. 'Oh no…' The staring eyes and awful colour told Maureen that it was too late. Standing up, she called for Ellie, but there was no answer.

What to do? Tom – She must fetch Tom. She'd just left him in the shop, because he was working late. Tom would know what to do. Maureen could hardly see for the tears in her eyes and her heart was thumping unpleasantly. It was so terrible that she could scarcely believe it. Peter Morris had murdered Mabel – that's why he'd been in such a hurry to leave.

Maureen left the door as she'd found it and ran down the alleyway. She was feeling sick and dizzy, her hands shaking as she went into the shop on the corner, where Tom was preparing to leave. He'd been stocktaking and had stayed late, which was the reason she'd been with him until this hour. If Peter hadn't come rushing out and nearly knocked into her, she wouldn't have thought of going to Mrs Tandy's back door, because she was already late for the children's bedtime.

'What's wrong, Maureen?' Tom asked, looking at her intently. 'Are you ill?'

'We have to telephone the police,' Maureen gasped and sat down in a chair. 'I just saw Peter Morris rushing out of Mabel's passage, so I went to investigate… She's dead… he's strangled her…'

'Bloody hell!' Tom said and looked shocked. 'I knew he had a temper, but I never dreamed— Should I go round…?'

'No, we'll just ring the police,' Maureen said. 'I shouted Ellie, but there was no answer. She may simply be out but...'

'He might have killed her too...' Tom looked sick. 'You sit there, Maureen. I'll ring the station myself and get them out – and then I'll ring your gran and let her know you won't be back for a while, because the police will want to know everything'

Chapter 22

Peggy looked at her friend in disbelief as Maureen told her and Janet the terrible news the next morning. It was just so shocking that a murder could happen in their lane – and awful that it should be a woman everyone liked.

'Mabel never harmed anyone. How could he do such a thing?'

'He looked wild, like a man possessed, when he knocked past me,' Maureen said and sipped the little glass of brandy Peggy had given her, because she'd been shaking when she told her, haunted by what she'd seen, even after a night spent without sleep. 'He's always had a temper, but I never thought he could do something like that...'

'It's a mercy Ellie and Beth were not there,' Janet said. 'Does anyone know where she is?'

'No – but the police say she must have packed a case because things had been taken out of drawers in a hurry, and the pushchair was gone. They think it may have been a row over her leaving that resulted in the murder.' Maureen gulped, still visibly in shock despite the hours that had passed.

'I feel sick,' Peggy said. 'I was only in the wool shop yesterday morning, talking to Mabel. She was sayin' that business had picked up a bit recently. She'd sold a few knitted things that she'd made herself – and some of the bits you took her, Jan. You know, she gave me two pounds for you for Maggie's things...'

Maureen was crying now. 'I can't believe she has gone, Peggy. She was such a good friend to me, to everyone. I called in most days to have a chat. She was so happy with Ellie and the baby and talking about what she planned to buy for Beth... she loved that child...'

'What will Ellie do now?' Janet asked. 'She can't live there again...' A shiver ran through her. 'Who would want to live there after what has happened? It was bad enough when Violet's son attacked his own mother, but she got better – but poor Mabel is dead...'

'It's horrible,' Peggy agreed and looked at Maureen. 'You must have had such a fright, Maureen. Are you all right? I mean in your condition...'

'Gran insisted on calling the doctor to me when I got home just in case,' Maureen admitted, 'but he said there was no harm done. He advised me to rest, but I couldn't stay in bed. I just kept walking about all night, making tea I didn't drink. Life has to go on, as we all know – and Gordon is being moved to the London today, so I shall want to visit him this evening, if he's up to it...'

'You're very brave,' Janet said. 'I think it would give me nightmares...'

'Don't be silly, Janet.' Peggy gave her a warning look. 'Maureen isn't goin' to let this upset her – are you?'

'I shall try not to for the sake of the children and Gordon,' Maureen said. 'Gran was upset enough over Violet – and she knew Mabel better than any of us really. They were friends years ago. She was very upset last night and I had to comfort her, but what can I say to her? A murder in Mulberry Lane is something no one wants to hear about.'

'It was strange about Knocker James last year,' Janet said. 'He'd been causing us all a lot of bother, but then someone killed him... I've always wondered about that.'

'The police thought it a gangland killing...' Peggy reminded her.

'Yes, but it was odd...'

'I wondered if Peter had anything to do with that,' Maureen said. 'Well, you know how nasty he was to Ellie... and he does have a violent temper. And now Mabel had been murdered!' The friends looked at each other anxiously.

'If he could kill once he would have no trouble killing again,' Janet said, nodding. 'He's a dangerous man. I just hope he doesn't come back here...'

'The police said they would interview him, that's if they can find him. Of course, they aren't saying he was the one that murdered her – although I saw him rushing out like that and – and she was still warm. They said it could only just have happened when I found her...' Maureen looked sick. 'And they want to interview Ellie – but no one knows where she is either...'

'I should've thought your testimony was proof enough,' Janet said, looking angry. 'Besides, if he was innocent he would go to the police himself.'

'Not according to the inspector I spoke to last night. He says it may constitute a case for prosecution, but the evidence is only circumstantial at the moment...'

'Poor Ellie,' Peggy said. 'If she ran away in fear, she will feel dreadful when she knows about Mabel.'

'But where has she gone?' Janet asked. 'Has he murdered her as well?'

'Oh, don't!' Maureen begged.

'Where would she go?' Janet demanded. 'I didn't think she had a family.'

'She had an aunt, but they never got on. Besides, Peter could easily have found her there.' Maureen looked thoughtful. 'I don't know of anyone else – unless...' She shook her head as the others looked at her. 'No, I shan't say yet, because I don't want to get anyone else into trouble... but I know that Ellie will feel this is all her fault.'

'I came down as soon as I knew, because I didn't want you to hear it on the wireless or read it in the paper,' Sid said and took Ellie's trembling hands in his own. They had gone for a walk towards some woods, leaving Beth in his sister's big friendly farmhouse. It was cold but bright and the earth in the fields was hard beneath their feet, because of an overnight frost. 'I've spoken to my general and he's given me a couple of days off. I can take you back to London if you wish...'

'I couldn't go to her house...' Ellie's eyes were drenched in tears as she looked up at him. 'Mabel was so good to me – like a mother – and he has killed her. He told me he would if I defied him, so it's all my fault…'

'No, my dearest girl, it isn't,' Sid said. 'I've spoken to the police and they say the man who attacked me the other night is a known killer, though they've never been able to pin anything on him. He kills to order, Ellie – and he confessed that he was paid to attack me. He wouldn't name the man who paid him, but they think it may have been Peter.'

'Why?'

'Because they were known associates before the war – Peter was a member of a gang, Ellie. They worked for a man who extorted protection payments from nightclub owners and bookies, market traders – and just before the war started their boss was murdered in his own club. They think someone wanted to take over his patch. No one was arrested for it, but Peter and his friend Herbie – or Scarface as he liked to be known – were suspected, though no proof was found – and then Peter joined the Army and his friend disappeared.' He paused and looked serious. 'The police know I had an interest in you – and they're half convinced he is Mabel's murderer, but the wheels of justice are always slow. They've got a warrant out for him, but until they have the proof they won't commit themselves.'

Ellie shuddered. 'I knew he had a temper, but when I first met him he was lovely to me. I never suspected anything like that – and he was always buying me things…'

'You didn't wonder where he got the money?'

Ellie shook her head. 'He said he had a good job working for a man who needed him at all sorts of strange hours…' Her eyes widened as she looked at Sid. 'He was a gangster, wasn't he? That's why his mother warned me not to upset him… Did Peter have Knocker James killed?' Ellie remembered the way Peter had acted when he'd discovered she'd been raped, furious at first, ranting about killing the man who'd violated her, and then was suddenly all smiles. It made sense if he'd arranged for Knocker to be murdered. 'Perhaps, we'll never know.' Sid put his arm about her, comforting her as she trembled. He frowned. 'Herbie Collins died of his wound the same night as Mabel was murdered. I killed him, Ellie. I'm a bodyguard, as I told you before, and I carry a gun. I was attacked and so I shot him in the shoulder. I called an ambulance and thought he might live, which he did for long enough for the police to confirm my story – but then he died… it turns out he had a terminal illness and he wasn't strong enough to fight the trauma. I doubt if he even knew he had the cancer; the doctors told me it is a silent killer until the last weeks.'

'Oh, Sid…' Ellie brushed away her tears. 'I don't blame you for what you did. They would've killed you if they could…'

'Yes, I know. Yet I could be killed any time while on duty, Ellie. I do a dangerous job, even if it doesn't seem that way – but I'm good at it, which is why I was given the job. I didn't intend to kill that man, just to take him down – but I don't regret it. If anyone attacked my general when I was on duty I would shoot to kill.'

'It's your job…' Ellie looked at him uncertainly. 'What about Peter – would you kill him if he came after you?'

'I should defend myself – and you,' Sid said. 'I told you I wasn't afraid of him, Ellie, but I don't like killing for its own sake. I would maim rather than kill if I could, as I intended with Scarface...'

'I think Peter may try to kill me if he knows where I am...'

'The police in London want to talk to you,' Sid said. 'I told them I would fetch you rather than have them come here to my sister's home, and you can stay at the house with Tom and me – he has another bedroom you can use. Once you've cleared this mess up, I'll fetch the rest of your things and I'll bring you back here – or I could find you a home of your own if you'd rather.'

'Your sister is lovely. She was so kind to me when I arrived after all those hours changing trains,' Ellie said, 'but she couldn't keep me here for long, because she has her own family. I have a job and friends in Mulberry Lane – but I'm not sure what to do. I'm afraid Peter will come after us again.'

'The police want to question him,' Sid said. 'You'll be safe enough with Tom and me ... and you can come back to Christine afterwards, if you want. She's told me she will be happy to have you.'

'I'll return to London if I can stay with you and Tom,' Ellie said, but she was nervous. 'I can't go to the house again, Sid. I can't bear to think of Mabel lying dead on the kitchen floor – and it was my fault. If I hadn't run away, she would still be alive...'

'You mustn't blame yourself,' Sid said. 'You were the one in immediate danger. No one would have expected him to murder an innocent woman...'

'I'll never forgive myself. She loved me…' Ellie sobbed.

'I know,' Sid put his arms about her, holding her close as she wept. 'I'm so sorry, love. The police will get him and he will pay the price, believe me.'

'It won't bring her back, though, will it?' Ellie looked up at him. 'I'll never forgive myself for leavin' her alone that night.'

Sid nodded, understanding what she didn't say. She blamed him for insisting on taking her away, because if they'd been together perhaps the tragedy might have been avoided.

Peggy was making jam tarts when Maureen called in one morning later that week. Everyone in the lanes was still shocked by the news of Mabel Tandy's murder. It had been in the newspapers, side by side with an article banning people from going to within ten miles of the coast from the Wash to Land's End. The whole country was on high alert, some folk said from fear of imminent invasion, others said the numbers of armed forces were so large that some big offensive was being planned. Either way, tension was in the air and with men in uniform wherever you went it felt like being in a military camp. Some folk were even whispering that Mabel had been murdered by an advance party of German infiltrators!

Maureen had Robin in his pushchair and he was sucking at a biscuit she'd given him. Peggy made her welcome, as usual, telling her to put Robin in the playpen with Freddie and Fay.

'How are you feeling now, love?' she asked.

'A bit better,' Maureen said and grimaced. 'I've stopped crying all the time, but I feel numb now... as if I'm in limbo.'

Maureen released the straps and lifted her son into the playpen, where he started to grab at some bricks until Fay snatched them away from him. He stared at her and moved away, turning his attention to Freddie, who handed him a rather sad-looking teddy bear.

'Fay doesn't like sharin' her toys. I think she'll be a right little madam in a couple of years...' she broke off as Laurie entered the kitchen.

'Hello, Maureen,' he said. 'I was sorry to hear about Mabel – that was a terrible thing.'

'Yes, I couldn't believe what had happened...'

'Must have been quite a shock,' he said and picked up the newspaper. 'Anyway, how is your husband? I like Gordon; he's a decent chap...'

'He was very tired the first night he arrived, as you may imagine. I only stopped for a few minutes, but I visited yesterday and again this mornin' and he seems better. He's still on penicillin and he says it makes him feel a bit sick, but it is marvellous at dealin' with infection. His leg is so much easier than when I saw him in Portsmouth.'

'That's wonderful. I did read about a marvellous new drug that was savin' lives in the papers. It will make such a difference to the treatment for our troops,' Peggy said and placed a tray of plum jam tarts in the oven as her husband left them to return to the bar, where he was changing barrels. 'Has Tom told you that Ellie is stoppin' with him and Sid for a while? I was so relieved when Sid told me she was safe. They arrived late last night. Sid popped in to tell me before he left for work this mornin'...'

'No, I haven't been to the shop today,' Maureen said. 'What made Ellie come back? I should've thought she'd be too scared of Peter...'

'Sid told me that the police wanted to talk to her, to get her side of the story. He didn't want them goin' down there to his sister's house, so he promised to fetch her. I don't know how long she's stoppin'.'

'She must feel so bad. I'm sorry for her, Peggy. She's had a rough time one way and another...' Maureen said, swallowing hard as tears threatened. 'Peter is a killer, I know it and I shall tell anyone who finds fault of Ellie...' She glanced at the playpen. 'Freddie and Robin are gettin' on well – but I don't think Fay likes it much.' Even as she spoke, Fay pinched her brother on his chubby little leg and made him cry out. He turned his big eyes on her reproachfully but didn't try to retaliate. However, Robin threw the teddy at her and she yelled in anger as it struck her in the face. Maureen acted swiftly and whisked her son from the playpen before war broke out. 'I'd better go, Peggy. I only called in to tell you that Gordon was settling in fine...'

'Fay, stop that,' Peggy said and picked her daughter up, giving her a tap on the leg. 'Naughty girl...'

'Kids!' Maureen laughed. 'We shall have them all runnin' wild in the lanes before long, Peggy. Goodness knows what mischief they'll get up to then...'

Peggy smiled and put Fay back in the playpen as her friend left. Fay was such a jealous little madam, just like

Maggie. The two of them were very possessive and there had been fights over various toys already; Janet did her best to control her daughter, who was bigger and stronger, though Fay instigated most of the quarrels.

Peggy stroked the head of her little boy. Freddie was so much gentler and easier to please than his sister, reminding her so much of Able with his smiles and loving ways. Peggy found Fay a little difficult to control at times, which had never happened with either Janet or Pip – but then she was older and she felt tired sometimes. Laurie helped with them a bit, but she never asked him for anything for the twins, because she felt guilty. They weren't his and it was only natural that he would resent being asked for help with them, so she took what he gave but she didn't ask.

He returned to the kitchen just as she set the freshly baked tarts under a glass dome. 'Ah, they're ready,' he said and bit into one. 'Lovely, Peggy. No one cooks quite like you.' He looked down at the twins with a frown. 'Everything all right with these two?'

'Oh, they were squabbling with Robin Hart,' Peggy said. 'Maureen looks so tired and drained. It really upset her finding Mabel like that...'

'It would upset anyone...'

'She has enough to worry her with her husband so ill.'

'Yes, poor chap.' Laurie seemed genuinely sympathetic and Peggy sighed. He was trying to mend the breach, but it was hard to forget all that had happened between them.

Peggy looked at him. 'Do you need any help in the bar?'

'Janet popped in just now to say she's puttin' Maggie to bed for her rest and then she'll come down for the lunchtime rush. Why don't you have a sit-down, love? You've got the twins to look after... you can help me this evenin' when they're asleep.'

'Yes, all right...' Peggy smiled at him. Laurie was being considerate lately and there were times when it almost felt good between them again. 'Thank you – and thank you for botherin', Laurie.'

'You know I care about you,' Laurie said and moved closer. He looked down at her. 'I wish so much these past years had been different, Peggy...'

'Yes, so do I,' she said and held her breath as he bent his head and kissed her on the cheek.

For a moment she was tempted to kiss him back on the lips. Surely there was nothing to keep them apart any longer – and yet something inside her held back. She had forgiven Laurie for his affairs, she was sure there had been more than one, but she wasn't ready to be his wife again. She didn't think she ever could be, because her heart belonged to Able, even though he could never return.

Chapter 23

Tom left the recruiting office with a grin a mile wide on his face. They had finally allowed him to sign on. He'd been given his cadet uniform and told that he would be getting his official papers for the regulars before long. Whistling, he strode back to the lane, feeling as if he were on top of the world.

Sid was just about to leave when Tom came into the kitchen of the house. Sid saw his look of satisfaction and smiled. 'I told you they would have you in the cadets like a shot – got your uniform then?'

'Yes and they say my call up papers should be here in a few weeks.'

'Good.' Sid patted him on the shoulder. 'I have to report for duty, but I hope everything goes well for you, lad...'

Tom left his uniform in his room and then hurried across the road. Maureen had stood in for him for a couple of hours, but he knew she would be looking for him to return as soon as possible.

She glanced at his face as he walked in. 'Everything went well then, Tom?'

'I've got my uniform now and I've signed on. My call up papers will be through soon – and then I'll be off...'

'You say that as if you can't wait to go and leave me...' Maureen pretended to be put out and then burst out laughing as she saw his face. 'No, I don't mind, Tom. I know it's what you want...'

They broke off as the shop door opened and Violet entered. She gave Maureen a sour look and then slammed her rent book and some money on the counter.

'My Harold would turn over in his grave if he knew the way I'd been treated by his daughter,' she said with a sniff. 'Forced to pay rent for a home that should rightfully belong to me.'

Maureen just stared at her while Tom signed the book and she went off with a glare, banging the door behind her. After the door had closed, Tom winked at Maureen and she exploded into laughter again.

'It's a good thing you were here or I might have lost my temper,' she said and Tom grinned.

'You've been more than good to her,' he asserted. 'I reckon most would've kicked her out after what she and that son of hers did.'

The door opened and Anne walked in. She looked at them in amusement. 'What are you two laughing about then?'

'Violet was in here complaining again,' Tom said. 'I'm used to her but Maureen caught the brunt of it...'

'Oh, her...' Anne's expression showed what she thought of Maureen's stepmother. 'I don't know why Hilda let her stay on after her son robbed you like that...'

'She had nowhere to go when she left hospital and Gran felt sorry for her – but I'd hoped she would find somewhere before this...'

Tom took Anne's list and placed the items on the counter. She packed her basket, paid and left with Maureen. The two women stood outside in the lane for a moment and chatted. Tom tidied the shelves and shook his head over empty spaces that couldn't be filled these days, but it still couldn't take the smile from his face. He had joined the cadets and now he'd joined the regulars and he would get his papers soon. He couldn't wait to get started.

Janet opened Ryan's letter. He'd been away on business for some days, but he was expecting to be in London now for a few months and he wanted to see her. Ryan had telephoned a few days previously and invited her to dinner one evening the following week and she'd told him she would go, but now his letter was telling her that he wanted so much more than just a dinner date.

You know how much I care for you, Jan. I'm not sure if you realise that I think of you all the time and wish I could be with you and Maggie. She feels as if she's mine, perhaps because I knew her when she was a babe in arms – and I'm lonely. I'm in love with you, Jan. It isn't just that I want a family again. I was torn apart by my feelings for you when we were both married. And I do know that it is too early for you to think of marriage again, but I hope you will one day in the not too distant future...

Janet crumpled the letter and let it drop on her bedroom floor. She wanted to cry, shout and scream all at the same time. It was so unfair. Why couldn't Ryan be content as her friend? She needed his friendship badly and he'd given it, but he wanted so much more and she wasn't sure she could give him the love he craved – and deserved.

To marry him just for the home she needed would be wrong. It was Rosemary's motive for her second marriage: she wanted a life, to be taken out, looked after, provided for and cared for. Janet wanted those things too, but she also wanted to *feel* love again – the kind of love she'd felt for Mike at the beginning of their romance.

'Oh, Mike…' she whispered and bent her head as the tears came. It was a long time since she'd cried, because anger had filled her, driving out the weakness that brought tears. 'Mike… why?'

There was no answer. There never could be an answer. Janet had to face up to the situation and decide for herself. At one time it would have been easy to sleep with Ryan, and perhaps if she let herself go it might be again. She'd been keeping herself on a tight rein for a long time, but maybe it was time to start thinking about a new life.

Janet bent down, picked up the letter and smoothed it out. She had to be fair to Ryan. Either she let him into her life or she had to send him away for good. Janet decided that she would tell him how she felt when they met for their dinner date and then see what fate brought… after all, not every woman got a second chance for happiness.

*

'Ellie, I had to come round,' Rose said when Ellie invited her into Tom's parlour. 'I know you've been through a terrible time recently and I wanted to say I'm sorry – and I don't blame you. Some woman claimed it was your fault and I gave her a ticking-off…'

'I am to blame in a way,' Ellie said and tears wet her cheeks. 'But Peter is wicked, Rose. You've no idea what he threatened; he was going to kill Beth and me. I thought he would leave Mabel alone once I'd left…'

'It's not your fault and you mustn't feel guilty…' she hesitated, then, 'I don't suppose you want to go – but I've got those tickets for the social tomorrow night…'

'I'm not sure,' Ellie said uncertainly. She hadn't wanted to open the door, but Rose had been friendly in the past, so she'd reluctantly invited her in. 'I don't know who would look after Beth…'

Rose was talking again, forcing Ellie to listen, to shut out the clamour of her thoughts and her guilt. 'Peggy isn't going this year. I asked her and she said she couldn't be bothered with it this time – so she might have Beth if you asked her. Do come, Ellie. Otherwise I shall have to go on my own, because Maureen isn't going either…'

'I'll have to ask Sid and Tom what they think…' Ellie wavered, because Rose was so persistent, but she could just imagine what folk would say and the looks they would give her if she dared to show her face. They were all blaming her for the death of a popular woman. A little shudder went through her. 'I don't want to go if it's disrespectful to Mabel. The police won't let us have her funeral yet – they say it can't happen until they've got someone for the murder…'

'Surely we all know who did it?' Rose said. 'It wasn't your fault that your husband was a bully and a wrong'un, Ellie. I didn't know him, but everyone says he had a bad temper.'

'Yes, but if I hadn't run away he would have hurt me not Mabel…' Ellie swallowed her sob and rubbed at her eyes. 'I don't think I can go – it would look so uncaring. You should ask someone else, Rose. Perhaps Janet Rowan would like to go with you…'

'Well, she did say she'd thought about getting a ticket,' Rose said. 'If you're sure, I'll ask her…'

'I couldn't enjoy myself and I would spoil your evenin',' Ellie told her. 'And people would blame me – some already do. I was spat at in the market this mornin' and two of my regular customers at the hairdresser's crossed the road rather than speak to me…'

'That just isn't fair,' Rose protested. 'I do know what that is like, Ellie, believe me. I've had people turn against me because… of something that wasn't my fault. You mustn't let them get to you. Hold your head up and ignore the insults; they're just ignorant. It's why I came round, to show you I'm on your side.'

'It's not easy, but I'll try,' Ellie said. 'I shall go back to the country in a few days. The police wanted me to stay in London until they'd finished gathering evidence, but after that I'm leavin'…'

'You're not coming back to live in Mulberry Lane?'

'I couldn't…' A shudder ran through Ellie and her hands trembled. 'Every time I look at her shop I feel like burstin' into tears. I loved her, Rose. Mabel was so good to me. I don't know how I would've got through the last couple of years if she hadn't taken me in...'

'I'm so sorry, Ellie,' Rose said. 'I just wanted to help, but I suppose it is just too soon. I'm sorry you're leaving.'

'I'm sorry too, because I liked my job and I had friends here, but it's time for me to make a new start somewhere else...'

Leaving Ellie in Tom Barton's house, Rose crossed the street to the pub. She no longer worked for Peggy but called round sometimes when she knew that Laurie Ashley would be in the bar. She liked Janet and perhaps she could make use of Rose's spare ticket, especially as it didn't look as if Jimmy would be home for a while.

'Would you keep an eye on Maggie if I go to the social with Rose tomorrow evenin'?' Janet asked her mother a little later. 'I haven't been out much for ages, but if it's too much to ask...'

'Of course I don't mind if you go out in the evenings,' Peggy told her with a smile. 'I'm glad if you can make friends and start to enjoy life again, love. You used to think the church social was boring, but you'll probably have fun with Rose.'

'She told me that Ellie was to have gone with her, but of course she isn't up to it just yet. I popped in to see her yesterday for a few minutes – did you know some people are cuttin' her in the street and one woman spat at her in the market.'

'I told Maureen that some folk were blamin' her for it all,' Peggy said. 'We know the truth, Jan, but to others, Peter seems a brave young man doin' his duty out there – and she's been branded the cheatin' wife.'

Janet looked serious. 'I know it looks bad for Ellie but I think she had a lot to put up with, Mum. She says she's goin' away as soon as the police say she can and I don't blame her.'

'Do you remember when Ryan stayed here that night during the Blitz?' Janet nodded and Peggy sighed, because it brought back memories for her too. 'If anyone had seen him leaving that morning your name might have been dragged through the mud too, love. People have sharp tongues and suspicious minds.'

Janet nodded thoughtfully, then, 'Mum, what would you think if I did decide to get married again— Oh, not just yet, but in time?'

'I should be happy if you were,' Peggy said. 'I know what happened was devastatin', Jan – but life has to go on, my love.'

'I know. I never thought Rosemary would marry again, but she has made up her mind. I'm not sure how I feel or what I want just now – but Ryan is taking me out next week and...' She broke off and sighed

'You like him – and you enjoy being with him, don't you?'

'Yes. I didn't think I would ever stop hurtin', Mum – but it is easing slowly. That's why I'm goin' to this social with Ellie. It's a start to livin' a normal life again...'

'Yes, you go and have some fun,' Peggy said and smiled at her lovingly. 'I've no intention of goin', so it's no trouble for me to look out for Maggie. I'll be listenin' out for the twins at the same time – and Anne has some free time again now that Kirk has gone off on his trainin' course so she will be helpin' out in the bar...'

Jan nodded. 'Anne is glowin', Mum. I don't think I've ever seen anyone so happy. She told me the doctor has confirmed she's pregnant...'

'Yes, I know,' Peggy agreed. 'She really does want this baby, Jan. I mean most women want their babies once they're on the way – but Anne is so intent that it frightens me a little. I fear for what might happen if anythin'... But I'm not even goin' to put that into words.'

Janet nodded, knowing exactly what her mother meant. Anne was walking on air and if anything happened to the baby... well, it didn't bear thinking about.

Anne paused outside Mabel's shop, looking at the closed notice in the window. It had been the only shop of its kind close to the lanes and the market was the nearest place to buy wool now, but the stall was only there on a Friday. The women of the lanes would miss both Mabel and her shop.

'Anne,' Maureen said, coming out of the grocer's as Anne was hesitating on the pavement outside the wool shop. 'Yes, it's so sad, isn't it?'

'It was awful for you finding her like that,' Anne said. 'You must have been so upset, Maureen.'

'It was terrible, but I've seen death at close hand a few times now, so it didn't upset me that way – only that a good friend had been murdered. I feel sad but mostly angry – and I want to see Peter Morris punished.'

'Yes, let's hope the police charge him when they find him.'

Maureen nodded. 'Are you on your way to visit Peggy?'

'Yes, but I was just thinking about the wool I asked Mabel to put aside for me,' Anne said. 'I bought six ounces, which is enough to work with for the moment, but she'd promised to keep another ten ounces of white and five of a pale lemon. I'm not sure where I can get a match.'

'This is your first pregnancy,' Maureen smiled. 'I remember finding the first time a bit daunting – but you look really well.'

'Yes, I am – and I'm excited and nervous at the same time. 'I've found a nice cot, almost new, and a pram…'

'Good. I was meaning to ask, because I had a lady who had one to sell in the shop the other day.'

'I've found most things I'll want – nappies and blankets, and a shawl. It's mostly clothes I lack…'

'I expect you will get a lot of presents when the time comes. I did…'

'I want everything to be ready on time…that's why I need that wool…'

'Wait for a while, because I may be able to get the wool you put by soon…' Maureen paused. 'I'm goin' to try and take over the lease of Mabel's shop when the police have finished with it. Obviously, it will be put up for rent again – and I'd like to carry it on more or less as it is. I've got a few ideas to make it more profitable…'

Anne was surprised. 'Could you face goin' round there after what happened?'

'Mabel was my friend,' Maureen said and looked her in the eyes. 'We got on so well and I don't believe her ghost will rise up in anger because I take over her shop. I think she would be pleased – and we don't want any more empty shops in the lane.'

'Who will run it?' Anne was curious now.

'I'll advertise for a woman,' Maureen said. 'We don't want a very young girl – but perhaps a war widow who needs a home and a job she can manage. She would have to know about the murder, but if she's the right one she won't be put off by what happened...'

'You seem to have thought it all through,' Anne said in wonder. 'Well, I hope it works out for you. I'll see what I can find elsewhere, but I should like that wool I put by – if you do get the lease and the stock. I wonder who that belongs to?' She frowned. 'Did Mabel have any family?'

'That's something we have to discover,' Maureen said. 'I know we haven't even had the funeral yet and it would be too soon to think about things like this normally, but I should be sorry to see the shop close down. We've got two empty shops in the lane as it is... and once they're left for a few years it's very expensive to do them up.'

'Yes, that bakery is a shambles,' Anne said. 'Peggy told me she had a look round it a few weeks back, but it's in an awful state. You'd think whoever owns it would have kept it in better shape.'

'Some people just don't bother.' Maureen shook her head. 'Who wants to spend money on a property that might get bombed?' Since February the German planes had been attempting to raid the docks and factories, but the RAF was shooting most down before they got near.

'We haven't had any raids locally for a while,' Anne said but crossed her fingers. 'Perhaps Hitler is fed up with us because we're too stubborn.'

'I doubt he can spare the manpower at the moment,' Maureen said, falling into step beside her as they walked up the lane together. 'But I wonder what else he has in store for us. The papers are warning he has a powerful new weapon – just when can we expect Hitler to unleash that, I wonder.'

Chapter 24

'I'm just going out for an hour or so, Peggy,' Laurie said. 'I've got a couple of errands to do. Would you mind looking after the bar for me? I shan't be long…'

'Of course I don't mind,' Peggy said. 'The twins have tired themselves out at last and they're both sound asleep. I'll be glad to have a little time behind the bar for a change.'

'I'll listen out for them,' Nellie said and nodded to Laurie. 'No need to rush, Mr Ashley. Me and Peggy can manage…'

'Good. I just need to speak to someone,' Laurie said. 'Anythin' you need from the shop, Peggy?'

'No, I'm fine. Tom is bringing my order this evenin'…'

'Right, I'll see you later then.'

Laurie took his scarf from the hallstand and his heavy Army coat, shrugging it on as he left through the bar and went out into the lane. No need to tell his wife that he was going to the doctor yet. That cough he got, mainly in the night, was a bit of a nuisance, but Peggy either hadn't noticed or she hadn't mentioned it to him.

He saw Maureen and Anne standing just outside the old bakery, talking and smiling together, and he was about to call out a greeting when something alerted his instincts. A man was staring fixedly at the two women from across the road and, as Laurie hesitated, the man suddenly made a run at one of them, his arm upraised.

Maureen screamed and jerked back as the man struck at her with what looked very much like a long knife. Laurie didn't hesitate or pause for thought. He rushed towards the man and tackled him from the back, his arm around the throat of the assassin. Maureen was staring at them, her face white and unable to move, but Anne had run into the cobblers' shop and was yelling to Bob Hall to call the police.

Laurie knew that the man who had tried to injure his wife's best friend was younger and stronger than he and he was in a fight for his life. The man threw Laurie off his back, muttering obscenities as he turned to face him. His eyes were wild with a kind of madness and in that moment Laurie recognised Peter Morris, and that he'd meant to kill Maureen, because of what she'd seen the night Mabel was murdered.

'Don't be a bloody fool,' Laurie panted as Peter stabbed at his chest with the knife. 'The coppers will throw away the key when they get you…'

Peter didn't answer. His face was contorted with ungovernable rage and Laurie thought he probably wasn't aware of what he was doing. Hunted by both the police and the Army, he must have brooded on his wrongs and let them fester inside him. Laurie might have felt sorry for the bloke if he hadn't tried to kill an innocent woman. No decent man could let him get away with that.

Laurie cried out with pain as he felt the knife stab his chest, but he refused to let go of his opponent as they grappled for the weapon. He caught Peter's arm and tried to twist it, to force the blade from his grasp, but the younger man was so much stronger.

'You're a damned fool,' he grunted, but his breathing was harsh and he could hardly find energy enough to continue the fight. Laurie knew that his strength was waning and unless help arrived soon he would come off worse in this fight. 'Give up before the cops get here.'

Suddenly, there was the sound of a police whistle. Laurie didn't have time to look round but felt relief because he knew that he was losing the struggle. Peter had heard the piercing noise, but he was determined to inflict as much pain on his opponent as he could and he plunged his blade into Laurie's chest just as the whistle sounded again, much closer, and then, someone in an Army uniform, charged at Peter's back and struck him with a lump of wood between the shoulders.

Peter grunted, turned to meet the new opponent and caught the full force of the next blow in his face. It felled him and he went down, falling between Laurie and the person who had delivered the blow.

'Tom Barton…' Laurie muttered, astounded at the sight of the lad dressed in his uniform just as the faintness swept over him and he fell forward to be caught in Tom's arms.

'Tom, are you all right?' Maureen said, coming up to them.

'I'm OK; he didn't touch me,' Tom said. 'It's Mr Ashley that's badly injured…' His eyes went over her. 'Are you all right, Maureen? I saw that devil run across the road, but I didn't realise what he was after until I heard the screams and shouts.'

'His eyes...' Maureen was pale as she saw Tom turn to Bob Hall and ask him for help in supporting Laurie Ashley, who was bleeding profusely. 'The look in his eyes... I think he was half crazy.'

'Are yer all right, mate?' Bob asked of Tom. 'You'd best bring Mr Ashley into my shop until the police and ambulance get 'ere. We don't want him frightenin' the ladies next door...' He jerked his head towards the pub, but he was too late. After asking Bob to call for the police, Anne had run into the pub and Peggy was coming towards them, her face white with shock.

'Bring him inside,' she said, looking anxiously at the blood seeping down his arm and on his hands. 'I'll try and stop the bleedin'.'

Just as Peggy spoke, they heard the sound of more police whistles and this time two burly police officers came charging up the lane. Everyone started to talk at once until one of them blew yet again. They asked a lot of questions, and then handcuffed Peter, who was just beginning to stir. By the time the constables got round to permitting Peggy's request to remove Laurie to the pub, an ambulance had pulled into the lane.

Laurie was now lying on a blanket on the ground with Peggy bending over him. She'd pressed a tea towel that someone had given her to the wound inside his coat, but it wasn't helping to stop the blood, because the knife had gone deep. It had fallen from Peter's grasp when Tom hit him and one of the policemen had now picked it up and wrapped a handkerchief round it.

Alice had brought the blanket out and was busy telling the police that she'd witnessed everything, from Peter Morris's attempt on Maureen's life to Laurie's gallant effort to stop him, and Tom's brave charge to the rescue.

'Regular 'ero, Tom were,' Alice said. 'He went fer the bugger like anythin'.'

Now the ambulance men took over. Laurie was tended to and placed on a stretcher before being carried into the ambulance.

'You go with 'im, Peggy,' Nellie said. She'd followed Peggy out, as had most of the pub's customers. 'We can manage for a while. Don't worry about anythin'.'

'I'll stay and 'elp Nellie,' Alice said. She looked at the police constables. 'You'd best come inside, officers. It's bloody freezin' out 'ere and we can tell yer just as good inside…'

One of them looked at her as if he was about to protest, but everyone had made a general move towards the pub, and a Black Maria had arrived. Three officers jumped out and Peter Morris was half carried, half shoved into the back before it drove off again, leaving the first two officers on the scene in charge of taking statements. All the lunchtime customers of The Pig & Whistle were gathered at the door watching and there was a babble of voices as they rushed to praise Laurie Ashley and Tom Barton for their courage and to decry Peter Morris for his wickedness.

'Bloody hero, Laurie Ashley was,' one of the customers said. 'And Tom – bloody good job, mate. He would've done for Ashley if yer 'adn't charged 'im from behind.'

'I tried blowin' the whistle a police officer gave me,' Tom told one of the constables. 'I hoped it would scare 'im off, but when it didn't I went for him, because he was tryin' to kill Mr Ashley…'

'It was lucky that Mr Ashley was walking down the street,' the constable said, 'and even more fortunate that you heard what was goin' on, Mr Barton.'

'I didn't see him go for Maureen, but I heard her scream and I grabbed the lump of wood I keep handy in case anyone tries to rob the till…'

'I see…' the officer scribbled busily. 'Fond of takin' the law in yer own hands, are yer?'

'No – but you need to be prepared in case the Germans invade,' Tom said, realising he'd been too frank.

'In the Army reserves, are yer?'

'Yes, I am,' Tom said proudly. 'I put me uniform on today because I'm goin' trainin' when I leave off work this evenin'.'

'Proud of it, I should think,' the other officer said. 'Leave it out, Bill. This young man is the hero of the day; don't be makin' him out to be a wrong'un. I know him well…'

'Right…' The constable turned his attention to Bob Hall. 'You raised the alarm, sir?'

'Yes, but my nephew's wife came and told me to ring the police. She was with Mrs Hart when she was attacked and ran to me for 'elp. As soon as I'd let your people know, I went out to see if I could do anythin', but Tom had already knocked the bugger down.' Bob hid his hammer behind his back, knowing that the police wouldn't take kindly to his choice of weapon.

The police officer was busy scribbling. 'We heard the rumpus and came as quick as we could, but you'd already done our work for us – as far as I'm concerned you should have a medal for this, Tom Barton. We need men like you on the force...'

'I'd be in the Army if they'd have me,' Tom said. He looked at Maureen, who was still very pale and sitting down, listening. 'Are you all right? You should have gone to the hospital too. You've had too many shocks lately. We don't want you losin' the baby...'

Maureen took a small glass of brandy that Janet had just brought her and sipped it. 'It was frightening – but I owe Laurie Ashley my life. I do hope he isn't badly hurt. We've had enough death round here...' Her hand was trembling.

'Yes – you discovered the body the night Mrs Tandy was murdered...' the constable said and his smile had gone. 'You reported that you saw a man come rushing out and that's why you investigated, and that man was the same one that attacked you just now. I think we all know why. He blamed you for bringing the law on him and wanted revenge. From what I've learned of the man he seems to be that sort...'

'Oh, Maureen... I'm so sorry...'

No one had noticed Ellie enter the pub, but now everyone turned to look at her. She was crying and looked terrible, her face white and streaked with tears.

'It isn't your fault, Ellie,' Maureen said. 'I know what Peter is like because Mabel told me – and he attacked me because he realised I'd seen him running from the scene of his crime.'

'But if I hadn't run away, Mabel would still be alive.'

'We don't know that,' Maureen said and deliberately let her gaze travel round the room. 'Peter was determined to hurt you and he might have killed you, your baby and Mabel if you'd been there.'

Janet went and put her arm round Ellie, drawing her to a chair. 'Sit down, Ellie, and I'll get you a drink.'

'No, just a cup of tea if you have one…'

'I'll get it,' Anne volunteered and went off to the kitchen.

'Who is lookin' after Beth?' Janet asked.

'Sid is with her. He didn't want me to come over, but I had to know – is Peter…'

'Tom knocked him out, but he's alive,' Maureen told her. 'He was seen to attack me and he has injured Mr Ashley. I don't think the police will let him go any time soon.'

'You can be sure of that, Mrs Morris,' the constable said. 'He'll be lucky to escape a hanging, if you ask me.'

Ellie accepted a cup of tea from Nellie's hands, her own shaking, but she only sipped it a couple of times. Tears were trickling down her cheeks and, after a few moments, Alice got up and took her back across the road.

'Well, I think that's all pretty clear,' the friendly police officer said and closed his notebook. 'We may need to take a further statement from some of you – but I think this is an open and shut case…'

'And so I should think,' one of the customers said. 'I saw it all through the window – and I'll testify if asked. Peggy Ashley is a good woman and she didn't need this worry.'

Several others added their voices to his and names were taken. At last the officers left and Janet realised it was long past the mid-afternoon closing, which all pubs were required to do; they would open again at six in the evening. She rang the bell and people started to leave, some standing outside in the lane to further discuss what had happened.

'I'd better get home or Gran will worry,' Maureen said and looked at Tom. 'Are you all right to carry on this afternoon? You didn't get hurt?'

'It's Laurie Ashley's blood,' Tom said and looked at Laurie's daughter. 'Sorry, Jan, but I held him up for a while... he was still breathin', that's all I can tell you.'

'He's in the hospital,' Jan said and sat down heavily. The shock had suddenly hit her and she felt sick. 'I just hope Mum is all right...'

Hearing a wail from upstairs, Nellie looked at her. 'That sounds like Fay. I'll go, love. You get straight here.'

'I'll help you tidy up, Jan,' Anne said. 'It's all been horrid...' She looked pale but shook her head as Janet told her to sit down. 'I'm all right. He didn't even know I was there. It was Maureen he wanted to kill...'

'Thank God you were in time to help Dad.' Janet looked gratefully at Tom. 'I can't thank you enough.'

'It's all right,' Tom said. 'I just saw what was goin' on and went for him. I hope they hang the bugger!'

'I think we all feel the same,' Janet said and smiled at him.

'I'll be in with your order later,' Tom said. 'I'm goin' to walk Maureen home and then I'll return to the shop. I just hope I can get this blood off me uniform or the reserves' officer will kill me.'

He went off with Maureen, grinning like a Cheshire cat, and Janet looked at Anne, and then smiled with relief. 'Thank goodness for Tom Barton,' she said. 'You are all right, Anne? You don't want the doctor?'

'No, I'm fine,' Anne said. 'Come on, Jan. Let's get this straight so your mum doesn't have a mess to come home to.'

'We've managed to stabilise him,' the hospital doctor said to Peggy when she got to her feet at his approach. She'd been sitting on a hard chair in the corridor of the London Hospital ever since they took her husband away. 'He is still unconscious and breathing with the help of some oxygen, but for the moment he is stable.'

'Oh, thank God,' Peggy said and felt her eyes wet with tears. 'I thought they might lose him on the way here – there was so much blood.'

'The knife went deep,' the doctor said gravely, 'and it just missed his vital organs but the trauma will be significant. However, we've done all we can and we have every hope that after a period of sedation he will improve. I suggest you go home to your family and return when he is awake.'

'Yes, of course, thank you,' she said. 'Everyone will be very worried…'

'Your husband acted heroically, Mrs Ashley. To try and stop a knife attack is dangerous and brave – you must be proud of him.'

'Yes, I am,' Peggy said and bit her lip, because her emotions were all over the place. She was upset and relieved that Laurie was not dead, and she was grateful to him for doing what he had to help Maureen – but it all contrived to make her feel guilty. 'He – he is a good man…'

'Yes, Mrs Ashley, he is,' the doctor smiled at her. 'Now, go home and get some rest. I understand you have young twins and they take a lot of looking after.'

Peggy thanked him and left. She hadn't realised how late it was until she left the hospital and saw it had grown dark. All she'd been able to think of was Laurie fighting for his life and it had torn her apart, because once she'd been a young and loving wife and they'd shared so much. Those things didn't just go away, even if there were quarrels later in life – and Laurie had acted so bravely, without a thought for his own safety.

Remembering that she'd wondered if he might try to harm the twins when he first came home, Peggy was ashamed. She'd allowed her judgement to be coloured by Rose's tales of her father's brutality. Laurie had helped her with the twins and he was trying to be a good husband… it was her duty to be a good wife.

Peggy lifted her head proudly as she waited for the bus to come. Laurie had proved who he really was deep down and she had to put her pride aside, she had to accept that they'd both hurt each other and get on with her life. When Laurie came home, she would let him see that she was prepared to be a proper wife to him again.

'Mum, you look so tired,' Janet said when her mother walked into the kitchen. 'Do you want something to eat – a drink?'

'I wouldn't mind a cup of tea, love,' Peggy said and smiled. 'A nurse brought me one at the hospital but it was awful, besides, I couldn't have swallowed more than a sip. I thought he was goin' to die – and I felt terrible.'

'Dad was very brave,' Janet said. 'Maureen would almost certainly have died and Anne might have been injured as well, if that madman had had a go at her too.'

'What happens to turn a man's mind like that?' Peggy was almost too exhausted to drink the tea that Janet gave her.

'Maybe it was something to do with the war,' Janet offered. 'Killing the way the soldiers have to must brutalise a man – and yet it doesn't change all men or doesn't seem to…'

'Perhaps Peter Morris was always that way…'

'Maureen says she's been told he may have been involved with an attempt to kill Sid Coleman the other night and she's convinced he murdered Mabel Tandy.'

'Is Maureen all right?' Peggy asked. 'I was so stunned by what had happened to Laurie that I don't think I asked her.'

'Yes, she managed to avoid his first attack and then Dad went for him from behind. Apparently, he put his arm round Peter's throat and forced him to turn on him. He tried to get the knife from him, but Peter is young and stronger. Dad would undoubtedly have been killed if Tom hadn't gone for him.'

'Tom was brave,' Peggy said with a shudder. 'He could've been killed too. Once a knife goes into vital organs, it causes a lot of trauma and often results in death. Even if Laurie gets over this, Jan, he may not recover fully…'

'Oh, Mum…' Tears trickled down Jan's cheeks. 'I know I quarrelled with him and I was cross with him for upsettin' you – but I don't want him to die…'

'Nor do I,' Peggy said and held out her hand to her. 'I don't think I could bear it if he died without our havin' made up properly. We fell out of love, Jan, but that doesn't mean I don't still care for him. I care for him as the man who gave me years of a good life and two beautiful children – you and Pip…' She lifted her head. 'We have to tell Pip. He ought to come home and see his father. They quarrelled last time they spoke and they need a chance to make it up.'

It was a long night and the next day seemed to drag. Peggy phoned the hospital first thing and was advised not to come in but to ring again later. Next, she rang the number Pip had given her and spoke to Sheila.

'Pip needs to come if he can get a pass,' she told the young woman her son was planning to marry. 'Can you get word to him, Sheila?'

'Yes, I shall go up to the airfield and ask to speak to him,' Sheila said. 'I'm really sorry this has happened – and I know Pip will be upset. He's been in a bit of a mood ever since we left London, and I know it's because he quarrelled with his father, even though he won't admit it.'

'He needs to see him and make his peace, because otherwise he'll never forgive himself,' Peggy said. 'Give him my love – and you too, Sheila. You're always welcome to visit us.'

'Thank you. I might come up with Pip,' Sheila said. 'I can probably get leave, because I'm due a few days and I haven't bothered because Pip has been flying almost constantly…'

Peggy finished talking to the girl she had begun to really like. Perhaps Pip was young to think of marriage, but the girl he'd chosen would make a good wife for him and she hoped he could make peace with his father. If Laurie came through this he would surely see the sense of being on good terms with his family.

Pip rang her that evening when she returned from the hospital. Laurie wasn't yet conscious and he still had an oxygen mask over his face, but they'd allowed her to sit with him for a while. Peggy held her husband's hand and told him she wanted him to get better and her tears wetted her cheeks. Never had she wanted Laurie to die and this was such a waste. He didn't deserve to die because he'd done something brave.

She told Pip that the doctors were still saying it was touch-and-go.

'You should come home if you can, love,' she said. 'Your father needs us all and he may know we're there even if he isn't fully conscious – that's what Sister said. Besides, I'd like you both here…'

'We're coming on the early train,' Pip told her. 'He's pretty strong, Mum. I think he'll pull through – if you saw some of the injuries the men get when they're shot down, and the soldiers… Well, he's in the right place anyway.'

'Yes, they're doin' all they can for him,' Peggy agreed. 'I know his attitude to your gettin' married made you angry and I think you'd like to make your peace with him.'

'He was the one that wouldn't listen,' Pip said, 'but I shan't hold a grudge. I'll see you in the morning.'

Peggy hung up, closing her eyes as she stood by the phone, her cheeks wet. Sometimes life hurt too bloody much. Pip was blaming himself and grieving because of the quarrel with his father but too proud to admit it – and he really would hate himself if Laurie died in the hospital without making his peace.

Chapter 25

'Well, the police say we can have the funeral for Mabel,' Maureen said to Ellie that afternoon, several days after Peter's attack on her. It was late April now and the weather was a little milder at last, though it had rained in the night, making the pavements dirty and greasy underfoot. 'Normally, I should ask Peggy to have a little do for Mabel at The Pig & Whistle, but with Laurie still in the critical ward I don't think I can do that – so I've decided I'll have a few friends back to mine now and then we'll have a memorial do for Mabel when things are settled…'

'Yes, that would be much better,' Ellie said. 'I'll help you with the baking if you like. Tom won't mind if I use his oven. I'll cook some fruit pies with tinned apples and plums, and make some fairy cakes – if that will do?'

'Yes, of course, and I'll do the sandwiches, biscuits and tea,' Maureen said. 'I'm happy to do what little I can, because she was my friend.'

'Who is payin' for the funeral – buryin' and that?' Ellie looked upset. 'I ought to because she was so good to me, and I've got a few pounds that Mabel gave me…'

'We've had a collection in the lanes and everyone was generous, because we all liked her,' Maureen said. 'If you could put in about five pounds that should do it, Ellie – but don't make yourself short, because Mabel must have some money herself somewhere…'

'I have five pounds,' Ellie said and went to her purse. She took the money out and gave it to Maureen. 'This was Mabel's. I didn't want to take it, but she insisted. I'm so glad you arranged it all. I don't think I could…'

'Mabel Tandy was my friend and neighbour for years,' Maureen said. 'As it happens, the lawyers contacted me. Mabel made me her executor years ago and she never changed that, although she did alter her will… but I haven't been told the details yet. I understand there will be a little money and, of course, the stock – though the shop was only rented; on a long lease, about a hundred and fifty years, she told me once. That's why her husband put in a bathroom for her; it was like their own house, and the landlord didn't mind what they did, because he's not interested in the property.'

'What will happen to it now?' Ellie gave a little shiver. 'I couldn't go there again…'

'I'm hoping the owner will let me take the lease over,' Maureen said, deciding to be frank. 'We need that shop in the lane, Ellie, even if I sell other things as well as the wool. Mabel asked me recently what she ought to do, because she was worried about trade, and I told her to expand her stock in whatever she could find – and that's what I'll do if I get it. I might take in good second-hand clothes for women and sell them on for the moment, but after the war I'll make it a complete baby shop with everything a mother could need for her child, including the cot and pram and all the rest...'

'That would bring more customers,' Ellie said and a half-smile flickered in her eyes. 'Mabel would be pleased if you took over the shop, Maureen – but how will you ever have time to do it all?'

'I'll find someone to run it for me,' Maureen said. 'I've got ideas, Ellie, but I can't do anythin' until after the funeral – and until the owner lets me take over the lease, if they will.'

'I don't understand these things, Maureen – but would the lease belong to whoever she left her things to?' Ellie asked.

'That's a question I can't answer,' Maureen said thoughtfully. 'I shall have to ask the lawyer. He's comin' to the funeral and to mine afterwards.'

'Well, I'll buy the stuff I need and make the things I promised for the tea,' Ellie said. 'I shall be at Mabel's funeral, Maureen, but then I'm going back to Sid's sister in the country. He promised to find me a place of my own somewhere as soon as he can and I might set up a little hairdressin' business if I can find a proper nursery to leave Beth at while I'm workin'. I think I could go to women's houses and do their hair for them at home. I might even be able to take Beth with me...' she drew a deep breath. 'I have to put the past behind me, forget about Peter and what he did – and I can't do that here where everyone knows.'

Maureen nodded sympathetically. Mrs Stimpson who owned the hairdresser's had taken over her customers for a short time, but now another young woman was starting work there and Ellie might not have a job if she stayed.

'I may have to give evidence at the trial,' Ellie said, 'but I'll come up when they tell me…'

'Yes, I expect they'll want me to go to court too,' Maureen agreed. 'I'm just glad both Tom and I learned to drive. It will make things easier – though it's his birthday soon and I think the Army will be after him.'

'You'll miss him…'

'Yes I shall,' Maureen agreed. 'You should learn to drive, Ellie.'

'Sid will teach me if I ask him,' Ellie said. 'He has this job he can't leave for as long as he's needed, but… he's asked me if I'll marry him once I get my divorce from Peter.'

Maureen looked at her steadily. 'Ellie, you do know that Peter may hang for what he's done?'

Ellie nodded, her face drained of colour. 'I know and I feel guilty, Maureen. If I hadn't had Beth…'

'I don't think you can blame yourself for what your husband did, Ellie,' Maureen said. 'Peter must have had a bad streak in him, don't you think?'

'I've been told he was into nasty things – but when I married him I thought he was wonderful. I keep thinkin' it was me that changed him.'

'I've been told that he was in with some bad types before the war from one of the constables who arrested him. He came to see me at home so that I could sign my statement and told me in confidence a lot of things about Peter and his friends, but you don't need me to tell you…'

Maureen stopped because Ellie was already feeling bad enough.

Ellie nodded. 'Sid heard the same and he told me a bit of it – but I think I'll always blame myself for what happened to Mabel.'

'You may feel better after the funeral,' Maureen comforted, because she didn't know what else to say. Ellie hadn't deserved all that had happened to her, and she wasn't to blame for Mabel's death. Had she not run away, Peter might have killed Ellie, her child and Mabel, because Mabel would not have stood by and let him get away with it. 'No one but Peter is to blame for his crimes, Ellie. In time you'll understand that.'

Ellie nodded, though she didn't look convinced. Maureen felt sorry for her, but she couldn't stay any longer. She had to call into the shop and see if Tom needed anything. It was his eighteenth birthday in a few days and Maureen was going to give him ten pounds and bake a cake for him. She knew he would get his call-up papers soon and she was going to miss him in the shop and as a friend, but Tom wanted to join the Army with all his heart. Maureen would find someone to take over the shop – until another of her little plans could be put into place. Gordon might never be fully able-bodied again, but he could serve in a shop and talk to the customers, and as he grew stronger they could find other things for him to do – but that was for the future.

Maureen had to talk to Tom, and then she must give Robin his lunch before leaving him with Gran so that she could visit Gordon at the hospital. She was always busy these days, even though she'd stopped helping out at the hospital for the time being. Ellie was right to wonder how Maureen would find the time to run two shops, but the lanes needed Mabel's shop to stay open, and Maureen was looking to the future. She had two children and another on the way, and she wanted to give them all good lives. Hopefully, she would be able to buy the lease and the stock, though she might have to borrow some money from the bank to get it all. Gordon didn't have a lot of savings, so he couldn't help, though he'd split the rent from his house between her and Shirley now, and Maureen had always been good at managing.

She could ask one of her friends if they wanted to share in the business. She wasn't sure that Peggy would have time to get involved, and she couldn't ask her at the moment, but Anne might – and Janet had spoken about a little job. It might suit her to serve customers in the shop… or perhaps she would advertise for someone new, if she got the lease.

Maureen refused to worry about her problems when others had so much more to be upset over. Peggy was fretting over Laurie and both Pip and Janet felt guilty because they'd quarrelled with him in the past. Maureen sighed. They'd all had so much to put up with since the start of the war and it never rained but it poured – another of Gran's favourite sayings. A little smile touched her mouth as she thought of her grandmother, who was as tough as old boots and seemed as if she would live forever.

★

'He looked so damned vulnerable,' Pip told his girlfriend when they left the hospital together that evening. 'I felt as if I wanted to shake him, to make him wake up and get mad at me again…'

Sheila nodded, and clung to his arm, offering what comfort she could. 'I know, love. He's your dad and he always will be, no matter what happens between you – but you mustn't despair. I talked to one of the doctors and he says the signs are good. Mr Ashley is coming out of a deep coma and he should wake soon. Then they will be able to tell what damage the trauma did to him… and, according to the doctor I spoke to, the signs are that he will recover.'

'Thank God!' Pip bent and kissed her on the lips. 'All I could think about was that I'd fallen out with him and if I died I couldn't ever tell him that I loved him.'

'He knows, of course he does,' Sheila said and smiled up at him. 'He loves you too, Pip – he couldn't do otherwise, because you're very loveable…'

'You're biased,' he said and aimed a kiss at her nose. 'I haven't bought you a present for our anniversary yet; we've been together for a year next week, properly together. What shall I get you?'

'I don't mind,' she said and looked up at him mischievously. 'Your mum told me what to buy for you as a present – but I've got some ideas of my own.'

'I think we should have a little party to celebrate our engagement – and Maggie's birthday was last month, and the twins had their birthdays not long ago,' Pip said. 'We should have a party. There's no point in us all sitting around in deep gloom – and I'll have to go in two days' time. I can't ask for more time off…'

'I'll stay on to help your mum for a while,' Sheila said. 'I've got a couple of weeks' holiday due and I'll take them now, so I'll be with her until we know how your father is so that she can visit him more. If you can get a pass, you can come up for a few hours, if not you can ring me.'

'Janet thinks it's a good idea to have a small celebration,' Peggy said when Pip broached the subject that evening as they ate dinner in the kitchen. 'She thinks it will cheer everyone up a bit – and after Mabel's funeral, we shall all need it… and it's good to celebrate your happiness, Pip. And it's Tom Barton's eighteenth birthday too. I've told Maureen I'll do something special for him. He deserves it…'

'Mrs Tandy's funeral is tomorrow, isn't it?' Pip said. 'I don't think I'll go, Mum, if you don't mind. I didn't know her well. I'll man the fort here with Sheila while you all go – if you want to?'

'Yes, I do, and so do Janet and Anne. Maureen is just having a little affair at hers, because she wouldn't ask me to have it here – but I think we'll make the party a memorial to her as well as a birthday celebration. That way it means something more… And you're right, it doesn't help Laurie if I just sit about being miserable.'

'Sheila is staying on until the end of her leave,' Pip told her. 'I have to go back the day after tomorrow, so I'll look after the pub until you get back from the funeral, and then I'll visit Dad – and then I'll go. I'll ring often, but I don't think I'll get more leave for a while, and that will only be a few hours, because I've had this extra time off…'

'I needed you here – and you, Sheila,' Peggy smiled at them both. 'Thank you for staying, Sheila. It will help me cope with visitin' and the twins.'

'I'm not the cook you are,' Sheila said, 'but I can help and I'd love to learn from you.'

'Pip says you make lovely bacon sandwiches,' Peggy said and reached for her hand. 'Thank you for everything. It is a comfort havin' both of you here.'

'I'm glad to be of help,' Sheila said. 'You know I'll do anything I can.'

Ellie was sitting on the front pew with Peggy, Maureen, Janet and Anne and Alice. Tom had closed the shop for an hour and sat in the row behind. Mabel didn't have any close relatives, although the church was filled with folk from all over the lanes. Her coffin had been brought in covered with lots of small posies of flowers, which people had sent in genuine sorrow for the loss of a popular woman.

Afterwards, the friends held hands by the open grave and wept openly for the woman they'd loved as their neighbour for years. When it was finally over, Sid came to fetch Ellie in his car and he took Maureen and Anne too. Peggy and Janet walked back, but they'd decided not to go to the wake, because they wanted to get home to the children. Sheila was looking after them, but if all three decided to play up at once it would be difficult for her.

Alice tagged along with them. 'I'll have a drink with you, Peggy. I don't feel like goin' to the wake much. Mabel was younger than me and it don't feel right. I could do wiv a port and lemon, tell yer the truth.'

'You'll come to our little party tomorrow,' Peggy said and smiled at her. 'It's for all the children and Pip and Sheila too, Tom Barton also has a special birthday – and I decided it would be a way to honour Mabel...'

'Are yer sure?' Alice said doubtfully. 'With yer man in the hospital...'

'It won't change things,' Peggy said. 'Pip thought it might cheer us all up and after some thought, I agree with him. What Laurie did was brave. We should celebrate that and pray he'll get better.'

'Yes, perhaps yer right,' Alice said and nodded. 'It's been a rotten few years in the lanes, Peggy girl...'

'Yes, it has. We've had our share of trouble,' Peggy agreed. 'I just hope things improve soon. The papers say things are turnin' our way, but I'm not sure the Germans know it – they don't seem to be givin' in, as far as I can see...'

'Some would say it couldn't get any worse,' Alice said. 'Everywhere yer go there are men in uniform and yer just know somethin' is in the air, though no one tells us what it is. Bloody hell, Peggy, I need that port and lemon or I'll be down in the dumps fer hours.'

'It's not like you to be so down,' Peggy said. 'Come on in, Alice, and I'll get you that...'

She walked into the bar followed by Janet and Alice. Pip was on the telephone, and Sheila was watching him, as were most of the customers. Clearly something important was being said. Peggy's heart started to race wildly. Was it bad news?

Pip turned to her and she could see that tears were running down his cheeks as he replaced the receiver. 'It's all right, Mum,' he said in a choked voice. 'That was the hospital. Dad woke up an hour ago and he's had something to drink. They say he's out of danger... but there are a few things they need to tell us. I said we'd both go along at two this afternoon...'

'Oh, thank God!' Peggy said and gave a little sob of relief. 'I was so afraid he was goin' to die.'

'Well, bless yer, Peggy love,' Alice said. 'I'm right glad yer 'usband 'as pulled through. That cheers me up proper...'

'I think it cheers us all up,' Janet said. 'Here you are, Alice – one port and lemon on the house.'

'Well, I'm glad you're both here,' the lawyer said to Maureen and Ellie when everyone had left after sharing tea and sandwiches at Gran's house. 'You two are the principal beneficiaries in my client's will. Until a few months ago, Mabel Tandy had left her entire estate to you, Mrs Hart. She altered it after Mrs Morris had the child in this respect:

> To Mrs Maureen Hart, the lease of my shop, in the hope that she will carry the business on after my death.

To Beth Morris, the sum of twenty pounds, to be held in trust for her until she is eighteen.

To Mrs Ellie Morris, one half of the value of my stock, the other half to go to Mrs Maureen Hart. Also any money left in my post office account after settlement of any debts is for Ellie with my love.

To little Beth, I leave my few bits of jewellery.

Everything else goes to Maureen, also with my fondest love. We have been friends for years, dear, and I hope you understand why I left part of my estate to Ellie. And if she needs a home, you might let her stay on for a while.'

'Of course I understand,' Maureen said and smiled as the lawyer read the personal message out. 'I'm glad Mabel left you something, Ellie, and I don't mind a bit. She told me once that I was her choice to carry on the shop if she died and that's why I made up my mind to it straight away…'

'Oh, Maureen, I don't deserve it,' Ellie said. 'It should all be yours…'

'No, Mabel wanted you to have half the stock and her post office account,' Maureen said and the lawyer nodded. 'I'm not sure what the stock is worth, but I'll pay you half as soon as it's settled.'

'I have a good idea of its value,' the lawyer said. 'I did Mrs Tandy's accounts and her last estimate was seventy-five pounds, so that would make Mrs Morris's share thirty-seven pounds and ten shillings... though you could have it valued if you wish, Mrs Hart...'

'No, I shall pay Ellie that sum straight away – or I'll give it to you and you can,' Maureen said. 'I do want to keep the stock, as I told you, and if the lease is mine free of charge I can afford it all.'

'Yes, and I'm happy to tell you that Mr Brock is content to continue the lease in accordance with the terms of Mrs Tandy's will,' the lawyer confirmed. He smiled at them. 'He may even be open to an offer for you to buy if you are able at some future date.' He paused, then, 'It has been a pleasure to be here today, Mrs Hart – Mrs Morris, I know how fond my client was of you both. She'd loved Maureen for years, so it shows how much she cared for Mrs Morris that she changed her will...'

He gathered his papers, went through to the kitchen to thank Gran for the tea and sandwiches and then left.

Ellie looked at Maureen uncertainly. 'It is a lot of money for me, Maureen, but I feel I shouldn't take it...'

'You must. If you want to start your own hairdressing business it will help – and Mabel would be so hurt if you refused.'

'You really don't mind? I didn't know what she'd done, honestly.'

'I really don't mind. I was prepared to buy the lease, and to take a loan from the bank to do it if I needed to, but now I shan't have to. I have enough saved to pay you, and I can still manage to pay my way without borrowin'. The lawyer knows where you'll be stayin' and he'll send the money on to you.'

'Well, if you're sure,' Ellie kissed her cheek. 'I'd better get back. Mavis was lookin' after Beth for me, but I mustn't take too much advantage of her good nature.'

'You get off,' Maureen said. 'Keep in touch, Ellie – and come and see us sometimes if you can.'

'I'll write and send postcards,' Ellie promised, but Maureen noticed that she didn't promise to return to the lanes. Somehow she didn't think that Ellie would ever come back to Mulberry Lane. She'd stayed for the funeral, but now she would leave and she would probably put them all out of her mind – perhaps for Ellie it was the only way to forget the unpleasantness of the past weeks and years.

Chapter 26

'All gone?' Gran said when Maureen went into the kitchen to find Shirley helping to wash up all the cups and plates. 'Did it turn out all right for you, love?'

'Mabel left me the lease and half the stock. She left the other half to Ellie and her money, and her little bits of jewellery to Beth. I think everything else is mine – the furniture upstairs and down, which saves the expense of furnishing the living quarters…'

'So you're definitely taking it on then?'

'Yes, I want to do it, Gran – for everyone's sake. Another empty shop in the lanes would just about finish us for trade. Besides, it's what Mabel wanted – and the money it earns will be for the children.'

'If you earn anything. Mabel was struggling.'

'Yes, I know – but I've got new ideas,' Maureen said and smiled at her. 'You'll see, Gran. I'll keep it ticking over until after the war and then I'll make it wonderful. It's a lot better a shop than Dad's ever was. I can do more with it – and I shall… especially if I can buy it one day.'

'Yes, I reckon you will, lass,' her grandmother said, looking pleased. 'Well, if you're prepared to take it on…'

Maureen nodded. 'I'm not sure how much Gordon will be able to do when he gets out of hospital, Gran. Tom wants to join the Army as soon as they'll take him, which can't be more than a few weeks now – and shop keeping might be a good job for a man who can't do hard physical work... and I'd make Gordon his own boss. He'll be in charge and the profits his...'

'Yes, I guessed that was your plan for yer dad's old shop,' Gran said. 'So Mabel's place is goin' to be yours – your independence, is that it?'

'Yes, I think so,' Maureen said.

'What if I offered you the money to buy the property?'

Maureen stared at her for a moment, but then shook her head. 'Gran you can't – and I couldn't accept. You've given me too much already.'

'The money is coming to you anyway...' Gran nodded. 'I don't need it, Maureen, and you would look after me if I did – so why don't you invest wisely for the future?'

'You're a generous woman, but I won't let you do it,' Maureen said. 'That money is yours to use as you see fit. I want you to spend more on nice things for yourself, enjoy life while you can...'

'Just as yer like, love,' Gran said. 'As long as yer content and well, I don't care what 'appens to it...'

Maureen kissed her. 'I'm going to ask Janet if she would like to do a few hours in the grocery shop. If she says no, I shall advertise for an assistant. I'm lookin' for a young woman, perhaps a widow who needs a job and a place to live for the wool shop...'

'You'll never have a minute to yourself,' Gran said and looked at Shirley. 'You've been such a good girl helpin' me, love. I'm goin' ter give yer a shillin' fer sweets – you can go and ask Tom at the shop and tell him I'll bring me coupons in tomorrow...'

Maureen frowned as Shirley took her coat and the money and left. 'Do you think she'll be all right in the lanes? It's dark already...'

'Shirley will be fine. Most folk around here are honest, Maureen. You used to come to me and then go home in the dark. I don't think anyone will harm her and she's a sensible girl.'

'Yes, she is. I suppose I worry over her too much.'

'Aye, yer do, but that's love. She's growin' up, Maureen, and she'll be a beauty – to my mind, you'll need to worry more in a few years' time than yer do now...'

Maureen laughed and nodded, because her gran was a wise old bird. Despite the violence that had shocked everyone of late, the lanes were usually peaceful and most people were friendly, meaning girls of Shirley's age could walk freely without harm. It was when she started courting that she would be more at risk, but that was years away yet.

Maureen went upstairs as she heard a whimper from Robin. He'd had his tea when the house was filled with Mabel's friends and been fussed over by everyone. She'd put him to bed when he showed signs of tiredness, but now he was awake and needed attention from his mother. For a moment Maureen knew doubt, because taking on this new shop would mean that she was busier than ever and perhaps her son might feel neglected at times, but then she dismissed the foolish thought. The shop was her children's inheritance, their future, and she was sure to find someone to run it for her. She just had to be careful to choose well.

Mabel would be missed, and so would Ellie, although Mrs Stimpson had already found a girl to take her place in the hairdressing shop. Maureen hadn't visited as a customer yet, but she'd seen Carla, the new hairdresser, going in and out of the place, looking very smart in a navy blue skirt and twinset with a red jacket.

People came to the lanes, some stayed and some left, some died and others were born, most left their mark. Life went on for all those that remained. Maureen would visit Gordon that evening and tell him about the funeral and what Mabel had left them. She knew he approved of her taking over the shop, but she hadn't yet suggested that he might like to run her father's shop when he was able. Gordon was a still long way from coming home and even longer from starting work. He could just about manage the length of the ward on the crutches they'd given him and he was determined to walk again and not be stuck in a wheelchair, even though the effort caused him pain and left him exhausted.

She was so lucky to have him back in London, Maureen thought as she went upstairs to sweep her son from his cot and wipe away his tears. He was wet and she changed his nappy, chasing away his sorry looks with kisses and tickles so that when she finally put him back down he was laughing at her.

For a moment she thought about Rory, Robin's blood father, and wondered whether he would make another attempt to see him. She hadn't heard a word from him since the day she'd let him see Robin and she hoped he would forget both her and his son. She thought the Army had sent him somewhere overseas, not to fight but to work at headquarters. Unless there was an accident, he would come through unscathed. All Maureen wanted was a quiet life with her family and she prayed Rory wouldn't interfere with that when he came back again.

Robin had started whimpering again, even though he was dry and comfortable. She hoped he wasn't going down with anything and felt his forehead, but it was cool, so he didn't have a temperature. Maybe he was just out of sorts. Perhaps he'd noticed she was reserved and thoughtful recently.

Maureen sat with him for a while, telling him a story until he dropped off to sleep and then she went down to the kitchen. Shirley was back and she'd bought a stick of barley sugar for herself and an ounce of soft jellies for Robin.

'He's fast asleep,' Maureen told her. 'He'll have them in the morning, darling.'

'Mummy,' Shirley said suddenly. 'Why did that awful man kill poor Mrs Tandy? I liked her. She used to give me a biscuit or a jam tart when I saw her in the lanes.'

Maureen took Shirley onto her lap. She was a big girl now but they still had a little cuddle sometimes and this was certainly the time for it. 'He was a very angry man. He wanted to know where his wife was I think, and Mabel wouldn't tell him, because she was afraid he would hurt Ellie – and so he hurt her. I'm not sure if he meant to kill her or if he just got too angry…'

'Some of the children at school say it was Ellie's fault for goin' with other men – was it, Mummy?'

'I don't think so. No one knows what makes someone do a wicked thing like that, Shirley love, but perhaps the war had something to do with it – and perhaps he felt jealous…'

'Perhaps he was just a bad man. That's what Tom said when I asked him,' Shirley said and sucked her barley sugar. 'I think I'll marry Tom when I'm old enough. He's nice and he says I'm his best girl…'

Maureen laughed and kissed her head. 'You'll have a lot of young men after you when you're old enough to go courtin',' she said. 'Have you done your school homework?'

'Yes, it was just a page of sums and didn't take any time at all,' Shirley said and Maureen smiled, because she knew her husband's daughter was a clever girl. 'If I don't marry Tom, I might be a teacher like Anne – or I might be a doctor.'

Maureen laughed and sent her up to bed with a kiss and permission to read for half an hour. Gran had put the kettle on and they settled down to a fresh cup of tea and a chat.

'Peggy is havin' a little do round hers tomorrow; it's for Maggie, the twins, Sheila, Pip, Tom's eighteenth, and Mabel in a way,' Gran said. 'I've got a gift for Tom and you can give it to him. You go to Peggy's, Maureen, and I'll look after the children.'

'I don't see why we shouldn't take them with us so we can both go for a short time,' Maureen said. 'I shall visit Gordon in the afternoon and I'm going to take them both with me. Sister says they can stay for a few minutes. Anne is coming with me, and when he's seen them, she'll take them down for a cup of milk in the café across the road...'

'She's hopin' her husband will be home for Easter; I expect they're both excited about the baby,' Gran said and nodded as Maureen got up to wash their cups. 'Well, I'm off to bed, love. Perhaps we can all look forward to a peaceful night... At least they seem to have stopped bombing us for a while, so we might get to sleep all night. Mind you, we've been lucky in the lanes this time.' In the mini Blitz of the last months, the Germans had mainly targeted factories and docks, unlike the real Blitz in 1940 to 1941, which had devastated the heart of old London.

'We'll never truly be at peace until the war ends,' Maureen said. 'I've got my husband home and he won't be fightin' again, but there are thousands of women who don't even know whether their men are even alive...'

'Let's hope this year will see the end of it. I did hear a rumour that there's talk of a new offensive from the Allies this summer, but there's all kinds of tales these days.' Gran sighed. 'Oh bother, I'm not goin' ter think about war. Let's have a good time with the kids at Peggy's little do and forget it all.'

*

'Well, that's wonderful news,' Maureen said the next day when Peggy told her that Laurie was sitting up in bed looking pale and sorry for himself, but over the worst. 'When will he be able to come home?'

'Not for a couple of weeks at least,' Peggy said. She frowned and glanced over her shoulder. 'I haven't said anything to Pip or Janet yet, but the doctors said they need to investigate his chest further. They've dealt with the damage inflicted by that knife, but it seems that Laurie may have a problem with his lungs. It seems they've discovered a shadow and he was coughing quite a bit before this happened...'

'Oh no!' Maureen stared at her in dismay. 'He hadn't said anything about it?'

'No, but he has been away for a long time,' Peggy said. 'He hasn't complained, though I did hear him coughing a lot at nights— What do you think it means?'

'I'm not sure,' Maureen replied thoughtfully. 'It could mean various things or it may be just a poor X-ray. I shouldn't worry too much until the doctors have done all their tests...'

'Do you think it could be lung disease?'

'It might – but, as I said, sometimes preliminary tests suggest all sorts of things. I'm not a doctor, Peggy. I still have another exam to take before I can call myself a proper nurse.'

'You knew enough to spot something was wrong with Freddie,' Peggy said. 'If the doctor hadn't sent him to hospital he might have died, because for a while they thought the hole in his heart might not close…'

'But it did and he's fine,' Maureen said. 'So stop worrying about Laurie until you hear what the doctors say when all the tests are done.'

'He was coughing in the bathroom the other day, but I hadn't taken much notice…' Peggy said. 'It couldn't be TB, could it?'

Maureen frowned. 'I don't think there's as much of that about as there used to be, but of course it is a possibility…'

'His uncle died of consumption, which some folk now call TB, years ago, just after the first war,' Peggy said. 'Laurie never seemed to show any sign of it though…'

'Well, just wait and see what the doctor says,' Maureen advised. 'We none of us know when something like that will happen, Peggy. There's no way you could have known… and nothin' you can do.'

'No, I know, but it's stupid,' Peggy said. 'I feel so protective of him all of a sudden – after what he did…'

'I'm alive because of it,' Maureen said. 'I shall visit him now he's over the worst and thank him, Peggy. He was so brave – and so was Tom.'

'Yes, thank goodness for Tom's quick thinking.' Peggy laughed and shook her head. 'I'm daft. I should be thanking God Laurie's alive, not worrying about things I don't understand.'

'Yes, we both worry too much,' Maureen said. 'When I first saw Gordon's leg, I thought he might never get over it, but they can do a lot of wonderful things these days with the new treatments.'

'Yes, I know,' Peggy agreed. 'Are you or your Gran comin' this evenin'?'

'We're both comin'. We're going to bring Shirley and Robin. They can go to bed later for once and that way we might get a few hours' sleep before they're awake and runnin' about…'

'Yes,' Peggy said. 'I want to show Tom how much we all appreciate him, make a fuss of him. Maggie will be there, of course, because it's partly her birthday party, but I don't think I shall let the twins stay up long once they've had something to eat. Fay can move fast these days and she would be in the coal bucket in no time…'

Maureen laughed. 'Why do young children love nibbling at coal? Robin grabs at it if he gets a chance, though I don't remember Shirley ever taking any notice – but of course she was older when I had her…'

'Ellie came to see me before she left,' Peggy said. 'She told me that Mabel had left her some money, but she said you were takin' over the shop – is that right?'

'Yes. Mabel left me the lease and half the stock, so I don't have to borrow for it,' Maureen said. 'I didn't say before because you had enough on your mind, Peggy. I was goin' to ask Janet if she would like a few hours in the shop – do you think it might appeal to her?'

'I'm not sure she knows what she wants to do,' Peggy said. 'She was determined she was goin' to find a place of her own, but she has decided to wait for a while…'

'Did she go out with Ryan the other evening as she'd planned?'

'Yes. At first she wanted to cancel it, because of what happened to Laurie – but then she agreed when Anne offered to help in the bar. I don't know what happened because she hasn't mentioned it... but she seems very thoughtful...'

'Well, I'd best get back to Gran and Robin, and Shirley is done with school for the weekend. We're goin' to visit Gordon this afternoon. Anne is comin' too so that she can have them for a while after they've seen their father...'

'I'll see you this evenin',' Peggy said, 'and I'll tell Jan you're goin' to take over the shop and you'd like her to do a few hours a week, if she wants...'

Maureen nodded and left. She was thoughtful as she walked home. It would be a bitter pill for Peggy and her family if the doctors discovered that Laurie had a serious illness. He'd escaped being knifed to death by a fraction, and if he was ill for a long time that would be a hard thing for Peggy to accept, but perhaps it was all a mistake. Maureen knew that sometimes X-rays were not quite what they seemed and they could be misread, which was why the doctors had chosen to do further tests.

Chapter 27

Janet looked at the beautiful diamond and sapphire ring Ryan had given her when he took her to dinner earlier that week. He'd proposed, as she'd known he would and she'd told him she would marry him but couldn't think of leaving her mother while her father was so ill. At least this time she was over twenty-one and did not need to ask her father's permission.

'Wait and ask me again in a few months,' she'd said, but Ryan had insisted that she take the ring.

'I can wait to get married, my darling,' he'd said and leant across to kiss her softly on the lips. 'I thought you might turn me down – but you've made me so happy. There's nothing to stop us being engaged, is there?'

Of course there wasn't and she'd acknowledged it.

'I couldn't leave Mum in the lurch at the moment,' Janet had said and touched his hand. 'I do care for you, Ryan – and I think I might be in love with you. I believe I always have been a little bit, but I had Mike... and I still love him. I always shall.'

'I'm not asking you to forget he ever existed,' Ryan said. 'Neither of us could ever forget our pasts – but we both deserve a future, don't we?'

'Yes, we do,' she said, 'and Maggie needs a father. She's very strong-willed and I need help controlling her sometimes. I do want to be your wife, but I can't marry you until Dad is sorted.'

Her father had still been unconscious when she'd told Ryan he must wait, but Janet hadn't changed her mind about rushing into marriage now that he appeared to be over the worst. She didn't want to lose Ryan, but if she admitted the truth to herself, she wasn't ready to marry him for a while. Her father's condition was an excuse she could use to hold him off, but she knew he would expect her to be wearing his ring when he came for the party that evening.

Janet stared at the wedding ring Mike had put on her finger. She was reluctant to take it off and yet perhaps it was time. For as long as she wore it, she was chained to the past and to regret. Taking a deep breath, she slid it over her finger and placed it on the bed beside her. It lay there reproaching her as she slipped on Ryan's expensive ring. The light made it sparkle and glow and she knew it was far better than her mother's engagement ring, more expensive than any other woman in the lanes wore.

She tore it off and replaced her wedding ring and then pushed the engagement ring on next to it. If Ryan asked why she was still wearing Mike's wedding ring she would tell him it wouldn't come off.

★

The party was a much quieter affair than the one Peggy used to hold at Christmas. She'd invited only her closest friends, most of whom lived in Mulberry Lane itself. Several children were there – Shirley and Robin, Maggie, the twins – also Tom, Rose, Anne, Alice, Maureen and her gran, and one or two others from the lanes, as well as Pip and Sheila, Janet and Ryan.

Ryan had taken charge of the older children and organised a board game for them, which kept them out of mischief, though not by any means quiet. Janet smiled as she watched him award sweets as prizes and thought what an excellent father he would be. She was glad that she'd agreed to become engaged to him, and though he noticed that she was still wearing her wedding ring with his diamonds, he hadn't said a word about it. Janet didn't think anyone had noticed, until Maureen caught her hand and looked at her.

'What a gorgeous ring,' she said. 'I don't think I've seen you wear this before?'

'No. Ryan gave it to me...' Janet said and blushed. 'We're sort of engaged, but we're not gettin' married for a while...'

'Congratulations, Jan. Ryan seems really nice,' Maureen said and nodded.

Janet laughed. 'I've been hopin' no one would notice, but that's daft... Yes, he's lovely, and I'm very lucky to have found love again – but I still feel it's too soon.'

'Mike loved you and you certainly loved him,' Maureen said. 'From what I knew of him, he wouldn't grudge you future happiness, Jan. You should take it while you can. The way things are at the moment, none of us knows what is goin' to happen or how long we have to be happy. Hitler could start another bombing offensive at any moment. I'm just so glad I married Gordon when I did, because if he'd been wounded before we married, he might have been too proud to ask me to share his life.'

Janet nodded, thoughtful, because what Maureen said was right, but she moved off with her tray of used glasses. It was good that Maureen approved, but she was still reluctant to take the plunge. A few more months wouldn't hurt anyone.

'I'm so happy for Jan,' Maureen said as she went to say goodnight to Peggy later that evening. 'I know she wants to wait a bit for the weddin', but I'm glad that she has started to move on.'

'Yes, I suppose so – if she has…' Peggy sighed. 'She should be bubbling over for joy – but she's still wearin' Mike's weddin' ring. When she takes that off, I'll know she's really ready to move on.'

Maureen kissed her cheek. 'Don't worry too much, Peggy love.'

'Are you goin' this early?'

'We have to put the children to bed,' Maureen said. 'Otherwise they'll be too tired in the morning. I'll see you tomorrow before I go into the hospital…'

'Yes,' Peggy kissed her cheek. 'I'll be visitin' Laurie as much as I can while Sheila is here to help look after the twins. Pip has to leave first thing in the morning, but she's stayin' on for a while.'

'She's a lovely girl,' Maureen said. 'I'm glad you get on with her, Peggy, because I can see that Pip is mad about her and she loves him.'

'Yes, he is and I'm happy for them both. I don't understand why Laurie didn't see it. I can only hope he will once he comes out of hospital...' Peggy looked at her. 'You're not too tired, are you? You ought to rest as much as you can, because you've only got a couple of months to go and you look a bit weary – are you happy about the baby, Maureen? I mean, I know it's difficult with Gordon ill...'

'I feel excited when I think about what is happening,' Maureen said and placed her hands on her swelling belly. 'I hope so much that it's another boy, for my husband's sake. He's wonderful with Robin, but every man wants his own son. If Gordon can come home by the summer, I'll have all I want...'

'That's good.' Peggy smiled at her and gave her a brief hug. 'Take care of yourself and your family, Maureen. Love is so very precious and it's only when we lose it that we realise how much it means...'

'I'm sure things will work out for you and Laurie,' Maureen said. 'I know you loved Able and you fell out with Laurie – but you have another chance...'

'Yes, perhaps,' Peggy agreed. 'I don't want Laurie to die, Maureen. That much remains of what we once had, but I'm not sure what else there is left... Of course I couldn't let him down while he's ill...'

Maureen nodded, understanding that she couldn't solve Peggy's problems with platitudes or friendship. Peggy had to face whatever the future held, as they all did.

Taking Robin in her arms and calling to Shirley to join her, she and Gran went out into the dark night; there were no stars and the blackout was still in force, making it hard to find your way even with a shaded torch. Maureen felt content as she led her family safely through the streets and ushered them into their warm kitchen.

'Well, I thought Peggy looked a bit down,' Gran said as she set about making a jug of hot cocoa for them all. 'Worrying about her husband, I expect...'

'Yes, I expect so,' Maureen said. 'Gordon loved seeing the kids this afternoon – and I'll pop in again tomorrow on my own. Sheila is there for Peggy at the moment, so she'll be able to visit Laurie every day. She's a nice girl and just right for Pip I think...'

'Janet has found herself a good one too,' Gran observed and poured the cocoa into mugs, distributing them to Shirley and Robin and putting Maureen's on the table. 'I saw that ring she was wearing – it must be worth a fortune...'

'Yes, but money doesn't buy happiness,' Maureen said.

'You tell that to some of the women in the lanes,' Gran said robustly. 'There's a good few as could do with a few pounds to keep the wolves away...'

'We all need enough money for food and to pay the rent,' Maureen said. 'But I wish I thought Jan was really happy – I hope she hasn't said yes just because she thinks

Maggie needs a father or she's afraid it might be her only chance…'

'I dare say she knows what she's doin',' Gran said and smiled at the two sleepy children. 'It's up to bed with you pair or I'll take my slipper to you.'

Shirley giggled, but Robin looked at her wide-eyed, only half understanding what she was saying. He made no protests as his mother picked him up, carrying him upstairs to his cot. She kissed him goodnight as Shirley hovered, watching.

'Now you too, love,' Maureen said as she turned the light off in Robin's room, leaving only a faint night light burning. 'You'll be too tired in the morning for your homework and you've got a test next week…'

'It was lovely seein' Dad,' Shirley said happily as she skipped ahead of Maureen into her bedroom. 'Will he be home soon, Mummy?'

'Not quite yet, darling,' Maureen said as she unbuttoned the pretty dress Shirley had been wearing for the party. 'But he is gettin' much better and I think we shall have him home in two or three months. I know that seems ages away, but we must be happy he's comin' home.'

Shirley nodded solemnly. 'My friend Carol's daddy isn't coming home. She said her mum told her there was no God and it's her birthday next week, but she's not havin' any presents at all, because her mum can't afford to buy her anythin'.'

'Oh, I'm sorry,' Maureen said and put her arms about her as tears pricked her eyes. 'Do you know where Carol and her mummy live?'

'Yes, of course,' Shirley said. 'Can I take her something – one of the lovely dresses you make for me? She doesn't have a best dress…'

'We'll take a cake and visit them,' Maureen said. 'If her mummy is pleased with the cake, I'll make Carol a new dress – and perhaps I can help her mum somehow. I promise I will if I can – but people are proud, Shirley, and they don't like it if they think they're being patronised or offered charity, so we have to be careful…'

Maureen was proud of her daughter. Shirley would be eleven on her birthday, but sometimes she seemed older and wiser than other girls of her age.

Shirley nodded. 'I share my sweets with Carol sometimes, but her mum gets cross and tells her not to take them because she can't give anything back.'

'That is very sad,' Maureen said and hugged her. 'Let's see what we can do for your friend, Shirley. We are very lucky in this family, and we must see what we can do to help Carol and her mum.'

'You're the best mummy in the world,' Shirley said and hugged her. She ran to get in bed, pulling the covers up near her throat. 'I love you, Mummy.'

'And I love you, darling.' She tucked Shirley into bed and kissed her. 'Don't worry, my love. I'll think of something to help them…'

'I know, because you're so clever…'

Maureen laughed and went out. Her little girl was growing up and she was glad to see that she cared for others. Maureen had heard that Vera Brooks, Carol's mother, had lost her husband to the war and she'd been meaning to go round. Before she was married, Vera had worked on the counters at Woolworths, which meant she was used to shop work. If Mrs Brooks was interested, she could offer her a job and perhaps a new home over the wool shop.

She would have to be careful how she put her suggestion to the grieving widow, because Vera was proud and would hate to be offered charity, but a job was something that would enable her to hold her head up – and Maureen was genuinely in need of at least one full-time assistant.

'What do you think Mabel?' she asked softly, and her throat closed with emotion as she thought of the woman she'd known as her neighbour all her life and loved as a friend. It still hurt badly that Peter Morris had so wantonly taken Mabel's life, but Maureen felt she was doing something worthwhile by keeping the shop going for the residents. 'Will she fit do you think?'

In her mind she could see Mabel nodding and smiling. She'd been a kind woman and she would have wanted to help another widow if she could.

Chapter 28

Peggy finished clearing the dirty dishes into the kitchen and sighed. Nellie had helped with washing-up earlier, so there wasn't that much to do and she was going to leave it for the morning.

'It was a good party. Do you want me to wash the glasses now?' Janet asked, entering the kitchen with some leftover food.

'No, I think we'll leave them for the morning,' Peggy said. 'Nellie and Sheila washed most of them and these won't take long tomorrow. Have you sorted out Maggie's things for her nursery school?'

'Yes, days ago,' Janet said and came to put her arms around her. 'Ryan gave me a huge present for her. I think it's a doll's house… but I'm half afraid to give it to her. She had lots of presents for her birthday and she's being spoiled.'

'Where on earth would he get somethin' like that?' Peggy asked and shook her head in wonder. 'He's goin' to spoil you both, you know.'

'Yes, if I let him,' Janet said and sighed. 'I hope you don't mind he insisted on givin' me this now?' She looked at her ring. 'I mean with Dad still in hospital and all…'

'Your father will be pleased,' Peggy said. 'He will look after you; give you a nice house and clothes – and more children. And he's the father Maggie needs.'

'Yes, but does it seem too soon…?' Janet looked anxious and uncertain. 'I don't want anyone to think I'm uncaring…'

'If you're happy, nothin' else matters,' Peggy said. 'I think you do love him – or you will once you stop feelin' guilty that you're alive and Mike isn't…'

'Mum!' Janet looked at her as if she'd struck her.

'Well, it's true, isn't it?' Peggy gave her a straight look. 'You're my daughter, Jan, and I know you. Mike is dead and you stuck by him when a lot of girls would've said enough was enough. Now you can start to live again and to be happy. And that makes me happy…'

'What about you, though?' Janet said. 'Maureen has everything she wants, or she will have when Gordon gets home. Anne is over the moon with the thought of her new baby later in the year. Pip and Sheila are happy. Ellie has gone off to a new life in the country and Rose is engaged to Jimmy… but what about *you*?'

'What about me? I'm all right. I've got you, Maggie and Pip and the twins, and I'm happy for my friends… what more do I need?'

'Something just for you,' Jan said. 'I know Dad wants to make things work between you – but is that what you really want?'

Peggy met her questing look. 'To be honest, I'm damned if I know, Jan. I know what I'll do and that is to carry on the same as usual – but what I want…' She shook her head.

'Is it still Able?' Janet asked, putting her arms about her. 'I know you really loved him, Mum. I just wish he'd walked in this evenin'...'

'Oh, Jan...' Peggy gave a little sob. 'It was so simple once. I was angry with Laurie and I would've left him if Able had come back even a few months ago, but now... I'm not sure if I could leave Laurie even if Able did come back, not after what he did...'

'Dad was so brave, and I know what you mean. I went to see him at the hospital to tell him I loved him and I couldn't stop cryin' when he apologised to me for refusin' Mike when he asked if we could get married, and for hittin' him when we told him I was pregnant... Pip has made it up with him too...'

'Let's go to bed, love,' Peggy said, her eyes stinging because it was suddenly all too much. 'We'll talk tomorrow...'

She followed her daughter into the hall, but went into the bar just to make sure everything was as it should be. Her gaze went round the room. She'd locked the door earlier, so there was no need to try it... But something was lying on the floor just inside the door. A white envelope – big, like a birthday card. Someone must have dropped it on his or her way out. She walked over to pick it up, turned it and saw her own name written in a bold script she knew instantly.

Able had written this card! Peggy knew it instinctively, even as she tore it open to find a pretty card with roses on the front. There was no verse inside, just an inscription:

To my beautiful Peggy with all my heart.

Yours forever, hon. Love you, Able – and I'm glad you're happy...

Peggy went cold all over and her heart stood still. She looked at the envelope quickly but there was no postmark. The card had been hand-delivered – Able was alive! He was alive and he'd been in the lane this evening... only moments ago, because this hadn't been here when she'd locked up.

Peggy fumbled with the locks, throwing the door open and rushing into the lane, his name on her lips. The unlit street lamps gave her no light, but the moon sailed out obligingly from behind a bank of dark clouds to show her that the lane held no shadowy figures waiting for her to appear. If Able had delivered her card himself, he hadn't stopped to see what she did about it.

She stared each way, willing him to appear, but there was nothing, no movement, and she went in again and relocked the door, trembling and feeling sick with shock.

Able was alive! Why had no one told her before? Why had there been no letters, no word from anyone?

Making her way upstairs, Peggy entered her room and sat on the bed. Silent tears were dripping down her cheeks. She looked at the card again and then held it to her breast as she let the sensations flood through her – sheer joy that he was alive, disbelief that no one had told her, bewilderment that it could have happened like this and faint hope.

But there was no address on the card. There was no way she could contact Able...

Even if Able was alive, it didn't mean he still wanted to be with her. He'd said that he loved her and he was glad she was happy... but she wasn't; she wasn't happy and never could be without him.

'Able...' she whispered as she lay down on her bed and turned on her side, curling her knees to her chest as she held the card to her and wept. 'Oh Able, why didn't you come in, my love – why haven't you written to me or been to see me?'

Why had there been no communication of any kind? Was this a malicious joke? Yet she knew that bold scrawl. It was on the notes and letters Able had sent her while they were together.

If he loved her, why hadn't he come in to speak to her? How long was he in the country for? Would he come to see her another day when there weren't so many people around?

Peggy's thoughts were whirling round and round in her head as she tried to make sense of it all. Could she let herself believe that Able had come back from the dead? Should she? How was it possible? Yet she knew that in war and with the Atlantic between them letters could go astray, though he could have phoned... but... The questions followed thick and fast. There was no denying this card and there might have been others... letters that went astray.

Peggy curled up like a ball, hugging herself and thinking long into the night. Even if Able was alive, even if he still loved her and wanted her – how could she leave

Laurie now? With the shadow of a terrible illness perhaps hanging over him and everyone praising him to the skies for his bravery in saving Maureen from a knife attack – how could Peggy ever turn her back on her husband now?

The truth hit her like a bolt of lightning. She was trapped, because her own sense of what was right and wrong wouldn't let her desert Laurie if he needed her. His act of bravery apart, he was her lawful husband and it looked as if he was going to be ill for some time; he would need care and love if he was to get through what could be a terrible ordeal.

Maureen had pretended that she didn't know what was wrong with him, but Peggy had a good memory. She'd lived in the East End of London all her life and she'd known plenty of people with consumption. TB was a killer still. If Laurie had that it would be awful for him, even though they could do more for patients now than they had when his uncle died.

Peggy got up and went to the bathroom to wash her face. She looked at herself in the mirror and faced the truth. Once upon a time she'd loved Laurie so much that she'd thought her love would last a lifetime. Now all she felt was a pale shadow of that love, but it was still there – and it would make it impossible to leave him while he needed her.

Even if Able came to her and asked her if she would go away with him, Peggy knew she couldn't. Her life was here at The Pig & Whistle, taking care of Laurie and the pub, and her children – all of them.

'I loved you, Able,' she whispered to the night as she looked out of the landing window at the empty lane. 'I still love you and I think I always shall – but it's too late.'

Chapter 29

'Shirley said it was Carol's birthday tomorrow,' Maureen said as she offered the sponge cake she'd filled with jam and butter cream. She was standing outside a terraced house with peeling paint on the door and the window frames, and the street looked far worse than any of the lanes around Maureen's home, though the nets were clean in most houses in the street. 'I made this for her because she's such a good friend to Shirley.'

Vera Brooks looked at her but she didn't smile. She hesitated as if she was on the verge of shutting the door in Maureen's face, but then she relented and stood back to invite her in. The first thing Maureen noticed was that the kitchen was spotlessly clean, even though everything in it was old and shabby, the bright yellow cloth on the table had been neatly mended, but it was clean, as were the nets at the windows.

'It's very good of you, Mrs Hart. I know Carol gets on well with your Shirley at school...'

'Please, call me Maureen. I hope you will all enjoy the cake...' She saw the little girl in the playpen. Carol's younger sister was clean, but her dress was clearly old and much washed. It was quite obvious that Vera could hardly put food on the table, let alone buy new clothes for her children. 'I wondered... if I could possibly ask you a favour?'

'Me – do you a favour?' Vera looked at her in disbelief. 'I'm sure you don't need my help, Mrs Hart...'

'Oh, but I do. I really do,' Maureen said and sat down at the pine table, even though she hadn't been invited. 'I need someone to serve in the wool shop. I expect you heard what happened to Mabel Tandy?'

'Yes, of course,' Vera Brooks said. 'That was a wicked thing...' She hesitated, then, 'Would you like a cup of tea?'

'Yes, that would be lovely.' Maureen ventured a smile as the other woman filled a kettle and put it on the range to heat. 'Mabel was a good friend, Vera. I knew her when I wasn't much bigger than your little one. She used to knit me cardigans and give me one of her tarts when I went round to visit, and I miss her very much.'

'Well, of course...' Vera looked at her, clearly curious now. 'Are you really goin' to keep the shop open?'

'Yes, I hope to. I shall sell wool and used baby clothes, as Mabel did, and perhaps take in good-quality women's clothing to resell – on a sale or return basis with commission for the shop. After the war I want to make it a proper baby shop. I'd like to sell cots and layettes and even pushchairs and less expensive prams – the sort that most mothers in the lanes can afford.'

'What a wonderful idea,' Vera said and for the first time there was a flicker of a smile in her eyes. 'But why have you asked me to serve in the shop? There are plenty of young women who would be much better at it than I should...'

'I don't think so,' Maureen said and looked her in the eyes. 'Most of them earn more than I could offer at the factories – but I was hoping that you might live over the shop and accept the living quarters as a part of your wage. I could pay thirty shillings a week plus the flat...'

'Thirty shillings and the flat...' Vera looked at her in disbelief and then a little sob escaped her. 'I pay fifteen shillings for this wretched place. I've been so worried... My landlord told me that if I was late with the rent again he would throw me out...' A tear rolled down her cheek, but she brushed it away impatiently. 'My sister-in-law would have Milly for a few hours during the morning, but she works in the afternoons...' Her eyes narrowed in suspicion. 'Did Carol tell Shirley that I'd been lookin' for work?'

'No, she told Shirley she didn't think she would have a present for her birthday, but nothing more.' Maureen's gaze was steady and open. 'I'm not offerin' you charity, Vera. I do need someone to look after the shop. I know you have children, but we could make it work, I'm sure we could. The little girl could be with you most of the time, and there's a playpen you can have. And I would prefer someone like yourself rather than a young girl who might leave at a moment's notice... Besides, not everyone would be prepared to live and work there after what happened...'

'Because Mabel was murdered?' Vera looked thoughtful for a moment, then, 'I'm not frightened of ghosts, Maureen.

Besides, I knew Mabel and liked her. She wouldn't harm anyone, alive or dead. I used to go there when I had the money to buy wool for knitting. Sometimes, I just went for a chat and a cup of tea.'

'So will you at least think about accepting my offer?'

'No, I shan't think about it,' Vera said and Maureen was sharply disappointed, but then she laughed as Vera stood up and came round the table to offer her hand. 'I'll take it and I'd like to move in as soon as possible please…'

'I'm so pleased!' Maureen cried, surprised and delighted at how quickly Vera had decided. 'I'm sure one of our neighbours would have Milly for a few hours in the afternoons if you wanted, Alice or Mavis are always ready to oblige – but I don't mind if she stays with you in the shop. She can have her playpen just as Beth used to… as long as you're sure.'

'Yes, I'd like to give notice here this week and move in next,' Vera said. 'If I could meet you there one day – not tomorrow, because that's Carol's birthday and now I'll be able to get her a little something. I've been terrified of spending what little I have, because my Roger's pension from the Army isn't much and I had to fight to get it. I keep thinkin' they might take it away again… because I can't prove we was married. The registry office where we took our vows was bombed during the Blitz and I couldn't find me lines, so they said I wasn't entitled…'

'That's so unfair,' Maureen said. 'Did you find the marriage certificate in the end?'

'No, I think it got lost when we was bombed ourselves. I had to swear on oath I was Roger's wife and me sister-in-law had to swear that she was a witness and even then they grudged it to me...'

'As if it was your fault it got lost,' Maureen said. 'So many people have lost documents, photographs and sometimes all they owned in this wretched war. The authorities should make it easier for us rather than trying to put obstacles in the way.'

'Well, that's what I said, but I had to argue for months before they would let us take the oath and then what they gave me was hardly worth havin'. I tried goin' to work, scrubbin floors, but Milly took sick and I couldn't leave her. She has only just got over it...'

'I'm sorry you've had such a bad experience,' Maureen said. 'We all have enough troubles without having to jump through hoops for some petty little Hitler in an office.'

Vera nodded emphatically, her mouth grim. 'I'm not the only one who's had trouble,' she said, 'but now it looks as if my luck has turned.'

'I think it will be good for both of us,' Maureen said. 'Once the war is over and I can build up the shop, I'll make you my manageress on more money, and take on an assistant.'

'Well, we have to get it up and runnin' again,' Vera said practically. 'There may be some women who won't feel like shopping with us because of what happened to Mabel – but that shouldn't last long.'

'I think once people see that you're prepared to live there they'll realise it's foolish to feel uncomfortable – and lots of women have wool put by, which I think they will want to buy. It isn't easy to match the colour if you don't buy from the same batch. Once the ice is broken they'll come back again and again.'

'I've been caught that way with matchin' wool shades more than once,' Vera agreed. 'Now, I think I'd better make that tea, Maureen and talk some more about the future.'

'I think that was lovely of you, Maureen,' Peggy said when she told her that Vera Brooks was going to run the wool shop. 'I saw her in the market one day and she looked tired to death. Her husband used to drink here before the war and he brought Vera in sometimes for her birthday or Christmas. I felt sorry for her when I heard he'd been killed, not long after it started – and her with two young children and another on the way. She lost her baby...'

'I didn't know that,' Maureen said and put protective hands to her stomach. 'I wanted a woman I could trust not to run off five minutes after she takes the job, and I think Vera is just what I need. Young girls come and go – but she will need a few hours off on Saturdays and perhaps some afternoons...'

'I think Janet would do a few hours,' Peggy said.

'It would be a help until I get over havin' the baby,' Maureen said. 'Gran says I'm takin' on too much, but I've always liked Mabel's shop and I think we need it in the lanes. And I'll be losing Tom to the Army soon... I'll need a full-time assistant there for a while.'

'Why don't you ask Rose?' Peggy said. 'She hates the factory – she told me so this mornin'. I think she might take on a few hours in either shop...'

'I'll speak to her then,' Maureen said. 'I'm not sure if they will let her leave essential war work altogether, but they might let her do part-time...'

'She told me they are slowin' down production where she works,' Peggy said. 'She was one of the last in, so they may be glad to let her go – and she can always do some volunteer work at night...'

'Yes, I've had to give up for the moment, but the WVS are always glad of new helpers...'

'You do far too much.' Peggy said. 'I'm in agreement with your gran there – but I'm glad you're keepin' the wool shop open. If we let all the shops go we'd be a ghost ship.'

'It's a pity someone doesn't open the old bakery,' Maureen remarked. 'Not as a bakery, but as a shop of some kind – I'd like to see it thriving again.'

'Well, you never know,' Peggy said, 'perhaps someone will find a use for it one day.' She'd thought of it herself, even gone as far as looking through the back windows, but now her thoughts were confused and uncertain. If Laurie had consumption she couldn't desert the pub while he needed her – and if Able was really alive, perhaps he would come back one day, and perhaps next time he would come to see her.

It was on the tip of her tongue to tell Maureen about the card she'd received on the night of the party and yet something held her silent. Why hadn't he come to see her – and why hadn't he written to her before this? She decided to keep her news to herself for the moment.

Peggy could accept that he might have been wounded and ill for a long time, but surely he could have got a message to her? She wasn't sure what that card meant – was it just a sentimental card without substance behind it – and what did Able mean by saying he was glad she was happy? Who had told him that? No one had mentioned seeing him and Reg hadn't brought her any letters from America.

Perhaps she would ask him next time he called.

'Reg, I'm expecting a letter from America,' Peggy said when her cheerful postman brought a pile of letters the next morning. 'I don't suppose there's one today, is there?'

'Not today, Peggy,' Reg said and grinned at her. 'Good news was it the other time? Laurie said he'd pass it on – how is he by the way?'

Peggy went cold all over. She had to dig her nails into the palms of her hands to stop herself demanding to know when he'd given her letter to Laurie. Yet she couldn't betray herself or him, because she knew Reg couldn't resist passing on gossip if she revealed that her husband had kept her letter.

'I think he's recovering well,' she said. 'He bled a lot, but the knife didn't go in as deep as it might have...'

'Well, give him my best wishes,' Reg said. 'I'll look out for that letter for you, Peggy. Bring you some veg from the allotment once I can get on it – been too wet these past few days, but there's new greens comin' up...' He grinned at her. 'Summer is just round the corner. This bloody war has to end soon, love.'

Peggy thanked him and he went on his way whistling. For a moment she was too angry to move, because she knew that Laurie had kept an important letter from her. Had he read it – or had he simply destroyed it?

Feeling the fury build inside her, Peggy went upstairs and into the bedroom her husband was using. She started by searching the chest beside the bed, but there were only underclothes, his jumpers and shirts and a driving licence in the drawers. Next, she went through every jacket and every pair of trousers in the wardrobe, but there was no sign of anything resembling a letter – just a used train ticket and a receipt for some sandwiches at the railway station.

She was about to leave empty-handed when she saw the suitcase on top of the wardrobe and went over to pull it down. She opened it and discovered it had several papers that her husband had clearly been working on. At first she thought they were the solutions to a crossword and then realised that they must be codes – secret codes. Was that what Laurie had been doing in Scotland? Surely, he ought not to leave them in a suitcase where anyone could find them? Peggy thought they ought to be burned but put them to one side as she made a thorough search of the suitcase. She found the envelope in a side pocket and drew it out with trembling fingers. It was of the same thin paper used for mail sent from abroad and it was clearly addressed to her.

She drew the sheet of paper out and read the message inside.

Dear Mrs Ashley,

Able has asked me to write to you, because just at this moment he isn't well enough to do it for himself. He is most anxious that you should know he is still alive and to explain that he was ill for a very long time and in a Swiss hospital where few people spoke a language he understood. He couldn't leave his bed and was too ill to think properly. It is only now that he has been transferred to America that he is in a position to think about contacting you.

Able hopes to be out of hospital in a few months and if he is well enough, he will come to London to see you. In the meantime he sends his love and hopes that you are well. He asked me to write this because he believes that you would wish to know he is alive.

Able's true friend, Captain Roy Barclay.

'Oh, Able…' Peggy's eyes stung with tears, because the letter had not been written by her lover but by a friend, which meant at the time it was written he'd been very ill. 'My love…'

She looked at the date at the top of the letter – it had been written in the summer of 1943 but it couldn't have been delivered for months afterwards, because Laurie hadn't come back to London until January 1944. Like so many other letters from overseas, it had been mislaid somewhere and delivered months late. It happened all the time with mail from serving soldiers, but it was just bad luck that it had been delayed all that time and then fallen into Laurie's hands.

How could he keep it from her? Peggy was angry that he'd opened her letter, read it and then hidden it from her. If it hadn't been for the card, she would never have asked Reg, never have known what Laurie had done.

The letter itself was impersonal, but it meant too much to Peggy to know that Able was alive after all this time. She'd never given up hoping for it, she'd believed it was a forlorn hope but now...

What must Able think when she hadn't replied? He must believe she didn't care – that she was back with her husband and happy. It was what he'd put in the card he'd pushed through her door. It could only be that someone had told him she was back with Laurie... he might even believe that the twins belonged to her husband. Why wouldn't he? Everyone else did... and she hadn't written to him about them before he went missing, preferring to tell him in person.

No wonder he hadn't come in, Peggy thought. He'd just let her know he was back in London and that he loved her. Able thought she was happy, but she wasn't. She loved him and she wanted to be with him... Laurie had forfeited all call on her loyalty after what he'd done. Peggy would have forgiven a lot of things but not this – it was so cruel not to let her know that Able was alive. If he'd just told her, she would have seen him through his time of trouble but now she was so angry she could explode.

Peggy put her husband's papers back in the case and returned it to the top of the wardrobe. She took the letter with her as she left the room. She must let Able know that the twins were his and that she loved him.

The address given in the letter from Able's friend was a hospital in Virginia. Peggy vaguely recalled that Able had once told her he had property there. It was too late to write to the hospital after all this time, because she believed Able must be here in London – and yet it was her only way of contacting him.

No, there was a box under her bed! Peggy had forgotten it because she'd left it untouched, not wanting to pry into Able's private life. Now, she decided that she would open it and look for something, anything that would help her make contact with him. Able should know that the twins were his… even though she felt conflicted. If Laurie was seriously ill she would feel duty-bound to stand by him for a while at least. Peggy was still very angry with him and was tempted to leave, but until she could contact Able she needed to stay here so that he could find her – but she was certain of one thing: even if she felt obliged to keep the pub running for the moment for everyone's sake, she would never let Laurie back into her heart or her life.

As she walked towards her bedroom, eager to find the box and discover what she could, a cry from the twins' room told her that Fay was awake and screaming for her. She halted and went to see to her daughter.

Looking down at her red face, Peggy couldn't help the tears that slipped down her cheeks as she picked Fay up. 'Your daddy is alive,' she whispered so softly that not even the child could hear. 'He's alive… he's alive…'

The words were dancing in her head and her tears were happy ones, because no matter how difficult her life might be in the future, Able was alive and suddenly nothing else mattered.

Chapter 30

'Yes, I'd love to work for you, and I don't mind whether it's in the wool shop or the grocer's,' Rose told Maureen that morning as she caught her on her way to work. 'They've told me I'll be on short hours next month, so I'll tell them I want to leave. If I have to do war work, I'll join the WVS in the evenings. I don't mind what I do, but I'd love to work for you.'

'I'd be satisfied with afternoons for now,' Maureen said, 'but I may have extra hours for you soon – Tom has his papers at last. He has to report on the fifteenth of May and he's over the moon.'

'Yes, I'll bet he is,' Rose said. 'I like Tom a lot, Maureen. I think the folk of the lanes will miss him when he goes.'

'I certainly shall,' Maureen said. 'I don't know how I would have managed without him at the shop. I'm hoping Gordon may want to do a few hours when he's able, but that won't be for months. In the meantime, I'll take on part-time assistants to help out. Janet is willing to do a few hours – so with her and Vera at the wool shop and you at the grocery counter, I shan't have to do too much myself.'

'You won't be able to soon,' Rose said and laughed as Maureen sighed and put a hand to her back. 'You must be almost there…'

'Not too long now,' Maureen said, 'but babies come when they're ready and it could be any time.'

'I should think you're exhausted, what with visitin' the hospital, lookin' after your grocery business and settin' up a new one in your condition…'

Maureen laughed. 'I like to be busy, but I must admit I've had more than I want just recently. However, it's all falling into place now. Vera likes Mabel's furniture, so she's going to sell a lot of hers and keep what's in the flat. She says hers won't bring much, but she'll be glad of a few extra pounds…'

'Things are hard these days for women like her,' Rose said and sighed. 'She's lucky you came along, Maureen.'

Maureen shook her head in denial. 'No, I'm lucky to have got her. Vera worked in Woolworths before she married and she's very good at a lot of retail stuff. I'm very pleased she will be taking over Mabel's shop. Shirley is happy because her friend has a new dress her mum made her for her birthday and they'll be close enough to each other to pop round on a Saturday morning.'

'Well, that's nice,' Rose said and smiled. 'I had a letter from Jimmy this morning. He is coming home next month. We're going to get married with a special licence and have a couple of days at the sea, because he'll be posted overseas then…' She hesitated, then, 'I was wondering if Tom would let us take over his house, at least until he and his father need it again.'

'Ask him. It would be up to his landlord, of course – but you could hear what Tom says.'

'Yes, I shall, because we'd like to have our own home once we're married.'

'I'm pleased for you, Rose,' Maureen said. 'That's the first bit of good news we've had round here for a while…'

'Yes.' Rose frowned. 'I know what you mean. I just heard last night – about Laurie Ashley. The hospital diagnosed consumption and he has to go away to the sea somewhere for a cure because he can't risk giving it to his family… that's rotten for Peggy again, isn't it?'

'Yes, it is,' Maureen said, 'but Anne has decided to move in with her until Kirk gets home. She doesn't like living alone and Peggy invited her to stay, so she'll be able to help out nearer to the birth – and she's letting her flat out for a few months at a time.'

'Oh, I hadn't heard that,' Rose said and felt pleased. 'I'm glad Peggy will have help – and it will be better for Anne to be with friends rather than on her own in that flat. I think she would like to sell it and buy something else – and of course she is out of a job now.'

Women teachers were not supposed to marry. As it was wartime, Anne's employers had turned a blind eye when she got married, and now the law was being relaxed, and women were about to be paid as much as their male colleagues, but Anne had decided to leave at the end of the month because of the baby. Perhaps after the war was over and Kirk came home, she could take it up again, but it meant that Anne might even be available to do a few hours at Maureen's shop once her child was born, and she'd be around a lot more. It would be lovely to see her most days. No matter what life threw at them, the women of the lanes stuck together and helped each other. It was the only way to get through these dark times.

'Well, I'd better run or I'll be late,' Rose said and grinned. 'Not that it matters, because if they sack me I won't have to work out my notice.'

Maureen smiled and waved as the pretty girl made a dash along the lane. She turned in the direction of The Pig & Whistle. There was just time for a chat with Peggy before she went home and started to help Gran prepare lunch.

'I'm glad Anne is moving in with you for a while, Peggy,' Maureen said. 'I didn't like to think of her alone in that flat when the baby comes…'

'She'll be company for me – and it will be better for her,' Peggy agreed. 'I'm having her room thoroughly cleaned and aired, even changed the curtains and boiled all the linen, because she's going to have the one Laurie was using. I've packed what he doesn't need and put it in the attic…'

'Oh, Peggy, I'm so sorry,' Maureen said and her eyes were moist as she looked at her friend. 'We've had more than enough to grieve us without all this on top…'

'Yes, I know,' Peggy said. 'I think it's worse because of what Laurie did – if he hadn't acted so promptly and so bravely, I might not be talkin' to you now, Maureen. I shall always be grateful to him for that despite all the rest…'

'I know. I'll always be grateful to him for that as well,' Maureen said. 'I wish I could wave a wand and make things better for us both.'

'It's different for you,' Peggy said. 'You're in love with Gordon and you can't wait for him to get better so he can come home. I want Laurie to recover, of course I do – but I've made up my mind. I shan't live with him ever again. I'll keep the pub goin' for him until he's well again, but I don't love him. I can't after what he's done…'

'What do you mean?' Maureen asked. She could see the dark shadows of a sleepless night beneath her friend's eyes and knew she was holding back her tears. 'What has Laurie done to hurt you like this, Peggy?'

Peggy hesitated and then took a thin piece of paper from her pocket. She handed it to Maureen. 'Laurie kept that from me – read it…'

Maureen read it, giving a little exclamation and looking at Peggy in disbelief. 'You think this means Able is alive?'

'He was when that letter was written,' Peggy said. 'I've written three letters, Maureen, explaining that I've only just got this – two to America and one to an address in this country I found in the box his friends gave me, but I don't know if any of them will reach him… or even where he is, though I think he may have been here in London quite recently, but he probably believes the twins are Laurie's and that I'm happy.'

'Oh, Peggy, it's wonderful that Able is alive – but how could Laurie do that to you? How could he be so selfish as to keep news like this from you?'

'Laurie only cares about himself,' Peggy said bitterly and then shook her head. 'No, that isn't fair – but he hasn't behaved well over this. He knew how much it would mean to me to learn that Able was alive. When I'll ever be able to join him is another matter... but he's alive and he still thinks of me.'

'It says he loves you in this letter,' Maureen said and returned the piece of paper to her. 'What will you do if Able comes to you and asks you to leave Laurie?'

'I don't know...' A sob escaped her. 'I want to be with him – but I couldn't walk out on Laurie when he's ill. Pip would never forgive me and I don't think Janet would approve either. The pub would fold and Laurie would be left with nothing. I have to stay here for a while – but I'm not sure Able is free to ask me a question like that or whether he still wishes it. This letter was sent months ago, though... I had a card from him on the evening we held the birthday party. That's what made me suspicious and when Reg told me there had been a letter from America I started searching. It wasn't hard to find...'

'Able was here in the lanes?' Maureen was astounded.

'I don't know for sure. Someone else might have delivered it for him. If it was him, why didn't he come in and ask for me?'

'Perhaps...' Maureen shook her head, then, 'Most people thought the twins were Laurie's... Able might believe you've made it up with your husband and forgotten him.'

'That's what I'm afraid of,' Peggy admitted. 'I still love him, Maureen. Is it too much to ask for a little happiness when this is all over? I know I can't desert Laurie yet, but he will get better… won't he?'

'As your friend, I'll say yes, of course he will,' Maureen said. 'As a nurse, I can't be certain. It depends how long he's had the disease and how bad it is – and he might be able to come home, but he might never be truly fit.' She hesitated, then, 'I'm not sure Laurie will ever be allowed to run a pub again, Peggy. Have the doctors asked you and your family to have some tests done?'

'Yes, they have…' Peggy stared at her and then nodded. 'Yes, they wouldn't let us run the pub if we had it – and Laurie may be considered a risk in future, because TB is an infectious disease, and if you've had it, you could still carry it…'

'You'll have to take the tests, of course,' Maureen said, 'but I don't think any of you have it – in fact I'm pretty sure you don't. Laurie was away during the time he was infectious and I imagine that people he knew up there in Scotland might be more at risk of havin' picked it up than you. It's lucky he was away all that time…'

Peggy nodded. 'I feel a pig for sayin' it, but I'm glad he was away and I just hope he hasn't passed it to any of us…'

'I shouldn't worry over that much,' Maureen said. She leaned forward and took Peggy's hands in hers. 'It will work out, love. Just hang on in there – and do what you have to do, but in the end, you owe it to yourself and the twins to choose Able if you get the chance.'

*

Tom glanced round the shop. He would be leaving soon for training camp and had been given his first choice of being in the Army, like his dad. Jack was expected home for a few days before Tom left, and he and Sid would sort out what to do over the house. Rose wanted to take it on, but that was up to Tom's father and the landlord and Sid could move in with Mavis if Rose and Jimmy took over the house.

Tom had heard the rumours of a big new offensive in the summer; there were a lot of Americans over here now and various manoeuvres were taking place off the coast in Devon. It was all top secret and although rumours of a disastrous attack by E-boats had circulated in April, no one knew anything for certain and the papers were not allowed to report it.

Walking into the stockroom, Tom thought about the cash box he'd found hidden under the floor some months previously. He still hadn't told Maureen, because Violet was living upstairs and he was afraid his soft-hearted boss would give whatever was in it to her father's widow, when Tom was sure Harold had intended it for his daughter.

Maureen didn't need it at this time, but Tom knew there was a possibility he wouldn't come home and he had to tell her – but not yet. He would leave a letter with Peggy and ask her to give it to Maureen if anything happened to him. Satisfied with his solution, he decided to go home and write the letter now. Peggy would keep it safe and, if Tom was killed, Maureen would know that he'd tried to look out for her.

He picked up an evening paper. The news was on the second page. Ellie's husband Peter had been found guilty of murder and would hang. Everyone in the lanes would be pleased about that, and Tom was proud of the part he'd played in his arrest.

Locking the shop door after him, he paused to look up and down the lane. It was a nice warm evening and the sun was shining, softening its shabbiness. This was home and if Tom survived the war he would return one day and start a business of his own.

As he crossed the street, Irene from the hairdresser's came up to him.

'You'll be off soon,' she said. 'I'll miss seein' you around, Tom.'

'I'll be back like a bad penny,' he said. ''Sides, you've got a boyfriend now, Irene.'

She nodded. 'Yes, Mick is all right,' she agreed, 'but I'd still rather it was you.'

Tom laughed and waved his hand as he went round to the back door of his house. Sid was already in and had the kettle boiling. Sid would be relieved over the news about Peter, because it would mean that he and Ellie could marry when she was ready.

Tom's heart hadn't broken when Rose told him she was marrying Jimmy, but it still hurt. He was glad to be leaving for the Army. It was time for him to move on.

Maureen caught the bus to the hospital. She had so much to tell Gordon, and some things that she must keep to herself for the time being. It had made Maureen want to weep for pity when Peggy showed her the letter Laurie Ashley had kept from her, because it was such a cruel thing to do. Peggy had been forced to bear too much heartbreak of late and Maureen wished with all her heart that she could do something to ease her friend's suffering.

Yet perhaps the knowledge that Able was alive would be enough to get her through the hard times ahead. The war was not yet over and none of them knew what might happen. The Germans had tried a mini Blitz in February and though the occasional raid still went on, few of their planes got through and what damage was done was mostly to docks or coastal, but according to the papers there was worse to come. If Hitler's secret weapon really flew, it could bring death and despair to London all over again.

As she left the bus and walked into the hospital grounds, Maureen put her sad thoughts away. Gordon was improving daily and she had great hopes of having him home before too long, at least by July or August. Shirley was happy because her friend Carol was no longer in such a miserable situation, and Maureen was eagerly awaiting the birth of her second child.

She was such a lucky woman! Maureen felt that her glow of happiness must be visible to everyone as she walked into the ward and saw Gordon sitting out in a chair beside his bed. He was waiting for her visit and she saw the eagerness in his face as he became aware of her walking towards him.

She bent to kiss him softly on the lips. 'How are you today, my love?' she asked softly. 'You look better.'

'I am, much better,' Gordon assured her. 'I've been to the end of the ward on crutches and I took a few steps on my own – and they say if I keep improving, I can come home in a month, by the end of June anyway...'

'Oh, Gordon darling,' Maureen said, feeling that her happiness was perfect. 'That's wonderful. Everyone keeps asking when you're coming home – and Gran says we'll bring a bed downstairs to the parlour so that you don't need to go up the stairs until you're truly well again.'

'It may not be as long as we feared,' Gordon said and she saw the pride and confidence was back in his eyes. 'I'm doing really well, Maureen. I probably shan't need a wheelchair at all...'

Maureen sat on the edge of the bed, putting the fruit she'd bought on his bedside locker. Her heart was full because this was the man she loved so much and she knew that he was prepared to fight for their happiness and to make a good life for them all.

Maureen had her man on the mend and his terrible wounds were healing well, in large part to a wonderful new treatment that had cleared up the infection in his leg. She had the future to look forward to and there was so much promise for her and her family. If there was one small shadow on her horizon it was Peggy's heartache. All she could do was pray that her friend would one day be as happy and content as she was – and perhaps there was a way. There was always a way to get through the bad times if you tried. Peggy didn't give up and her friends would support and love her, and perhaps soon this rotten war would be over and then things might begin to sort themselves out.

Maureen would be there for her, just as she'd always helped everyone else. Peggy was more than the local landlady; she was loved, admired and needed. Maureen felt the shadows lift, because somehow she knew that whatever happened, Peggy would fight through as she always did. The folk of Mulberry Lane would help her just as she had helped them and surely one day she would be happy again... Once the Germans were beaten and that surely had to happen soon because the Allies were beginning to turn the tide on all fronts. In a year or so it might be all over and the folk of Mulberry Lane could begin to build their lives once more. Maureen was eager and willing to work hard to make a good life for her family and her beloved husband, and she knew Peggy would do the same for her family. She prayed that Anne's child would be safely born and that Kirk would come home to his wife and child.

Maureen's smile could have lit up the entire ward as she leaned forward to kiss her husband. Surely they had weathered the worst Hitler could throw at them and things would get better soon...

Hello from Aria

We hope you enjoyed this book! Let us know, we'd
love to hear from you.

We are Aria, a dynamic digital-first fiction imprint
from award-winning independent publishers
Head of Zeus. At heart, we're avid readers committed to
publishing exactly the kind of books we love to
read — from romance and sagas to crime, thrillers
and historical adventures. Visit us online and discover
a community of like-minded fiction fans!

We're also on the look out for tomorrow's
superstar authors. So, if you're a budding writer
looking for a publisher, we'd love to hear from you.
You can submit your book online at ariafiction.com/
we-want-read-your-book

You can find us at:
Email: aria@headofzeus.com
Website: www.ariafiction.com
Submissions: www.ariafiction.com/
we-want-read-your-book
Facebook: @ariafiction
Twitter: @Aria_Fiction
Instagram: @ariafiction

Printed in Poland
by Amazon Fulfillment
Poland Sp. z o.o., Wrocław